Destiny's Fate

Written by Ashley M. Lovelis

My dedications:

I dedicate this book to the depression I suffered in my teenage years, but more so to my amazing husband who inspired all of the love that Destiny and Jade have for one another. Thank you so much, baby for loving me with everything you have, and for helping me through everything. I love you so much, Adan Chavez.

Chapter One

I am living in a pit of misery. I just finished dealing with one of the worst days at work that I've ever had to be a part of. Driving home from work, I think about all of the shit I've had to deal with over the last two months, starting with finding out from the doctor that I've been diagnosed with high blood pressure. Then today I got screamed at by my boss. I was having a panic attack and bawling on the store floor in front of a dozen customers because I was too stressed out and overwhelmed. I'm about ready to give up.

And on top of everything else, I'm moving into a new apartment with my best friend from high school, Jade, this weekend and have to finish unpacking my things. Yay.

Thinking about everything crappy going on in my life, I start to zone out a little bit, imagining what the world would be like without me in it. While thinking about that world, I forget that I'm driving for a few seconds and when I realize what's about to happen it's too late. My car swerves into the next lane in front of a semi truck.

Within seconds I'm thrown forward through the windshield because I forgot my seatbelt. And the last thing I remember before going unconscious is hoping that this kills me so the mental pain and torture can end.

****

Destiny flies through her car's windshield, landing on the road surrounded by glass and her own blood. The driver of the semi truck rushes out of it and runs to the front of the truck to see what happened. When he sees Destiny's bloody and torn up body on her car he starts to panic.

He yells for his partner to get up there and to call an ambulance. "Bruce!!! Get your ass over here!!! Call an ambulance!!! I think this chick is dead."

Bruce comes running from the cab and as soon as he sees the sight in front of him, he gags and throws up in the middle of the street. It takes a few moments for him to gain his composure.

When Bruce has finally stopped dry heaving, he calls 911. "H-hello. This is Bruce Carter. I work for Jacks Trucking. My buddy and I were just drivin our route and... and we hit someone. This girl, we didn't even see her car before we could try to stop... and we hit her. She's pretty bloody and bashed up. We need an ambulance out here. Now. Cuz she might be dead."

The operator calmly asks Bruce, "Sir, where are you located? As soon as I know your location, I can send an ambulance and a few officers over to help you and the young lady."

"W-we're on the east side of Highway 14. There's a forest on the side where we wrecked into her. The last mile marker was mile 45. Please hurry."

"Yes sir. They're on the way now. I'm going to stay on the line with you until they arrive. Just talk to me. Okay?"

Bruce shudders heavily, trying to breathe. His friend comes over to make sure he's okay and mouths to him, "I'm keepin' an eye on her. I've got a rag, tryin' to keep the blood down."

Bruce nods. "My friend is holdin' a rag on her to try to keep her from bleedin' out so much. But there's just so much blood everywhere already. It looks like a scary slasher movie. This feels unreal, man. It just happened out of nowhere. We were just drivin' to Richmond from Hankersville and then BAM!!! This car just showed up out of nowhere."

The operator listens as Bruce talks to her, telling her the details. After he's done talking, she says, "It's okay, Bruce. Accidents happen. It's not your fault. And it's very good that your friend is using rags to stop her bleeding. Just try to stay as calm as you can. The ambulance and officers are on their way. They should be there any minute."

As the operator continues talking to Bruce, Destiny starts to convulse on the ground in front of the semi truck, her mouth bubbling.

"Are they almost here!?!? The girl's mouth is bubblin' now. And I don't know what to do."

"Just have your friend check for a pulse on her neck and make sure she's still breathing. They're just a couple of minutes from your location. If she's still breathing and has a pulse, she's still alive.'

Bruce hollers over to his friend to check for a pulse and breathing. His friend puts his fingers to her neck and feels a slow heartbeat. He puts his hand to her chest and it's moving up and down slowly telling him that she's still breathing.

"She's breathing, but just barely. And her pulse is real slow."

Bruce lets the operator know just as sirens sound, nearing the scene. An ambulance pulls up along with a few squad cars.

The paramedics rush over to where Destiny is laid out on the road in front of the truck. They begin applying direct pressure on her wounds to stop the bleeding. As the bleeding slowly stops, a couple of the paramedics grab a gurney. They bring it over and put Destiny onto it so that she can be placed in the ambulance.

As this is happening, a few of the officers are talking to Bruce and his friend, asking for details on what happened.

One officer says to the two shaken up men, "My name is Officer Miller. This is my partner, James. Can one of you tell us exactly what happened?"

Bruce's friend nods and recounts the entire ordeal to the officers, going over everything he can remember.

As they go over the details with the two officers, the paramedics finish getting Destiny hooked up to the IVs and heart monitor in the ambulance. Once they have gotten her secure, they get in the vehicle and begin driving to the hospital.

****

Destiny's POV: "Hey, babe. How did it go at the publication meeting for work today? Did you get approved?" Jade smiles at me as I come through the door.

I beam at her, exclaiming, "Yeah, babe. I got approved. They're going to publish my article in TIME magazine. They absolutely loved it. I showed them my article about fiction novels and television shows and how much they help shape the lives of the people who read or watch them. They were absolutely fascinated by my take on it. So many people's lives and personalities are shaped around what they read and watch. Even what they see through the media. It's not even funny."

Jade comes over to me, smiling as she leans over to give me a big hug and a kiss on my lips. "I'm so proud of you, sweetie. You're going to make it big with all of your articles on psychology and the human mind. Hopefully one day soon you'll be able to study people's minds and help them with anything that's troubling their psyche. Just keep going and working hard, Des. I'm very proud of you and all the hard work you've put in. In fact, we should go out to dinner to celebrate the start of your career."

"Let's. I'll go get changed out of my work clothes and put on my best dress and heels."

I give Jade another small kiss on her cheek and head over to the bedroom to start getting ready for the night out on the town.

When I get in there, the first thing I do is pull my hair out of the wavy bun on the back of my head, shaking my head from side to side to help let it down. I undo the buttons on my blouse, letting it fall off my shoulders as I go over to the closet to find my sexiest little black dress. My favorite one, lacy along the collar with a silky smooth bodice. It has little scarlet red roses printed down the sides of the skirt. And it has a nice V neck to show off my cleavage.

I let my slacks fall off my butt and my thighs as I slowly pull the dress over my head. Right as I get the dress all the way over my head, I notice Jade standing in the doorway.

I grin cheekily at her. "How long have you been standing there?"

"Oh just long enough. Long enough for it to feel really hot in here. How about before you finish getting ready we have a little fun?"

Laughing, I go over to her, wrapping my arms around her neck and kissing her slowly.

"Baby, you're so sexy when you're turned on. If you wanted me so much while you were watching me, you should have just asked me to stop what I was doing and get on the bed."

Jade's cheeks begin to burn red from my touch. After I remove my lips from hers, she grabs my hand and slowly walks me over to the bed. Laying me down on the mattress, she slides my dress up slowly and gets down on her knees.

She looks at me with a steamy look in her eyes as she pulls my satin panties down off of my waist and buttocks, pulling them down my legs. She starts to kiss my inner thighs, making me shudder with ecstasy.

"O-o-ooh baby. You know just what I like." I wrap my fingers through her hair as she slowly makes her way up to my pussy, nipping my thighs along the way. Jade starts to flick her tongue along my opening while she slides her index and middle finger inside of me.

Jade stops for a second and whispers in a sultry voice, "You like this?" She licks her lips before slowly inserting her tongue into my pussy.

Gasping, I grip the bed sheets. I can feel her tongue going deep inside me, hitting every spot. She licks up and down, back and forth until I just can't take it and explode onto her face.

Breathing heavily, I sit up as she cleans up the mess I made with her tongue. After she's finished she gets up and slides my panties back up my legs and over my ass.

I shakily get up from the bed and give her a sweet kiss on the lips. "Baby, that was wonderful. And a great way to start off tonight. Now let's go off to Renaldo's L'Amor and have a nice dinner and talk about the amazing future we're going to have after our careers start."

Jade smiles and grabs my hand as we both head to the door. I put on my heels and grab the keys and my wallet as we head outside.

I smile to myself, thinking, This is the woman I'm going to marry and grow old with and it's going to be amazing.

We both get in the elevator, heading down to the first floor. When we get there, the receptionist at the desk greets us both with a big smile. "How are two of my favorite tenants this evening? What are you all so dressed up for?'

I exclaim, "I'm getting a psychology article published in TIME magazine and we're going out to celebrate."

"Oh wow. I'm so happy for you. It's great that they're going to publish your article. I'll definitely have to read it as soon as it goes onto the shelves."

"Thanks, Kathy. If you want, I can get you one of the first copies and bookmark the page for you."

Kathy comes from behind the counter and gives me a hug. "I'm proud of you. Getting your career started. I'll do the same someday. But for now I'm running the front desk here. I love it though. Now you two go out and have some fun. Paint the town. Just go wild and celebrate."

I nod, "We will, Kathy. Maybe we'll bring you back a drink so you can celebrate with us when we get back. But for now, have a good night."

Jade and I exit the building and head over to the car park. Holding Jade's hand, I smile over at her when she's not looking. I have the most beautiful girlfriend in the world.

We make our way over to our cute little yellow, flowered Volkswagen Beetle. I open Jade's door for her and give her a kiss before she gets in. After shutting her door, I make my way around to the driver side and climb in, turning the key in the ignition. Once I get seated, I turn the radio on to my favorite song, Don't Stop Believing by Journey.

Both of us sing at the top of our lungs to every lyric. To anybody else it probably sounded like a couple of screeching cats getting beat against a wall. But to me it's the most beautiful sound on the planet.

We sing the entire ride until we get to L'Amor. From Journey to Queen to Ozzy Osbourne. The entire ride I just can't help but admire how beautiful my girlfriend's voice is and notice how radiant the lights from outside the car make her.

When we arrive at the restaurant, we're met at the entrance by Francis, our favorite valet.

He greets us with a cheeky little smile. "If it isn't my two favorite patrons. How are you two ladies doing on this fine evening?"

I respond with a smile, "Well I just got approved for publication in TIME magazine. I wrote an article about how various media shapes people's personalities and they accepted it to be published in the next issue. So we're having a night out on the town to celebrate my accomplishment."

Francis beams. "Congratulations, girl. I'm proud of you. At least your making a career out of your dream."

Jade laughs teasingly at him. "I'm sure you'll be able to do the same. You just have to get started. What is your dream, anyway?"

"Well ever since I was a little boy I've always dreamt of being a famous singer. But I never pursued it because my parents said it was foolish. So here I am... a valet at the most prestigious restaurant in New York. Making a few hundred a week parking cars."

I look at Francis and tell him, "You know what? Screw what your parents told you. I bet you sound amazing when you sing. And I'd be willing to bet a hundred bucks you'll be the next Freddie Mercury. I say you should go after your dreams. When I get paid for this article, I'll give you the money to go to the nearest recording studio and record your first song."

Francis gives me a great big hug and cries out, "Thank you so much, sweetie. If I get accepted, I'll credit you for my success. now you two go in there and celebrate your success. Get anything you want. Drinks, appetizers, dessert. It's all on me. And if you all end up hammered and need a ride to the next party location, tell the maitre'd to get me and I'll escort you beautiful women anywhere."

Smiling, I tell Francis, "Can do, hun. And hey, I'll buy you a couple of drinks and a slice of fondue cake if you want.

He agrees as he gets into our car to take it to park.

Going inside, the maitre'd escorts Jade and I to our table by the window. There's a candle lit on it and a little bouquet of flowers in a vase. We get seated and order our drinks, chardonnay and Jack Daniels whiskey on the rocks.

Jade looks over at me with a gleam in her eyes. "So babe, tell me a little more about what the magazine said about your article. What all did the like about it"

"Well when they read my article they said that I had some brilliant incites into the way media influences the public and the way they think. I'd written that there are so many different things that affect the way the human personality forms. People's favorite shows, they influence people to act similar to the way their favorite characters act. Even speaking like them sometimes. Or doing things that their favorite celebrities have done, whether it be hobbies or crazy off the wall things. The publishers for TIME magazine were enthralled with what I said in the article. They told me almost immediately that it was going to be published so that I could show people how easily their minds are influenced."

After I finish explaining to Jade what they told me, she squeaks with pure glee. "I'm so freakin' proud of you, babe. You're going to be a well renowned psychologist. Hopefully soon you'll have your own psychology office and patients and you'll be helping people understand themselves and their minds better."

We continue talking about the future possibilities of my career when the waiter brings over our drinks.

"Are you ladies ready to order or would you like a few more minutes?"

I glance over at Jade and she smiles, replying, "I think we're ready. I'd like a Ceasar salad, a medium filet steak with a side of a baked potato and green beans. What would you like, baby?"

I laugh. "I just want a New York strip done medium rare, side of macaroni salad and side of fresh sautéed zucchini and squash. Also, can we have an appetizer of baked brie?"

"Of course, ladies. I will be right back with your appetizers and salads."

The waiter walks off with our menus, leaving us to ourselves, the sweet music playing in the background.

Smiling, I stand up and walk over to Destiny, grabbing her hand as I begin towards the ballroom floor. When we reach the center, I put my arms over her shoulder and begin swaying to the Beethoven symphony playing through the speakers.

We sway at first, moving slowly with the music. Each step we take, I begin to twirl Jade to the music until all that fills the room is just the music and the two of us.

We continue like that for the next few minutes until the piece ends. After we stop dancing, we both make our way to the table where the waiter is waiting with our salads and appetizers.

When Jade and I sit down, we thank him and begin eating.

I start in on the small salad that I ordered, adding a little bit of Italian dressing to it to give it a little bit extra flavor. Taking the first bite, the lettuce has a nice crispy crunch. The taste is fantastic.

"How is your salad, baby?' I stop eating for a few seconds to ask Jade how hers tastes.

"It's great, sweetie. But I'm about to be done with it so that we can share this brie. What do you think?"

I nod, smiling as I put my salad fork down as I move the plate of brie pastry to the center of the table. I scoop up a forkful, reaching across the table to put into Jade's mouth. She moans with satisfaction as the pastry touches her tongue.

Watching as she chews, I take a bite of it as well, closing my eyes as I enjoy the flavor in my mouth.

Each of us alternate giving the other bites of brie until it's all gone. After we finish eating, the waiter arrives with our food.

"Here are your steaks. Would you like me to take the empty plates and get them out of your way?'

I tell him yes as he begins gathering the empty plates.

Jade and I start in on our meals after he leaves. We spend the next twenty minutes eating and enjoying our steaks and side dishes.

****

After we've finished our meals and our drinks, Jade and I order dessert to-go. We get a couple of orders of chocolate fondue cake, pay for the bill and head outside to get our car from Francis.

"Hi, girls. Got anything else fun planned for the evening?"

Grinning, I tell him, "We're probably going to go to the club down the road for a little dancing and a few more drinks. Then we'll probably take a walk in the park and sit in the grass to eat our dessert."

Francis shakes his head with enthusiasm. "Well you two have lots of fun. I'll probably have a drink after I get off in honor of your success. But don't get too wild. We don't need you guys getting arrested."

"Don't worry. We won't do anything stupid like shoot fireworks off the Empire State building. We're just gonna have some fun." I laugh as I get into the car with Jade.

We drive off down the road to Club Chaos, the most popular club in town.

It only takes a few minutes to get there, and when we do, it's packed. Everybody and their brother is at the club.

We get in the line to the entrance to wait, all the way around the corner of the building. Jade and I start talking to the people in line in front of us, a cute girl and her boyfriend until we are able to reach the entrance to the club.

The guy is the first to speak as he asks us, "What are you guys up to tonight? Out just to have fun or are you celebrating something?"

"Celebrating. I just got an article accepted to be published in TIME magazine. So we're spending the night out on the town."

The guy hoots, "Yeah!!! Me and Sasha will have to check it out. My name's Jake. Hopefully this line won't take too long so we can all get inside to party and have some fun."

****

After a few hours out at the club, Jade and I drive over to the park to have our dessert from the restaurant.

We get a little throw blanket out of the trunk, laying it out across the grass. I open the dessert trays, but as soon as we go to start eating, a bunch of pigeons swoop down, trying to attack our food.

DESTINY'S FATE

"Ahh!!!!!!" We both scream as we jump up to run from the swarm of pigeons attacking.

Chapter Two

Jade's POV: I'm starting to get worried about Destiny. She was supposed to get home two hours ago so we can start unpacking her boxes.

I get up off the couch and grab my phone from the kitchen counter. I unlock it and go to my recent contacts. I click on Destiny's name and hit the call button.

It starts to ring, ringing once, twice, then after the third ring, she finally answers.

I start speaking. "Destiny, where are you? Do you expect me to unpack your stuff all by myself?"

There's silence for a few seconds. Then someone else responds back. "Hello? Who is this? Are you a friend of Destiny's?"

I start panicking. "Who are you? Where is Destiny? What happened to her? Is she okay?"

The person on the other end answers, saying, "This is Dr. Drew. Your friend Destiny was in an accident on the highway. She's at St. James hospital. You should come up here so that I can explain the situation to you."

My heart drops after what he tells me. All I can picture in my head is Destiny splattered on the highway. Her skull smashed in and arms and legs broken every direction.

"Hello? Are you there?"

I shake myself out of my thoughts. "Yes. I'll be right there. My name is Jade Shay, by the way."

I hang up the phone, and gather my purse and keys then head out the door.

Once I get in my car and start the ignition, the radio starts to play mine and Destiny's favorite song, *Don't Stop Me Now* by Queen.

I turn it up, blasting it because I know that whatever condition Destiny is in, she won't let it stop her. I know it won't.

****

When I arrive at the hospital, I go inside and walk over to the front desk.

"Hi. I'm Jade Shay. I'm looking for Destiny Morgan. She was in a car accident on the highway. I spoke with Dr. Drew briefly on the phone."

The nurse looks at her computer, typing for a few seconds. "It looks like Destiny is in the critical condition unit down Hall E. In room 524. Dr. Drew should be in there with her."

"Thank you so much."

After getting Destiny's room number from the nurse I quickly make my way over to the elevator and go up to the fifth floor.

I press the button to call the elevator down and stand impatiently as I wait. It takes a few minutes for it to get to this floor. When the door finally opens, I press the button for the fifth floor and wait for the doors to close so it can start moving up.

It seems to take forever for the elevator to make its way to the fifth floor and I can't help but worry about what condition Destiny will be in when I get to her room.

The elevator finally reaches the fifth floor and as soon as the doors open I hurry and make my way around the corner to Room 524 where Dr. Drew is walking out.

I rush over to him, trying to steady my breath.

Before I even get the chance to speak, Dr. Drew stops me. "Hello. Are you here for Destiny?"

"Yes. I'm her best friend and roommate, Jade Shay. How is she doing? Is she going to be okay?"

He looks at my upset expression before speaking. "We should probably go to my office to talk."

Taking a deep breath, I swallow a knot in my throat before starting to follow him down the hall. I'm honestly terrified of what he is going to tell me.

We reach his office where he tells me take a seat across from the desk.

Once I'm seated, he sits in his chair and pulls out a file folder from the top drawer. He sets it down on top of his desk and opens it to look at the papers inside.

"Destiny Morgan was brought in in critical condition after being impacted in her car by a semi truck. She was thrown through her windshield because she wasn't wearing a seatbelt. After the paramedics and ambulance arrived, she was found on the road.

Her head had hit the pavement first and it was cracked open exposing her skull and some soft tissue. Her body was bruised and had cuts and tears in her skin from going through the glass. She broke a couple of ribs as well as her right femur, and tore through a few ligaments throughout her body. She's in critical condition right now but she's stable."

After the doctor finishes speaking, I take a deep, shuddering breath. *I can't believe that my best friend could be dying right now.*

After a few moments of trying to calm my breathing, I finally speak. "Do you know how long it will take before she wakes up and will be able to fully recover?"

"Destiny sustained some severe head trauma when she was thrown from her car. It could have killed her. I'll have to conduct a few MRIs and CT scans to determine what's going on in her brain. Once I do that, I can give you an estimate on when she'll wake up. I'm going to take her down in about an hour for an MRI and I can call you after it's done if you like."

I shake my head before telling him that I'm not going to leave her side for a second. She's my best friend and I need to know that she'll be okay.

"I am not leaving her until I know what's going to happen. No matter what. We have been best friends since we were both in kindergarten. If I was in her place, she would do the same thing for me."

Dr. Drew nods his head. "I completely understand. Would you like to go back to her room and sit with her until I come to take her for the MRI?"

"Yes. She needs someone to be there with her."

I stand up from my chair and follow the doctor back to Destiny's room, trying to ignore the loud silence emanating through the long, white hall.

After we reach her room, Dr. Drew tells me that I can take a seat in the chair and he'll be back in an hour to take her for the MRI.

Once he's left the room and closed the door behind him, I turn to look at my best friend. She looks so different, tubes sticking into her from her IV, heart monitor, and various different machines. She almost looks like a specimen waiting to be experimented on.

And the room doesn't help either. It's so plain. There's nothing on the walls. The furniture is one dull grey hospital recliner and two black plastic chairs. White walls that look faded from years of wear and tear. And a small TV mounted on the wall across from Destiny's bed.

All I can think about is, *What if she doesn't wake up? What if she does wake up but is left paralyzed? What if her brain or motor functions can't work right?*

I can't stop going over scenarios in my head, so to try and stop myself from panicking or worrying too much I decide to put on some music. I turn on my Queen Pandora station and just listen to the music as it flows through my ears, and hopefully through Destiny's ears.

Song after song goes by, my mind trying to relax with the music.

****

After what feels like hours of listening to music, the door opens and Dr. Drew walks in with two nurses to take Destiny to get an MRI.

"Hello. Are you ready for us to take her for the MRI scan?"

I turn the music off before standing up. "Yes. Is it alright if I come with her and watch through the window?"

"You may. You could sit in the room with her also, but you would have to take off anything with metal because the machine will pull it and could malfunction."

I do as he says before following him into the MRI room.

When we get there he transfers Destiny from the bed onto the bottom of the machine before sliding it in. I watch as Destiny disappears inside the tube before I go to the chair that's sitting across from the machine.

It whirs up a few moments later as it starts to scan her brain and her body for internal damage.

I just hope that she'll wake up safe.

Destiny's POV: Jade and I run full speed as the pigeons take over our food, laughing the entire time. I look over my shoulder at the birds and can see them flocking at the food we left behind.

We reach the lakeside further away from where we set up the blanket and food. We both sit down in the grass together and lay down next to each other. I grab ahold of Jade's waist, pulling her next to me before sliding in for a kiss on her maroon lips.

I kiss Jade with a passion, feeling the warmth grow between us.

"Mmm." A sigh releases from my lips as I start to run my hands along her body.

I can feel her face starting to get warm from my touch. As we're still kissing, I slowly start to slide my hand under the waistband of her pants.

I pull away for a moment and smile with hunger in my eyes. "My baby's burning for me. We should get home and get these clothes off."

She smiles darkly at me as she says, "Okay, babe. Let's go home."

We both get up from the grass and start walking to the car. It only takes us a few minutes to get to the yellow bug and once we get there, Jade grabs me by the waist. She pulls me closer and starts to suck on my neck, leaving little red marks all along the side of it.

I can feel my knees trying to buckle under the sensation of her kisses. God, I just want to fuck her right now.

I can feel myself falling victim to her touch as she moves her way down my torso, caressing my breasts. As she continues to use her hands and the feeling of her skin on me, she opens the door on my side of the car to let me in.

"Let's go home now and I'll show you what all I can do, baby."

We both climb into the car and she starts driving us home to our apartment. The entire ride there, Jade has her hand rubbing on my thigh and going really close to my crotch. It takes everything I have in me to not move her hand up to the center between my legs.

Each turn we go around on the roads makes me want it more. I want to feel her hands touch my skin, feel her lips on mine. Our clothes coming off as we make sweet, passionate love in our apartment. I just want to feel her body against mine.

When we get to the apartment building twenty agonizing minutes later, Jade and I both get out of the car and head inside, making out the entire way up to our apartment.

Once we're there, Jade unlocks the door and we both continue kissing as we make our way inside.

I start unbuttoning her jacket and pull it off her shoulders, tossing it onto the couch. As I kiss my girlfriend's lips, I slowly slide us down to the cushions where I start moving my hands along her body. I touch every inch of her as we kiss, eventually placing my hand inside her pants as I start teasing her.

"Come on, babe. Stop teasing. You know I want it, and I know you do, too." Jade starts to pull my shirt over my head, squeezing my boobs through my bra.

My eyes close as I feel the pleasure spreading throughout my body. She begins to kiss her way down my body, leaving little maroon lipstick marks on my skin. I can feel her breath when it reaches my waist as she pulls my dark blue ripped jeans off. Her warm breath brushes against my purple lace panties as she slowly licks me from the outside.

She looks up into my eyes with this sultry expression. "How badly do you want it, babydoll? Do you want me to take it slow? Or be wild and ravenous?"

My hands immediately grab her hair.

I try not to moan as I say, "I want it now, baby. Show me what your mouth and fingers can do."

As soon as I say this, Jade grabs my panties and pulls them down. She starts to kiss my lips, leaving wet marks on my skin before she opens her mouth to use her tongue. When her tongue goes inside me, I feel my body start to go weak. I can feel every sensation that she gives me.

I can't even let any sound out because the pleasure has taken over my entire body. I move my body with her mouth as her tongue moves through me.

When my legs start to shake a little, Jade picks up her head.

"You really want me, baby. You really want me. Well don't worry. You can have me." As she says this, she stands up and slowly pulls her tank top and jeans off of her body.

Jade climbs on top of me on the couch, grinding her body against mine and putting pressure on mine. Her legs wrap around my waist as she presses her entrance against mine.

I grab Jade's hair, pulling her face down to me as I kiss her with wild, crazy passion. My body presses into hers as our pussies collide, thrusting against each other. I can feel how wet she is as I slide my fingers inside her.

I put two in first, slowly inserting them inside her as she grinds on top of me. My fingers move carefully as I touch her clit.

Her mouth moans into mine as my fingers move in and out of her.

"You like this, baby. Don't you?"

Jade's body tenses up beneath mine as she orgasms. "Ohh ohh!!! Don't stop!!! Don't stop!!!"

My fingers and my body keep going until I feel her cum into my hand. I kiss her a few more times before looking into her beautiful brown eyes.

"I love you so fucking much, baby."

She smiles at me as she gets up from the couch. "I love you so fucking much. Do you want me to go get us a snack from the kitchen?"

I nod my head as I go to the bedroom so that I can grab us both some clean underwear.

When I get back to the living room, Jade is back with a bowl of buttered popcorn and two cups of coffee sweetened to perfection. I grab the television remote and start to look for a movie to watch. I go to the suspense movies to see if there's anything good that we could watch.

Misery... Shutter Island... Green Mile... All really good movies.

"What do you think, baby? Do you want to watch any of these?"

"We can watch Green Mile. That's one of my favorite movies."

I settle into the couch next to Jade before I press play on the remote control.

We lay together, picking on each other as we watch the movie until eventually we fall asleep in each other's arms, crashing on the tan couch.

Jade's POV: I sit in the MRI room with Destiny and watch as the machine scans her. The loud noises coming from the machine are so loud and intimidating. Every few minutes, a different sound comes from it.

Each time one noise stops, I think to myself that she'll be done with her scan soon, but then another starts up.

****

A few hours later

After Destiny's MRI scan is finished, I follow Dr. Drew back to Destiny's room.

He stays for a few minutes to make sure that she is still stable and lets me know that I can stay for as long as I want to, and that if I need anything I can press the call button. He or one of the nurses will come and help.

Once he leaves the room, I sit down in the chair next to Destiny's bed. Looking at her makes me sad, seeing her so broken and helpless.

I can't believe that just this morning Destiny was going to work and was awake, vibrant, and full of joy. Now she's unconscious and in a coma for God knows how long. My best friend might never wake up and I don't know what to do.

I'm trying not to think about the worst case scenario, but I can't help it. And I want to be here by her side until she wakes up, but I know I'll have to leave at some point. I hate seeing all those cables, tubes, and machines connected to her body. She looks like a lab experiment.

After thirty minutes of sitting and thinking about everything that has happened since this morning, I decide to go home for a while and try to get some rest for the night.

I look over to Destiny laying in the bed before I reach over to hit the call button.

After a few moments, a nurse walks into the room. "Hello, my name is Christine. Is something wrong?"

"No ma'am. Nothing's wrong. I just wanted to let someone know that I'm going to go home and rest for the night, and I didn't want her to be left alone. Can you let Dr. Drew know?"

Christine nods her head as she says, "I can. He's going to make sure and take great care of Destiny for the night. And if there happens to change during the night I will call you immediately."

When Christine finishes talking, I stand up and grab my purse. As I leave the room I look around at everything around me: all the doctors and nurses going from room to room, patients with IV machines connected to them, and the white walls.

Everything is so white here and seems so impersonal, almost as if everyone here is either a specimen or a scientist poking and prodding at them.

I continue walking down the hall until I reach the front doors. Once I get outside, I burst into tears, worrying like hell about my best friend. I don't want her to die.

I can feel heat rising up inside of my chest as the sobs rip out of my throat. My body feels weak and broken knowing that I can't help Destiny. That I wasn't with her when this happened. That I'm not the one in that hospital bed.

My chest heaves as I keep crying out. I can feel myself starting to breathe harder and faster before I fall to my knees on the ground.

Before I know it, I'm laying on the concrete with my face to the ground as people walk by staring at me.

It feels like time has stopped completely.

I can't do anything to help her except wait. And worry. And cry. And agonize, knowing that my best friend could be dying.

I lay on the concrete just crying my eyes out as cars and people pass by, staring at me like I'm crazy. I can hear some comments from people saying to ignore the crazy lady. Some people whispering rude things about how I'm making a scene.

But I don't care. I don't give a freaking rat's ass what anybody says because my best friend is in a coma and I can't do anything.

Before too long it starts to pour down rain, making me feel a thousand times worse. More miserable with worry and fear. And I don't care that I'm getting soaking wet from the rain.

I sit up from laying on my knees and just sit as the rain continues to come down over me. Lightning starts flashing in the sky and thunder cracks from the black clouds in the sky. It feels like the world is falling apart around me.

I sit there, letting the rain come down on me, for what feels like hours as the sun fades from the sky. My body feels weak, and begins know it, everything around me turns black.

****

"Hey. Are you okay? I found you laying on the ground in front of the hospital. What happened?"

A man is standing over me as I wake up. I look around myself to see where I am. I'm laying on a couch under a warm blanket. The room is cozy looking, with wood colored walls, a fireplace going, and pictures of various things on the walls.

The man is looking down at me with worry written across his face. He has dark brown hair falling over his forehead. His eyes are a deep brown color, and his frame looks strong but gentle.

I try to sit up before I open my mouth to speak. "Where am I? Who are you?"

"You're in my house. My name is Gregory Miller. I found you lying on the ground outside of the hospital doors in the middle of the rain. I brought you here instead of taking you into the hospital because I felt like you would be better off in a warm house. And I wanted to be able to make sure that you were going to be okay."

I take a deep breath. "My name is Jade and, well... my best friend is in the hospital right now in a coma from a car accident that she got into this morning. Seeing her in there knowing that there's nothing I can do to fix anything broke me. I just broke down as soon as I left the hospital to go home."

Gregory sits down in the chair across from me as he lets out a sigh. He looks at me with kindness on his face before saying anything.

After a few seconds of silence, he opens his mouth to speak. "I can't help with your friend, but if you want I can take you home so that you can rest in your own bed. I don't want you driving yourself in this emotional state."

I nod my head before asking if I can use the restroom to clean up.

"It's down the hall, first door on the right. And if you need anything, I'll be in here."

Once he's finished speaking, I get up and walk down the hall to the bathroom. I go inside and shut the door before turning on the water from the sink.

As I look at myself in the mirror, I notice how much I look like an absolute wreck. My face is splotchy and red. There are black circles around my eyes from crying through my makeup. And my hair is knotted all to hell from the rain.

I put my hands under the water and splash some up onto my face to try and cool off. I do my best to clean it off with my hands. I rub my hands against my eyes to get off as much of the black as I can. Then I grab the soap bottle and put some in my hands. I lather it onto my face, scrubbing the makeup and red spots on my face.

It takes me a few minutes to get all of the soap off of my face before I head back to the living room.

When I get back into the room, Gregory stands up and walks over to me. "Are you okay? Are you ready to go to your house? Or do you want to sit in front of the fire some more?"

I make my way over to where he's standing before I answer his questions.

"I'm alright. I think I would rather stay here for the night because going home to an empty apartment would just make me cry more."

"I understand. Is there anything you need or would like?"

I think for a few seconds then say, "Is there any way that I could get something warm to drink and maybe some dry clothes?"

"Of course. I can make a pot of coffee and you can borrow a t-shirt and sweatpants for the night. Let me go grab the clothes and then I'll start the coffee, okay?"

I nod my head and sit down on the couch, wrapping the blanket around myself.

As I'm sitting under the blanket I take a better look around the room. Looking at the pictures on the wall, they look more like detailed paintings than just pictures or photographs.

One has the image of a mountain range next to a lake and another looks like a self portrait. All of the paintings look absolutely amazing.

A few seconds later, Gregory walks back into the room with a large Journey t-shirt and a pair of navy blue sweats.

"These were the first things I grabbed. How are you feeling?"

"I'm feeling okay. I was wondering, where did you get these paintings? Or did you paint all of them? Because they look amazing."

He smiles brightly as he says, "I did. I took professional painting classes in high school and college. I learned techniques that were used by Van Gogh, Picasso, and even some of the lesser known painters. I haven't ever shown anybody else my work. You really like it?"

I nod my head as I stand up. "Oh yes. These are absolutely amazing. I thought they were photographs when I first saw them."

"Well thank you. Oh and here are the clothes for you. You can go to the bathroom to change and I'll go make the coffee."

I take the clothes from Gregory and make my way over to the bathroom so that I can change out of my wet clothes.

Once I have the door closed, I start peeling off my wet shirt and pants. They plop onto the floor when I drop them. I grab the t-shirt he gave me and pull it over my head and arms, then pull the sweatpants up over my legs. As soon as I have the clothes on, I can already feel my body getting warmer now that I'm not wearing wet clothing.

As I make my way back out of the bathroom to the living room, I can already smell the fresh coffee.

I get back to the living room and sit down on the couch as Gregory comes out of the kitchen with a black mug in his hands.

"Hey how do you like your coffee? I have a few different creamers: regular, vanilla, hazelnut, and mocha. And I have plenty of sugar and milk."

"I'll just do some milk and vanilla creamer. Thank you so much."

Once he goes back to the kitchen, I lay back on the couch and place a blanket that's laying on the couch over my legs. I lay there as I try to relax my nerves until Gregory comes back from the kitchen with the cup of coffee.

He hands it over to me as soon as he comes back. "Here's your coffee. Give it a few minutes to cool off before you drink it."

He sits down on the chair again before asking if he can turn the TV on for me.

I blow a few times over the coffee cup as I nod my head yes. "You can. You can put anything on."

Gregory turns the TV on and puts on a movie about some couple trapped in the middle of the ocean on a fishing boat. I try to pay attention to it and watch, but my eyes keep drifting in and out of consciousness.

After about thirty minutes of trying to watch the movie, my eyes can't stay open any longer and eventually I fall asleep on the couch.

Chapter Three

Gregory's POV: I finish watching the movie before I get up and shut the light off so that Jade can sleep. I head down the hallway to my bedroom after getting the light turned off and turn on my lamp so that I can read some before I go to sleep.

Once I get to my bedroom and the lamp is on I crawl into bed and get under my sheets to lay down. As I lay under the covers trying to focus on my book, I can't help but think about what Jade told me about her friend in the hospital.

What she said about what happened to her friend, I think about the fact that I was the officer who showed up at the accident. That is was one of the people who responded to the scene of the accident.

I didn't think that later I would be housing that poor girl's best friend while she's in the hospital on life support. But I will help Jade as long as I need to, because I don't want her being alone through this even if we just met.

I want to make sure that both of them will be okay.

****

The next morning I wake up and use the bathroom before going to the living room to check on Jade. When I get in there she's sitting up on the couch and scrolling on her phone with the blanket still laying on her legs. After a few seconds, she notices that I've gotten up and am in the room.

She turns and looks at me. "Good morning. I just woke up a few minutes ago. How did you sleep?"

I stretch my arms up, yawning, before I can answer her. "I slept alright. How are you feeling?"

Jade brushes some of her dark hair out of her face. "I'm feeling alright. But I woke up around one this morning because I was crying in my sleep. I spent most of the night awake afterwards just trying to take my mind off of everything that happened yesterday."

After she's done talking, I walk over and sit down next to her on the couch. "Everything will be okay. I'm sure of it. Your friend is probably just dreaming and probably can't even feel any pain right now. Do you want to go see her after I get you some coffee? Or before?"

"I think after I drink a cup. Because I still need to calm down some more after waking up late last night."

"Okay. I'll go make some and be right back. Unless you want to join me in the kitchen and chat while it's brewing?"

Jade stands up as I make my way to the kitchen, following behind me.

I go over to the coffee pot next to the sink and start filling it up with water. I can feel her watching me from the table as I fill up the pot and get the coffee started brewing.

As I grab the filter and place it in the machine I decide to break the silence. "So, you spent the night on my couch last night. Can I learn some more about you, Jade? I know some from what you told me yesterday, but I don't know anything really about *you*."

I can hear her let out a deep sigh before she says anything.

"I grew up in small Winters, North Dakota with my mom and dad. I was an only child so I was incredibly awkward when I started trying to make friends after starting school. I met Destiny after I got to kindergarten, where we became best friends. She was basically my only friend throughout my entire childhood. I was always a quiet person, though. I'm not one to easily express my feelings or my thoughts.

"After graduating high school, Destiny and I moved here to Connecticut. I started pursuing a career in writing and publishing once we got here and started working with a local publishing agency.

"I started working there because I want to try and become successful with my writing, maybe one day becoming a highly successful author."

As Jade talks, I finish getting the coffee brewed and bring a cup over to the table where she's sitting. "Nice. I'm glad that you met her and were able to have a friend with you all your life. I'm really glad that you were able to start working towards your career. What kind of topics or genres do you write about?"

"I typically write fiction stories or manuscripts based around the people and events in my life. I've even written some stories about my childhood, but they're not nearly as detailed as others." Jade stops to take a few sips of her coffee.

I smile genuinely. "It sounds like you have a vivid imagination. I've never met anyone who writes or does anything creative other than myself."

Her eyes begin to wander around to the couple of paintings on the walls in the kitchen, examining them closely. "Well you are really talented because your paintings are so detailed and look fantastic. It must have taken years to get that talented. I could never paint like that."

My face beams with pride as Jade compliments my work. I get up after taking a few sips of coffee and grab a painting from the wall next to the table.

It's a painting of a beautiful lakeside in the fall surrounded by deer grazing and drinking from the lake. In the background there is a forest of different trees that are shades of orange, yellow, and red.

"This is my first painting after I started to hone in my skills. I wasn't sure how good it would turn out, so I really appreciate that you like my art."

Jade and I continue talking about our work until we finish our cups of coffee. After we're both done, I wash them out in the sink before asking if she wants to go see her friend at the hospital soon.

She tells me that she does, so I go to the bedroom and get dressed before we both go out to the car.

Jade's POV: After Gregory gets dressed, I follow him outside and climb into his car so that I can go see Destiny. I know that there's not much chance that she's woken up, but I hope and pray to Apollo and Asclepius that there's some kind of change for the better.

My mind wanders around as Gregory drives to the hospital, thinking about Destiny. Thinking about if she's going to wake up, and what I'll do if she doesn't wake up.

Destiny has been my best friend since before I can remember. I met her when we were in elementary school the first day. She was the first kid who said hi to me and wanted to be my friend. After that, we spent damn near every day together and had every class together until graduation.

We went through everything together, from puberty and first periods to boy problems and heartbreak. From financial issues to family problems and everything in between. She even stayed in the hospital with me when I had to go through surgery for my kidneys.

As I'm thinking about Destiny and what could happen to her, my thoughts are broken by Gregory.

He taps me on the arm as he pulls the car into a parking space. "We're here. Are you okay?"

I nod my head. "Mostly. J was just thinking about Destiny and what would happen if she doesn't ever wake up."

My body shakes when I say that and I turn my head down as tears start to fall from my eyes.

I close my eyes, fear filling my brain with worry. "I just... She's my best friend. I can't lose her."

I feel his hand when he places it on my shoulder, squeezing me in a slight hug.

"Hey, she'll be okay. I have this feeling that everything will be fine. Do you want to go inside and see her now?"

"Yes. I do. I want to see her. Even though I know she's broken and small right now. I just want to see her face."

Gregory gives me a small smile of reassurance before he gets out of the car . He comes around to my side and lets me out.

Once I get out of the car and the doors are locked, we start making our way to the hospital entrance. It's much brighter outside than it was last night when Gregory found me crying in the rain. There's also a lot more people about.

I walk with him through the doors past the colorful pots of azaleas and over to the front desk. The woman behind it looks over from her computer screen and greets us.

"Hello. How can I help you?"

"We're here to visit my friend Destiny. I was here last night with Dr. Drew after she was brought in."

As she scans through the computer for a few moments I'm looking at the little trinkets on the desk. A little plastic bear wearing a bowtie is sitting next to the pen cup which is painted with pink and purple streaks. A vase with fake flowers is next to the window. And a variety of cute stickers are on the glass.

After a few minutes of her going through the computer she stops typing and opens her mouth to tell me what's going on.

"So Destiny is going to have surgery this morning because during the night her body was starting to go into shock and her brain was going into an abnormal neural rhythm. She's still in her room for a few more minutes so you can still see her before they take her in for surgery."

As soon as she's done speaking I grab Gregory's hand and haul ass to the elevator.

I press the button to go up to the fifth floor. Once the doors are closed, my right leg starts to shake with anxiety waiting for the elevator to reach the floor.

After what feels like an eternity, the doors finally open.

I run out as soon as the doors are open enough and run as fast as I can to my best friend's room with Gregory right behind me.

When we get there, Dr. Drew is walking towards her door.

It takes me a few seconds to catch my breath once I stop running and am standing in front of him. My chest is going up and down quickly with each breath going in and out of my lungs.

Once I am finally able to breathe normally again I ask him, "What's going on? Why does she need surgery? She was stable last night. Is she going to be okay?"

I don't want to stop asking questions but he grabs onto my shoulders and stops me before I have a panic attack.

"She was, but at about 2:20 this morning when her nurse Alice went in to check on her she started to code because her brain was going into seizures from too much neural activity. I need to go in to try and stop it. Try to control the neurons so that they can go back to a normal state."

As soon as he finishes explaining what's going on I follow him into the room. I walk over to her bed and place my hand on her arm.

When I look at Destiny she looks so sad and frail just laying there on the bed with her arms in bandages and her left leg in a cast. She almost looks like a ghost of herself because her face is so pale . Her smile that was there when she left home this morning is nonexistent. Her hair looks dull and lifeless just laying behind her head on the pillow.

I reach my arms around her body and squeeze her into a hug, being careful not to squeeze too hard. I can feel a few tears falling from my eyes as soon as I let go.

"Please be okay, Destiny. Please."

After I stop hugging my best friend, Dr. Drew tells me that everything will be okay before a couple of attendings come in to help take her to the operating room.

God, I hope that she'll be okay.

Destiny's POV: I wake up the next morning to my sweetheart nuzzling her head against my chest. As Jade pulls close, I lean my head down and give her a kiss on her forehead. Her eyes flutter gently before opening.

Her mouth opens in a yawn as she says, "Good morning, babe."

"Good morning, beautiful." I give her a kiss before sitting up. "Do you want me to go make the coffee?"

She smiles at me, her cheeks pink with happiness. "I say we go out and grab coffee from our favorite coffee house in our pj's. How does that sound?"

I give Jade a kiss before I tell her that it sounds great.

Before we get ready to leave and go to Jay's Kaffeine House, I go into the bathroom to wash my face, brush my teeth, and brush my hair. I turn the warm water on and splash it across my face, then grab the bar of soap to start scrubbing my face.

As I scrub my face and wash it off I think to myself, God this feels so fucking amazing.

My eyes are closed while I wash my face off and rinse the soap off my face, and while I'm finishing getting rinsed off, I hear the door open. Before I can turn around, Jade grabs my hips and presses her body up against mine. I feel her leaving kisses along the back of my head and neck, making me feel warm.

"Mmm, your so gorgeous in the morning, baby." She starts running her fingers through the tangles in my hair as I turn around. "You are just so fucking perfect."

I give my girlfriend a kiss on her pink lips as I lean in close to her. My lips move with hers as we kiss each other with pure affection. My heart starts to speed up a little as a smile spreads across my face.

Jade and I kiss each other for a few more moments, running our fingers through each other's hair. I kiss her lips softly before I pull away. Once we stop kissing, I grab my toothbrush and put some toothpaste on it and run it under some water so that I can brush my teeth.

As I brush back and forth across my teeth I glance at Jade in the mirror while she's brushing her hair and making faces at me. I finish brushing my teeth after a few minutes and bend over to spit in the sink, running the water to help clean out my mouth.

Once all the toothpaste is gone, I grab my dark blue towel from next to the sink and dry off my face. I finish getting the water dried from my face before tossing the towel in Jade's face playfully. Before it can drop to the floor, she grabs it and tosses it back.

She laughs with a cute smile on her face. "I love you so fucking much, baby. Are you ready to go get coffee now?"

"Of course, babe. Let's hit the road."

I go into the bedroom and slide my sneakers onto my feet and grab Jade's shoes for her. After I grab her shoes and take them to her, she puts them on and we head out to the car.

Jade and I go down the elevator and out to the parking lot where our yellow bug is parked. Since I'm going to be driving, I go ahead and climb into the driver's seat while Jade climbs into the passenger seat. I turn the keys in the ignition and turn up the radio so that we can listen to Three Doors Down until we get to the coffee shop about ten minutes away.

****

Jade and I just pulled into the parking lot at Jay's Kaffeine House where there are at least a dozen other cars. Once I get the car into park, we both get out and head inside.

I grab the door and hold it open for my sweetie so she can walk inside and follow after once she's through the door. We both walk over to the counter where Jay is standing behind the register.

He smiles at us when we walk over. "Hello, girls. It's good to see you two this morning. Do you want your regular orders? Or would you like to try my new cinnamon vanilla frappucinno? Also I just finished baking a pan of cherry chocolate chip muffins if you'd each like one."

"Thanks, Jay." I turn to Jade and ask, "What do you think, babe? Do you want to try those?"

"Heck yeah, baby. Those both sound great."

Jay gives us both a huge smile as he starts making our drinks. "Here are the muffins, girls. I'll bring your drinks over to your table in a moment."

I grab the muffins from the counter and go with Jade over to our usual table.

After we both sit down, I take a bite of my muffin. As soon as the flavor hits my taste buds, my eyes widen from the taste of the cherries and chocolate.

"Oh my god! This is freakin' delicious."

Jade takes a bite after I say that and she doesn't even swallow before exclaiming, "Holy crap on a cracker! This is absolutely amazing."

We were going to just sit and chat, but the muffins are so good that I can barely think. It's even better than her muffin.

It's just so crumbly from the bread, but so moist and gooey from the chocolate chips and the warm juice coming from the cherries. I don't think that I have ever eaten anything this scrumptious in my life.

As I finish eating my muffin, Jay walks over with our coffees.

"It looks like you two really liked the pastries. Here are your coffees. I hope you enjoy them just as much."

Jade thanks him through a mouthful while wiping her mouth with a napkin.

I smile at her as I take a drink of my coffee.

"Mmm this is good too. Just the right amount of vanilla to cinnamon. It's so sweet I might go into diabetic shock from breakfast. How does yours taste, babe?"

"Mine is great, baby. I love the cinnamon and the vanilla together. I'm so happy that we came to get coffee and breakfast this morning. And hopefully we'll be able to go do something downtown for the rest of the morning until you go to work at noon."

As we continue sipping on our coffees we both keep talking about what we could do before I go into work. I mention a craft fair that's going on all week that we could go to. Or the local museum. Or even the crystal and spells shop.

After talking for thirty minutes about what we could do before I go to work, we both finish our coffees and get up from the table. Before we go out the door I tell Jay bye and that we'll be back tomorrow morning for our coffee.

I walk with my girlfriend to the car and let her get behind the wheel because she's driving us to our morning destination.

"You choose what we do before I have to go in. I just want to spend the time with you doing whatever you choose."

I turn towards Jade with a smile on my face before kissing her and getting in on the passenger side of the car.

She starts driving and turns onto Turner Street towards downtown. "We're going to the craft fair this morning, and the crystal shop once you get home. Does that sound good, baby?"

"Of course it does. I said that I'd love anything this morning."

****

We arrive downtown about twenty minutes after leaving the coffee shop and it's already bustling with people at barely nine o'clock in the morning.

There are kiosks and stands and activity areas going down the next eight blocks and my heart is racing with excitement over all the fun things we could do. The first one that catches my eye is a painting booth with blank canvases and a variety of paints to use. I point it out to Jade and we walk over to the person running the booth.

"Hi. Can we each paint something for each other?"

The woman turns towards us and hands us each a paintbrush. "You can. You can each paint your own canvases or you could paint together or even on each other. Just not on me because as you can see I have enough paint on me for everyone."

I take a look at her clothes and her apron, along with her shirt and pants, and they are covered in splotches of paint.

After we tell her that we'd each like to do a painting, she points us to our canvases and tells us that we can go wild if we want, and we can mix whatever colors we choose.

I look at the paints in front of me and think before I choose my first color of paint. After thinking for a few seconds I grab the violet paint and the red paint and squirt some onto the pallet next to me. I start mixing them together before putting anything onto my canvas.

I begin to paint streaks across the top to make a dark background. I slide the brush along the canvas until the paint from the brush has faded and has almost a wispy look. Next I take the red paint and the yellow paint and begin to paint little flowers along the bottom of the canvas, tapping the brush in little speckle spots across the canvas until there's a field. Then I get some blue paint and place it across the middle.

I put a few clouds across the sky, paint a few mountains in the background, and finish by painting a silhouette of Jade and I walking away. After I finish the painting I grab a small brush and sign my name in the corner of the canvas then rinse off the brush.

I take a look over at Jade's canvas to see how her painting is coming along, and what I see is absolutely beautiful. On her canvas she's painting an abstract portrait of my face with hers slightly behind mine.

I can feel my cheeks turning pink as I watch her finish her painting.

It takes her a few more minutes to finish her artwork, but as soon as she's done I go over to her and give her a huge hug from behind.

"I love you so freaking much, babe. Your painting is absolutely amazing and I can't believe how much detail you put into it. You even put the speck of grey in my right eye. And the freckles. It looks absolutely amazing."

Jade looks over to me with the biggest smile on her face. "Thank you so much, baby. And look at yours. You did amazing at the silhouette and the colors. I love you so fucking much."

She reaches over and gives me a soft kiss on my lips before we both grab our paintings and go back to the car so I can go home and get ready for work.

About thirty minutes later when we've arrived at the apartment, I make my way into the bedroom to get changed into my work clothes.

I get a black blouse out of the closet along with a pair of jeans. When I set them on the bed so I can start getting changed, I feel Jade come up behind me and start pulling my pajama shirt off.

"Come on, baby. You can be a few minutes late to work today, right?"

I giggle a bit as she starts running her hands along my body before sliding my pants down my legs. Her hands move along every inch of skin before slowly sliding underneath my panties, her fingers moving along my lips.

A slight moan escapes from mouth as she slides her fingers into me, slow and sensual. Jade's finger move slowly in and out of my entrance, putting pressure against the skin inside me. I start kissing her neck as she maneuvers me onto the bed.

I kiss all along her neck and down towards her breasts as her fingers move in and out of me. All I can think about in this moment is Jade and her wonderful touch. Her skin is so warm and pink.

I start moving down her body with my mouth, leaving kisses and small bite marks from nibbling her skin. As my mouth reaches her waistline I pull her panties down a little bit, licking her skin. I swirl my tongue across her warm, soft pussy while she keeps fingering my insides.

Every thought leaves my head as I focus on only her and I and what we are doing in this moment: loving each other.

I don't stop using my mouth in between Jade's legs until I can feel her legs starting to shake. Her freckles on her legs are almost vibrating underneath my mouth as I leave small kisses with my lips.

Her fingers are still inside me when I sit up, moving in circles around my g-spot. I smile at my baby when she pulls her fingers out a few seconds later, and she smiles back before giving me a few soft kisses on my wet lips.

"I love you so much, babygirl," I tell her as I get up and put my work clothes on.

After I finish getting dressed, Jade grabs a clean t-shirt from the closet to put on, a black shirt with a tie dye picture of a pentagram on it. She slides on her dark blue skinny jeans afterwards while I go to the kitchen to finish getting ready for work.

I grab my hair brush and run it through my hair quickly before grabbing a bottle of water to bring with me to work.

Jade walks over to me after coming out of the bedroom and wraps her arms around me in a hug. "I love you so fucking much, baby, and I hope that you have an amazing day at work today. And tell Sherry that I said hi once you get to the office."

I pick up my keys, wallet, and phone as I give her one last kiss before I leave for work.

****

When I get to work at the office I'm greeted by Sherry as soon as I get inside.

"Hey, girl. How are you doing this morning?"

I can feel a huge grin spreading across my face as my mind thinks back to what Jade and I did before I left the apartment. "I am doing fantastic. Jade and I had coffee and breakfast at Jay's diner earlier and had a blast at the craft fair downtown."

Sherry smiles at me as she goes to grab a box of papers from underneath her desk and sets them down in front of me. "Awesome. Did either of you make anything cool?"

"We both painted a picture. I painted a sort of landscape with a silhouette of us walking towards the dusk sky and she painted a portrait of us."

She nods her head in approval as she says, "You two are such a great couple, babe. I won't be surprised if this time next year you guys are engaged to each other."

I giggle as I grab the box and take it to my office so that I can start looking over the papers in it.

As I start looking through them, I can see that they are all reviews of my article from TIME magazine. And each one is raving about how great it is. How the author, me, should be writing more than just magazines articles. That I should be writing books, novels and novellas.

I take out my headphones as I finish looking over the reviews and turn on my computer. I open up Microsoft Word and start trying to brainstorm a story idea so that I can try to come up with an idea for my first novel.

About thirty minutes after reading the reviews, I manage to write almost three pages on the computer. I ended up just writing about Jade and I, using different names of course. Writing about our relationship and our love and everything that we can picture in our future.

I spend the entire rest of my day in the office just writing. By the time it's almost 5:00 I've managed to write almost thirty pages on the book that I've started.

By the time I gather my things to leave, I have written almost 150 pages. When I walk out of my office and go to the front to leave, I go over to where Sherry is and give her a hug. "I'll see you tomorrow. Have a great night, Sher."

"You too, hun. Stay safe out there and tell Jade that I said hi."

I laugh as I walk out the door. "I will. Thank you."

We both walk out to our cars and hit the road home. While I'm driving, I turn up the radio and jam to Evanescence until I pull up in front of the apartment. After about twenty minutes of driving, I arrive home. When I unlock the front door and walk inside, I see Jade already passed out on the couch.

I grab a warm, red checkered blanket and place it over Jade's body before giving her a small kiss on the lips.

I whisper to her, "Goodnight, babygirl. I love you," before I go to the bedroom and get out of my work clothes and into bed for the night.

Chapter Four

Jade's POV: It has been at least seven hours since Destiny was taken into surgery and I'm starting to get really worried. I've been pacing back and forth since the doctors left with her, and each hour is just making me more and more antsy.

I keep trying to sit down and watch the TV that's on in the waiting room but I can't. I haven't said a word to Gregory since the first hour either, and I can tell he's getting worried about me.

I sit down after walking around the entire room again and grab a magazine from the table to try to read but end up just flipping through the pages. My mind can't stop racing with worry and anxiety so I decide to go ask the nurse if there have been any updates on Destiny.

I walk over to the desk where a blonde woman in bubblegum pink scrubs is sitting behind the window. "Has there been any updates on my friend Destiny Morgan's surgery? She's been in there for over seven hours."

The woman looks up from the computer for a moment to answer me. "Let me see here... The last update that was given was that Dr. Drew is almost done and going to be sewing her up soon. They should be taking her up to recovery any minute, then he'll cometell you how the surgery went."

I let out a sigh of relief knowing that her surgery is almost finished. I walk back over to where Gregory is sitting halfway awake on a chair so that I can tell him the news.

"Hey Gregory, wake up. They should be bringing Destiny out of surgery soon then they'll be taking her into recovery."

He opens his eyes and yawns as he starts to sit up from the chair. "That's great. Hopefully everything went well and she'll be all right. I'll be right here with you until the doctor gets here. Don't worry. Everything will be okay."

I sit back down with Gregory on the chairs and try to relax while we wait for Dr. Drew to come talk to us. As we talk, my mind wanders for a while, zoning out until the doctor shows up.

I watch the news on the TV to try and get my mind to focus. Right now they have the anchors on there doing a newscast of a local celebrity.

After fifteen minutes of watching the news, Dr. Drew shows up.

He walks over to where we're sitting and begins speaking. "Destiny is in recovery now from her surgery. The surgery went really well. I was able to get her neurons to calm down in her brain. There was some swelling when I went in, but I was able to get it to go down and back to normal. She is still in a coma but the muscles and nerves in her body have started to twitch, so there is a chance that she could wake up soon."

"Oh my god!!! Can we go see her soon?"

"You can. Just follow me to the recovery ward."

Gregory and I both stand up and follow Dr. Drew to recovery. We have to go down a few hallways and pass by a few rooms on the way to see Destiny.

When we get to her room she's laying peacefully on the hospital bed. She still looks broken but has a little more color in her cheeks. It almost looks as if she has a smile on her face.

I reach down and run my hands across her face as I walk up to her bed, feeling every curve of her skin.

I close my eyes as I bend over to give Destiny a hug and say into her ear, "Please Destiny, please wake up. You're my best friend and I can't function without you. I love you and want to hear your voice and see your bright eyes and smile again. Just please come back."

As I go to stand up, Gregory comes over and gives me a hug. "She's going to be okay. I just have this feeling that Destiny is going to wake up soon. We can stay here all day with her if you want. I don't have anywhere that I have to go today."

I nod my head to say yes. Because I am not leaving her side until she wakes up. I need to be here when she does.

Dr. Drew comes over next to Destiny's bed where we're standing and says, "You two can stay here all day. I'm going to be coming back in a few hours to see if there is any progress on her state. If either of you need anything, you can press the call button for the nurses station."

He walks out of the room and closes the door after he's finished speaking.

I stand next to Destiny's bed looking down at her. She just looks so different and lifeless being unconscious like she is.

I feel Gregory place his arm around my shoulder as a tear falls down my face. He pulls a chair over next to the bed so that I could sit down next to the bed.

"Here. Sit down. I'm going to go down to the cafeteria and grab us each some jello to eat. That way you have something in your stomach while we're here."

My head turns towards him as I say, "Okay. I'm just going to be sitting with her while you're gone."

When he closes the door behind him, I sit down in the chair next to Destiny's bed.

I reach out and grab her hand as I start to speak. "Destiny, I don't know if you can hear me or not, but I have been a complete wreck since I got the phone call about your accident. You make me happy every damn day and these past two days without you have been miserable. I need you to wake up. I need to see your happy face again."

I close my eyes while I continue to talk. "You have to wake up, because without you I'm nothing. I don't really have a purpose or reason without my best friend in my life."

After I say this, I feel a small twitch of her hand in mine. My eyes open quickly and I squeeze her hand tight. I reach over with my hands and run my right hand across her cheeks, waiting for her to move again.

I start to speak softly to her to try and get a reaction from her. "Babe, I know you're here and that you can hear me. I felt your hand move. I just need something to tell me that you're going to wake up soon. Anything. Please."

My eyes watch for any kind of movement. I sit, watching for any twitches or movements. As I watch Destiny's face for a few minutes, waiting for something to happen, I see her mouth start to move. Small sounds start coming out from between her lips.

"Babe. Babe," it sounds like she's saying.

I grab the remote next to the bed and start hitting the call button frantically. I grab ahold of her hand as I start calling out to get someone to come in here.

"Nurse! Nurse! I need somebody to come in here!"

After a few seconds a nurse comes through the door, looking frantic. "What happened? Is everything okay?"

I stand up before saying, "Her hand twitched and she spoke for a moment after I talked to her. Do you think that she's going to wake up soon?"

The nurse goes and grabs a little flashlight from the nurse's station. When she gets back, she starts shining the light into Destiny's eyes, trying to see any movement in her pupils.

"Her eyes have a little more life to them, so she may be close to waking up. But it could also still be hours or even days before she wakes up."

I nod my head as I reach my hand over towards Destiny. "Okay, ma'am. Thank you."

When the nurse has left the room, Gregory walks through the door with the jello cups.

"What happened? Is she okay?" He sets the tray down and comes over to stand by my side.

"She's okay. I think that she might wake up soon because she kept saying something under her breath and her hand twitched in mine."

Gregory smiles at me. "Just keep talking to her and holding her hand. She'll wake up in no time. I know it."

Destiny's POV: The next morning I wake up to Jade being next to me under the covers. I lean towards her and give her a kiss on her cheek.

"Good morning, baby. How was your night?"

Her eyes open slowly, a smile spreading across her face. "It was wonderful. I'm glad you made it home from work safe. Are you ready to go on an adventure today?"

I look at her with confusion on my face. "Adventure? What are you talking about? We both have work today."

"I know. But your work is going to send you back to where you belong soon. You'll see when you get there. Now get dressed and go see."

I get up, confused as shit about what Jade means, and get dressed to go to work at the office.

The entire time I am getting ready to go, Jade is just sitting there on the bed like a robot in rest mode. I try not to think too much of it but feel concerned the entire time until I leave for work at 8:30.

When I get to the office, everything seems off. Every office is empty and void of anything, almost like it's been abandoned for years. I see Sherry when I get inside, but something seems off about her, too. Her face almost looks like Jade's.

"Good morning, babe. Are you going to wake up soon? Jade's waiting for you."

"What the hell is going on? Am I dreaming or going crazy?"

As soon as the words come out of my mouth everything around me starts to change. Sherry starts to fade along with the office. Everything swirls around me as the light starts to become brighter, almost white, blinding me.

I don't know what's going on, but everything keeps getting brighter and continues to change around me. As everything moves around me, the office changes into a white hospital room before my eyes. I see Jade sitting next to me, holding my hand.

I blink my eyes a few times trying to focus. As soon as I do this, her eyes pop wide open.

"Destiny!!! You're awake and you're alive!!! Are you okay? Do you feel okay? I was so worried about you. I thought you were going to die after you got into the car crash. I'm so happy you're awake."

She gives me a big hug after she finishes shooting out questions.

I look around for a few seconds, trying to get my brain to focus on what's going on. My right leg is in a cast and my torso is wrapped in bandages. My head is freaking killing me. And there's a strange guy standing next to Jade.

"What happened to me? Why am I in the hospital? Who is this?"

"You got into a car accident on the highway with a semi when you were driving home yesterday afternoon. You were in a coma after you were brought to the hospital and had surgery earlier today because of hyperactive neurons in your brain. This is Gregory. I met him last night outside of the hospital when I was crying and worried about you. He's been with me all night and all day."

My brain is starting to hurt from all the information. "Holy crap! What the hell?"

I was only dreaming that Jade and I were a couple and that I worked in an office as a writer. Everything felt so fucking real.

"I'm going to call in your doctor so that he can come check on you. Okay?" Jade tells me this as I break from my thoughts.

I nod my head as she presses the call button on the remote next to my bed.

My eyes turn to look at Gregory. "Thank you for being here for my friend while I was in a coma. I'm glad that she had someone with her for comfort and support."

His face turns up to a half smile. "I just wanted to make sure she would be okay, and that you were going to wake up. Even just for her. I found her crying outside of the hospital entrance in the rain. I wanted to make sure that she would be all right even though I didn't know her."

A big smile crosses onto my face as I say, "Thank you, Gregory. I really, really appreciate it. A lot." I turn toward Jade before continuing. "Jade, I am so freaking happy that you were here when I woke up."

As I'm speaking, the door opens and a doctor walks in, a clipboard in his hand.

"Well hello. My name is Dr. Drew. I see you're awake now. How are you feeling? Any pain or soreness? Headaches?"

"Just sore under the casts and bandages. I have a slight headache from the lights after waking up, but other than that I feel okay."

I take a glance towards Jade. "I'm incredibly grateful that my best friend was here for me the last two days while I was out. When am I going to be able to go home?"

He takes a look through my chart for a few moments before answering me. "We still need to keep you here for at least a few days of observation to make sure that you haven't suffered any blunt trauma to your skull, but once we're certain that you are able to function well enough mentally, you will be allowed to go home. And you will be sent home with a wheelchair and crutches for your broken leg."

"Okay, doctor. Thank you so much." I pause for a second before I ask, "Is there any way that I can go outside in a wheelchair to sit in the moonlight with Jade for a few minutes? Just to get some fresh air."

Dr. Drew nods his head. "Of course."

He goes out into the hallway and brings in a wheelchair after a few seconds. "Here you go. You can take this down the elevator and go sit out in the courtyard with your friend."

After he tells me this and leaves, Jade and Gregory both start helping me into the wheelchair.

Jade moves the cover and grabs around my arms and shoulders and he grabs my legs. They carefully maneuver my body from the bed into the chair.

Gregory makes sure that I am situated comfortably in the seat before telling Jade and I that he's going to stay here while we go outside. "You two need some time together, so I'll let you all go by yourselves. I'll stay up here in case the doctor or nurse comes back."

I smile, happy with how understanding and kind Gregory is being towards both Jade and myself.

As Jade starts pushing me out of the room and down the hallway my mind starts to think back on the dream I was having while I was unconscious. It felt so fucking real.

I honestly thought that that was my life. My real life. I was happy and in love with my best friend.

I look up towards her, beaming with real happiness in my eyes. I'm thinking about what I want to say to her. About the dream life that we had while we are riding down to the first floor on the elevator. Because I felt truly in love in it and I honest to god want that feeling to become real.

"Hey, Jade? When we get outside I want to talk to you about everything I dreamed about while I was out, because it's important."

She reaches over to the panel on the wall and presses the STOP button. "What do you mean? What did you dream about?"

I give her a nervous smile. "I dreamed about us. You and me. But we were more than roommates. We were girlfriends and in love. When I thought that was my life, it felt amazing. It felt perfect."

Jade looks at me with slight shock and awe on her face. "Holy crap, Des. Do you feel like those feelings were real?"

"I do. They felt beyond real. They felt right. What do you think about all of this?"

Her mouth opens and closes a few times like a fish's mouth before she can even say anything.

"Uh-uhm... Holy fucking shit!!! I think it sounds amazing. Because to be honest, my mind has been telling me that there should be more with us. I've felt like I wanted to be more than friends since we both graduated from high school."

I start to laugh and cry tears of joy. "Really!? Oh my god!!! Are you serious!?"

"Yes, Destiny. I am dead serious. I would love to be your girlfriend if you really want that."

"Yes. I really do. I would love that a lot."

As soon as I finish my sentence, Jade bends over and gives me a kiss on the lips. It feels absolutely amazing to feel her lips on mine.

Our lips move together like we have been kissing each other every day for years. It feels right. Her lips are so warm and soft. They taste like cherries from her lip gloss she wore yesterday.

My tongue glides across her lips as she pulls away slowly, tasting the sweet cherry lip gloss on them. My eyes open and turn up to look at her before I open my mouth to speak.

"That felt amazing, baby. It felt so freaking right kissing you. It was like what I felt in my dream, except this time it was real. I love you so freaking much, baby, and I'm so glad that I had that dream."

Jade's face lights up with a sweet smile across her lips. "I had been thinking for a while about asking if you would want to go out for a date, but I was always too chicken to ask. So thank you so freaking much, Destiny."

A giggle escapes from between her lips as she presses the button to make the elevator start moving to the bottom floor again.

When it reaches the first floor and the doors open, zhe starts pushing my wheelchair down the hallway towards the direction of the cafeteria.

"I figured that you I would take you to get some food before we head back up to the room because you need some real food to eat instead of the feeding tube that you had for two days. We can go see what they have for dinner in the cafe."

It takes a few minutes for us to reach the cafe. When we get there people are scattered at the circular black metal tables eating from trays.

Jade pushes me over to the food counter and grabs a tray for our food.

There are all kinds of fresh sandwiches, some fried chicken strips, burgers, soup, salad. Some chips, fries, tater tots, and then jello and a few chocolate desserts.

I take a look at everything before I tell Jade, "We can grab a couple of ham and cheese sandwiches and bags of Lay's potato chips with a bowl of jello and some water to drink. Then we can make our way back up to the room."

"Okay, baby."

Jade places our food onto the tray and thanks the man behind the counter when he hands her two bottles of water. Once Jade has gathered our food and waters, she places the tray across my legs so that I can hold it while she helps me back up to the hospital room.

It takes much less time to get up there than it did to go down the elevator this time.

About five minutes after we leave the cafeteria we arrive back in my room. We are greeted by Gregory when Jade opens the door to push me into the room.

"Hi, girls. Is everything okay? You all were gone for a while."

I feel a smile spread across my face. "Everything is absolutely amazing, Greg. I just had to talk to Jade about something that I had been thinking about since waking up."

His eyebrows furrow into little creases across his forehead. "O-kay."

Jade starts helping me out of the wheelchair and back onto the bed, and Greg gets up to help get me back into the bed.

Once I am situated comfortably on the bed, Jade slides the bed tray over my legs and sets the food tray down so that I can eat. I pick up the sandwich first and take a big bite of it. The mayonnaise oozes from the sides of my mouth as I bite down.

It takes me about five minutes to finish my sandwich before I start on the chips and jello. By the time I'm about done with my chips the door opens and the doctor walks in.

"Well hello, Destiny. I'm Dr. Drew. How are you feeling, Destiny?"

I smile when I tell him, "I'm feeling great," and glance in Jade's direction. "I am really happy, doctor."

Chapter Five

Destiny's POV: Dr. Drew comes over to my bedside and takes out his stethoscope. "That's really good. Is it okay if I check your vital signs right quick?"

"Of course, Dr. Drew."

He smiles and gently presses the stethoscope against my chest after putting the ear pieces inside of his ears. He listens for a few seconds, moving it around my chest.

After listening to my heartbeat for a few seconds, he places the stethoscope on my back. "Take a deep breath for me."

I breath in through my mouth and out through my nose. I do this a few times as he places the stethoscope in different spots on my back listening to my lungs.

When he's done listening to my breathing he takes off the stethoscope and places it around his neck. "Your heart and lungs sound really healthy. I'm going to check your blood pressure now and then I'll leave you and your friends be for the night."

He puts the blood pressure cuff around my arm and starts tightening it until it's tightened all the way. It releases after a few seconds.

He looks down at the monitor and says, "Your blood pressure is 135 over 73. That is really good considering everything you have been through these last couple of days. I was expecting it to be almost 200 over 150."

When Dr. Drew finishes checking everything, he leaves the room and tells me that he will be back to check on me again in a few hours.

Once he's left the room and the door is closed behind him, Jade comes and sits next to me on the bed. She wraps her arms around my body in a hug.

"I am so freaking happy that you are okay, Destiny. I was so worried about you that I couldn't stop crying."

I give her a huge grin before saying, "Well I'm back now, baby. And I'm going to make sure not to go anywhere any time soon."

I plant a sweet kiss onto Jade's lips before she pulls away.

A few seconds after our kiss I turn my head and look over to where Greg is sitting in the chair, a look of awe across his face. He looks as if he's just seen a ghost.

"Holy crap! Where did that come from? I thought that you guys were just friends."

Jade and I both smile before she answers him.

"We were. But when we left earlier to talk, we both realized that we wanted more than that. That we love each other and want to be together. So that's what we are now. Together."

A smile spreads on his face, showing a dimple on the right side of his mouth. "Well damn. I'm happy for you guys. You both look really happy."

"Thank you," I say, my cheeks blushing pink. "It actually wouldn't have happened if not for the dream that I had while in the coma. So even though I'm still in a lot of pain after the accident, I'm glad that it happened. Because otherwise

Jade and I wouldn't have realized that we love each other and wanted to be in a relationship."

"Wow. I'm really happy for you two. Do you think that I should grab some dessert or something from the cafeteria or store to celebrate your new relationship?"

I let out a small laugh. "Sure, Greg. You can go get some chocolate ice cream. We'll just be hanging out here."

When I finish talking he gets up from his chair and leaves the room, leaving Jade and I to ourselves.

She looks at me with a slight hint of mischief in her eyes. "What do you want to do while he's away? Do you want to kiss some more or talk about what we're going to do after you're discharged in a couple of days?"

"We can talk some about what we're going to do after I can go home. I know that I'm not going to be able to go to work for at least a few months after I go home because of my broken leg and bruised ribcage. But I don't care, because in done with those jackasses after what I dealt with the other day."

"I'll be able to take care of you and help with everything at home and get you everything you need, baby. Don't worry about not working. I know you told me that they'd been pissing you off lately, so I'm glad you're not going back."

My face lights up. "Thank you so much, Jade. I love you so fucking much."

She gives me a kiss and hug. "Of course, Des. I'd do anything for you. As soon as you're out of here, me and Gregory, are going to take you to the house and make sure you're nice and comfortable in the bed."

Gregory walks into the room with three bowls of chocolate ice cream and plates of cake.

"Here's the celebration dessert, girls. Did I just hear my name?"

Jade laughs for a second then says, "Yeah, I was just telling Destiny that as soon as we get her home that we would both make sure that she's able to be comfortable on the bed, and that I will take care of her the whole time that she's incapacitated."

"Yes. And if you girls need help with anything during the healing process, Destiny, I can come help out."

I tell him, "Thank you, Greg. I really appreciate it. A lot."

I lay back against the pillows and turn the TV on, scrolling through channels until I come upon Friends. It's the episode "The One Where No One Is Ready."

I start watching the show with Jade and Greg until my eyes start to get drowsy.

Jade's POV: I finish eating my ice cream and cake when I notice that Destiny has fallen asleep.

As I throw my plate and spoon away I lean over to Greg and whisper, "I really, really appreciate everything."

"No worries. I know we just met last night, but it feels like I'm the protective older brother for both of you. I'd do anything to help you both out just to make sure you're okay."

****

I wake up the next morning to whispers between Destiny and Gregory.

"You really think so?"

Gregory whispers back, "Oh yeah, she'd do anything for you."

After a few seconds of eavesdropping I open my eyes and stretch, letting them both know that I'm awake.

"Good morning, guys. How did you both sleep?"

I stand up and go over to Destiny giving her a good morning kiss.

"Hello, beautiful. I slept great. Has Dr. Drew been in yet to see you this morning?"

"He hasn't yet, but it's barely six o'clock."

I sit back down as Gregory tells me, "You have an amazing girlfriend here. We were just talking about you while you were asleep. She told me that ever since you guys met in elementary school that you have been basically inseparable."

I can feel my face turn beet red in embarrassment. "Well she was my first friend and my closest friend. If Destiny wasn't in my life I don't know what I would do."

All three of us continue to talk until the doctor comes in for Destiny's morning check.

"How are you feeling today, Destiny? Any soreness or headaches?"

I turn my head to look at my babygirl as she answers him.

"I'm feeling extremely well rested. I fell asleep fast last night. I have had a slight migraine since waking up, though. Do you think that has anything to do with head trauma?"

Dr. Drew takes a look at Destiny's chart. "Hmm... I may have to take you in for an MRI in a little while after your breakfast is brought in and you have been able to eat. Because having a migraine might mean something happened through the night that needs to be taken care of as soon as possible."

I can see Destiny's chest start to move faster with her breathing. She starts to hyperventilate as a panic attack comes on.

Dr. Drew tries to start calming her down by telling her that it's most likely nothing but he just wants to be sure. I come stand next to her, caressing her arm and sliding my hand across her hair.

"Everything will be okay, baby. I know it. Try not to worry. Besides in a few minutes your breakfast should be here."

Destiny takes a deep, wavering breath. "I trust you. As long as you are here, I will be okay."

As soon as Destiny is able to get her breathing back to normal and calm back down, the doctor asks to take her vital signs again. He also asks if he can take some blood so that he is able to get her labs tested and make sure that everything is on the up and up.

It only takes him a few minutes to do everything and get her blood drawn.

"Amelia should be in in a few minutes with your breakfast. I'll be back in about an hour to take you for an MRI scan."

****

Destiny's POV: I look up as the door opens and Dr. Drew walks in.

He greets me and asks, "Are you ready for your scan?"

I nod my head before he helps me into the wheelchair so that he can take me to get the MRI.

As he gets ready to take me out of the room Jade gives me a kiss and tells me that she'll be waiting with Greg for when I come back. I tell her that I love her and will be back in a few hours after the scan is finished.

When Dr. Drew and I are out of the room and on the way to the MRI room he asks me, "How are you feeling?"

I sigh in content. "Doctor... I feel amazing because I have had Jade here with me this entire time. The migraine is still bothering me a little, but because of her and Gregory I have been able to ignore it."

"Okay. Well hopefully this scan will help us find out what's causing the migraines. I am very glad that your friends have been helping you. We're about to arrive to the MRI room. As soon as we get there I'm going to have to place you onto the bottom of the machine and we'll get started."

A few seconds later he pushes me into a room with a large metal machine that has a metal bed in front of it.

When we get into the room, a nurse comes over to help get me onto the bed from the wheelchair and get me laid just right. She places a pillow underneath my legs to prop up my broken leg.

"There you go, sweetie. This way your leg can stay propped up while you are inside the MRI machine. As soon as it starts you'll be slid back into the machine. When the scan begins it's going to be loud. If you would like, I can place some earplugs into your ears to muffle the sounds."

I thank her and accept the earplugs.

Before she puts them into my ears she also tells me, "About halfway through the scan I am going to have to give you a small injection of medicine. The entire scan should only take a couple of hours. But it should be done in what feels like no time. Are you ready?"

"Yes ma'am. I'm ready."

She goes out into the computer area before the scan begins. After a few moments the machine slides me back inside.

"There's going to be a red light before the first scan begins, so you may want to close your eyes."

I do as she says and close them before the red light appears. Then a second later the machine starts to make noise. It sounds like loud thumping at first and it's really ear-rattling, so I'm glad I have the earplugs.

My eyes close as I try to just focus on the noise, trying to make a rhythm out of it. My mind and brain begin to relax as the sounds wash over me. After a while it feels like I fell asleep with my brain still active, listening to the machine.

Almost an hour has gone by when the nurse stops the machine and comes back in. "I'm here to give you the injection. How are you feeling?"

As she wraps a rubber band around my arm to check for a vein I tell her, "I'm really relaxed. The noise was actually putting me to sleep a little bit."

She starts tapping the inside of my elbow to try and get a vein to the surface. "I'm glad, sweetie. I think I may have found a vein. I'm about to try and get the needle in and it may sting a little."

As she carefully presses the needle into my skin I do a fast intake of breath.

"I'm so sorry, sweetie. It's almost over."

After she says that she grabs a cotton ball and vet wrap. She places the cotton ball on my skin as the needle comes out and then wraps the vet wrap around my arm.

"There we go. Now I'm going to go back in there so that we can finish the scan."

When she's back on the other side of the window I'm slid back inside the machine. My eyes close as the noise starts back up, focusing on the rhythm of it. My mind relaxes and zones out until the machine is done with the scan.

About an hour later when the scan is finished, Dr. Drew comes back into the room.

He comes over and helps me back into the wheelchair. "I'm going to take you back up to your room. Then I'll go take a look at your scans and come talk to you about them."

As we make our way back up to my room my mind starts to think about everything that's changed since the car crash.

How I'm going to be in a cast and bandages for at least a few months. How I'm going to have to do physical therapy for a while once I'm free of the bandages. The new friend Gregory who Jade met. And my new relationship with Jade because of my realized feelings after having the dream in my coma.

I zone back into reality when Dr. Drew pushes me through the door to my room.

As soon as we're through the door Gregory and Jade stand up and help him get me back into the bed and lay the blankets back over my legs.

"I'll be back in about thirty or forty minutes to give you the results of the scan." After he finishes telling us this, Dr. Drew leaves the room and closes the door behind him.

Jade comes over after he's gone and asks me, "How was the MRI?"

"It was good. The machine was loud during the scans, but somehow I was able to relax and almost fall asleep during the entirety of it. And the nurse was really nice."

"I'm glad, baby. Do you think that everything is going to be okay with the results?"

I think for a second before answering.

"I'm not sure. Because I don't know what could have been causing the migraine or what could be there. Inside my brain. And I'm worried."

I'm trying not to cry as Jade comes over and gives me a hug. But as soon as her arms are wrapped around me I break down in sobs.

"I don't know what could be wrong and I'm scared. I'm terrified that something even worse could be going on in my brain."

Jade sits up and grabs me by the shoulders. "Listen baby, I'm sure that it's nothing bad. It's probably just migraines and nothing to worry about. Let's just relax until Dr. Drew gets back with the results of your scan."

Gregory comes over and gives me a hug also. "Whatever happens, try not to worry. Because I know that you can make it through anything. You are incredibly strong."

I let a weak smile cross my face. "Thank you guys. I'm just ready to get out of here and go home."

****

We all keep talking about everything that has happened until Dr. Drew shows up thirty minutes later.

"I just finished going over your scans, Destiny, and I didn't find anything out of the ordinary. Just some active brain waves full of thought. I also didn't find any damaged tissue or trauma in your brain. Everything seems to be perfectly fine in there. I don't believe that there is anything serious causing the migraines."

I let out a huge sigh of relief. "Oh thank god, doctor. I was so freaking worried that something was wrong with me."

Dr. Drew smiles. "There is nothing to worry about. You're just going to be here for a few more days for observation and then you'll be able to go home. You will of course have to come back in a few months to get the cast removed from your leg and then start on physical therapy to start walking again."

After the doctor finishes telling me what's going to happen and leaves the room, Jade comes over to me and says, "I'm so fucking glad that nothing is wrong. Do you want me to get you anything? Or do you need anything?"

I lay back against the pillows and close my eyes as I tell her and Gregory, "I think that I want to get some rest for the next few hours and am probably going to take a nap. You guys can stay or go do something if you want. "

Gregory stands up and says, "We'll stay until you fall asleep, then we'll probably go hang out in the courtyard for a while. That way it's nice and quiet."

Gregory's POV: Jade and I leave to go down to the courtyard as soon as Destiny falls asleep.

After we're out of the room and the door is closed I ask Jade, "You seem really in love with Destiny. How long have you thought that you might want to ask her to be your girlfriend?"

As we're walking, she looks over at me and says, "We have been friends since we were kids and spent almost every single day together. She was the person I trusted through everything and told everything to. Destiny was the only person who was always there for me. I think that I started to get feelings for her the winter break after freshman year of college. I was supposed to go home but right before I was going to leave the campus to go to my parents house, I got a call that they were going to Las Vegas for the holidays. I had nowhere to go and was going to be stuck by myself for three weeks.

"Destiny could see that and offered to bring me to her family's for vacation. I went with her and rode the entire way to her family's house in New Hampshire a few hours away. And when we got there, everyone greeted me like I was family. I loved it. I felt welcome and wanted instead of forgotten and abandoned. I wanted to be able to spend every day with Destiny after that, because she made me feel loved."

Gregory smiles at me after I finish talking. "So why didn't you ask her to be your girlfriend any time sooner? I'm sure she would have said yes back then. Because it almost seems like she's felt the same way for a while considering her dream."

"I was just always terrified of being rejected by her and laughed at. So I'm beyond grateful that everything is turning out the way that it is despite the circumstances. Because I fucking love her with everything I have."

As Jade and I continue talking, we arrive to the courtyard.

We both take a seat on the wooden bench before I tell her, "I'm really happy for you both, even if it did take a few years for you guys to figure out how to tell each other how you feel."

After he says this, I notice that the sun is shining really bright and warm in the sky and birds are chirping. *It's a perfect day, even if it is being spent at the hospital. I am sure that everything will be absolutely amazing for these two girls. I just know it, and I'm happy for them.*

I sit there and watch the birds and people walking by with Jade for what feels like hours before she tells me that she wants to go back inside and make sure that Destiny is still doing okay.

"Okay, Jade. I think I'm going to leave the two of you alone for the rest of the day and overnight so that you can spend some quality time together. While I'm away, I can pick up anything you need and bring it up here. Snacks, clothes, or even board games to play."

"Thank you so much, Gregory. I appreciate your help and everything you have been doing to help us through all of this. I think we'll be okay on everything, but if I think of anything I'll call you."

Jade gets up and goes inside as I go out to the car and head to my house.

When I get there twenty minutes later, I get on the computer and open my emails. As soon as I get them open, I see a bunch of messages from my boss in Devan County.

The first email that shows up says, *Gregory, I need the report for the Connor case sent in right away.*

Every email after that is basically the same. I get started on writing out that report on the case as soon as I get through with my emails. It was a family of three who were killed by the psychotic father.

The man claimed to not have any idea what happened before he found them chopped up and tied to the tree in the front yard. Supposedly he had been out on the lake with friends, but none of them could verify his alibi.

As far as the evidence shows, it all points to him being the guilty man. Even the murder weapon was found in his shed, still covered in dried blood. He said that it was from him chopping up a deer he just butchered but no meat was found on the property, and the blood tested as his wife and children's.

I have been avoiding writing this report because of how much it makes my stomach turn thinking about the crime scene and seeing those poor innocent girls' body parts next to their mother's. Their eyes looked so terrified.

That's why I've been feeling so obligated to help Jade and Destiny out after everything they have been through. Because so much worse could have happened to Destiny when she got in that accident with the semi truck.

I didn't even realize until this morning when I woke up that I had been on the scene of her car accident after it happened. I saw how broken she looked on the asphalt and

I thought that she wasn't going to make it. I'm very fucking happy that she's okay and awake. Functioning perfectly except for her broken leg and bruised ribs.

I just want to be there for the both of them until Destiny's okay and able to go home. I want to know that they're both going to be okay and that nothing else bad happens to either of them.

****

It takes me all night to get the report done on the Carter case, but once I'm finished with it I feel like I can breathe again. Because I don't have to look at the gruesome photographs, evidence, or interview videos.

Watching the videos of Deacon Carter being interviewed made my stomach turn because he seemed so lacking of emotions. He didn't seem to care at all about what happened or the fact that his wife and daughter were dead.

After I type up the last bit of the report, I send an email to my boss asking when he wants me to get the report for Destiny's case sent to him. I still need to talk to the drivers of the truck that hit her vehicle, and I need to find out what all she remembers from the time of the accident. I really don't want to, but it's my job.

And I'm going to have to tell Jade that I was one of the officers that was called to the scene of Destiny's crash. That's the part that scares me the most.

Chapter Six

Gregory's POV: I fell asleep last night after emailing Jimmy about the accident report. I was so tired that I passed out as soon as my head hit the pillows.

When I get up and check the clock, it says that it's almost 8:30 in the morning, and I have at least ten missed calls from Jade. As soon as I'm up and wake my eyes a little bit I grab the phone and call Jade back. It rings about three times before she picks up the phone.

"I have amazing news. Dr. Drew came in early this morning to check on Destiny and told us that she can go home tonight. Her lab and MRI results showed that she doesn't have any serious trauma from the accident and that she seems like she's functioning well enough to go home and let her leg heal in her own bed.

"She will still have to keep the bandages around her torso because of the bruised ribs and stay in bed with her leg elevated. But he said that she's good to go home this afternoon."

I can feel my heart grow warm with happiness and a smile spread across my face. "Awesome! That's great, Jade. I'm going to try to come up this afternoon to help when she's discharged, but I can't come visit this morning because I have some work to do."

"Okay, Greg. Well we'll see you this afternoon."

I tell her bye before hanging up the phone.

After I've hung up, I get up from my bed and grab my police uniform out of the closet. I lay the button up shirt and pants across the back of my desk chair and go to the bathroom to take a quick shower.

I turn the water on to warm before taking off my clothes and climbing in.

The water washes over my body and my head as soon as I'm under it, easing all of my muscles and the tension in me. I let my body get covered by the water coming out of the showerhead before grabbing the shampoo so I can wash my hair.

I put some of it into my hair and massage my hands through it. I scrub it into my scalp before letting the water wash over my head.

My eyes close as soon as I'm completely under the water, my mind relaxing from the warm temperature.

It takes me about fifteen minutes to get my entire body washed off before I get out and dry off. Once I'm out of the shower and am completely dry, I go back to my bedroom and get my uniform put on.

I brush my hair back with some hair gel and put my hat on. Then I grab my boots, pull them onto my feet, and tie the laces into a military bow.

Before I leave to go to the station I make sure that I have my taser, baton, and gun in its holster. Once I'm sure that I have everything I head out the door and start driving to the station.

A few minutes of driving later, I arrive in front of the station and get out of my vehicle where I'm greeted by Lieutenant Jimmy Sanchez.

"Good morning, Sergeant Miller. Thank you for getting the report on the Carter case. And how's everything going with getting started on the case with the semi accident from the other day?"

A sigh escapes from my mouth as I tell him, "I haven't been able to get started on it yet but I'm going to call the drivers of the truck after I get into my office and ask when they can come in for an interview."

Sanchez tells me, "You better get on it because the hospital that the victim is staying in just called today and said she's being released this afternoon. We need to find out if she's going to press charges on them."

"Yes, sir. I'll get on it as soon as soon as I'm in my office."

I finish talking with Sanchez then go inside and look up the phone number for Bruce Edwards. Once I find his phone number, I dial in the numbers and wait as it rings.

After about three rings the phone is answered with a, "Hello? Who is this?"

"This is Sergeant Gregory Miller. Is this Bruce Edwards?"

He answers me, saying, "Uh... yes, sir. What's going on?"

"I am one of the officers from the accident you were in a couple of days ago. I was wondering if you and your friend could come in this morning for an interview about what happened."

"Oh shit. Yeah. I'll call Mike and we can come up in about an hour."

I get off the phone after Mike says that. After a few minutes of thinking about what I'm going to say when I have to ask if Destiny wants to press charge, I go to Sanchez's office to tell him that I've got the men coming in about an hour for an interview about the accident.

I knock on his door with my knuckles and wait a few seconds before opening the door and going inside.

"Lieutenant Sanchez? Bruce Edwards and his friend are going to be here in an hour for their interview. I'm going to be in my office writing a list of questions to ask while I wait for them to get here."

Sanchez looks up from his desk and tells me, "Good man. Call me before you start the interview process once they arrive so that I can be witness behind the glass."

"Yes, sir. I can do that, sir."

I go back to my office after I finish talking to Sanchez and get started with wrriting down my questions.

Bruce's POV: As soon as I'm off the phone with Sergeant Miller I think to myself, *Oh shit!!! I've got to call Mike and tell him what's going on.*

I dial up Mike's number and wait for him to answer. It keeps ringing for at least five rings before going to voicemail.

Gaw!!! Come on, Mike! Answer your freaking phone.

I hang up, not bothering to leave a voicemail that he won't answer. I get up and start grabbing clothes from my dresser to put on after I hang up. I get out a white t-shirt and black plaid button up with a pair of dark blue jeans.

As soon as I'm about to start buttoning my shirt I hear my phone ringing from my nightstand. I make my way over to grab it and see that it's Mike.

When I hit the button to answer the call I say, "Mike, get your ass up and dressed. We need to go to the police station. I just got a call saying that we need to come up for an interview about the crash from the other morning."

Mike starts talking mid-yawn. "Shit! Okay. I'll meet you there in thirty minutes."

****

I get to the station about twenty minutes later and head inside.

"Hi. I got a call to come in for an interview with Sergeant Miller. My friend Mike should be here soon, too. I was told that we both need to come up for the interview."

The man at the front desk tells me, "Sergeant Miller will be out shortly to come get you. Will your friend be here soon?"

I nod my head. "Yes, sir. He should be here in a few minutes."

"Okay. You can have a seat over on the bench by the front doors until the sergeant comes out to get you. If your friend isn't here by the time you have to go back, I'll tell him where to go."

After he finishes talking, I go and take a seat. As I'm sitting there, I start twiddling my thumbs while I wait.

For the entire ten minutes that I'm waiting I watch people come in and out of the doors. Officers, regular people, people in handcuffs following officers into the building. I feel like I'm going to go crazy when finally the door opens and Mike comes inside, right as an officer with the name tag Miller comes out from the back.

"Hello, gentleman. I'm Sergeant Miller. Are you Bruce and Mike?"

Mike and I walk over to him.

I glance over at Mike before saying, "Yes. I'm Bruce, and this is Mike."

Sergeant Miller gives us a smile as he tells us, "Follow me. I just have a few questions to ask you two about the accident per my lieutenant. No need to be worried."

Mike and I follow him through a door and down the hallway. We go with him through the second door on the right. When we go into the room, we both have a seat in the chairs near the back wall, across from Miller.

"Okay, fellas. So that accident you got into the other day with the black Corolla... what can either of you tell me about the wreck?"

Mike speaks first. "I remember I was driving our route down the highway, then out of nowhere our truck crashed into this car that swerved in front of us. Bruce was the first out of the truck after I was able to get it to stop. He saw the girl laying on the road in front of her car, blood everywhere. She looked dead."

Miller writes down a few things on a paper in front of him before continuing.

"All right. Was it you or Bruce who called for emergency services after the accident? And which of you helped try and stop her bleeding?"

I swallow the lump in my throat before saying anything. "I called 911 after I got out and saw her on the road. I used a rag that we had in the truck to hold over her head wound. She looked so broken with her arms and legs laying limp on the ground. I was freaking out so bad thinking that we had killed her."

"Well you don't have to worry about that, Bruce. She was in a coma in the hospital for the last two days, but she woke up last night. She is actually going home tonight. But I am going to have to talk to her and find out if she wants to press charges against you or your company for payment of her medical bills or and possible mental damages. I just need your cooperation with me."

I can feel my mouth stutter before I answer. "Yes, sir. You have our full cooperation. Do you need us to stay here until you're able to talk to her?"

He thinks for a second before telling me, "It would be best if you stayed here so that you don't have to come back after I talk to Destiny Morgan. After this interview I am going to go to the hospital to see how she's doing and ask if she wants to press charges. So you guys shouldn't have to be stuck here for too too long."

"We definitely can stay here. Our route that we were running has been put off until everything is resolved."

"All right. Well I'm about to leave to talk to her before she gets out of the hospital, and I should be back within a couple of hours. If you all can just sit tight."

Sergeant Miller leaves Mike and I to so that he can go talk to the girl.

Gregory's POV: After I finish talking to Mike and Bruce about the accident I leave the room and go visit the Lieutenant to tell him how it went. I reach his office a few minutes later and knock on the door and go inside.

"Hi, Lieutenant. I just finished the interview with the truck drivers and am about to head up to the hospital so that I can find out if she wants to press charges on them."

Lieutenant Sanchez smiles with approval. "Good man. Keep on it and before you know it you might get promoted to lieutenant."

He laughs jokingly as he pats me on the back.

Once I finish telling Sanchez everything is leave to go back to the hospital to check on Destiny and Jade. God I hope that they won't be mad that I didn't tell them that I was at the accident and am an officer.

It only takes me a few minutes to get back up to the hospital. When I get there I go over to the desk and ask if Destiny is still here or if she's already been released.

The nurse goes over her computer for a few seconds before she says, "She was in recovery after waking up from her coma, but it looks like she's relapsed back into the coma. She had a slight seizure that caused her brain to go into unconsciousness."

"Oh shit!!! Where is she at now?"

"Room 321."

I grab my phone from my pocket and see that I have almost a dozen missed calls and texts from Jade.

I move as fast as I can to the stairs and run up two at a time until I reach the fifth floor. I turn to the left and haul ass to Room 541. As soon as I get there I run inside and ask Jade what happened.

"I-I don't know. We woke up a few hours ago and had breakfast." As she's talking, I can tell that she's trying to hide the tears behind her voice.

"The nurse came to draw some blood, then out of nowhere she started having a seizure and went back into a coma. Dr. Drew was here a minute ago and told me that her brain might be swelling from after effects of the wreck. But he'll have to take her back into surgery to find out and see if he can make the swelling stop.

"She was fine! Then all of a sudden... I don't know!!!" Jade breaks down into sobs before letting her head fall into her hands on her lap.

I hurry over and give Jade a hug. "It'll be okay. I know it will. She'll be okay and you'll be able to bring her home in no time."

Jade looks up after a few seconds and takes a look at me, confused when she sees me.

Oh shit! I'm still in my uniform.

"Are you a police officer?" she sniffles out.

"I am. I just came from the station, and I actually need to talk to you about something involving the wreck."

Jade looks at me with her eyebrows furrowed. "What's going on?"

I take a deep breath before I answer her. "I... I was one of the officers who was called to the crash. I just left the station from interviewing the drivers of the truck that hit Destiny. I was actually coming up here to find out if she wants to press charges against them. Do you want to press charges, Jade? Considering she's back in a coma?"

"Fuck yes!!! My best friend... My girlfriend is suffering still because of them. And they are alive and well. Screw them!"

Dr. Drew enters the room right as Jade starts to cry again.

"Hello, Jade. I'm so sorry that I wasn't able to stop the seizure and prevent her from going back into a coma. I am going to send my residents in in a few minutes to bring her back up for surgery. I am going to do my best to stop the swelling and wake her back up. Because I don't want her suffering. But I promise that I will do everything I can to get her back into consciousness and good health."

Jade hugs Destiny tight in her arms as tears pour out of her eyes. Her face looks so red and swollen from crying. Her eyes are red and puffy, shining from the tears in her eyes.

"I thought that she was going to be okay. I thought that she was okay. And it hurts that I can't do anything. I can't take her place in the coma. I wish that it was me in that bed right now. Because then she'd be awake and wouldn't be suffering."

I sit down on the chair next to Jade. "Listen to me. It's not your fault. If you were the one in the coma, she would be in your position. Worrying like hell about you. You just need to do everything you can to be okay for her until she *can* be all right. The doctor will do everything he can to help her wake up and get better. Just trust him."

Jade lets out a long sigh before she speaks. "Okay. Are you going to be able to stay here with me until she gets back from surgery?"

"I will. But I am going to have to call my lieutenant in a minute to let him know what's going on." I give Jade a hug from behind after telling her this.

A few minutes of quiet go by before Dr. Drew and his residents come to take Destiny to surgery. After they enter the room, he asks us if we're ready to let her go for surgery.

"Yes, sir. Please take care of her and help her to wake up. Please."

He nods his head in assurance as they move Destiny onto the gurney and leave for the operating room.

"Everything will be okay, Jade. I know it will."

I look into her eyes after they leave to make sure that she knows I'm telling the honest to god truth.

Everything has to be okay. It has to.

Chapter Seven

Destiny's POV: I'm about to finish writing the last chapter of my novel that I'm sending out to the publisher this weekend when Jade walks into the bedroom.

"Hi, sweetie. How's the book coming along?" She bends over and gives me a kiss on the top of my head.

"It's going really great, baby. I just finished the final chapter and just have to finish the editing before sending it to the publisher for review."

I hit the enter button to save everything before getting up from my desk chair.

Jade gives me a big hug, pulling me in close. "I'm so proud of you, baby. You're coming so far since sending in your first draft. Do you want to go out for drinks with the girls later? I can call them in a second."

I lean in and give her a small kiss on the lips. "I love you so much, baby. That sounds like a blast. We can go out at around five to get dinner and drinks with the girls."

After agreeing to go out with our friends, I go to the bathroom so that I can start doing my makeup and hair before finding some clothes to change into.

****

I walk out into the living room after I'm done getting ready. Jade is sitting on one of the bar stools next to the counter in the kitchen when I come out.

She's sitting there wearing her little lacy black dress with a pair of black heels. Her hair is hanging over her shoulders in nice bouncy waves, and her makeup looks dark and sexy.

As I make my way over to her she turns her head up to look at me, and a huge smile spreads across her face. "You look gorgeous, baby. Holy crap!" Jade lets out a laugh before continuing. "I'll have to make sure that the rest of the girls know that they can't have you. Because you're mine."

I go over to my baby and grab her in my arms before leaning in to give her a big kiss. My mouth meets her soft, warm lips as we kiss each other. My arms move along her body as I pull her close to me.

We kiss for a few minutes before a knock sounds at the door.

"It's us!!! Let us in!!!" Terri yells from the other side of the door.

Jade laughs as she goes over and answers the door. When she opens it, Terri, Chloe, and Deanna are standing there.

"Hi, girls!!! Are you all ready to go get drinks and some fun out on the town?" I grab my purse as I greet our friends at the door.

"Heck yeah!" Chloe shouts. "Let's have a blast in your honor, Destiny."

Jade and I follow our friends out the door and head down to the lobby so that we can grab a cab.

We get outside and everything outside is thrumming with activity as the nightlife of the city ventures out. People are everywhere, walking through the streets, moving from store to store in the downtown area.

Jade and our friends are all buzzing with excitement because of my publication and I can feel a smile spreading across my face as I listen to them. They are my best friends and are all beyond proud of me.

As we stand on the sidewalk waiting for a cab I say, "Thank you so much guys for your support through all of this. It took months to be able to finish writing Journey in Fate, and I could not have done it without you guys' help."

I pull everyone in for a group hug. Jade gives me a kiss on the cheek as Terri, Chloe, and Deanna wrap their arms around me, squeezing tight.

As we pull out of the hug, Terri tells me, "Girl, we are here for everything. No matter what it is. You got that?" She smiles brightly, her cherry red lips flashing in the light.

I chat with the girls about the book and everything that is going to happen with my new publication until a cab pulls up.

When the car stops, Chloe opens the door and lets me get in the backseat first before everyone else climbs in. Once we're all in the cab and seated, Jade tells the driver to take us to Jack's Pub on Fifth Street.

I laugh and giggle with everyone until we get to the bar.

By the time we reach the bar it's already crowded and packed with people out partying. The music is blasting from the speakers playing Sweet Child o' Mine by Aerosmith when we walk through the door.

"Hell yeah! Come on guys, let's sing it!" I shout before I start belting out to the song.

My friends and everyone around me start singing along until the song is over a few minutes later.

As the song finishes, I can feel myself breathing heavily from trying to hold out the last notes. Everyone in the bar is cheering as I take a seat at the table nearest to me. Jade sits down next to me and Terri, Chloe, and Deanna follow, sitting around the circular table.

After a few seconds, Tiff, our regular waitress, walks over and greets us. "Hi, gals. That was awesome. Are y'all out celebrating somethin'?"

Deanna points over to me before she says, "This one just submitted another book to her publisher so we decided to come here to celebrate and have fun."

"Nice, Destiny. How many books does this make? Fifty?"

My eyes close in laughter. "I love you, but no this is number five. Thanks for over exaggerating, though."

Tiff smiles at me as she says, "Well then your first drink is on the house. What would you like?"

"Just a strawberry rum mixed drink." I look around the table at the others. "What about the rest of you? What are you guys going to drink?"

Jade and Terri chime in that they'll have the same. Chloe gets a piña colada. And Deanna decides on strawberry wine.

Tiff writes down all our orders before leaving to put them in.

Jade grabs my hand after Tiff is gone and I turn to look at her, smiling with pure happiness. She looks at me her face turning more serious.

"Destiny... we have been together since basically the start of our freshman year in high school. I have loved you through everything. Through family issues and self doubt. And now you are becoming a well-known author throughout the country. I am going to be here with you through anything life throws our way."

I can feel my face growing warm as Jade speaks.

"Destiny, I want you for the rest of my life... our life. Destiny Anne Morgan, will you marry me?"

My eyes open wide and I can feel my mouth agape. I can't think or say anything because I'm so freaking happy.

I try to say something, but my mouth won't move because I'm in a state of pure happy shock. After a few minutes of all my friends staring at me I finally lean forward and plant my lips on Jade's.

Our lips move together in ecstasy. My hands move up to her hair as I run my fingers through it. I kiss her for what feels like forever before moving away from the most wonderful kiss I've ever had.

I take a shaky breath before I am able to say, "Yes, Jade. Yes!!! I will marry you! I love you so fucking much, baby."

Cheers sound off around us as all of our friends congratulate us.

Deanna gives me a hug first. "Congratulations, sweetie. You two have been made for each other since long before I met you. I can't wait to see the day you both get married."

Chloe and Terri get up from their seats and come around to give me hugs. They both congratulate Jade and I, smiling with happiness.

"Congrats, babe. You guys are meant for each other," Terri tells me. "You have got the greatest girl ever. I couldn't be more proud of either of you."

Chloe is the last to congratulate us before Tiff comes over with our drinks.

"I can't believe this. First we were here to celebrate your new book, and now we're celebrating you guys getting engaged. Holy crap."

As Chloe gives Jade and I hugs, Tiff walks over with our drinks. "What's going on? Are we celebrating something else now?"

Jade beams as she tells her, "I just proposed to Destiny and she said yes. So hell yeah we are. Can you grab us a round of tequila shots?"

Gregory's POV: I can't believe that Destiny's back in a coma. Jade looks so miserable with worry for her. I've got to call the lieutenant and tell him what's going on and that Destiny's friend wants to press charges against Mike and his friend.

I stand up and walk over to where Jade is sitting so that I can give her a hug. I wrap my arms around her neck and she grabs me around my chest, holding me tight. I can feel her body shaking and shuddering while she tries not to cry.

"Listen to me, Jade. I'm going to give my lieutenant a call in a few minutes and let him know that you want to press charges against the truckers and hold them accountable for Destiny being in this coma."

Jade sniffles a couple of times before she lets go. "Okay, Greg. Thank you so much for being here to help Destiny and I. I don't know how I would be handling things without having you here for support."

I slide my hand up and down her back gently before moving out of the hug. "I'll make sure that Destiny gets the justice she needs, whether she's in the coma or awake and well. Those assholes will get what's coming for putting her in the hospital. I promise you that."

She nods her head at me as I open the door and go into the hall so that I can call Lieutenant Sanchez.

Once I'm in the hall, I pull my cellphone out of my pocket and dial his number. I wait for a few rings before he picks up the other end.

He answers the phone by saying, "Hello, Sergeant. Have you talked to the girl yet?"

I take a deep breath. "Sir, I went up to the hospital to speak to her and she's back in the coma. Her friend says that she wants to press charges against them. So I'm going to have her come down to the station with me in a few minutes to fill out the paperwork."

"All right, Miller. I'll be waiting here with the paperwork until you two get here."

"Yes, sir." I hang up the phone and go back into the room with Jade. She looks up at me as I enter the room, looking like she was deep in thought before I walked in.

I make my way over to her and place my hand on her shoulder. "I just finished talking to my lieutenant and told him that you want to press charges against the drivers of the semi truck. But you'll have to come to the station so that you can fill out paperwork."

She turns her head to look up at me. "I can come with you. I don't know when Destiny will be out of surgery so I have time."

Jade gets up from her chair and grabs her purse before following to come with me.

We go to the elevator and make our way down to the first floor. I lead the way out to my cruiser in the parking lot. Jade follows me and looks at me with wide eyes when she sees the police car.

I go around to the passenger side and open the door so that I can let Jade into the car. Once she climbs in and is settled in the seat, I go around to the driver side and get in. I buckle my seatbelt and put the keys in the ignition before starting the car.

For the first few minutes after I start driving to the station, neither Jade or I say anything. Just the sound of my radio going off as I drive through traffic.

My mind can't stop racing, thinking about Destiny being unconscious again in the hospital and having to get surgery for the second time. She's going through hell because of that crash and her best friend, her girlfriend, is miserable with worry for her.

I break away from my thoughts as the light between Fair Street and Shumaker Street turns yellow, slowing down as it becomes red.

I let out a deep breath before deciding to break the wall of silence. "Jade, I'm just as worried about her as you are. I know that she doesn't seem like she's doing better since the accident but she is. She looked broken and like there was no chance she could survive. But obviously she can and will survive because she was awake. Even if she's not now, her waking up shows that she *can* wake up again."

"I know that she'll wake up, but the fact that she's back in a coma, it kills me. When I thought that she was fine and was coming home, I was so freaking happy. Especially since we're more than just friends now. I just don't want to lose her."

Her voice quivers while she talks and I can hear the sadness in her tone.

"I just want Destiny to get justice for what happened."

I nod my head in understanding as I pull the car into the parking lot of the precinct. As I get the car parked near the doors, Jade unbuckles her seatbelt and starts getting ready to climb out.

I get the car parked and get out before I lead Jade over to the doors and use my ID card to get them open.

I walk over to the front desk and tell Cheryl that I'm taking Jade back to the lieutenant's office so that she can sign some paperwork in regards to Destiny Morgan's case. That she's pressing charges against the men who drove the truck.

Jade follows me down the bright hall to the back. We make our way down the left corridor until I stop in front of Lieutenant Sanchez's office.

I knock lightly on the door before he answers with a holler of, "Come in."

His head is turned down, nose buried in a stack of papers on his desk. After a few seconds he looks up to greet Jade and I.

"Hello, Miller. Is this Jade Shay?"

I glance at her for a moment before I answer, "Yes, sir. This is Miss Shay. She's here to sign the paperwork and press charges against Mike and Bruce."

Lieutenant Sanchez hums in acknowledgment as he shuffles through the stack of papers on his desk. He moves a few of the pages around before gathering up the papers that Jade needs to sign. He places them into a neat stack then grabs a pen from the blue cup next to his computer and places it on top of the stack of papers.

I pull out a chair so that she can take a seat. I sit down in the chair next to her before Sanchez looks up to talk.

"So Miss Shay, are you sure that you want to press charges against these men? Because once you do there's no turning back."

I see Jade shuffle a little bit in her seat as she thinks. I can tell that she's really nervous about actually pressing charges against them because she hasn't even met them. I know that she wants to, though. I know that she wants to protect Destiny.

After a few seconds she says, "Yes, I am. Because they are the reason that my best friend is in a coma at the hospital right now. I want her to get justice for what happened."

Lieutenant Sanchez slides the papers and pen across the desk before he begins to explain where she needs to sign and what's going to happen afterwards.

"So you just need to sign a few pages letting the state know that you are allowing Sergeant Miller to place the charges against Bruce Carter and Mike Sanders. After you have signed and filled out everything, they are going to be placed into holding and we will get a trial date set up for the case."

Jade's POV: I glance down at the police report in front of me as I pick up the pen. Reading through it, it almost feels as if I was there at the scene. The description of Destiny's body lying on the road after crashing with the semi truck is almost clear in my head.

The victim, Destiny Morgan's body was lying limp in the road when I arrived to the scene of the accident. The drivers of the semi truck were bent over her, trying to stop the bleeding caused by her being thrown from her vehicle into the road.

Paramedics arrived a few moments before myself and the other officers.

They were already bringing out equipment so that they could get Miss Morgan into the ambulance.

Reading the words on the paper makes it feel that much more real, because Destiny could have died. She should have died. Yet some how she's still here, even if she's not awake. But the fact that she could have been killed... I have to hold those drivers accountable for what happened. Because for all I know Destiny might not wake up again.

I pick up the pen and sign in the places that I'm told to as tears start to well up in my eyes.

After I have finished signing the paperwork I let out a deep sigh of satisfaction knowing that this is the start of getting the necessary justice for the love of my life.

Chapter Eight

Jade's POV: Lieutenant Sanchez gathers the paperwork from the desk and grabs a stapler from his desk so that he can fasten then together. I feel a small smile of satisfaction cross my face as he files the report into the computer.

"What's going to happen now?" I ask Gregory and the lieutenant.

Gregory stands up and says, "Well for now, they are going to be held in the jail until the courts are able to get a trial date set up to try them for the accident. Until then, I can take you back to the hospital so that you can wait for Destiny to get out of her surgery."

I can feel warmth and happiness inside me when he says that. I get up from the chair when he finishes speaking and follow him out the door as Lieutenant Sanchez grabs the papers from the desktop.

The lieutenant pushes his chair out as he tells me, "I am going to get this filed in the system and sent out to the courts. Once they receive them, they will decide when to hold the trial for Miss Morgan's case."

I nod my head as Greg and I go down the hallway and head back towards the lobby.

Greg leads the way out to the parking lot after we get back to the front of the police station. When we get outside, it's still really sunny and warm with a slight breeze blowing through the air. Everything feels so much more calm now that the men who hit Destiny's car are going to get their comeuppance.

She's going to get her justice.

After I get to the car, Gregory comes around to the passenger side and opens my door and helps me into the vehicle. I get seated and buckle my seatbelt as he goes around to the driver's side of the car.

As soon as Greg starts driving the car down the road, I hear him let out a deep breath before he opens his mouth to speak.

"I'm going to make sure that Destiny gets justice for her injuries and the state she's in, and that you are able to see her every day until she wakes up and can go home."

I reach over and gently grip his hand in mine. "Thank you so much, Greg. I am so glad that you're helping both of us because I really don't think that I would be able to handle any of this without you. So thank you."

As he drives down the road back to the hospital, we have to slow down a few times for traffic along the way.

Fifteen minutes go by before Greg and I reach the hospital. After he parks his car, we both make our way inside. We walk over to the front desk and ask the nurse behind it if Destiny is out of surgery yet.

She gets on the computer and types for a few seconds before saying, "She's still in surgery but you can wait in the waiting area upstairs until she's brought out to recovery if you like."

My heart sinks as soon as she says that Destiny is still in surgery. *This surgery seems to be taking a lot longer than the previous one. What could be going on? Is something wrong?*

I can feel my brain starting to go into panicked thoughts as I speed over to the elevator and start mashing the button for the third floor until the doors open.

As soon as they open I get in the elevator with Greg right behind me. I hit the button for the third floor and start tapping my foot as it moves up slowly. As the elevator goes up, I try and focus on the faint music playing in the background.

It feels like forever before it finally stops to let us out, but once the elevator doors open I rush out. I run down the hall straight to the waiting area and up to the desk, my eyes wide in panic.

The man behind the desk looks up quickly as soon as I'm in front of him. "Are you okay, ma'am? What can I help you with?"

I take a deep, shuddering breath. "My best friend, my girlfriend, Destiny Morgan has been in surgery for the past five hours and I haven't heard anything. I'm really worried that something could be going wrong. Or that something bad has happened. Do you know anything?"

"Give me a few seconds and I can go find out what is going on. I'll be back in a few minutes." The nurse stands up from behind the desk and walks down to the double doors where he disappears.

I know that everything will be okay. It has to be.

After the doors are closed, Greg comes over to me and wraps his arms around my shoulders in a gentle hug. "She's okay. We just have to wait and see what Dr. Drew says after he's finished her surgery and Destiny is in recovery. But try not to worry too much. Okay?"

"All right."

I can feel my heart beat in my chest as I move out of the hug. I make my way over to the seating area and take a seat with Greg while we wait for the nurse to come back out.

I know that everything will be okay because Destiny is strong. She's strong as hell, but I still can't help worrying like hell. I just want her to wake up again and everything be okay, and eventually go back to normal. But I don't care how long it takes because I am not leaving her for even a second.

My mind just can't stop racing through worst case scenarios every second that I wait. Because for all I know Destiny could be brain dead or paralyzed. She could be suffering permanent trauma in her brain.

My chest starts to heave as my thoughts keep whirling around through every worst situation that could happen.

I can feel myself starting to hyperventilate as my body begins to shake from anxiety and worry. My vision starts to get blurry as my body shakes. I don't even know what's happening around me until I feel arms wrap around me.

I know it's Gregory's arms but my mind almost feels like it's Destiny hugging me. Like she's right next to me.

I want her next to me again, need her here, awake and okay. Destiny can't leave me.

Destiny's POV: Tiff brings over the shots of tequila from the bar and sets them down on the table in front of all of us. She sets one down in front of each of us, a big smile spread across her face.

"I'm so proud of y'all. You two have been beyond happy together since the day I first met y'all and now you're getting married." Tiff bends over and gives Jade and I each a tight hug.

Jade smiles at her as she says, "Thank you so much, Tiff. Destiny has been my one and only since the day we first started dating. She's my world and I just couldn't wait any longer to ask for her hand." She turns to me before continuing. "Baby, you make me so fucking happy."

I let out a small laugh and grab Jade, pulling her in for a kiss. Her lips feel so warm and soft against mine. My eyes close as she leans into the kiss, deepening it.

It feels as if Jade and I are the only two people in the world, and it feels absolutely fantastic.

The kiss lasts for a few minutes before we both pull away. I look into Jade's eyes and can see the light bouncing off of the beautiful amber flecks in her irises. I could stare into them all day.

"I love you, Jade. So much. And I can't wait to spend the rest of our lives together."

I pick up my shot glass and lift it up. "Here's to us, babe. A toast to our life together and everything we will accomplish."

Jade, Jasmine, Deanna, and Charlie all lift up their shot glasses and clink them against mine. "To Jade and Destiny!"

Each of us down our shot and set them on the table before we start to chat about wedding plans.

Jade starts off first with, "So baby, what do you see our wedding looking like? Because I want everything to be perfect for you, Destiny. I don't care what it is. I will give it to you any way possible."

I think for a few seconds as ideas go through my head. I hadn't thought about my dream wedding since I was in high school before we even met.

"Honestly I want a dark princess themed wedding. Royal and regal but with cobwebs and dark colors all around. I want it to be held in front of all of our loved ones, but I want it to feel like it's just us two up there under the wedding arches."

I can hear the others gasp and squeal in delight after I finish describing the way I see our wedding looking.

My face feels warm with joy flushing through it as Jade grabs my hands in hers. She pulls them towards her and gives them a kiss.

"No matter what it takes, that will happen, sweetie. I'll make sure of it. Make sure that our day is the most special day for each of us. Because I want it to be absolutely perfect. Just so that I can see your amazing smile."

Jade and the girls and I start bouncing ideas off of each other to try to get ideas rolling.

We talk about everything and brainstorm for hours, talking about locations, setup, flowers, colors, everything under the sun to get started with the planning. And by the time last call comes we've already gotten almost everything pictured for what Jade and I want the wedding to look like.

I am so beyond happy to have the best friends and the best fiancée in the world.

When we go to leave the bar and head back home I am slightly stumbling from getting a little more drunk than I intended, so Jade has to try and hold me up on the way to the car. She's giggling too from drinking.

By the time we reach the cars with the girls, Jade and I hoop and holler our byes to our friends before we climb into the VW.

I can feel the giddiness inside me bursting at the seems as Jade fumbles with the ignition. After a few seconds of fighting to get the key in she gets the car to turn on and starts pulling out of the parking space.

The car is moving suuuper slow while Jade drives us out of the parking lot and onto the main road. It feels like we're barely moving. But the music blaring from the speakers feels like it's coming out a lot faster than normal. As if it's going twice as fast as we're moving.

My brain feels fuzzy and my vision blurry until we finally reach the apartment building where I have to climb out of the car.

Jade helps me out after she comes around to my side of the car and helps me get in through the doors of the building. We go up to the apartment in the elevator and about fall down at the foot of the door when we reach it.

As soon as Jade and I get inside the apartment we go into the bedroom and collapse on the bed before passing out.

****

The next morning I wake up to the smell of fresh coffee coming from the kitchen, helping me float awake. I follow the smell and find Jade sitting next to the bar counter with two cups of coffee sitting in front of her.

"Good morning, baby. How did you sleep?"

I reach my arms up and stretch them over my head, a yawn escaping as I open my mouth to answer my baby.

"Good morning, babe. I slept like I was on a fluffy pile of clouds. How are you feeling?"

Jade stands up and hands me my coffee. "I am feeling amazing and beyond filled with joy after last night. You made me so freaking happy when you said yes."

After I grab the mug I take a few sips of the nice, warm caramel flavored coffee as a grin shows on my face.

"I cannot wait to spend the rest of forever with you, babygirl. And I cannot wait to start getting ready soon for our big day, because it is going to be absolutely amazing. I love you so, so fucking much."

I sit down next to Jade on the next barstool and set my coffee down on the counter as Jade turns on the speakers to play our music loud and proud.

Queen starts blaring out We Will Rock You and we both start belting out the lyrics, stomping and clapping to the beat of the music. I sing and dance with Jade while drinking my coffee until the clock reaches ten o'clock.

We both have to start getting ready to leave for work soon so I go to our bedroom and grab a loose violet blouse out of the closet and a pair of black office slacks. I start getting dressed while Jade is in the bathroom doing her hair in the mirror.

I can see her face around the door as she sweeps the makeup onto her face, making her beauty multiple and become even more visible. She just looks so fucking gorgeous.

Five minutes later after I finish getting dressed, I make my way into the bathroom with Jade and give her a kiss on the cheek.

"I love you so fucking much, babygirl. I wish that we could spend the whole day together here at home, but I'm about to leave for work in a minute."

Jade turns around and moves her hands up to my cheeks, pulling me in close for a kiss on the lips.

"I love you so much, babe. I hope that you have an amazing day at work. I'll be heading to my office in about twenty minutes."

I can feel myself smiling as I give her another kiss before I go grab my keys and purse and head out the door.

Chapter Nine

Jade's POV: My eyes open from resting for a few hours while waiting for Dr. Drew to bring Destiny back out from surgery. Gregory is sitting in the chair across from me when he notices me stirring awake.

"Hi, Jade. How are you feeling?"

I stretch my arms up over my head, letting out a yawn as my arms stretch up in the air. My eyes blink a few times before I can focus my vision and answer his question.

"I'm feeling okay. Just a little groggy. Has Dr. Drew come in at all?"

I can see the slight tension behind Gregory's eyes before he opens his mouth to speak. "He hasn't, but the nurse across the hall came and told me that he should be in here soon. We just have to be patient."

I nod my head as my heart sinks in my chest. "Okay." I pause for a moment as a sigh escapes my lips. "Hopefully he won't be too much longer."

My mind keeps running through every bad situation. Destiny could be brain dead. She could be paralyzed. She won't still way to be girlfriends. She might want to move back out. She might never want to speak to me again.

As each thought becomes worse and worse my breath starts to speed up and I can feel myself starting to hyperventilate. All I can see is the worst of the worst happening and it feels like everything is crashing down around me.

My body begins to shake. My vision starts to become blurry. I can sort of see Gregory coming over to me fast but all I can feel is panic in my chest, rising.

After a few minutes, all I can see is black. I barely feel Gregory's arms when he places them around my shoulders to try and hold me steady. The door to the room opens up while he holds me in a hug, and Dr. Drew comes inside.

My chest begins to move slower with my breathing as I try to focus on him. When he sees me, he walks over quickly and pulls his stethoscope up to his ears, placing it over my chest.

As he listens to my heart for a few seconds he asks me, "Are you okay?"

I take a shuddering breath. "Yes, sir. Is Destiny okay? Did her surgery go well?"

"The surgery went well, but I did have to stop some brain bleeds. She's in recovery now. She is still comatose, though. I don't know when she's going to wake up again, but she's very strong and seems to be fighting everything with all that she's got."

A long breath that I didn't know I had been holding releases from my lungs. I feel the tension in my body dissolve a little, knowing that Destiny is okay right now even if she is still in a coma.

"Thank god! Am I going to be able to go see her soon?"

"You can come see her now if you like. I'll take you over to the recovery unit so that you can visit her and see how she's doing."

I stand up with Gregory by my side and follow Dr. Drew down the hall and through the double doors at the end. We walk past a few doors until he stops and opens a door on the left.

As soon as I walk in I see Destiny laying on the bed with her leg propped up in the cast. She's hooked up to an IV line and heart monitor and has stitches in her skull near the front of her hairline.

My baby looks so helpless just laying there.

As I look at her I can't help but feel like I should be the one lying there. She should be up and awake and I should be the one suffering. I just want her to wake up and for us to get her justice for the accident.

Dr. Drew tells me, "She is stable right now but when she was in the operating room the brain bleed that she had took a lot of work to stop. And there is still some damage to the tissue in her brain from the trauma she suffered. So for now it's best that she is unconscious so that her brain can try to mend."

I sit down in the chair next to Destiny and turn to look at her small, beautiful face. "Thank you so much, Dr. Drew. You have no idea how much I appreciate everything that you are doing to help her."

He tells me that I'm welcome before leaving Gregory and I alone with Destiny.

"Greg, do you know what's going to happen with the charges on those truck drivers? Do you know when the trial date is going to be set?"

I can see the thoughts whirling through his mind before he answers.

"Well the report and charges have to be sent in to the courts so that the judge can decide on a date for the trial. But until then we just have to wait."

"Okay. Do I need go ahead and try to find a lawyer soon?"

"I would, so that you can get her case established. Because otherwise you'll have to hire a public attorney. Then you would have to rely on the hopes that they can win her case and get a settlement for her medical bills and emotional trauma."

I nod my head as I reach my hand towards Destiny and brush her dark blonde hair from her face.

Destiny's POV: As I leave the apartment building to go to work, I watch Jade's car pull out and head towards the highway going left. I drive out behind her and go right and head towards my publisher's office downtown.

I turn up the radio dial so I can hear the music playing from the speakers. For the next twenty minutes I drive with the windows of the bug rolled down and the music blaring as I sing along to every song.

Traffic on the roads seems fairly easy to get through as I breeze through each stoplight. Before I know it, I'm already pulling up to the entrance of the Woodhouse Publishers building.

I drive around to my parking spot on the left side of the building and pull in, putting the car into park.

After I get my seatbelt unbuckled, I take the keys from the ignition and grab my purse and water bottle to take inside. I grab my writing folders and my laptop before shutting and locking the doors to the car.

I walk over to the building entrance, my heels clicking on the sidewalk, and scan my ID card to get inside. When I get into the lobby of the building, I'm greeted by James Nolan, one of the head editors for the company.

"Good morning, Miss Morgan. How are you doing this morning?"

I wave and give James a big smile as I say, "I'm doing fantastic. Last night, my most recent book was picked up to be published. I've just got to finish getting the editing done and finish the cover design."

His face lights up with happiness when he tells me, "Congratulations. If you need any help with editing, I'm your man."

I thank him as I make my way over to my office and set down my things on the desk. First I open my laptop and pull up the word document with my manuscript file in it.

I begin looking through every page to see what details or mistakes need to be corrected and start going through, page by page, and edit what I need to. The first part that I start with is fixing some plot details that I wrote in the beginning that I changed later on in the story to make it better.

I had written that my main character, Bonnie, was going to go through a wormhole to a completely different universe, but later on I made that universe a parallel of hers, messing with the initial idea. But because I had written from then on out in that perspective, I have to change the beginning to match it.

A few hours go by with me editing the details that need to be fixed, and by the time I'm through with almost fifty pages of work I hear a knock at my door.

"Come in," I say, not looking away from my computer.

"Hello, Miss Morgan. How is your editing coming along?" Shane Williams, my publishing manager asks.

I pick up the laptop from my desk and show Shane what all I have gotten done so far.

His eyes scan across the screen as he scrolls through the pages, skimming over my edits. As he reads, I hear a few sounds of approval here and there.

After a few minutes, he stands up and turns his head to look at me. "Well Miss Morgan, it looks like you are making great headway with the editing process. You are working amazingly fast."

"Thank you so much, sir. I always try my hardest to get everything done when I need to be done by or before the deadlines. So until I leave at five, I'm going to be working my ass off to get as much finished as possible."

Shane smiles and gives a nod of approval. "You are an amazing writer. Your books have all gotten so popular over the last five years that you are becoming the next Virginia Wolff with a twist. If you keep it up, you might even become another Stephen King/Mary Higgins Clarke."

My cheeks turn a slight pink as he walks back out the door, leaving me to continue working. I go through every page, fixing any little detail that needs to be changed, whether it be a story detail, incorrect grammar, or sentence structure.

My mind flows with the work, feeling as if I'm becoming one within Bonnie's story and life. As if I'm a character within the novel.

As each hour goes by, I get further and further into my editing. By the time it's almost five o'clock I look back through everything that I've accomplished so far. I make sure that what

I have done is acceptable to me before deciding to close the document for the day and go home.

I go over to Shane's office and tell him that I'm heading home for the day and will continue editing tomorrow morning. He tells me to take my time and to try not to rush my work then thanks me again before I leave to go home.

I make my way to the door and go back out to the parking lot. I walk to my car with all of my things in my arms and hit the button on my keys to unlock it.

Once I get all of my things set in the passenger seat, I make my way around to the driver's side and climb in to start the car. I turn the radio up, playing some Evanescence from the speakers once the ignition has started.

The entire ride home I jam out to Wake Me Up Inside, Bohemian Rhapsody, Crazy Train, and Don't Stop Believing. I listen to all of my favorite songs as I drive back home to 54 Maple Street where the apartment building is.

By the time I reach home, I can see Jade's car is already there in her parking spot across from our apartment building.

I get the bug parked and get all my things so that I can head inside where my fiance is. As I walk from the car to the elevator inside, I pass by our neighbor David and his beautiful pit bull Georgia.

"Hi, Destiny. How are you doing? Did you just get home from work?"

I bend over and scratch Georgia's head. "I'm doing great. I did. How have you been doing?"

John smiles as Georgia wags her tail. "I have been doing really good. We just finished our daily walk to the park and back. And Georgia here has been as happy as she can be."

"Awesome. Well I hope you both have a great rest of your day." I pet Georgia one last time before getting into the elevator.

As the doors close, I press the button to go up to the eighth floor then wait until it stops.

When the door opens back up I walk out into the hallway with my things in my arms. I go all the way down the hallway to our apartment 8G. Once I reach the door, I get my keys and unlock it to go inside.

I'm greeted by the smell of warm bread and potatoes with cheese.

I take a deep breath, my eyes closed, as I ask Jade, "Mmm. That smells delicious, baby. What all are you making for dinner?"

Jade walks over and gives me a hug and kiss before she answers me. "I'm cooking sweet rolls, cheesy potato casserole, and going to start frying some chicken soon."

I take another deep whiff of the air as I go over to the bedroom so that I can get changed into something comfortable.

I grab a loose fitting black t-shirt and a pair of violet sweatpants to put on. First I pull off my blouse and switch it for the t-shirt. I pull the t-shirt over my head slowly and slip it down over my breasts and my stomach, letting it fall loose around my body.

Then I slide my slacks down from my waist and let them fall to the floor. I grab my sweatpants to pull them on, but my hands are stopped when I feel Jade's soft fingers come into contact with my warm skin.

"Baby, you are so amazing," Jade whispers into my ears. "Dinner's almost ready if you want to come help me fry the chicken in a second."

I smile as I pull my sweats on over my thighs and backside. "Let's go cook that chicken."

Jade gives me a kiss on my cheek before I follow her out to the kitchen. As soon as we reach the kitchen the smell of rolls and the cheesy potatoes hits me like a delicious wave.

I go over to the counter where the raw chicken is sitting and grab a bowl to mix the flour and oil in to make the breading. I grab the eggs from the fridge and break a couple into the bowl then add a cup of water and start mixing it together.

Jade comes over and grabs the flour, pouring some onto the cutting board before we start costing the chicken breasts in it. We coat each breast into the eggs and milk, then Jade grabs out the breadcrumbs and helps me start rolling the chicken in them.

After we finish getting the breading on the chicken, I turn on the fryer and put the breasts in a couple at a time to cook.

As the chicken is frying, Jade turns on the stereo and puts on some Three Doors Down for us to listen to. The first song that plays is Kryptonite.

I grab ahold of her hand and start singing with the music and dancing with my baby. We dance with each other and cook the chicken until it's ready. Then once the potatoes are ready to come out of the oven, I grab a pot holder and put them on the counter to cool off some.

Jade grabs the plates down while I start taking all of the food over to the table.

Once we both finish setting up the table, Jade and I sit down and start putting food on our plates.

I grab a couple of pieces of chicken, a roll, and a couple scoops of potatoes. I get the butter knife and butter my roll then wait for Jade to get her food.

"This looks so delicious, baby. You know that you didn't have to do this, cook all this food. We could have just ordered takeout and eaten on the couch in our pajamas."

Jade looks over at me as she finishes getting her food. "I did this because I am incredibly proud of you for everything that you are accomplishing. You have made it so far since we left high school. And I am making headway in my company also. This afternoon I got a call from corporate and it was Mr. Daniels. He called me down to his office and told me that he wants to put me in charge of the legal department at the company. So this is in celebration of both of us."

My eyes widen in excitement. "Holy crap, babe. I can't believe this. You were in data analyzing just last week and now you're the head of the legal department. I'm so glad that you're making it so far up at Daniels and Associates. And I can't wait for us to get married and really be starting out lives together.

"What did Mr. Daniels tell you about the change in your position?"

Jade swallows a bite of chicken then says, "He said that I am going to be in charge of everything under the legal department: keeping track of casework, keep track of the money that comes in and goes out, and also any HR work that has to be done. Whether it's worker's compensation, harassment, or anything of that matter. I'm now in charge of everything under legal."

"Awesome, baby. I know you'll do great once you get started and learn everything."

Jade and I keep talking about both of our jobs while we eat dinner with the stereo still playing in the background.

About twenty minutes later, we have both finished our food. I get up and take our dishes over to the sink and fill it up with soap and water. I place the plates and cutlery into the sink, then start scrubbing them with the sponge.

While I'm washing the dishes, I hear Jade turn on the TV to watch Supernatural. I listen to it in the background while I scrub and rinse the dishes. I finish washing all of the dishes after ten minutes and get the remaining food put into the fridge. Once I'm done with everything, I join Jade on the couch.

When I get in there she's laying under a blanket. She looks so cozy and cute all snuggled up underneath the blanket like that.

"Hi, babygirl. Which episode is this?"

She looks over to me with a smile on her face. "It's the episode where Jack first shows up. He's so cute and innocent when he was first taken in by Sam and Dean.

I go into the living room and join her on the couch and crawl under the blanket. While watching Supernatural, I eventually fall asleep in Jade's arms. Right as I fall asleep, I can feel her hand going through my hair before my eyes eventually fall closed.

Chapter Ten

Gregory's POV: It's been a week since Jade signed to file the charges against the drivers of the semi truck, and a week since Destiny fell back into a coma. And every day Jade looks more miserable waiting for her girlfriend to wake up.

The court hasn't gotten back to me about the case and when the trial will be, so I'm going to have to call and find out what's going on.

I grab my phone from my pocket and dial the D. A. office and wait for someone to answer.

While I wait for the phone to be picked up I think to myself, *God, is Destiny going to be able to wake up soon? I just hope that everything with her will be okay and that she'll get her justice from what happened because of that accident.*

As I finish thinking, the phone continues to ring a couple of times before it's answered.

"Hello. This is the Fairview, Connecticut D. A. office. How can I help you?"

"This is Sergeant Gregory Miller. I am calling about the Destiny Morgan case and I was wondering when the trial date would be set."

There's a pause before she answers my question. "Sergeant Miller, it looks like the trial has been set for Wednesday, July 21. So Destiny Morgan can come to give her statement and we can get started on the trial procedure."

I let out a deep sigh. "Ma'am, Miss Morgan is currently in a coma for the second time since the accident. Her roommate will be the one presenting her case on the stand."

"Oh okay. That's fine. Is there anything else that you need to know, sir?"

I tell her that there isn't and thank her before I hang up the phone.

A week until the trial. I've got to call Jade and let her know.

I dial her number and she picks up on the first ring. "Hi, Jade. It's Gregory. I just heard from the courthouse that the trial is going to be held next Wednesday. Have you been able to find a lawyer to represent Destiny and her case?"

"Yes. I managed to get ahold of my friend Derek Johnson who's a lawyer and he told me that he could represent Destiny. Thank you so much for helping with everything. I'm still up at the hospital with her. Nothing much has happened except that her heart rate and vitals are all still stable."

"Damn. I'll be up there shortly to be with both of you guys."

After I hang up the phone, I get up from my desk at the police station and start making my way outside. When I'm passing through the lobby, Sergeant Linda Cooper gives me a smile and tells me to have a good rest of my day.

I tell her the same thing and go outside to my car.

Once I get it unlocked and get behind the wheel, I drive out of the parking lot and start heading towards the hospital so that I can be with Jade and Destiny.

The entire time I'm driving the only thing I can think about is what crap it is that Destiny and Jade are having to deal with all of this. That accident shouldn't have happened and Destiny should be awake and all right. Living her life with Jade.

Fifteen minutes go by before I reach the hospital. I go inside as soon as I get my car parked and hurry upstairs in the elevator.

As I run down the hallway I can hear the sound of loud sobbing coming from Destiny's room. When I get there and rush inside, I see Jade sitting next to the bed with her head in her hands as tears stream down her face.

I make my way over to her and kneel down, placing my right hand on Jade's shoulder. My hand gently grips her shoulder blade in reassurance.

"Jade, I know that you're worried like hell and in a lot of pain from it. But I want you to know that I am going to do everything I can to help you guys get justice for all of this. Make sure that those guys pay for what they have done to both of you."

She sniffs a couple of times before looking up from her lap. "Really, Greg?"

"Yes. And I know that she will wake up again because she loves you too much to leave you. Trust me."

I can see the tears in Jade's eyes and the shining reflection of the light as she turns to look at me. She looks so sad and pitiful. I want to take all of this away from both of them. For them to get their happy life back. Because this sucks like hell and it hurts seeing Jade so broken every day.

"Jade, I want to take all of this away. And I hope that the trial next week will help to get that started. But you have to keep talking to Destiny every day and try to get your voice to wake her up. Touch her hands, her skin, show her that you are still here. I'm sure that you showing her your love and affection will help her to wake up soon."

Jade lifts her head from her arms and turns towards me. "Greg, do you really think so? She's just been laying there in her coma. She hasn't even moved since she went back unconscious from having that seizure. I hate seeing her like this."

She places her right hand onto Destiny's arm on the bed and rubs her hand across it. "I just hope that Destiny is okay and will wake up soon."

I grab Jade's other hand and tell her, "Listen to me. She'll be okay. I promise."

Jade's POV: Greg tells me, "Listen to me. She'll be okay. I promise."

"I know. I'm just worried like hell. And I need to go talk to Derek in a little bit to try and get prepared for the trial on Wednesday. And there's only five days left until then."

Greg pauses for a moment while he thinks then says, "I'll go down to the station so that I can talk to the lieutenant about what is going on with everything. Also find out what all I need to get done to prepare for the trial. You can go talk to Derek while I'm up there."

I nod my head before standing up from the chair. I lean down and give Destiny a kiss on her lips before grabbing my purse and walking out the door.

Gregory walks out behind me and follows me to the first floor. When I walk out with him, he takes me to my car and makes sure that I'm okay before he goes to his car across the lot.

As soon as I get my seatbelt buckled and start the car, I drive out onto the road.

I drive for about ten minutes before I get to Derek's law firm. After I get there I go inside and walk up to the reception counter where Sharon is sitting behind the desk.

She smiles at me, little dimples showing in her cheeks. "Hi, Jade. How can I help you?"

"I just need to go up to speak with Derek Johnson about my friend's trial that he's representing her in next Wednesday."

Sharon tells me, "All right. I can give him a ring and let him know that you're here." She grabs the phone and presses a few buttons before waiting for an answer.

A few seconds later she gets an answer from Derek's office. I can't hear what he says but Sharon says "Uh huh" and "Okay" a few times, then she hangs up the phone.

After she puts the phone down, Sharon tells me that I'm good to go up to his office.

I thank her before making my way over to the elevator and go up to the third floor. I get off of it a few seconds later and walk down to the second door on the right. When I reach Derek's office, I reach my hand up and knock.

"Come in!" Derek calls from the other side of the door.

After I get the door open and go inside, I greet Derek with a hello.

"Hi, Derek. I'm here to talk about Destiny's case and her trial on Wednesday. What are you planning to bring up to them?"

There are papers spread out on his desk that he was glancing over before I came in. He shuffles them back together quickly before looking up at me.

'Well I've been looking over everything from the accident report and the charges that were set, as well as the evidence brought up from the cameras in their truck. It looks like when the accident happened that they weren't fully paying attention to the road in front of them. Because their cameras were turned off at the time of the accident."

When Derek tells me this I can feel panic running through my brain as I think about the fact that things could have gone so much worse. *She could have ended up a splat on the ground.*

I zone back into reality, breaking from my thoughts when Derek snaps his fingers to try and get my attention.

"Hey. Hey, it's okay. She's still alive. She may be in a coma, but she's still alive. And those guys were negligent with their driving. They should have been paying more attention to the road in front of them. I'm going to make sure to get Destiny what she deserves for what happened."

"Okay, Derek. Thank you so much for helping represent Destiny and her case. What all are you going to bring up to the jury? How are you going to try and prove that they were at fault for putting her through that accident and into the hospital?"

I can see the gears turning in Derek's mind as he's thinking through everything before he answers my question.

After a few seconds, he looks at me and says, "Jade, these guys were negligent in their driving. They could have tried to stop and swerve the other way from Destiny's car, but they didn't. Granted, they called the ambulance and police after the accident, but they still could be held accountable for causing the accident to happen. I am going to do everything in my power to prove that they were at fault for what happened. And they will be held accountable for their negligence. Because they fucked up. Bad."

I can feel my face turning up into a smile as Derek says that. *Hopefully with him as her lawyer, Destiny will be able to get justice for what has happened to her.*

"You really think that you can get them with the evidence that you have? Because if she ends up suffering permanent damage from the accident, she'll have hell trying to pay her medical bills. And I know that she'll probably have trauma and PTSD from the crash after she recovers. I just want her to be able to get some kind of justice after everything she's having to go through. It's bullshit."

Derek turns his eyes towards me with sincerity before he opens his mouth to speak. "I am going to do everything in my power to get those assholes to pay for what they've done. I promise."

I can feel a smile spreading across my face as I stand up. Derek walks around his desk and grabs my hand in his as he pulls me in for a hug. As he's hugging me, I can feel the warm sunlight hitting my face through the window.

After a few seconds I pull away and brush a few strands of hair out of my face. "Thank you so much, Derek, for being so helpful with Destiny's case. You are the only person I would ever trust to be her lawyer or my lawyer. So thank you."

"You're welcome, Jade. I would do anything for you two. Even if that meant joining the shady side of the law." He laughs out loud, his chest rising as he chuckles deeply. "Now you should go back up to the hospital so that you can be with Destiny."

I nod my head before telling him bye as I leave his office, then make my way back towards the elevator.

As I go back down to the lobby I can't help but think what could have happened to Destiny had the accident been worse.

She could have been mangled from flying through the windshield. Her skull could have busted open on the asphalt, killing her instantly. She could be permanently paralyzed or even brain dead.

But she's not. She's only got a few broken bones and is stuck in a coma that she may or may not wake up from. I'll just have to wait and see what happens. Until then, I am going to be right by her side every day at the hospital, watching for any signs of consciousness.

I walk out to my car a few minutes later and get on the road back to the hospital.

It's about 4:00 in the afternoon as I'm driving down the road, and rush hour traffic is starting to get busy. I end up stuck behind a large black Silverado with cars slowly pulling forward around me.

I pull to a stop as the lanes surrounding me fill up with cars. Traffic is stopped by the red light ahead. I can feel myself getting anxious to get back to the hospital quickly, but I'm going to have to wait for the lanes to move forward.

The light changes to green after what feels like hours and I follow behind the truck until I'm able to get through the light, stopping a few more times beforehand.

Once I'm past the light and onto the straightaway on Shepherd Street I push my right foot down on the gas pedal and drive as fast as I can until I see the hospital coming up on the right.

I change lanes until I am in the right turning lane and pull into the parking lot. I drive around to the side of the hospital where Destiny's room is and pull into a parking spot a few rows from the doors.

I take a few deep breaths before getting out of the car and head into the hospital.

When I get inside I walk over to the nurse's station and ask her if Destiny is still in the same room.

The nurse turns from the computer to look at me. "Let me check really quick for you."

She types for a second on the keyboard before she gives me an answer. While she's typing, her face has an expression of slight concern on it.

"Hmm... It looks like she's still in the same room but currently she's getting a CT scan. But the scan should be finished soon. They took her back probably thirty minutes ago."

I thank her as I run over to the elevator and ride up to the third floor where Destiny's room is.

It only takes me a few minutes to get back to her room and when I open the door it's still empty from her being taken to get the scan.

I can feel my chest gaining pressure as my breath starts to speed up a little bit. *What if something's gone wrong? What if something happens to her?* My thoughts are running through all of the worst case scenarios as I wait for her to be brought back from getting the CT scan.

My eyebrows furrow as I try not to let my thoughts get carried away and try not to cry.

I wait for what feels like forever before the doors open and Destiny is wheeled back into the room on a gurney.

Dr. Drew, along with Destiny's nurses push the gurney into the room before they greet me and start moving her back onto the hospital bed. They lift the sheet underneath her and carry it carefully from the gurney to the bed, then gently set her down onto the mattress.

Once she is laid back on the hospital bed, Dr. Drew hooks her IV and heart monitor back in as he starts to tell me what is going on.

I can feel the intensity before he even says anything.

"Destiny was having some severe hyperactivity that was causing her to seem like she was having epileptic seizures. When I got her in to start the scan it looked like her brain was overflowing with serotonin waves going in and out through her temporal lobe. There was also some excess blood flow that I noticed. It stopped after a few minutes but I have to keep an eye out for any signs that it may come back. Because if her brain is overflowed with blood, it could cause permanent damage."

As he's telling me all of this, all I can think is that the worst is happening. My mouth widens as my eyes start to fill with tears. I can feel myself trying not to burst out in sobs.

It takes me a few minutes to be able to regain composure before I say what I want to say.

Once I am able to breathe normally again, I ask the doctor, "Is she going to be okay? Do you know if Destiny will be able to wake up again?"

I can see Dr. Drew thinking before he answers me.

"The activity that I saw during the CT scan showed that there is a lot of activity running through her mind while she is unconscious. It showed that she is not brain dead and that she can wake up. I just don't know when. That will be determined by her and her brain's willpower. You can see her eyes moving behind her eyelids which means that she's actively dreaming."

I open my mouth and take in a deep, shaky breath. "Thank you, Dr. Drew. I really hope that she's able to wake up soon. But until then I'm not leaving her side for anything."

He gives me a half smile before telling me that he's going to go down to his office and look back over the scans again. See if there's anything significant that he might have missed.

After Dr. Drew has left the room and closes the door, I look over at Destiny laying on the bed with her eyes closed. I can't help but think that she is in pain and that's the reason why she went back into a coma: to help her not feel the pain in her body.

Chapter Eleven

Jade's POV: It's been two days since I spoke to Derek about the trial and what his stance is going to be. Greg was here yesterday to keep me some company with Destiny for a few hours, just to make sure I'm okay.

It's Monday morning and I have been sitting in the hospital room with Destiny since Friday afternoon. She's been laying there looking sweet and peaceful, her hair splayed around her head on the pillows. She looks like Snow White almost, her hands laying next to her body, her dark blonde hair laying in waves behind her head.

As I'm sitting there gazing at my best friend, my girlfriend, the door opens, Dr. Drew coming inside.

He's holding a clipboard in his hands when he walks through the door.

He looks towards me with sympathy in his eyes as he opens his mouth to speak. "Good morning, Jade. I'm here to see if there's been any improvement during the night. Can I come over to check her vitals and look at her eyes?"

I slump down in my chair, my eyes hooded from exhaustion and sadness. "Yes, sir."

"Hey, I'm sure that everything is okay. That she's still alive and well in there. Her body is just trying to protect her from feeling every ounce of pain that was caused by the accident."

Dr. Drew walks over and gives me a slight hug before going over to Destiny.

He grabs his stethoscope and places it onto her chest. He puts the ear pieces into his ears and listens closely to her heart and her lungs, moving the stethoscope a few times.

His face turns a little serious before removing the stethoscope from her chest, and I can feel my heart start to race with worry.

Dr. Drew turns to me as he says, "Her heart rate has slowed down quite a bit and her breathing is extremely low. I'm going to have to keep an eye on it over the next few hours to make sure it doesn't slow down any more or if it comes back up to normal."

"All right." My eyes feel like they want to fill with tears as he takes out his little flashlight and starts to look into Destiny's eyes.

He has her eyelids lifted open as he's looking into her pupils. After a few moments he turns off the flashlight and lets Destiny's eyes fall closed.

"Her pupils are slightly dilated, and her eyes are moving a lot. She's certainly still alive and has a lot of activity going on in her brain right now, so I can tell you that she's not going to go anywhere any time soon, if at all. And I am certain that your being here has been helping a lot."

"Thank you so much, doctor. I don't want to leave her side at all until she's fully awake and conscious. If anything were to happen and I'm not here, I don't know what I would do."

Dr. Drew lets out a sigh as he tells me, "I know that you don't, but you really should go home at least for a few hours to get some actual rest and food. Because you look exhausted. You look like you haven't slept for days and that's not good. "Call your friend Greg to come pick you up, because you shouldn't drive until you are more rested."

I breath out shakily and tell him, "I will. I'll ask him to come get me and take me home. But please, if anything happens, call me. Please."

He nods his head before walking out the door.

As soon as it closes behind him, I pick up my phone from the armrest next to me and dial Greg's number on the keypad. I hold the phone next to my right ear with my elbow resting on the chair while I wait for him to answer.

After almost five rings I'm about to hang up, but then he answers.

"Hey what's going on? Is everything okay?"

"Yes, but Dr. Drew told me to call you and ask you to pick me up. He wants you to take me home so that I can rest for a few hours and get something to eat. Do you think you can come get me?"

"Of course I can. I'll be there in about ten minutes in the cruiser."

Greg's POV: I get off the phone with Jade and start getting my boots on next to the couch. After getting the laces tied tight, I grab my keys and wallet then head out the door.

As soon as I get to my car in the parking lot, I get in and start driving to the hospital. I can't help but think about the toll that Jade's health is taking with her worrying so much about Destiny waking up. She's been losing weight and her face has been sinking in a little every day as she's staying awake damn near 24/7.

That's not good. She needs rest and she needs to try and relax herself.

****

When I get to the hospital I immediately go inside and up to Destiny's room to get Jade.

I walk past a few doctors and nurses taking care of other patients who don't look nearly as bad as Jade does. As soon as I reach the room and go inside, I see just how bad Jade has gotten.

Her dark hair has become frazzled and stringy. Her eyes have dark circles around them. The skin on her face looks tight. And her clothes are hanging loose from her body.

I rush over to her and grab her by the shoulders. "You need to get some actual rest and some real, nutritious food in your stomach. You look like a corpse. I know that you want to be here for Destiny, but you need to be taking care of yourself too. Because if you don't, you'll end up in intensive care with feeding tubes and steroids being pumped into you."

Jade looks up at me from where she's sitting. "I know I do. But I can't stop worrying so much about her. Especially with the trial coming up in a few days. I've never seen the faces of the truck drivers, but I get the feeling that seeing their faces might make me feel even worse knowing that they are responsible for her being here, stuck like this for god knows how long.

I lean over and wrap my arms around her, picking her up from the chair. I help Jade gather her few things while she bends over slowly and leaves a kiss on Destiny's pale lips.

She slides her hand across Destiny's before turning toward the door to follow me.

Jade looks like she can hardly stand and might fall over any second.

When she starts trying to walk to the door, I wrap my right arm around her waist to hold her up as she walks. At first I can feel her tense up beneath my touch, but after a few seconds she relaxes and lets me help guide her to the elevator.

It takes a few minutes for us to reach the elevator, but as soon as we're able to get inside she goes over to the closest wall and falls against it.

I hold onto Jade's hands as the elevator goes down to the first floor and make sure that she's not going to collapse. I can feel her squeezing mine in hers, trying not to lose her grip when the elevator stops and does a slight bounce before the doors open.

Before Jade can start trying to walk, I bend over and place my left arm under her legs, my right arm behind her back, and pick her up from the floor.

"You're not walking all the way out to the parking lot. You can barely stand on your own. So I'm going to carry you to the car and upstairs to my apartment so that I can make you some food before you rest."

I look down and see her opening her mouth as she mumbles, "I-I can do it. I can walk."

She tries to get free from my arms while I walk but her arms are so weak that they're shaking. After a few seconds she gives up and lets her head lay against my chest while I carry her to the cruiser.

I place my arms underneath her legs and pick her up off the ground. Jade's head is laying in the crook of my neck as I walk out to the parking lot with her in my arms.

She feels so fragile from being so exhausted. *I know that she wants to stay up here with Destiny until she wakes up and can leave the hospital, but she needs rest and food. Because otherwise she'll end up in the hospital from malnourishment and exhaustion.*

I get to the car finally and have to be careful as I try to open the door because I don't want to drop Jade.

I grab the keys from my pocket with my left hand while my right arm holds her up. I reach down and carefully unlock her door then get it open. After the door is open all the way I maneuver her into the seat, trying not to hit her head on the roof of the car.

Before I get in on the other side, I make sure that she's secure and get her seatbelt buckled around her.

I close her door nice and quiet then go over to the driver's side and climb in, turning on the ignition. The engine turns and comes to life with a purr as I buckle my seatbelt. Once the car starts, I can hear Jade mumbling something under her breath in her sleep.

It almost sounds like she's saying something like, "Destiny... wake up. Come back."

I wish that there was any way I could help to reassure her. But I know that there's not much I could do without being able to somehow get Destiny awake and out of the hospital. I know that that's all Jade needs. She needs her best friend and girlfriend to be okay.

I know that Destiny will wake up when she is able to. When her body feels okay for her to be awake and conscious. Because I've seen victims of other car accidents who were in much less critical condition than her who have stayed in the hospital, in a coma or not, for months or years before being better enough to go home.

As I'm thinking about both Destiny and Jade's wellbeing, I reach my apartment building. I get out and go over to the passenger side so that I can open Jade's door and wake her up enough to get her to my apartment.

Her eyes open slightly as she blinks, trying to regain consciousness. She looks around in confusion as she wakes up.

"Where am I? What's going on?"

I reach down and grab her hand so that she can stand up before answering her questions.

I look into Jade's eyes that are surrounded by dark circles. "You're at my apartment, Jade. We're going to go up there so you can get some food and well-needed rest. You have been awake for days without rest and you need to get some sleep before Destiny's trial on Wednesday."

Jade nods her head in acknowledgement as she tries to stand up, her eyes falling back closed as I grab onto her so she doesn't fall.

I wrap my arms around her waist, pulling her inside to go up to my apartment. I have to hold a firm grip around her as we walk because her feet are barely lifting from the ground.

Once we reach the apartment I open the door and get her inside and onto the couch, laying her against the cushions. As soon as her head hits them her eyes are closed and her breathing turns shallow.

I grab a blanket from the closet and drape it over her and making sure that she's covered before going to the kitchen.

When I get in there, I grab the ingredients to make her a quesadilla on the stovetop.

I get the cheese and butter out of the fridge and the tortillas out of the pantry and set everything onto the counter. I turn the front burner on with the skillet over it.

After I grab a tortilla out of the package, I lather it in butter with a knife then place it in the pan on the burner. The butter starts to sizzle as soon as it touches the skillet. While the butter is starting to brown the tortilla, I grab the cheddar and start sprinkling it across the tortilla.

The quesadilla only takes a few minutes to cook since I've got the burner on high. I grab a spatula and fold it in half before putting it onto a plate.

I grab the plate from the counter and carry it into the living room, holding it under Jade's nose to try and wake her up so that she can eat.

Her nose twitches some as the smell of the food reaches her nostrils. She starts sitting up as her eyes open. When she's finally awake enough to focus she grabs the plate out of my hand.

A smile crosses her face as she tells me, "Thank you so much, Greg. This smells delicious."

I sit down on the chair across from her as I ask, "How are you feeling? Do you feel any better from your nap? And how's the food? Do you like it?"

Jade takes a big bite from the quesadilla, the cheese stretching from the tortilla. She swallows it after a few seconds and answers my questions. "I'm feeling better. The food is really good. It's so warm and cheesy. It's the first thing that's good that I have eaten in the last few weeks. So thank you so much for making it for me."

I turn on the TV while Jade eats her food, putting it on a random episode of *Supernatural*, the one where Sam and Dean are having to get rid of the rabbit's foot.

I managed to turn it on right after it's starting. After we watch Sam lose the foot and start having bad luck, Jade starts to laugh and smile each time something happens to him.

It makes me happy to see that she's smiling right now. Because she doesn't need to be letting herself feel miserable while Destiny is in the hospital.

I just want to see her happy, whether I'm the cause of it or not.

Chapter Twelve

Destiny's POV: I wake up to the sound of bacon sizzling and the scent of waffles cooking in the kitchen. I push my arms behind me to help get my ass off the couch. I toss the blanket over the cushions before I make my way out of the living room to where Jade is standing in the kitchen wearing only an oversized t-shirt and pink cotton panties.

As soon as I am standing behind her, I wrap my arms around her neck and lean around to kiss her cheek. "Hi, babe. What time did you get up and start cooking?"

Jade sets the spatula down next to the pan of bacon and turns around to look at me before she answers my question with a sweet, soft kiss on my lips. "I got up around six thirty. I didn't want to disturb you because you were sleeping so peacefully, so I decided to surprise you with a breakfast of bacon and waffles."

"You are so awesome, baby. I love you so much, and I can't wait to eat this delicious food after it's done cooking. Do you need help with any of it?"

Jade looks at me with a sparkle in her dark green eyes. "Well if you want, you can get some eggs started in the bigger skillet. Any way you want them. Scrambled, fried, poached, et cetera. That way we'll be eating breakfast made by both of us. How does that sound?"

I give her a cheesy smile with a thumbs-up as I walk over to the fridge and take the carton of eggs out.

I get the skillet and place it onto the left front burner as I turn it on. Then I grab the bread out of the cabinet and cut holes into four slices before getting out four eggs. I place two slices of bread into the skillet after putting some butter on them. Then I crack two of the eggs and pour the whites and egg yolk into the center of the bread.

The eggs and bread begin to sizzle in the pan as they start to cook. After a few minutes, I flip them over to cook the other side until they become a golden brown color.

Once the first two eggs in a nest are finished cooking, I put the other two in the pan and start cooking them. It takes only about six minutes for these ones to cook since the pan is already hot.

As soon as they are finished, I place two pieces onto one plate and two pieces onto the other plate. I can feel Jade eyeing them over my shoulder as she finishes with the waffles and bacon, putting them onto their serving plates.

"Those look delicious, baby. We haven't had eggs in a nest in a while."

I smile as I turn around. "I figured it'd be nice to have this with the waffles and bacon you made instead of just regular scrambled eggs like we usually eat. Is everything about ready to be served up onto plates?"

"Yes, ma'am. Bon apetit. You can get your plate ready first. I am going to get some more coffee in my mug before I get my plate."

As my baby grabs her coffee cup and goes to refill it from the pot next to the sink, I place four slices of bacon onto my plate and grab a second plate to put my waffles on. Then I get the jar of peanut butter out of the pantry along with the syrup.

I get a knife and fork from the silverware drawer and carry both of my plates to the table after setting the peanut butter and syrup into the center of the table.

Using the butterknife, I spread a nice layer of peanut butter onto each waffle before pouring syrup onto them. As soon as I'm done, I start digging into the waffles.

I cut the first bite and put it into my mouth, the warm syrup running down my throat. "Mmm... these waffles are delicious, baby. You did amazing."

Jade makes her way over and sets down her plates along with her coffee cup. She places another cup next to my plate. She slathers peanut butter and syrup onto her waffles before she starts to cut into the eggs in a nest that I made, her eyes closing as she chews. Her cheeks turn a warm red as she finishes eating her first bite.

She turns to look at me before continuing to eat and says, "Baby, these eggs in a nest are amazing. The toast is perfect, and the eggs are so gooey and runny. I might just need an extra piece of toast to dip into what's left of the yolk. I love you so much, babygirl."

Jade and I continue eating in satisfied silence until our plates and cups of coffee have been emptied completely.

Once I finish mine, I stand up and gather the plates from the table and make my way over to the sink. "You made the food, so I am going to clean the dishes and put them away if that's alright, baby."

"Of course. So long as I can observe and watch your cute butt going back and forth."

I let out a laugh as I turn on the hot water and start filling up the sink. I grab the sponge and dunk it under the water before squeezing some soap onto it. I scrub the forks and spatula first, using the sponge to get all the grease and grime off them.

As I wash each dish thoroughly, I can hear Jade behind me playing on her phone.

"Whatcha doin', babe?"

She lets out a giggle as she says, "You'll find out in a second, babe. Don't worry."

I rinse off the last plate before filling the pans we used with soap and water when I hear music starting up behind me. Music from a particular song that we heard last night on a particular television show.

A big grin covers my face as I say over my shoulder, "Is that what I think it is?"

As soon as the words have escaped my lips, the lyrics start playing from Jade's phone. "Carry on my wayward son, there'll be peace when you are done. Lay your weary head to rest. Don't you cry no more."

At that point, both Jade and I are singing with the lyrics, including the guitar. "Do do do doo, do do do doo!!!"

About halfway through the second verse, Jade comes to stand behind me and starts swaying our bodies to the rhythm of the song. My eyes close as we're singing and dancing together. I forget that I'm washing the dishes after another minute.

The sprayer that was in my hand ends up being used as a guitar pick and not thinking about it, I end up spraying water on myself.

I scream out in surprise and drop the sprayer while Jade jumps back and laughs at me.

I stand in front of the sink, dripping wet while giving Jade an evil look. "You did that on purpose. Now I'm wet." A pout crosses my lips in fake sadness.

"I did not. And really? I couldn't tell. Well now we better go get you out of those clothes before you freeze to death. Wouldn't want you catching a cold, would we?"

I can see the devious look in her eyes as she grabs ahold of my hand and starts pulling me towards the bedroom. Every step that I take, I can feel my heart beating faster and my insides beginning to throb as a warmth grows in my lower region.

As we get closer to the bedroom, I start purring under my breath like a wild kitty.

Jade looks at me over her shoulder. "Don't worry, my kitty. You'll get what you want in a second. I'm going to tame my little putty tat."

We get to the bedroom where she pulls me inside, leading me towards the bed. Jade turns around and starts kissing my lips slowly as she pulls me close, moving her hands along my damp torso. She starts pulling my t-shirt up, grabbing at the clinging fabric.

As she pulls the shirt free from my body, I start pulling my shorts off and begin kissing my baby feverishly. I collapse onto the bed as soon as she has the shirt free from over my head.

Jade begins kissing my neck, slowly making her way down towards my bare breasts. She opens her mouth and starts to lick around my nipples, nipping my skin each time a moan escapes my throat.

I start grinding my body underneath hers as she continues messing with me, torturing me. I can feel myself getting more turned on as Jade keeps playing with me, using her tongue in all the best ways before she starts to use her fingers.

My back arches under her touch as I moan out, "Oh do me already!"

My eyes open for a moment as Jade plants a deep kiss on my lips. A smile crosses her face, making her look like the devil she is before she says, "As you wish, my lady."

Jade pulls my panties off my butt and down my legs, followed by hers and wraps her legs between mine as we connect to each other in lust and passion. Pure ecstasy. Our bodies press against each other as we kiss and grind against each other. I can feel the pulse vibrating between us as we move together.

All I can see in this moment is the warmth that encompasses both of us. The love in Jade's eyes is growing deep and dark as we move together as one. I can feel myself gripping Jade closer towards me as I try to feel every inch of her body against mine.

I kiss Jade with passion as my hand moves down between us and starts sliding between her legs, my fingers moving inside her.

"You're really wet, baby. I can make you wetter if you want."

Jade looks down at me as she bites her lower lip between her teeth. Her body grows warm as I slip a couple of fingers between her lips, moving them around her g-spot.

I can feel her starting to tremble under my touch.

"Do you want me to take over, baby? Get on top? Because I can."

Jade's eyes open slowly as she stutters out a yes. As soon as the word is out of her mouth, I grab my baby and wrap her legs around my waist, flipping us over.

I start kissing her wildly as my fingers move inside of her. Our mouths move as one while I slide my fingers frantically inside of her, bringing her to orgasm a few times. I can feel Jade gasping for breath as her body shakes under my touch.

As each breath escapes her lips, I place a kiss onto them to replace it until she is a puddle of mush beneath me.

After a few more minutes of pleasuring my baby, I climb off of her and wrap my arms around her body.

"How was that, baby?" I smile at my fiancé while she tries to sit up and catch her breath. I can feel her body still shaking when she falls back onto the mattress.

"That was amazing, baby. You always make me feel like I'm on cloud nine. I love you so goddamn much."

Jade pulls me close and gives me another kiss before she tries to stand up again. I help her up because I can feel how much her body is still shaking and her knees are trying to buckle under her weight.

Once we are both standing, I look at my baby and say, "How about we get a shower together before going to town? That way we don't smell like lust and sex. Instead, we'll smell like lavender and shea butter. How's that sound?"

"That sounds great, baby. Then we can go to town and have fun browsing the stores and shops around downtown. And maybe talk to people about possibly getting your next book on their shelves for sale."

I wrap my arms around Jade and give her a hug and quick kiss before grabbing some clothes to take into the bathroom with me. "I love you so fucking much. Thank you for being so supportive of me, baby. You are amazing and I cannot wait for the day that we are able to get married."

"No, you're amazing for having such a creative mind inside your head. You come up with all these amazing ideas and just run with them. You are the most amazing woman I could have ever met, and I am so glad that I get to call you mine. I love you so much."

I grab Jade's hand and pull her towards the bathroom so that we can get in the shower.

As soon as we get into the bathroom, Jade goes over to the shower and turns it on. She gets in first and I follow right behind her.

The warm water runs over our bodies as soon as we're under it. I can feel my body relaxing again as I start running my fingers through Jade's hair, wetting it throughout. I caress my fingers through each strand, making sure it's all fully wet before I grab the shampoo.

I put some into my hands and lather them together before I start to put it in her hair, massaging the shampoo into her hair and against her scalp.

"How does this feel, darling? Is this soothing?"

"Mmm... yes. It is very soothing. Your touch feels amazing, whether in a sexual way or a sensual way. This is incredibly soothing."

I continue to massage Jade's scalp as I start to rinse the shampoo out of her hair. "Are you ready for the conditioner, baby?"

She nods her head as I finish getting all of the shampoo out of her hair.

I finish rinsing the shampoo out of her hair and grab the conditioner bottle. I put a dab of it in my hand then lather it up. Once I get it lathered up in my hands, I start rubbing the conditioner into the ends of her hair. I run my fingers through each strand, coating her hair before I start to rinse it out.

After a few minutes of lathering the conditioner all the through, I finish rinsing the it all out.

"How does your head feel, sweetie? Does it feel like I got it clean enough?"

Jade smiles at me as she answers. "Oh yes, baby. My hair feels nice and clean. And my scalp feels very relaxed. Now it's your turn. Then we wash our bodies."

Jade grabs the shampoo bottle and pours some out, lathering it in her hands before she starts to massage it into my hair and scalp. As her fingers run through my hair, I can feel my skull beginning to relax because of how soothing her fingers feel in my hair.

She continues to massage my head until my hair is fully lathered from the shampoo, then begins rinsing it out. Her hands run the water through my hair, rinsing the shampoo out completely after a few minutes. As soon as she's done, she gets the conditioner and starts putting it in my hair.

Her fingers run along the ends of my hair, putting conditioner on each strand until it's fully coated. Jade uses the water to rinse the conditioner out for the next few minutes before it's completely gone.

"How does that feel, baby? Are you relaxed?"

I let a sigh of satisfaction come out of my mouth before I answer her.

"Oh yes, baby. I feel so relaxed after that scalp massage. Now we can soap each other up and wash the sweat and sex off our bodies. Do you want to do it at the same time to be a little faster?"

Jade smiles at me as she grabs the body wash. I hold my hand out and let her pour some of the body into it before she pours some into her hands. We both start lathering each other up, starting at the chests and making our way down and around our bodies.

I massage the soap along Jade's skin as I lather up her breasts, her stomach, and her thighs. I move my hands around to her back and soap up and down until I reach her taut butt.

I squeeze her butt in between my hands, getting as much soap onto it as possible before I move back around to the front. My hands move between her legs as I soap up her lips before slowly soaping in between them.

I make sure to get Jade nice and clean before we start rinsing the body wash off of each other's bodies.

Once we're both fully rinsed off, Jade and I climb out of the shower and get dressed.

I put on a comfy pair of purple cotton underwear and a matching bra topped with a plain white t-shirt and black jeans. Jade puts on a matching set of lacy black underwear and a bra before she puts on a hot pink t-shirt that says "Sexy Babe" on it and a pair of faded denim skinny jeans.

"Are you ready to go, baby?" I walk out of the bathroom and grab my keys from the kitchen table.

Jade comes out of the bathroom with a brush in her hand, running it through her hair. She comes over and gives me a quick kiss on my lips before she answers me.

"Yes, babe. I'm just gonna brush your hair right quick and grab us both a pair of shoes from the bedroom then I'll be ready to go. Go shopping with my sexy baby. How does that sound, darling?"

I give Jade a huge smile, my cheeks turned a deep pink. "That sounds amazing, baby. I love going anywhere with you because you are the love of my life and you're my best friend. I love you."

"I love you, babygirl," Jade says as she starts running the brush through my hair.

After she's done, she goes to the bedroom and grabs us each a pair of converse sneakers, black for me and pink for her to match her t-shirt.

I go over to the couch and put mine on, then grab my phone from the coffee table. Once I'm ready, I follow Jade out the door.

She gets in the driver's seat before I can get over there. When she closes the door, I give her a look while she laughs at me before I give in and go over to the passenger side.

Once I'm in the car I hand the keys over to Jade and buckle up my seatbelt. She turns the car on and as soon as it starts, she turns the radio on. Rockstar by Three Doors Down is playing when the radio blasts from the speakers.. After my ears adjust for a few seconds, I start singing along with the song.

Jade starts driving down the road, laughing at my off-key singing. "You're so cute, baby. Even If you do sound like a dying cat being thrown at a wall."

"Hey! Rude. I sound great, thank you very much. Where are we going first?"

She turns the car down Green Street. "You'll see, baby."

I let a groan of impatience come out before I continue listening to the music, watching the buildings go by through the window.

We pass by The Mug Barn that we always go to for new coffee mugs every few months, pass by Vanessa's Vintage, and a few other stores before Jade finally stops the car, pulling into a parking spot in front of Frank's Woodworks.

I turn to look at my baby as my mind fills with curiosity. "Why are we here? You can't carve for anything without trying to carve yourself."

Jade looks at me with a sparkle in her eyes as she says, "Well baby, we have been officially together for almost three years now and since we just got engaged last night, I figured I would take you to get a few things. I called Frank yesterday morning after I decided that I was going to ask the question and asked him if he could make something special for us. Something that commemorates who we are."

My mouth drops as happiness fills my entire body. I follow Jade toward the door and go inside behind her.

"Hello, ladies. How are you two doing this morning?' Frank greets us as we get inside.

We walk over to the counter where he's standing before I tell him, "We are doing amazing, Frank. I know you already know, but last night Jade asked me to marry her, and I said yes." I wrap my right arm around Jade's waist and pull her close.

Frank grins as he says, "I am so happy for you gals. I knew you would say yes. I'm guessing y'all are here to pick up your surprise?"

Jade nods her head. "Yes, sir. Is it ready?"

"It took all day and night, but it's ready. Let me go into the back to grab it for you, sweetheart."

Frank walks away and goes tgrough the door that leads to the back while Jade and I stand next to each other, beaming with joy. I don't know what she asked him to make for us, but I can't wait to see what it is.

After a few minutes, Frank reemerges through the door with a little wooden figure in his hands. He sets it on the counter so that we can look at it.

It's a carved figurine of both Jade and I standing next to each other, with each of us wearing an intricately detailed gothic style gown. There's a book between us with the words Together Forever carved out in the pages.

I pick it up to look at it more and on the bottom are our names carved out in a calligraphy style font.

Once I set it back down on the counter, I turn and look at Jade with tears in my eyes. "You had Frank make this for us? It's beautiful, baby. It's incredible."

"And thank you, Frank, for making it. I can't believe that you were able to make this. It's incredible. Thank you so much."

Frank gives me a smile. "It's no problem at all. You two make a gorgeous couple and I can't wait for the day y'all are able to stand on that altar and get married. I am very happy for both of you."

I pull Jade closer and give her a kiss on her cheek. "We can't wait either. Thank you again for making this for us. It will be sitting on display in the bedroom until the day of the wedding. Then it will be our centerpiece for our bridal table."

Frank comes out from behind the counter and comes over to give Jade and I both a big hug. "I am so proud of both of you. Y'all are both making it so far in this world together and now y'all are going to get married."

He gives us each a kiss on the cheeks before asking, "What are you two going to be up to for the rest of the day? Anything fun planned?"

"*Well, we're going to go shopping at some more of the stores around here, then probably go grab something to eat from The Lunch Bar,*" *says Jade as Frank wraps our figurine in paper and puts it inside a bag for us to carry with us.*

He hands the bag to me. "*Here you go, hun. That way it can't break while you're carrying it with you. I hope that you two have a great day out shopping.*"

Jade and I thank him again before we walk out the door with the bag. I'm still smiling as we walk down the sidewalk, gazing at the various shops that are around us.

"*Where do you want to go next, baby?*" *I ask her as we pass by the local coffee shop.*

She turns towards me with a sly grin on her face. "*Do you want to go in there to grab some coffee then stop by the crystal shop? We could each pick out a few crystals and maybe some jewelry to buy each other.*"

"*That sounds great, baby.*" *I turn toward the coffee shop with Jade and head inside.*

It's already filled with people drinking coffee at tables and eating muffins and other pastries. As we walk inside, we make our way over to the counter to order our drinks.

The woman standing behind the counter greets us with a nice, cute smile. "*Hi, this is Brew Tastes. What would you like to order today?*"

I look over the menu that is over the counter for a few seconds before I decide what I am going to order. I look over at Jade to see if she's ready to order.

After a few seconds, she nods her head to let me know that she's ready. She orders first, getting a mocha bean cappuccino with no foam, and I get a caramel mocha frappucino with extra foam. The woman tells us that our drinks will be ready in a few minutes once we finish give her our drink orders.

I give her my name before I walk with Jade to sit down at a nearby table to wait.

I sit down across from her with an expression of affection spread across my face.

I think to myself, Jade looks so cute in her t-shirt with her hair all wavy over her shoulders. I can't believe that as of last night I am engaged to the love of my life, the woman of my dreams, my baby.

Jade breaks my thoughts, as she says, "Are you ready to start planning our wedding soon? We'll have to grab the girls to help with getting everything planned and decided once we start. That way we can have outside help with the planning."

"I am ready to start planning the wedding. Because we'll be planning the day that we will be bonded together in matrimony, as wife and wife. It will be an amazing day, and the sooner it comes, the better. I love you so freaking much."

Jade gives me a smile. "I love you so freaking much, babygirl. I can't wait for the day that we get married to each other."

I grab her hand from across the table and plant a sweet kiss on the back of her palm. I look up into her eyes as she smiles at me.

After a few moments of just gazing into each other's eyes, my name gets called by the barista. Jade and I stand up from our chairs and go over to the counter to grab our drinks.

We thank her after she hands us our cups and head back outside. We start walking down the street until we reach the crystal shop, Witch's Passion.

As soon as we reach it, I grab the door and open it for Jade, letting her go ahead of me. I walk inside with Jade next to me and am almost immediately hit with the strong scent of lavender and jasmine from the lit incense. I take a deep breath, letting them wash over me.

I pull Jade behind me, making my way towards the display of polished rocks that are to the right side of the store. As we get closer, I can see one rock that sticks out to me.

It's probably five inches tall and two inches wide. It's shaped similar to a cloud and is the color of midnight and sapphire. It's gorgeous, and I have to buy it for Jade.

I make my way over to the counter where the rock is and greet the woman standing nearby. "Hello. I was wondering how much that beautiful midnight colored stone is right there, because I would love to buy it for my fiancé here."

The woman gives Jade and I a smile while she reaches down and pulls the stone out from underneath the counter.

She sets it in front of us as she says, "This stone costs about $24.99. It's a unique type of opal that was unburied from an archaeological site just outside of town. I feel like it has some distinct character that is shown in its colors and shape."

I grab my wallet out of my handbag so that I can pay for it, but before I do, Jade stops me and points at a crystal in the next display over. A crystal that's dark blue colored in the center and multi-colored along the outside of the points. It almost looks like it's not even real.

Jade tells the woman, "I would like to purchase that crystal over there for her. That way we'll have each bought each other something." She pauses and looks at me before continuing. "How does that sound, babygirl?"

I let out a laugh as my face turns into a blushing smile. "Okay, baby. That sounds good. So long as you let me buy you something else pretty to make it even since you already gave me this ring on my finger."

"Deal."

The woman goes over to the other display and grabs the crystal to bring over to the register along with the stone. Before she rings them both up, she looks at us with kindness in her eyes.

"I am so happy for you two. In fact, I am going to give you each a 50% discount on the final price of your items as an engagement gift."

I open my mouth to tell her no, but she stops me before I can say anything. "Nonsense. It's on me. Don't worry about it. Besides, I own this shop. Your total is $12.49."

I thank her as I grab my card out of my wallet and slide it through the debit machine.

Once the payment goes through, she rings up the crystal for Jade. It comes through as $10.24 as the final price. Jade gets her card and slides it through to pay. Once the machine beeps, our things are wrapped up and put into a paper bag for us.

Jade and I both thank the woman as we walk out the door back to the street and continue on our shopping adventure through downtown.

As we're walking down the street, I can hear music coming from around the corner. We reach the other side of the corner and it looks like a festival is being held . There are crowds of people and a few stages scattered in the grassy area.

Jade and I quickly run across the street to the park and are greeted at the entrance by a man wearing a black cloak.

"Hello. Did you hear the music playing in the park?"

I nod my head as the sound of the music grows louder across the park. "Yes. We were shopping around the corner and heard the music. We were curious what's going on today?"

He shakes his head in understanding as he starts to explain. "Well, there's a battle of the bands competition going on down near the lake. So far everyone has been pretty good. There's been rock, classic and heavy metal, pop music, country, alternative, reggae, and classical bands. Each band has to play and perform their own original songs and have their own instruments. You can come watch or you can even enter if you want. You would just have to find some instruments to play on."

"Okay," Jade says as he hands us a pamphlet with the names of the judges of the competition.

After he walks away, Jade looks at me with excitement in her eyes. "We should enter the competition. I still have my bass and your keytar in the trunk of the car. We could perform Shaking the Devil Down. We'll blow the metaphorical roof of this park."

"Hell yeah, babe. That's probably our best song that we've written together. Do you want to go to the car and grab the instruments while I go sign us up for the competition? Or I can grab the instruments and you sign us up?"

Jade's face beams as she says, "I can grab the instruments and you can go over to sign us up."

Before she walks away, she wraps her arms around me and gives me a kiss. "I'll be right back, baby."

Once Jade is headed across the street, I start walking over to where the crowds are near the lake. I make my way over to the sign-up table that's at the back of everyone.

"Hi. I would like to sign my fiancé and I up for the battle of the bands competition."

The man sitting at the table grabs a pen and hands me a clipboard. "Just put down the name of your band, what song you will be performing, and what music genre it falls under. Once you are ready, your band can go behind the stage area with your instruments to wait and be called out to perform."

I take the pen and clipboard from him and put down our band's name, Sweet Angels. I write down the name of our song and put our band as fitting the alternative metal genre.

After I hand them back to the man, I start making my way towards the stage. I pull out my phone from my pocket and call Jade to let her know where I am going to be when she gets back.

She answers on the second ring. "Hi, baby. I just got the instruments out of the trunk."

"Okay, sweetie. I got us signed up and the man told me to go behind the stage area with the instruments once you bring them. We have to wait there until they call us out to perform."

"Got it. I'll be there in a few minutes." Jade blows me a kiss before she hangs up the phone.

I make my way towards the crowded area and push my way through people as I try to get to the stage and go behind it where the other bands are waiting to perform.

When I finally manage to get to the backstage area, I walk around until I find a spot to sit in the grass until Jade gets here. I sit and listen to the music coming from the stage while I sit in the grass.

Deep guitar riffs, fast drumbeats, and a voice that's screaming the lyrics out, but also harmonizing the words with the music. They perform for a few minutes until the finishing *chords, signaling that the song is over. As it ends, the band that was performing gets off the stage and comes to the back.*

I stand up as they walk by where I'm sitting. "Hey, that was really sick and awesome, guys. I loved it. What's your band called?"

The singer comes over to me and shakes my hand. "Thanks. We're called Dusk Til Dawn and our song was Bleeding Your Hearts. We've been playing together for a few years, since we were still in high school. What's your name?"

As he asks this, Jade walks over with our instruments in her arms. I grab my keytar from her and tell him, "My name is Destiny, and this is Jade. We're Sweet Angels and we're going to perform our song, Shaking the Devil Down. We've been performing casually together since we first started college back in 2013. Mainly at small events or tattoo conventions."

The guitarist nods her head in satisfaction. "Awesome, babe. I'm sure y'all will kill it up there once they call you. Just be confident and play from your soul. Ignore the noise, and just focus on the music and your voices and you'll suck everybody into your sound."

"Got it. Thank you for the advice."

Each of them give Jade and I a pat of encouragement before they leave to join the crowd in front of the stage.

I sit back down in the grass with Jade while we wait for our band to be called to the stage.

She looks at me with confidence in her eyes. "Are you ready for this, baby? We haven't performed on stage since the summer before our third year in college."

I smile at her as I say, "We've got this. We may not have performed together on stage in a few years, but we have the rhythm that comes from us just being together. Once we're on that stage, everybody else will disappear and it will just be us out there with our sound. Our music. We're going to knock them dead as soon as we start to play and sing with our voices rising through the air."

Jade sets her guitar down on the ground and leans forward, giving me a deep kiss. "God, I love you so much. You are amazing. I don't think that I could actually do this if it weren't for you."

We sit, listening to the different bands performing for another thirty minutes before our name is finally called.

The announcer calls out through the microphone, "Here's Sweet Angels and their song, Shaking the Devil Down!"

Jade and I grab our instruments and make our way to the stage, walking around the curtain to the front. We make our way to where the microphones are at in center stage and start to play.

I begin with a slow rhythm on the keyboard on my keytar, playing the opening notes as Jade starts to sing into her microphone. As I play, I move the notes smoothly from low to high as the crowd starts to gear up with our sound.

Jade sings out, "Shake him good, shake him deep. Shake him til his soul quakes. Bring the demon down to his knees. Grab his horns. Take his hooves. Tie him up until he's yours!"

I sing the final chorus with Jade and strum my chords into an echo as we end our song a few minutes later, the crowd in front of us screaming in a loud encore.

The announcer hollers our band name one more time as we make our way off the stage to join the crowd of people surrounding the stage. Jade grabs my hand as we reach the stairs and walk into the audience.

As we're walking, I can feel myself trying to catch my breath before I can say anything to her.

After a few seconds, I'm finally able to breathe and speak. I turn towards Jade with a huge grin on my face as I say, "That was amazing, baby. We haven't performed like that in years. I don't even care if we won. I'm just glad that I got to have fun with you. Doing something that we love."

"I love you so damn much. Let's listen to the rest of the bands until everybody's done. Just sit out here in the park having fun with everyone around us."

For the next few hours, Jade and I sit with everyone listening to the different bands playing, jamming out to each of them. As the sky starts to turn to dusk, the last band finishes playing, and the judges hand their cards to the announcer on the stage.

He makes his way towards the center of the stage and looks at the winner's cards.

"Coming in third place is... Dusk Til Dawn! Congratulations, guys! Come up and claim your prize!"

They make their way through the crowd and go up onto the stage. He hands them a bronze trophy as he pats each of them on the backs in congratulations.

After they have grabbed their trophy and make their way towards the back of the stage, he announces second place. "In second place we have Comin' On Home!"

A group in flannel and cowboy boots makes their way to the stage and grabs their trophy from him.

"And finally, in first place we have... Sweet Angels for performing their kickass song, Shaking the Devil Down. Get on up here, girls."

Jade and I look at each other in awe as we make our way to the stage.

As we 're walking, I holler to Jade, "I can't believe we won first place! We freaking won!"

I climb the steps with her onto the stage and go over to the announcer so he can hand us our gold trophy. As we reach him, we both start thanking him, the judges, and everyone who watched us perform.

Jade speaks first into the microphone. "Thank you so much, everyone. We honestly didn't think that we would stand a chance of winning. So thank you all. This was an amazing experience that we will never forget."

I take the gold trophy from the announcer as the audience cheers for us before we get off the stage.

Jade and I start walking our way back across the street as the event winds down in the park.

Once we reach the next square over, Jade pulls me in the direction of a diner on 5th street. I follow her inside with the trophy in my hand.

I go over to a table with Jade and sit down across from her.

I grab ahold of Jade's hands across the table and ask her, "What else do you want to do for the rest of the evening, baby?"

"Well, we can go to the mall after we eat and browse around. Would you like that, baby?"

I smile at her as the waiter comes up. "Of course I would, babe."

The waiter stops once he reaches the table and asks us, "My name is Gregory. Do you lovely ladies know what you would like to drink?"

"Just two sweet teas with honey, please."

"Yes, ma'am. I will be back in a few minutes with your teas."

The waiter walks away after he gets our drink orders. Once he's gone, I reach across the table and grab Jade's hands.

She looks across at me with a glitter of affection in her eyes. "Baby, this has been an amazing day. You are the most amazing and beautiful fiancé ever. And I cannot wait for the day that we are able to stand under the wedding arches and get married. The day that we say our "I do's" to each other with all of our family and friends watching and celebrating with us."

I give my wonderful woman a big grin, my cheeks turning to a blush. "Jade, you are my one and only. You are the love of my life. I love you so freaking, much, baby and want us to be able to start our lives together as soon as possible. Because I don't think that I would be this far in life if it weren't for you."

I give a gentle kiss on Jade's hands as the waiter comes back over with our drinks.

As he reaches the table, I catch a glimpse of a smile coming across his lips. He sets the glasses of tea down in front of us before commenting, "You two make a lovely couple, if I do say so myself. How long have you been together, if you don't mind me asking?"

Jade answers him with a smile. "Thank you very much. We have been together for four years now, and engaged as of last night."

"Oh wow. Well congratulations. Now have you decided on what you would like to order for your meal?"

I pause for a moment and look down at the menu. Hmm... Everything looks so good. The grilled club sandwich... the cheeseburger... the bacon and cheese sandwich...

After a few seconds of glancing over the items on the menu, I tell Gregory, "I think that I would like the grilled club sandwich with a side of macaroni salad." I look towards Jade and ask her, "What about you, baby? What are you feeling?"

She closes her menu after I ask and says, "I would like the cheeseburger with bacon along with a side of fries with ranch dressing, please."

He nods his head after we finish giving him our orders and grabs the menus from us. "Alrighty. I will have those out for you guys shortly."

As soon as he's gone, Jade looks at me and says, "Baby, I want to start planning our wedding together as soon as possible, because I want us to have it as soon as we can."

"Okay, baby. What do you want to talk about first?"

"Well, we haven't even told either of our parents that we are engaged to each other yet. We have to do that first, but I was thinking... where would you like to have the wedding?"

I take a deep breath as I think for a few seconds. I know that I want it to be outdoors, but I also would love to have it held either in a park in town or in the forests just outside of town. Either one of those would be perfect and so romantic.

I open my mouth and say, "Baby, I just want the perfect outdoors location. I want it to be somewhere that it can look like our own little fairy land with you in a beautiful, magical, shimmering white gown. What do you think, baby?"

As I finish speaking, I can see Jade's eyes starting to well up with Joy. She jumps up from her chair and comes around to give me a hug.

Her arms wrap tight around my neck as she says, "That sounds wonderful. Beyond perfect. You are perfect. All that matters to me is that I get to see your gorgeous face in front of me under the wedding arches, no matter where they are.

"We'll both be up there at the end of the aisle, in front of all of our friends and family, in the most beautiful setting. Both of will be wearing the perfect wedding dress with a bouquet of artificial flowers in our hands, because I want them to last forever. And we will have all the girls as our bridesmaids."

I can feel a tear roll down my cheek as Jade speaks, so I grab my napkin to wipe it away. My face is beaming so brightly that I feel like a star.

I let out a shaky breath before I can speak. "Baby, you are amazing. We will have the perfect wedding, and we will both be the perfect brides. I was wondering, would you rather our wedding to be in the evening or the morning?"

Jade stands up next to me and gives me a kiss before she walks back across to her side of the table. She smiles the biggest grin ever at me. "I think it should be in the evening. That way your gorgeous face will be glowing under the string lights in the trees and the sunrise won't be washing out your beauty. I want your face to be the main focus on the day that we get married."

I take a sip of my tea before I tell her, "That sounds amazing, sweetie. I want to see your face glowing in the moonlight and stars. You will be the brightest star that exists that night and every night. I love you so much, baby."

"*I love you with every beat of my heart.*" *A tear falls from Jade's eye.*

We sit staring at each other for what feels like forever until Gregory comes back, carrying our plates of food. Before he gets to the table, Jade and I both wipe the tears from our eyes.

When he gets to the table, he sets each of our plates down. "Here you go, ladies. Do you need anything else?"

"No thank you. This looks delicious."

He smiles at us as he says, "You are very welcome. If you need anything else, just holler for me and I will be right here."

Jade chuckles before he walks away. Once he's left, Jade and I both start digging into our food. I take a big bite of my sandwich and she takes a big bite of her cheeseburger.

"Mmm!" Both her and I moan in delicious satisfaction.

After I swallow my first bite, I tell Jade, "This sandwich is making my mouth water, it's so delicious. The bacon is so crisp and just the right amount of greasy. And the cheese is sooo gooey and melty."

Her eyes are still closed as she says, "Same. This burger is so juicy and melty. I think this is the best burger I have ever had. How have we never been here before?"

"I don't know, but we might just have to have this place cater for the wedding because damn is their food good. And the tea is the best."

I spend the next thirty minutes eating and savoring my food with Jade before we're both finished with our plates.

We pay for our food after we're both done and head out.

Once we get outside, Jade asks me, "Do you still want to talk to some of the stores around downtown to see if they would want to help sell your new book on their shelves?"

"*I do, baby. In fact, I'm pretty sure that I can think of a few places that would be interested. First let's go to Carl's Books and Things. Because he's been bugging me about it since I got the first page written.*"

She nods her head and follows me down the street towards Carl's. I grab ahold of Jade's hand and start swinging our arms between us.

Everything around us seems so bright outside. The tree branches swaying in the wind, the sun shining through the clouds. Even the birds are chirping happy little songs from their nests. It almost feels as if everything and everyone around us can sense the joy radiating from us as we pass by.

Everything is going perfect and nothing can stop us.

Chapter Thirteen

Gregory's POV: As I sit with Jade, watching Supernatural with her, I can't help but smile each time she smiles. It makes me happy that she's not letting herself feel completely miserable over her best friend being in the hospital.

It's Monday night right now and I have to do everything I can to make sure that Jade stays happy. At least until the trial comes up on Wednesday. Because then she'll actually have to see the faces of the two men who put Destiny in the state that she's in.

As we're watching season three, Jade eventually falls asleep on the couch.

I grab the blanket from the back of it and drape it across her body before I grab both of our plates to take to the kitchen.

When I get Jade's plate from the couch next to her head, a small hum comes from her mouth. I pull the blanket over her shoulders to make sure that she's covered. I walk out of the living room and go to the kitchen with the plates in hand.

I put the plates in the sink and start the water to rinse them before I get the soap to start scrubbing all the grease from the quesadillas.

Hopefully Jade will manage to get plenty of rest tonight, because I know that she probably won't get any rest tomorrow before the trial. She'll be a ball of stress and anxiety, and there will be nothing that I can do to help. I'll just have to do my best to hold her together.

After I finish washing the plates and set them to dry, I go back to the living room to check on Jade before going to brush my teeth.

She's still laying under the blanket all cozy, but her forehead is creased.

I walk over to her, trying to be quiet, and carefully give her a kiss on the forehead to try and make the worry disappear from her sleeping mind.

I look at Jade one more time before turning out the light and going to brush my teeth.

While I'm brushing them, I can't help but worry about whatever is going through her thoughts while she's sleeping. What she's dreaming about. Because whatever it is, it's upsetting her and worrying her even while she's sleeping. And that's not good.

After a few minutes, I finish brushing my teeth and washing my face. I go to my bedroom and climb under the covers to lay down even though I'm probably not going to get much sleep worrying about Jade.

****

Jade's POV: "Aaahhh!!!"

I jolt up from my sleep in a dead panic. I can feel myself shaking from sweat after waking up from a nightmare.

Barely a few seconds after I wake up, Greg bursts into the living room.

"Are you okay!? What happened!?" He has a panicked expression on his face when I look up at him.

I take a few seconds to try and calm my heart and breathing back down before I answer him. "I don't know. I was having a nightmare about Destiny. Right before I woke up I was at home with her having fun, and then out of nowhere this big, black truck runs through the house right over her. After the truck was gone, Destiny was just lying flat on the ground like a pancake and I could hear a heart monitor flatlining."

Gregory rushes over and wraps his arms tight around me. As he's rubbing his hand up and down my back in comfort, he says, "It's okay. Destiny's okay. It was just a bad dream. I'm going to sit out here with you until you tell me to leave you be. Okay?"

"Mm-hmm." I shake my head yes as I pull in closer to Gregory's chest.

I can feel myself shaking from how real that nightmare felt. I can still see Destiny lying on the tile, her blood smeared across the floor after being ran over by the truck. And the beeping... the beeping is still ringing loud as hell in my ears.

All I can think about is how she must have felt when she got into the accident.

As I keep going over and over the images in my head, my thoughts get broken by Gregory's voice saying something to me.

He pulls me up from his chest and looks me in the eyes as he says, "Hey... hey, everything is okay. Can you tell me what's going through your head right now? Tell me what you are thinking about."

I sit up after a few seconds once I am able to stop my body from shaking so much. I take a deep, shuddering breath as I try to speak.

I open my mouth and tell Greg, "All I can think about is what I saw in my dream and how Destiny must have felt... after the accident. How she must have felt so alone. I can't stop panicking and worrying that she's never going to wake up. That she'll either stay in this coma forever or that she's going to die, and her heart is going to stop. Or that she'll wake up and be braindead."

I feel myself starting to panic again as I start to stutter. "I-I-I... I just want her to be okay." My voice breaks as I start to sob, falling back into Greg's chest.

I can feel his arms tighten around me, trying to get me to stop shaking.

His mouth moves against my head as he starts to speak. "Jade, listen to me. Destiny will be okay. I know that she will. Because she's strong. Just like you are. She has been fighting since the moment it happened, and I know that she's not going to give in so easily. She's going to keep fighting until the day she wakes up and is able to go home with perfect health. You got that?"

I sit up and try to breathe in through my nose, sniffling. "I believe you. I do. My brain just won't stop going to worst case scenarios. It can't stop picturing her getting hit by that truck and dying in front of me in my nightmare. I'm terrified that I am actually dreaming and that she really did die on that highway."

"No. You are not dreaming still, and she is not actually dead. You are just worried, and that's understandable. But can you please trust me?"

I wipe snot from my face as I say, "Uh huh. I can try. Could you get me a few tissues, please?" I take in a deep, snorting breath as I try not to get any snot on Gregory or his couch.

He stands up and grabs a box that is sitting on the kitchen counter behind the couch. When he gets back to me, he pulls out a few tissues and hands them to me. I thank him then blow my nose and clean my face off.

After I blow my nose a few times and wipe it off, I thank Greg for being such a good friend to me. "Thank you so much, Greg. Thank you for being a friend and being here for me through all of this. Thank you for trying to make sure that I don't break. I really appreciate it. A lot."

"Don't worry about it. You don't have to thank me. I just want to make sure that you're okay... that you'll be okay. You're my friend and I want to make sure that you don't make yourself suffer worrying about Destiny."

"I'm trying to be okay, but I don't think that I will be unless I can see her or until she can wake up and be okay. Until she can come home. I just can't."

He nods his head. "Okay. Well I'm going to stay by your side until Destiny can wake up and be okay. Because I want to make sure that you are going to be okay. That you're not going to go into a deep depression."

"Okay. Thank you." I hug Gregory tightly once more before I let go. "I think that I'm going to try to go back to sleep and get some rest for the night. Are you going to go back to your bedroom? Or are you going to stay in here and make sure I'm okay?"

Gregory looks at me with sincerity in his eyes as he says, "I'll stay out here if you're okay with that. Because if you wake up from another nightmare, I want to be right here."

I look at him with a pleading expression in my eyes. "Can you please stay out here all night? Because I don't know if I will be able to fall asleep again after that nightmare."

"I'll stay out here with you all night. But please, try to get some rest. Because I want you to get *some* before Wednesday. I know you won't be able to get any sleep tomorrow night because you'll be stressing about the upcoming trial. So please... try to get some sleep tonight. I'll be right here in the chair."

I nod my head shakily, pulling the blanket up towards my chest.

I close my eyes as I try to fall back asleep. My thoughts start to slow down after a few minutes and my breath slows and becomes shallow before my mind shuts down and falls asleep for the night.

****

The next morning, I wake up to the smell of fresh bacon and coffee. I get up and go into the kitchen to see Gregory standing in front of the stove as he puts a few pieces of bacon onto a plate.

"Good morning, Greg. Thank you for staying in the living room with me all night."

He hands me a cup of coffee and a plate of bacon and eggs. "You're welcome, Jade. Here. I figured you should eat something."

I smile as I take a sip of the warm coffee, cupping the mug between my hands. As soon as the warm, sweet liquid hits my lips and goes down my throat, I feel my body starting to warm up. A shiver runs up my spine when the warmth from the coffee hits the pit of my stomach.

After I take a few more sips of my coffee, I start eating the eggs and bacon while Gregory sits across from me drinking his coffee. I take a bite of the eggs first, closing my eyes and savoring the fluffy texture of them while I chew.

"Thank you for the coffee and the food. This is the first real sustenance I have had over the last few weeks other than the quesadillas you made me last night. I really appreciate you taking care of me as much as you have."

Greg sets his coffee mug down on the table next to his chair before he speaks. "You don't need to thank me. You have been my friend since the day that I saw you crying outside of the hospital. I want to do what I can to help make sure that you're okay."

I feel myself smile slightly. *I don't think that I would be surviving and making it as well if I never would have met Greg. He's been my rock and support through all of this.*

"Do you want to go see Destiny in a bit after you've finished your coffee and breakfast? I don't have to go into patrol today or tomorrow, so I'll be with you."

I swallow the last couple of bites of scrambled eggs then answer. "Of course I do. I'll probably finish my bacon and take the coffee in a to-go cup if you have any. Because I want to go make sure that she's still okay."

I catch a glimpse of a half-smile on his face as he stands up to take his cup to the kitchen, but by the time I'm looking directly at him it's gone.

He comes back into the living room after a few seconds, carrying a little metal tumbler in his hand. He grabs my coffee off the table while I continue eating my bacon and pours what's left into the tumbler.

"There you go. That way as soon as you're done, you can slide your shoes on and we can go to the hospital."

I nod my head, my eyes half-closed as I put the last bite of bacon into my mouth. Once I get it swallowed, I grab my shoes that are next to the couch and slide them onto my feet.

"I'm ready to go now," I tell Greg as I stand up.

He tells me okay and grabs his keys and wallet from the countertop then I follow him to the door.

We make our way down to the parking lot together in a calm quiet. The entire way I can't help but think about the trial that's coming up tomorrow at ten. About seeing the faces of the men behind the truck. I can only picture them looking like dirty ass truckers with greasy beards and beer guts, but I know that that's not going to actually be how they look.

I walk with Greg all the way down to his car before he decides to break the silence.

"Hey... everything's okay. The trial will go great tomorrow and I know that they will rule in Destiny's favor. And I'm sure that she's still doing okay. Her mind is just keeping her at rest so that her injuries can heal without hurting her. Try not to worry too much."

I feel tears welling up in my eyes as I climb into the car. Before I open my mouth to say anything, I use my hands to wipe the tears away.

"I know she's okay... My heart just can't stop hurting and worrying about the worst-case scenario. The what ifs. I know that I should try to stop... I should stop. I just can't help it."

Gregory reaches over and grabs my hand before he puts the car into drive. He looks at me with a serious expression on his face.

"I wouldn't be saying this if I didn't believe it. Destiny will be okay. She is okay. I just have a feeling that she'll pull through this. Trust me, okay? Can you do that?"

After he stops speaking, he puts the car into drive and pulls out of the parking spot and onto the road.

My heart feels happy knowing that I have a friend like Gregory. Someone who's able to be there for me as support while the woman that I love is trapped in a coma at the hospital. I never thought when I was leaving the hospital that day that I would have someone next to me that would be willing to hell me as much as Gregory.

Especially considering both mine and Destiny's parents live in Scotland where they moved to retire a few years ago. They moved there after we both graduated from college and moved in together. Her parents haven't even been told about what's going on because I don't want them worrying and flying back here when I don't even know when or if Destiny will wake up.

My mind zones back into reality when I see that we have reached the hospital.

As soon as Greg gets the car into a parking space, I open my door and jump out, running inside as fast as I can. I run over to the elevator and press the button for the third floor as fast as I can.

The doors open after what feels like forever. By the time the elevator shows up, Gregory is standing next to me. I feel his hand place on my shoulder to try and calm my vibrating body when I try to run into the elevator.

He makes me walk at a normal pace onto the elevator, and when the doors close, he tells me, "Jade, I know that you want to get up there as fast as you can, but if you fall and get hurt, you'll end up having to stay here, too. And you won't be able to go to the trial tomorrow or come visit her as often."

"I know. I just want to see her beautiful face and make sure that she's okay and not worse."

After a few moments, the elevator stops at the third floor, and I get off as soon as the doors open. I rush down the hallway to Room 321.

I get there in less than ten steps and run in through the open door to see a nurse standing over Destiny, inserting a needle into her IV.

"What are you doing? What are you giving her?"

The nurse looks up after a few seconds. "I was just giving her some morphine to help ease the pain from her broken leg and her brain injury."

I hurry over to the bedside and grab ahold of Destiny's hand as I ask the nurse, "Has there been any change in her state? Has Destiny made any noises or said anything?"

"Well, a little while ago she was saying something that sounded like the word Jade, almost as if she was trying to call out to somebody, but that was all she said. Are you Jade?"

"I am. I'm her girlfriend. Did it sound like she was dreaming of something good? Or something bad?"

She looks at me after throwing the needle away. "It sounded like she was dreaming about something sweet. I'm sure that her mind is okay while she's in the coma. She just needs a way for her mind to cope and distract her from the pain that she's dealing with right now. The doctor is going to be in here in a few minutes to talk to you about some things, okay?"

I turn to Gregory with a look of panic on my face as I start to shake again. He quickly pulls one of the plastic chairs forward and places me down onto it.

The nurse grabs ahold of my hand to reassure me once I'm sitting in the chair. "Everything's okay, sweetie. He just needs to talk to you about something, but it's nothing bad. I promise."

I can feel my chest heaving as I start trying to steady my breathing. After a few deep breaths, I look at her and ask, "Are you sure everything's okay?"

"Yes, sweetie. Dr. Drew will be in to explain everything in just a moment."

I nod my head to her before she walks out of the room. I take a few more deep breaths before I try to say anything to Greg.

"What do you think he's going to come talk to me about, Greg?"

"I don't know, but I'm sure that it's nothing bad."

After a few seconds, the door opens, and Dr. Drew comes inside with a clipboard in his hands and a slight concerned look on his face.

He closes the door behind him before he starts to speak.

"Hi, Jade. Are you feeling any better than you were yesterday?"

I swallow deeply then say, "Yes, sir. I am. Greg made sure that I got some sleep and ate last night as well as this morning. What's going on?"

He looks down at the chart and tells me, "Last night, Destiny had a small seizure in her sleep. She's okay, though. It actually shifted some of the nerve activity in her brain and caused it to calm down some afterwards. She's okay right now, but I'll have to keep a careful eye on her to make sure that she doesn't have another seizure and possibly cause a brain bleed. Because if it happens again, that is possible."

My chest starts rising and falling again as I start to hyperventilate. Words are trying to come out of my mouth, but air can barely get down my windpipe.

Gregory gets down on his knees and looks directly into my eyes. "Hey. She's okay. He said that she's okay. We've just got to make sure that it doesn't happen again and possibly hurt her. But she's okay right now. Just try to calm down and try to breath. Okay?"

I take a big gulp as my breath starts to even out some. I hug Gregory around his neck and shoulders before I start sobbing.

I can feel the panic rising in me as I start worrying that she's going to start getting worse now. That Destiny's going to start going downhill instead of up. Everything just feels like it's getting worse and worse every day and it won't stop.

Before I know it, my eyes start to go dark, and I collapse on top of Gregory.

****

The next thing I remember, I wake up in a bed. I look around myself after blinking my eyes for a few seconds to try and get my vision to stop being fuzzy.

I see Gregory sitting in the chair across from where I'm lying.

As soon as he sees my eyes open, he jumps up and runs over to me. "Are you okay, Jade? How are you feeling?"

I take a few shaky breaths as I tell him, "I'm feeling all right. What happened?"

"Well a few hours ago, you found out from the doctor that Destiny had a seizure and if she has another one that it could make her worse. You started to panic and passed out from hyperventilating."

"I remember now. Am I going to be discharged before the trial tomorrow?"

Greg gives me a serious look. "I don't know, but I doubt it. Because they want to keep an eye on your vitals and make sure that you don't have another panic attack and pass out again. But don't worry. I called the judge and let her know what's going on and that you need to postpone the trial for at least a week until you're better."

My head falls in distraught. "Dammit... Okay. Can you check on her every few hours for me to make sure that she's still okay until I'm not in this bed anymore and can stay with her again?"

"Of course I can. I will. I'll do it for you and for her. Do you need anything or want anything?"

"I'm okay for now, I guess. I just wish that everything wasn't becoming more complicated every second. I just want her to be okay and be able to come home."

Greg comes over and gives me a huge hug. "I know you do. Everything will get easier. It'll just take some time and patience. But everything will turn out just fine. I promise. It may not end up how you're expecting, but it will all be okay."

I hug him tight. "Thank you so much, Greg. So much. You have no idea how much you have saved me from myself. Because before I met you and before Destiny ended up in the hospital from that accident, she was the only person I had. As a friend or otherwise. Because my parents don't live here. They live in Scotland and I haven't seen them since last summer. After Destiny got in that accident, I had no one. Absolutely no one. And it scared me. It terrified me. So thank you for being here to support me and comfort me through all of this."

Chapter Fourteen

Destiny's POV: Jade and I reach Carl's shop on Shade Street after a few minutes. We walk inside, holding each other's hands. I open the door, a bell ringing overhead as we walk inside together.

As soon as we're inside, we get greeted by Carl. "Hi, girls. How are you two doing today?"

Jade gives him a smile as she says, "We are doing wonderful today. We're slowly starting to plan a wedding that we're going to be having in a couple of years."

His eyes light up in surprise as he asks, "Who's wedding is it? Are y'all getting married?"

I hold up my left hand and show him the ring on my finger. "Yes, sir. She asked me last night at dinner with her and the girls after I announced my new book to everybody." I place my right arm around Jade's shoulder before I continue. "I am now engaged to this beautiful woman and have my sixth book out for publication."

Carl smiles at us. "Congratulations, you two. And congratulations on your book, Destiny."

After he gives us both a hug, Jade looks at me before she tells him, "Thank you, Carl. And actually, the book was the reason we came here. We were wondering if you would be interested in helping sell her book on your shelves."

"Of course I would. I would do anything for two of my favorite girls in town. Just let me know who to contact about ordering it to sell, and I'll push your book to anybody who walks through that door."

I let out a laugh as I walk over to a display of jewelry. Jade and Carl continue talking about my book as I go over to the display.

I start looking through the necklaces and bracelets and rings while Jade and Carl talk. There are so many beautiful pieces to choose from. Some of the necklaces have charms and some have stones inside intricate designs. There are charm bracelets and gorgeous rings.

As I am looking through the different pieces of jewelry on the display, a package falls off one of the hooks.

I pick it up and start looking at what's inside it. As I'm looking through the package, I see a rose gold necklace with an amethyst-colored stone inside a heart-shaped pendant. There is also a matching ring with a similar heart that has little swirls surrounding it. They're both beautiful.

While I continue examining the jewelry inside the bag, I hear Carl's voice behind me.

"Do you like those pieces, sweetheart? I got them from a friend who makes their own jewelry. Those are probably my favorite pieces from her. Would you like me to take them out so you can look at them."

"Yes, please," I say to him with a smile on my face.

I walk back over to where he and Jade have been standing and hand him the little bag.

Carl takes it from me and carefully opens it, pulling out both the necklace and ring. He hands them over to me, and I start really looking at each of them.

The violet stones on both the necklace and the ring start to sparkle in the light coming from overhead. They are almost glimmering, and they look beyond magical. They are so gorgeous, and I would love to see them on Jade.

I turn to Carl and ask him, "Can I put these on Jade to see how they would look on her?"

I can see a half-smile cross onto Jade's face as he says yes. I grip the clasp of the necklace between my fingers and open it before reaching around her neck to put it on her. I get it around the back of her beck and re-clasp it before letting it fall to her chest.

Next I take the ring between my fingers and grab ahold of Jade's left hand, sliding it over her ring finger. It fits her almost perfectly.

Once both pieces are on her, Jade smiles and begins to look at them for a few moments. She then looks up at me and wraps her arms around my neck in a tight hug.

"I love them so much, baby. They are gorgeous."

Jade looks so beautiful wearing the necklace and ring. And that smile... that smile on her face just lights up the entire room. I turn towards Carl and get ready to ask him how much they both cost, and as I do, he gives me this look.

"Together they are $75.99. But if you want, you girls can buy them for a discounted price of $50."

I look at Carl and tell him, "No, Carl. We'll pay the full price. I'll pay the full price. You work hard here, and you shouldn't have to lose money on us just because we're friends."

I pull my wallet out and hand him my debit card as I say, "Charge it for the regular price, not a discounted price. Please. We already got a discount earlier when she bought me a bracelet. I don't mind."

He shakes his head as he runs my card through the machine. After a few seconds, it beeps, and he hands me back the card.

"Do you want the receipt, ladies? Just in case you decide you're not satisfied with your purchase?" Carl lets out a deep chuckle.

Jade and I both laugh as she tells him, "No, we don't need it. We're very happy with this purchase. I am going to be wearing both pieces of jewelry every day until the day I die. So thank you, Carl."

He smiles at both of us. "What are you all going to do for the rest of the afternoon?"

I think for a second before answering. "We're probably going to go hang out with the rest of the girls at one of their houses for the rest of the day. Do some wedding planning."

"Good. That ought to be fun for you all."

Before Jade and I turn to head out the door, we each give Carl a hug in thanks and appreciation."

We walk outside and start making our way down the street together. I reach out and grab her hand in mine as we walk along the sidewalk, swinging our arms along between the two of us. A smile appears on my face, thinking about how incredibly happy I am with Jade right now.

"Hey, baby?"

I turn my attention towards Jade when she calls out to me. "Yes, baby? What is it?"

"Do you want to go down to one of the river or lake parks and see how one of them would look for a wedding venue? Because I want to try and start scoping out places to figure out where we are going to have the ceremony."

I give her a big, cheesy grin as I say, "Yes. Of course I do, Jade. We can go to each of them and decide which one would look best with decorations, seating arrangements, and a reception area for afterwards. Because I want it all to be perfect, baby. For you, and for myself. I love you so much, babygirl."

I pull Jade close and give her a kiss on her warm lips.

She starts kissing me back, her lips moving against mine with sweet passion. They feel so warm and soft on my lips. And as we kiss, I can slightly taste her strawberry flavored chapstick. So sweet and so delicious.

I slide my hands along her back as I kiss her a few more times before I end the kisses and pull away slowly.

"Let's go, babe. Let's go to James Park first and walk around a bit, see if that park could be a possibility." I hold her hand in mine as we start walking our way back towards where we parked the car a few blocks back.

Once we get to the car, I go around to Jade's side and open the door for her before I get in the driver's seat. I give her another small kiss after she's seated, then walk around to the other side and climb in the car.

I buckle my seatbelt and put the key into the ignition, turning the radio up after the car cranks on.

Before putting the car into drive, I ask Jade, "Are you ready for this, baby? We're officially about to start planning the details of our wedding."

"I am. I have been ready for this for a while now. You just didn't know it yet." A little happy laugh escapes her mouth after she says that.

"I love you so freaking much, Jade. You are the most amazing woman that I could have ever met and fallen in love

with. I am so happy that we're going to get married and spend the rest of our lives together."

I start driving the car as we listen to the music playing from the radio, singing along together in harmony. And hearing her beautiful voice makes me beyond happy because it shows me just how truly happy she is right now, in this moment.

We ride through town for about ten minutes before reaching James Park. When we get there, I pull the car into a parking spot near the entrance.

Jade and I get out of the car together and start walking towards the river, towards the center area of the park.

As we get closer to the river, I start to hear people in the distance. Children playing, dogs barking, and people talking. It all sounds so peaceful and happy.

When we reach the center of the park, Jade and I walk together towards the area in front of the river where everybody is. I glance at her when we stop and wrap my right arm around her waist, holding her close to my side.

"What would you think about getting married right here, baby? Us under a beautiful arch in front of the riverside with all of our friends and family out there, where all the people are at. Would you want that? Or would you want somewhere else?"

Jade scans the area in front of us before telling me, "Honestly I would be perfectly happy getting married to you in a gutter on the street if it meant I got to see your beautiful face in front of me." She pauses for a second before continuing. "I would love to get married here, but is it okay if we still go look at a few other parks just to make sure first, baby?"

I let out a little giggle. "Of course it is. I want it to be perfect for both you and me. I told you this. So let's go keep looking until we find the perfect park. Okay?"

We make our way back over to the car and get back in so we can drive to Madison Park.

When we start driving down the road, Can't Stop Me Now by Queen comes on the radio and we both immediately start screaming along with the lyrics, trying to sing as off-key as possible. We sing loudly the entire ride until we reach the park a few minutes later.

As soon as we get there, I park the car under the trees surrounding the parking lot.

Before we even start walking towards the park area, I can feel the happiness radiating off of Jade. I can feel how happy this is making her. And I love seeing her so happy.

We make our way to the center of the park as we both start looking around to see what areas would be best for the different sections of the wedding.

Jade stops me for a second and turns toward the trees in front of us. "Do you think those trees would look wonderful with tulle and ribbons hanging from them? That could be the altar area."

I smile at her and say, "Yes, and the aisle can lead from over there," I point at the middle of the grass coming from the other side of the trees. "We could have the seats in rows on both sides. And over there near the other side where the trees begin can be the reception area for tables, with the open area being for dancing and chatting with everyone."

"That sounds beautiful, sweetie. I love it. Let's get married here, at this park. It has that feeling. Just like I had when we first started dating."

I squeal in delight as I wrap Jade in a tight hug, slightly picking her up from the ground. "I love you so freaking much, babygirl. I can picture it now, and it looks absolutely amazing. You're amazing and I love you so, so much."

Gregory's POV: "Everything will be okay, Jade. I know it." I smile at her after pulling away from the hug.

She looks at me with an expression of fear in her eyes. "But how do you know? Destiny's in there all by herself while I'm down here stressing and worrying about her. I don't want her to be by herself. Because I know how much it sucks."

I reach out and grab Jade's hand in mine as I tell her, "She won't be by herself. I will go visit her every chance I get until you are okay to be released from the hospital. You need to worry about yourself first and foremost. Because otherwise you're going to end up killing yourself with worry. Do you want to try to get some more rest? I can go sit with her while you do."

"I guess. But I'm still worried like hell. I don't think I'll be able to get any rest even if I tried. "

I give Jade a serious look as I say, "At least try. For me?"

She nods her head and says okay before closing her eyes and laying her head back on the pillows behind her.

I make sure that Jade's eyes are closed before I stand up and leave the room.

God, I'm so worried about her. She's gotten better since the first day I met her, but at the same time she keeps sinking back into a depression each day that Destiny doesn't wake up. I just don't want her making herself miserable thinking that everything that's happening is her fault.

I walk down the hallway to the elevator. Once the doors open, I go inside and press the button for the third floor.

It takes a few seconds before the elevator reaches the third floor coming down from the sixth floor. Once the elevator stops and opens back up, I make my way down the hall to Room 321.

As soon as I reach Destiny's room, I see Dr. Drew coming out the door.

"Hi, Dr. Drew. What's going on? Is everything okay?"

He stops when he sees me and says, "I was just checking on her. Her heart monitor started beating rapidly and I came to make sure that she wasn't having another seizure."

My eyes widen in worry. "She wasn't, was she?"

"She wasn't. Her heartrate has calmed down, but I don't know what caused it to spike. So I have connected a monitor to myself to let me know if it rises again just in case she has another seizure. Because if she does, I need to be here immediately to make sure her heart doesn't stop."

I let out a sigh of relief. "Thank God. I don't know what I would do if I had to tell Jade that something happened with Destiny."

"I understand that. I can see how much Jade loves her."

"Yes, sir. I'm here for now to be with her while Jade tries to get some rest. And I may try talking to her and see if that could help Destiny in any way. Try to help bring her to consciousness."

Dr. Drew nods his head in understanding. "Okay. If you need anything or something happens, you can press the call button on the control next to her bed and either myself or a nurse will come to help."

I go into the room after he leaves and sit down in the chair next to Destiny's bed.

I look at her lying there, and she looks so helpless. I can't help but think about what she could possibly be dreaming about while she's in this comatose state. I don't know if she's reliving the accident over and over again. If she's having some other nightmare, or if she's having good dreams to keep her mind at peace while she's healing from her injuries.

As I'm looking at her small frame lying in the bed, I start trying to think of something to say to her that could possibly help her to wake up.

After a few minutes, I open my mouth and start to speak. "Destiny, I know you're still in there. I don't know why you're still in your mind instead of out here, awake, but you need to wake up. Because Jade... your best friend, your girlfriend... she needs you here. She's going deeper and deeper into depression every day that you don't wake up. It's killing me seeing her like that."

I sit with Destiny as I watch for any sort of movement from her, but nothing. I figured that would be the case, but I can be hopeful. I am hopeful that she'll wake up, and soon.

But for now, I'll just be here to watch and make sure that she's okay... and make sure that Jade will be okay.

I sit and try to come up with some way, any way that I could help Destiny to wake up, but I can't think of anything off the top of my head.

"I want you to wake up so that Jade will be okay. So that she won't be miserable worrying that you won't ever wake up. Please."

A tear rolls down my cheek as I say, "I love her. Even if she doesn't love me the same way. She needs you awake and okay. I'm worried about her going into a deep depression because you're not here with her."

I pause for a few seconds before I place my hand on the bed next to Destiny and tell her, "Jade is breaking more and more every day that you are in this state. Especially considering we just had to postpone the trial against the drivers who hit you because she's having to be monitored after a panic attack.

"Please hear my words and wake up soon. I don't want you or her suffering any longer."

I let my head fall towards the floor after I finish speaking to Destiny. *God, I hope that she will be able to wake up soon. Because I can't stand seeing Jade suffering so much, worrying about Destiny.*

I stand up after a few more minutes of just watching her lay motionless in the hospital bed and walk towards the door. As I leave the room, I think to myself, *Please... Wake up.*

I make my way down the hallway and go to the elevator. Once I'm inside it and the doors are closed, I press the button for the first floor so that I can go down to the cafeteria and get some fresh coffee and something to eat.

After a few seconds, the door opens to let me off and I start making my way down to where the cafeteria is.

I walk through the hallways, looking down at the floor until I get to the cafeteria because I do not feel like talking to anyone or making small talk. I just want to get there and get a cup of coffee and a snack. Be able to sit in silence while I think about everything that is going on with Destiny and Jade.

When I get there, there's maybe a dozen people hanging out and getting something to eat. I walk over to where the coffee bar is and grab a paper cup before I get in the small line behind a few other people

A few minutes go by before I'm at the front of the line and am able to get my coffee.

I pick up the coffee pot and fill up a paper cup, then add a bit of creamer and sugar from the bottles on the table. Once I have the cream and sugar in the cup, I get a little plastic mixing straw and mix it in the cup.

I take a sip of my "fresh" coffee before I make my way over to the cafeteria lines and grab a tray. As I swallow some of the coffee, the warm liquid hits my stomach, warming me up from the dread that's been sitting in my gut since I first started worrying about Jade.

It takes a few minutes before I am able to reach where I can start grabbing my food. When I am able to reach the food, I go ahead and grab a plain peanut butter and jelly sandwich and a bag of chips. I put them on my tray along with my cup of coffee and a napkin taking my food over to a table so that I can sit down and try to relax my thoughts about everything.

I sit down and unwrap my sandwich so that I can start eating. As soon as the white bread and peanut butter and jelly hit my tastebuds, I can feel them getting happy from eating something sweet and savory.

I close my eyes as I swallow the first bite of my sandwich and take another couple of bites. As I eat each bit of the sandwich, I can feel my stomach starting to fill up with something other than worry for Jade, and it feels really good.

Once I'm about halfway done with my sandwich, I pick up the coffee cup and start to chug some of it down my throat.

The coffee is very refreshing and warming my entire body as I drink it down. I set the cup back down onto the table after I drink about half of it, then start to eat some of my potato chips that I grabbed.

They are so salty and crunchy, but they definitely taste really good with the coffee and sandwich.

I finish eating all my food and drinking all my coffee after a few more minutes. Once I'm done with everything, I take my tray back over to the counter and throw the trash away.

As I'm on my way back over to the table to sit down for a few minutes before heading back up to Jade's room, my phone starts ringing in my pocket.

I pull it out and look to see who's calling, and it's Lieutenant Sanchez.

"Hello, Lieutenant. What's going on?"

"It's the judge. He just called about the Morgan trial. He told me that we will have to have the trial within the next week because otherwise we'll have to release Mike and Bruce. He doesn't want them trying to press charges against the city for holding them without reasoning. Even if we do know that they hit Miss Morgan's car."

I let out a groan of frustration. "Dammit! Okay. Well, I'll go let her friend know after she wakes up and have her speak to her doctor about letting her leave for the trial for a day. Because I don't know when she'll be able to be discharged after she had that panic attack."

"Okay, Sergeant Miller. Call me as soon as you are done talking to them."

"Yes, sir. Will do."

I hang up my phone and slam it down on the table in frustration. "Goddammit!" I was hoping to let Jade be able to try and relax for at least a week before she would have to stress and worry about the trial. But nope.

I pick my phone back up and check to see if I cracked the screen or not before getting up to go to Jade's room. It's got a small crack across the screen, but oh well. I am not worried about it right now. I can fix it later.

I rush back to the elevator and make my way back up to Jade's room on the sixth floor. After a few minutes, I get to the room and go inside to check on her.

When I walk inside, she's sitting up with a blank expression on her face.

As I get closer, she breaks from her trance and looks at my, her eyes glossy as if she's been crying.

"Are you okay, Jade? Were you crying?"

I can hear her sniffle before she says anything, wiping her face with her hand.

"I was asleep for a little bit but woke up because I was having that nightmare again, dreaming that the truck ran through the hospital this time. And all I could do was stand there and do nothing but watch."

I come closer and place my hand on her shoulder. "I'm so sorry, Jade. I wish that I could make those nightmares go away."

She smiles weakly at me before asking, "How was she doing when you went down to check on her?"

"She was doing okay. She's still out, though. I stayed with her for a little while and talked to her. I told her how you're doing while she's here, and told her how you need her to be okay."

"Thank you so much, Greg."

I smile as I tell her, "Then I went back down to the cafeteria and grabbed something to eat. Right before I was about to come back up here, I got a call from the lieutenant. He told me that the judge for Destiny's trial called him and said that we need to hold it before the next week is up because otherwise we'll have to release the truck drivers."

As soon as I say that, Jade's face falls in despair as tears start to fill her eyes. "Dammit! Do you think that I can be released from the hospital to go to the trial? Because I can't not be there. I can't not defend my best friend's life. I have to be there to help defend her case."

"That's the thing... I'm going to have to talk to your doctor to find out if you can be released, even for just a day, so that you can attend the trial."

I grab her a towel from the counter next to the wall so that she can blow her nose when I see her sniffle again. Then I sit down it the chair next to her bed while she sits in silence.

I can tell that she's thinking about what would happen if she can't go to the trial or if the trial ends up having to be pushed back more and they end up releasing Mike and Bruce from the jail. She just looks so small and so worried about everything going on. It's killing me inside because I hate seeing her like this.

A few minutes of silence go by when the door opens and Dr. Williams walks in.

"Hello, Jade. How are you feeling now?"

She looks at him, her eyes and face red from crying so much. "I'm okay. I'm just worried about my friend. I just found out that the trial for her case is going to have to be held this week. Is there any way that I could leave the day that it's held so that I can attend it?"

He walks over with Jade's chart in his hand as he says, "Hmm... maybe. So long as you're in a stable enough mental state to be able to go to the trial. Do you think you will be?"

"I know I will, because the trial is to help my best friend. To help get her justice from being put here after being ran down by a truck."

"Okay. Do you know when the trial will be held?"

Jade turns to me, her eyes pleading.

I open my mouth and tell him, "We don't yet, but it will have to be either tomorrow or Friday. Because otherwise the plaintiffs will have to be released and we won't know when we'll be able to hold the trial if that happens."

Dr. Williams lets out a sigh as he says, "Okay. Well let me know as soon as you find out so that I can get Jade discharged and out in time."

I nod my head. "Okay. I've got to call my lieutenant so that I can let him know."

He leaves after I tell him that, and I grab my phone out of my pocket so I can call Lieutenant Sanchez.

I turn to Jade as I start to dial. "I'm about to call Lieutenant Sanchez right quick. If you want, I can put the call on speaker so that you can hear what he says."

Jade nods her head as the phone starts ringing.

After a few seconds, he picks up with a "Hello. What did Morgan's friend's doctor say? Will she be able to be released for the trial?"

"Yes, sir. He just needs to know what time it will be tomorrow or Friday so that she can be released on time."

"I spoke to the judge and he said that it would have to be held tomorrow at eleven in the morning. Do you think that that will give him enough time to release her so she can come to the trial?"

I look at her and she frantically shakes her head yes before I answer him.

"Yes, sir. It will be. If not, I can try to kidnap Jade from the hospital so that she can attend the trial."

I hang up the phone after telling him this and tell Jade, "Can you press the call button to get your doctor back in here so that I can tell him what I was told?"

She grabs the little remote control and presses the call button. After a few moments, a nurse comes in.

"What's going on? Is everything okay?"

Jade looks at her and asks, "Do you think that you could get Dr. Williams back in here? I need to talk to him about something urgent."

The nurse looks at Jade and tells her that she can. She walks out of the room so that she can go find the doctor and bring him back in here.

I sit with Jade while we wait for a few minutes. After a few seconds of silence, I look at her and tell her, "Everything will be okay. I promise. We'll get you to that trial and we'll make sure that we do everything we can to get Destiny her justice for what those guys did To her."

She nods her head as the door opens back up, Dr. Williams walking back inside.

As soon as he gets in the room, he closes the door and asks, "So what did you find out? Were you able to find out when the trial will be?"

I tell him, "Yes, sir. It will be tomorrow at eleven in the morning. Do you think there's any way that you can get Jade released before then so that she can attend it?"

"I probably can. I'll have to get her discharge papers, but I should be able to. That way she can go home and get ready for it beforehand. I can go put it in that she's being released tonight and should be able to get that done before visiting hours are over for the night."

A small smile crosses Jade's face as she thanks him. "I really appreciate this. A lot. So thank you, Dr. Williams."

He shakes his head. "No need to thank me. You need to go to this trial, and honestly it will probably help you get some resolve once you are able to find out what the judgement will be. I'll put your discharge in and be back soon so that you can sign them and go home."

He leaves the room and closes the door behind him.

As soon as he's gone, I ask Jade, "Are you sure that you'll be okay going to the trial and seeing those guys face to face for the first time?"

Jade turns to face me with a serious look on her face as she says, "I'm sure. It will probably hurt me at first seeing their faces even though I have never even met them, but I have to go. For Destiny. Because I want to make sure that the trial goes the way it should and that she'll be given her justice before she leaves the hospital."

"Okay. What do you want me to do before you leave the hospital? Do you want me to do anything or help with anything?"

I see her face turn red before she says, "Do you think that you could go to my apartment and grab me some clothes to change into after I get discharged?"

"Of course I can. I'll just need the key to your apartment so that I can get inside."

"Can you hand me my purse so that I can get them out for you?"

"Yes. Give me a second." I walk over to the chair and grab her purse from the floor next to it and hand it to her.

She unzips the purse and opens it, reaching inside and grabbing her keys from one of the pockets before she hands them to me. "Here you go, Greg. Thank you."

I take them from between her fingers and grab my keys out of my pocket. "I'll be back as soon as I can. Call me if you need anything, okay?"

She says okay as I leave out the door and head to the elevator.

I get down to the car after a few minutes and climb in. As soon as I have the engine started, I start driving down the road.

I roll my window down so that I can let the wind hit my face as I drive. It feels so cool on my face that I don't even care that the outside temperature is in the mid-forties right now. I'm just glad that Jade will be able to go to the trial tomorrow morning.

About ten minutes go by before I reach the building for Jade's apartment. Once I get there, I park next to her building and head inside.

I take the stairs up to the third floor and make my way to her apartment. I get the keys from my pocket and unlock the door before heading inside.

After I get the door unlocked and open, I go in through the door.

I look around at everything inside and it looks like nobody has lived here for months. Dirty dishes piled up in the sink and trash scattered in the living room and kitchen. This is how Jade had been living after Destiny was brought to the hospital.

She's been more depressed than I realized. Holy crap.

I go over to the open bedroom door and turn the light on as I walk inside.

As soon as I'm in there, a funk hits my nose, almost as if somebody died in here. It smells like Jade had been staying in her bed all day, every day when she wasn't staying at the hospital. Like she had been laying in a depressive funk for weeks.

I walk over to where the dresser is and open the first large drawer to try and find some pants to bring her. I get out a pair of black yoga pants and then grab out a pair of jeans for her to wear tomorrow. Next I go over to her closet and grab a blue t-shirt and a slightly nice white shirt.

Now is the part I'm scared of: getting her underwear. First I'll get the socks, then a pair of underwear and a bra.

I open the first smaller drawer on the left, and let out a sigh of relief when I see that it's her socks. I grab a pair out, then go over to the next drawer. I open it slowly and carefully, hoping that both a bra and underwear will be in here so that I don't have to open a drawer for both her underwear and her bra.

I get it open, but there's only bras in it. I grab one as quick as I can and go to the next drawer. I open that one and get the first pair I touch then close it.

I gather all of Jade's clothes in my arms and head back downstairs so that I can make my way back to the hospital.

I drive as fast as I can to get to the hospital. It only takes me about five minutes this time, rolling through each stop sign and skipping the roads with traffic lights. As soon as I get there, I skid into a parking spot by the door and hurry inside to get up to her room.

As soon as I reach Jade's room, she sits up and I hand her the keys and her clothes from my arms.

My face turns red when I see her bra and underwear again. "Here you go Jade. I got you clothes to change into before you get discharged and some clothes for tomorrow. And I felt incredibly awkward getting you underwear and a bra. But I got them, too."

She lets out a small giggle as she looks at the clothes that I grabbed for her. "That's okay. Oh, and you accidentally grabbed sexy, lacy underwear and a half bra."

She starts to laugh even harder when my face turns into a tomato. "Oh my God. I'm so sorry. Do I need to go back and get you different ones?"

"No, it's okay. I just think it's cute that you're embarrassed by having to get my underwear and bra. Most guys would love seeing underwear and bras, so I'm kind of glad that you seeing and touching mine embarrasses you."

I feel the redness in my face turning into a different red. "Do you want to change into your clothes now or wait until he comes back with your discharge papers?"

"I'll wait until after Dr. Williams comes back to change."

She starts folding up her clothes that she's going to wear tomorrow before the doctor gets back.

After a few minutes of sitting with Jade, Dr. Williams comes back with the discharge papers in his hands.

He walks over and hands them to Jade. "I'll take out your IV, then you've just got to sign the first couple of pages. After that you'll be free to go home."

He goes to the counter and grabs a cotton ball and vet wrap, then comes back over and carefully pulls the needle from Jade's arm. Once he gets her arm wrapped, he hands Jade the papers and a pen so that she can sign them.

She takes them from his hands and starts signing. She signs a couple of lines on the first page, then signs at the bottom of the second and third pages before handing them back to Dr. Williams.

"You can go into the restroom to change into your clothes, and after that you're good to go home."

Jade stands up, holding the gown closed behind her as he leaves the room. She turns to me and says, "I'm going to go in there and change, then we can go back to your apartment for the night. That way I won't be at my apartment by myself tonight."

She grabs her clothes and goes into the restroom to change while I gather her few things so that nothing gets left behind.

She comes out a few minutes later and puts on her shoes so that we can head back to my apartment.

"Thank you, Greg, for helping me so much." Jade gives me a hug and follows me out the door so that we can go to the car and go back to my apartment.

We ride there in silence for about fifteen minutes. I can't help but think about how stressful tomorrow is going to be for her, and it worries me. Because I don't want her to end up breaking down at the trial.

When we get to my apartment, I get out and go around to help Jade out of the car. I grab the rest of her clothes and take her purse from her so that I can carry them inside.

I carry her stuff up the stairs, letting her go ahead of me so she can get up there first. As soon as we reach my apartment, I unlock the door and let Jade inside.

I set her things down on the couch before I tell her, "You can have the bedroom for the night so you can be comfortable if you want. I can sleep out here on the couch."

"Are you sure? I don't mind sleeping on the couch."

I give Jade a look as I say, "I told you this the first night we met, I don't care if I sleep out here. I would much rather you be comfortable and warm. If you need me at all during the night, just holler for me, I'll be in there in a second."

Jade nods her heads as she goes to my bedroom to lay down. "Good night. I'll see you when I wake up in the morning."

I tell her goodnight before I lay down on the couch for the evening.

I hope that the trial goes all right, I think to myself before closing my eyes to go to sleep.

Chapter Fifteen

Jade's POV: I look around myself when I wake up. As soon as I sit up, I see Destiny lying next to me in the bed. I feel my heart start to race as I reach over to tap her on the shoulder and try to wake her up.

But as soon as I do, her skin feels cold to the touch. I roll her over, and when I do, I scream because her eyes are empty and black.

"Ahhh!!!"

I wake up with a jolt, still screaming as loud as I can. "Ahhh!!! Ahhh!!! Ahhh!!!"

Greg bursts through the door and rushes into the bedroom, grabbing ahold of me. "Hey, hey, hey. Jade! It's okay. It's okay. It was a nightmare. It wasn't real. It was just your imagination."

He grabs me around my body and holds me close in his arms. I feel him start rubbing his hand up and down my back as he tries to calm me down, but my mind won't stop, can't stop, picturing Destiny in the nightmare. Her eyes were just gone. She was just gone. Never coming back.

"What was it? What happened?" Greg tries to get me to talk to him, but I can't stop shaking after having that nightmare.

I try to say something, but all that comes out is, "I-I-I... D-destiny... E-e-eyes... H-holes... Gone."

Greg hugs me tight as he tries to get me to calm down so I can try to tell him what I dreamed about.

It takes a few minutes of me trying to stop shaking and trying to catch my breath before I can finally say something.

"I-I woke up in my dream, and Destiny was laying beside me in the bed. I reached over to wake her up, but as soon as I touched her, she felt cold as ice. And when I rolled her over, her eyes were black holes in her skull. She was gone. Long gone. I screamed in my dream and then I woke up screaming still because the image wouldn't leave my head. It terrified me."

He hugs me again before telling me, "Hey, it wasn't real. It was just your mind trying to scare you. I promise that Destiny is okay. Do you want to get coffee and breakfast somewhere? My treat?"

I sit up and tell Greg, "Yes, that sounds good. I just need to do something to try and get my mind off that nightmare before we go to the courthouse for the trial in a few hours."

"Okay. Do you want to get dressed before we go? Or do you want to wait and get changed afterwards?"

"I think I want to go ahead and get changed, because I was wearing this in the nightmare."

Greg stands up as he says, "That's fine with me. Can I grab a clean t-shirt and jeans before I go back to the living room? I'm gonna get changed in the bathroom before we go."

He leaves me to get changed and closes the door behind him.

As soon as he's gone, I get up and take off my shirt to change into the white blouse. I place it on the foot of the bed before I grab my other shirt to put on. Then I take off my yoga pants and switch them for the pair of jeans that Greg grabbed me. I place the yoga pants with my blue shirt on the foot of the bed.

I slide on my shoes and go to the living room once I'm finished getting changed out of my pajamas.

When I get in there, Greg's already changed with his sneakers on. He comes over to me and places his hand on my shoulder.

"Are you ready to go get food and coffee?"

"I am. Let's go."

He grabs his keys and wallet from the counter, and I follow him out to go down to his car. As soon as we get down to where he parked his car, he helps me in before getting in the driver's side.

Once Greg starts driving, he asks me, "Where do you want to get food and coffee?"

"Honestly, I would be perfectly fine getting food from McDonald's. Just something to fill me up before we have to go to the trial at eleven."

He puts the car in drive and starts heading towards Alberts Street. Then he turns after a few blocks onto Oak Lane and heads towards The Pancake House.

He pulls into the parking lot and parks in front of the building a few minutes later.

"I figured this would be better than McDonald's. Especially since they have fresh coffee and food instead of processed everything. Does this sound good? Or do you want somewhere else?"

"Here is great. Thank you. Let's go inside."

We both get out of the car and go inside to the host stand.

"Hi, my name's Amber. Is it just the two of you?"

I tell her it is, and she grabs two menus and leads us over to a table across the dining area.

After we sit down and she hands us our menus, she asks, "Do you know what you would like to drink?"

"Just two coffees with cream and sugar, please."

"I'll bring your coffees out in a jiffy. In the meantime, y'all can look over the menus to decide what you want to eat."

She leaves to get our coffees and I start looking over the breakfast menu to see what looks good.

Hmm... do I want pancakes or an omelet or biscuits and gravy or just fried eggs, bacon, and toast? It all sounds so delicious right now and my mouth is starting to water. *I just want some good, savory food to get me through the day.*

I set my menu down after deciding what I want to eat and look over to Greg. "Do you know what you want to eat? I'm probably going to ask for the homestyle pancakes with a side of sausage and eggs."

Greg laughs heartily. "Well it seems like you have an appetite again. I'm probably going to get the loaded omelet with all the fixins. That way I'll be good to go until after the trial in a couple of hours."

"Okay." My head turns down after he mentions the trial. "I am not looking forward to this because I am terrified that there's a chance it won't go the way I am wanting it to. That they will go in favor of those guys. And if that happens, I don't know what I'll do."

Greg's face turns serious as he looks at me. "Jade, I know that the trial will go well. They have evidence against them.

You'll just have to be confident when you are on the stand for Destiny. And I won't be able to be next to you on the defense since I am the charging officer. Will you be okay by yourself up there?"

I take a deep breath. "I think so. I'm going to try to be. Try not to break down."

As I finish saying that, Amber walks back over with two cups of coffee in her hands.

She sets one in front of both me and Greg before saying, "Here are your coffees. Have y'all decided what you want to eat yet?"

Greg sets his menu down as he looks up at her. "I think so. She can order first. What did you decide on, Jade?"

"I just want the homestyle pancakes with a side of fried eggs and sausage." I hand her the menu once she writes down my order.

After Jade orders, I tell Amber, "I want the loaded omelet with everything in it and a side of hashbrowns, please."

Amber smiles as she takes our menus after we give her our orders. "Okay, honey. I will be right out with your food as soon as it's ready."

When she leaves again, Greg tells me, "I know you'll be okay up there on the defense. I know you're strong. You've just got to prove it to yourself. Do you think that you can do that? Because if not, you can break down on the stand. It will be okay if you do. You just have to be yourself up there and not let anybody tear you down. Okay?"

I nod my head. "Okay. I can be strong. I just don't know how strong I'll be when I see them for the first time."

"That's okay. As soon as the trial is over, and I finish what I'll have to do, I will be back to comfort you and take you back to see Destiny. I promise."

He stands up from his side of the booth and comes around to give me a hug. As soon as his arms are around my neck, I nestle into his arms, trying to get as much comforting touch as possible.

I am just ready for this trial to start and be over so that I can find out what is going to happen. So that I can find out whether it will come out in our favor or theirs.

"I just want all of this to be over. I want Destiny to wake up. I want her to be okay after everything that has happened to her. Because until I can know if she's going to be okay, I don't know if I am going to be okay."

Greg tightens his arms around me for a few seconds before he lets go. When he looks at me, his face is filled with emotions that I can't read. He looks sad and also worried. He looks confused and stressed out.

"I just want to do everything I can to make sure *you'll* be okay, because I've been worried about you."

As he sits back down across the table, I tell him, "I should be. I'll pull through everything just like I know Destiny will. I promise. Thank you for caring so much."

A few minutes go by of me and Greg just sitting in silence until our waitress Amber comes over with our food.

She sets my pancakes, sausage, and eggs in front of me first. "Here ya go, hun.... and here is your omelet and hashbrowns, sweetie." She sets Gregory's plate down in front of him. "Enjoy your food. I'll be back to check on y'all in a little while."

After she leaves, I take a sip of my coffee then put butter and syrup on my pancakes. I cut them up into bites once they are nice and covered with syrup and start eating my eggs first, smashing them into bits.

I eat them slowly, trying to sop up as much of the yolk that leaked out as I can while I eat each bite. What's left on the plate after I finish the eggs, I soak up with my sausage and eat them.

I finish my eggs and sausage after less than five minutes, and when I am putting the last bite of sausage in my mouth, I catch Greg staring at me.

"What? Are you okay?"

He stammers for a few seconds before he says, "Nothing. I've just never seen you eat like that. Especially not that fast. Are you okay?"

I set my fork down for a second. "I'm okay. It's just that when I'm nervous or worried, I sometimes eat a little faster. And it doesn't help that the food is so good."

Greg takes a couple of sips of his coffee before he says, "That's okay. I was just a little worried about you for a second."

I giggle quietly before continuing to eat my pancakes while he eats his omelet and hashbrowns.

Fifteen minutes go by before we are both finished with our food and our coffee. I finish sipping down the last few sips of coffee right when Amber comes back over with the check for our food.

"How was everything?" She sets the check on the table as she gathers our plates and coffee mugs.

Greg smiles at her. "Everything was really good. We both enjoyed every last bite. Thank you."

He hands her his debit card before I can try to get mine and split the bill. "Here you go. I'll be the one paying for everything."

Amber nods her head at him as she leaves for a minute to put the payment in from Greg's card. When she comes back and gives Greg his card back, she tells us to have a nice day before we both stand up to leave.

Once we are out the door and in the car, Greg starts driving us to the courthouse.

As he's driving, I can feel my heart moving deeper and deeper into the pit of my stomach. *I am just ready for this to be over with.*

He pulls into a spot and puts the car into park. Before he gets out, he asks me, "Are you sure that you'll be okay by yourself with just you and your lawyer up there?"

I take in a deep breath and let it out slowly as I say, "I'm sure. Besides, my lawyer is a close friend of mine and Destiny's. I'll be okay. I'm going to head inside and meet him so that he can tell me what he plans to start off with."

"Okay. I am going to go see the lieutenant to find out what I need to do."

Greg opens the door and we both walk inside, going in separate directions. As soon as I am through the doors, I see Derek standing about fifty feet away from the entrance to the courtroom.

When he sees me, he comes over to where I'm standing. "Hi, Jade. Are you about ready? We're going to have to go in in a few minutes before the trial starts so that we're prepared."

"I am. What do you plan on starting our side of the case with?

Derek leans over towards me and whispers to me, "The first thing that I am going to bring up is the fact that when they were driving down the highway before they even hit Destiny's car, they didn't have the driving camera turned on. That they are supposed to have it turned on any time they are on the road. We don't know what happened except through witness statements of the other drivers from the highway at the time because it wasn't turned on."

Once Derek tells me what he plans to start with, I follow him through the doors of the courtroom and over to the plaintiff table. After we sit down, he pulls a folder out of his briefcase that has documents in it for Destiny's case.

I sit next to him, trying not to let my anxiety show as I try not to tap the table too much with my fingers. A few minutes go by before others start to file into the courtroom, including the drivers of the truck and their attorney.

Seeing their faces makes my skin crawl because of knowing what happened to Destiny and what they did.

After a few minutes of everyone chattering, the bailiff enters the courtroom and announces the judge. "All rise. Please welcome Judge Connors to the courtroom."

The judge walks in and makes his way behind the stand. "Good morning, everyone. I am calling the case of Morgan versus Smith and Daniels. The plaintiff, Destiny Morgan, is being represented by Jade Stephens and attorney Derek Johnson."

"The case against Michael Smith and Bruce Daniels is being brought before us because of an accident they were involved in with Destiny Morgan, our plaintiff. The reason for this trial is because Miss Morgan was severely injured in that accident and has been in a comatose state since being put into the hospital.

"I am going to be bringing to the stand Derek Johnson to begin his questioning of the defendants."

Derek stands up and walks to the front of the courtroom. "May I have Michael Smith come to the stand first?"

I look over and see him stand up as he makes his way to the witness stand to be questioned. He looks scared but also a little bit pissed off, and that scares me a little.

As soon as he's seated, Derek says, "My plaintiff and I have evidence showing that you and your friend Bruce did not have the driving camera in your truck turned on when the accident occurred. Is this true, Mr. Smith?"

Michael looks at Derek after he finishes his question. "I think so. Me or Bruce might have forgotten to turn it on before we got onto the highway."

"Okay. Is it also true that you may not have been watching the road in front of you? You were the one behind the wheel, weren't you?"

"I was. I was contacting our boss on the radio when the accident happened and didn't have enough time to react by the time I saw her car in front of me. By the time I saw it, she was on the road and through the windshield."

Derek tells Michael, "Were you the one who got out and find Destiny on the road after the accident or was it Bruce who found her?"

"I found her. Bruce called 911 after I called him out of the truck."

After Michael tells Derek this, Derek tells him, "I am done questioning you for now. I am going to call up Officer Gregory Miller, the officer who was first on the scene of the accident. Officer Miller, can you please come up to the stand?"

I look over and see Greg walking up to the witness stand.

As soon as he's up there, Derek asks him, "What did you see when you first arrived at the scene of the accident with the paramedics?"

Greg clears his throat before he starts speaking. "When I arrived at the scene, Destiny was lying on the road, her body laying in a puddle of blood from her going through the windshield. Michael was trying to stop the bleeding from her head after it hit the asphalt."

"What did Michael and Bruce tell you about what happened?"

"They said that they were driving their route across the state when the accident occurred. That they were just trying to figure out what exit they were supposed to take next when Miss Morgan's car was in front of them."

"Did you get any evidence of foul play where she was after she went through the windshield?"

Greg thinks for a second before he answers. "It did look as if they had moved her from where she had originally landed. There was blood in one spot, then a small trickling trail on the road leading to where she was when I arrived."

Derek stops for a second to think about what Greg told him before he continues the questioning. "Now did you question them about this at the time?"

"I did not. I was just trying to get her to the hospital as soon as possible and get ahold of her emergency contact, Jade Shay, so that I could let her know what had happened."

As soon as Greg says this, I feel my heart sink. Greg lied to me. He never told me that he thought something might have happened like that. When I look over at him, I can see his eyes turned down in guilt.

"That was extremely negligent on your part, Officer Miller. Did you know that you could lose your job because of omitting evidence?"

"I did. I don't know why I didn't bring that evidence up about the accident. I guess my mind was just out of it that day."

"You may step down, Officer. Now can I speak to Bruce Daniels?"

He walks up to the stand and sits down before Derek begins his questioning of him.

Derek takes a deep breath. "So in light of this new evidence brought up by Officer Miller, did you or did you not move Miss Morgan to a different location from where she originally landed?"

Bruce looks out nervously to where Michael is sitting at the defendant's table before he answers. "Mike did. By the time I got around to the front of the truck and saw what had happened, he had moved body to lay in the middle of the road instead of in front of our truck."

"Did either of you know that she was still alive after the accident? Or did you both assume she was already dead when you saw her lying on the road?"

"Listen man, I thought she was vulture food as soon as we hit her car. Hardly anybody survives being hit by a semi-truck. I wanted to toss her into the trees where her car was and let people think that she just got in an accident and killed herself. But Mike wanted to try and help. He wanted to make sure she was okay. He's probably the only reason she's still alive, even if she is in a coma."

I can feel my face turning to shock when he says all of that. *He was just going to let her die. He thought she was dead and wanted to throw her away like she was nothing.*

I shake my head and continue watching as Derek tells him, "Bruce Daniels, you both are lucky that you called 911 and that Destiny Morgan survived that accident. Because if she hadn't you both would be on trial right now for voluntary manslaughter. Step down."

As I sit at the plaintiff table, trying not to cry, Derek calls me up.

"Can I please have Jade Shay, my client, to the stand?"

I stand up and make my way over to the witness stand, walking slowly. My head is whirling from everything that has been said so far by everyone.

After I sit down in the witness stand, Derek stands in front of me and asks, "What were you told when you were called about Destiny being in the car accident?"

I think back for a second before I can answer. "When I got the call, I answered thinking it was her, because we were supposed to be moving in together that day. But when I answered, I was told that she had been in a car accident on the highway and that she was in a coma at the hospital. I didn't know what to do or what to think."

"Did anything happen before she was driving on the highway? Or do you know anything that could have happened?"

"All I know is that she had just left work and was on the way to our new apartment to start unpacking boxes."

"Okay. You may step down for now. I am done with my questioning if the defense's attorney would like to ask anything."

I go back to my seat as Bruce and Michael's attorney gets up and walks to the front.

As soon as he's up there, he asks Greg to get back on the stand. "I would like to further question Officer Miller about what he saw after he arrived."

When Greg makes his way back up there, I can feel the tension radiating from him. He sits back down in the chair and waits for the attorney to ask him a question.

After a few seconds, he's asked, "So Officer Miller... you said that it looked like my clients had moved Destiny from where she was originally after the accident. Can you tell me why you didn't ask them about it? Why you didn't question it at all?"

"I had thought at the time that I was just imagining things. I should have questioned them about it. I know I should have, but I didn't."

"What did you think had happened before you got to the scene?"

I can see Greg thinking before he answers. "I had thought that they had crashed into Miss Morgan's car and were just trying to make it look less bad than it would have if they hadn't moved her into the road. But my mind was just focused on getting her to the hospital at the time and making sure to get ahold of someone and let them know what had happened."

"Did you not think about the fact that you *will* lose your job as an officer of the law because of being negligent? Did you think that you were helping Destiny Morgan or just helping yourself?"

Greg looks out towards me as he says, "I was being hopeful that my thoughts were wrong. That my eyes were tricking me. I thought that it was just an accident."

"Step down. Your honor, those are my questions."

Judge Connors stands up and says, "We are going to break so that the jury may discuss and determine a verdict.

Everyone starts talking as the courtroom empties for recess. I stay sitting at the table as I think about what I found out.

Derek turns to me as he's gathering his papers back into his briefcase. "What's wrong? They're probably going to rule in Destiny's favor. It's a shoo-in, almost guaranteed. Doesn't that make you happy?"

"It does, but I'm still sad because of everything that's come up."

"What do you mean, everything that's come up?"

I let out a deep sigh before I answer him. "Well Officer Miller, he's my friend. I met him the first night I was leaving the hospital. I found out later that he was the officer who had gone to her accident, but he never told me about the blood, about the fact that she might have been moved and he didn't question it. It feels like he betrayed me and I can't trust him. He's been the only person by my side since day one basically, and now I feel like he's been lying the entire time.

"I just don't know what to do now."

Derek places his hand on my shoulder as he says, "He was probably just trying to protect you. He probably didn't want to hurt you."

I feel my body shudder as I try not to cry. "I know, but I feel like I can't trust anyone now. I had nobody besides him helping me through everything that's been going on and now I don't even know if I have him for support."

I lay my head on Derek's shoulder as tears start to pour from my eyes. He holds me against his shoulder, trying to comfort me and make me feel better, but it's not working.

I cry for a few minutes on Derek's shoulder until I hear Greg's voice behind me.

"I am so sorry, Jade. I really am. I didn't tell you because I didn't want to hurt you, and it backfired."

I sit up and turn around to look at him. "You seriously hurt me. You could have told me, and it honestly probably would have made me feel better knowing that you were concerned about the circumstances behind the accident. But you didn't. It feels like you didn't think you could trust me. You have been lying to me since the day we met."

Derek stands up and says, "I'm going to give you two some privacy."

"What else have you been lying to me about? Is your name really Gregory Miller? Are you really a sergeant in the police department? Or did you lie about that too?"

"All of those are true. Well the last one isn't true anymore. The lieutenant just finished chewing me out for omitting evidence and fired me. I had to turn in my badge."

"Is there anything else you're hiding from me? Please tell me the truth. Don't hide anything."

I can see the gears turning in Greg's head before he answers me. "I didn't want to tell you yet, but as we've been hanging out, I have been falling in love with you. I didn't want to tell you because I know that you love Destiny. And I have been trying to push the feelings down, but they won't. Are you okay with knowing that?"

My face turns pink after Greg tells me this. "Holy crap. Are you serious?"

"I am beyond serious. Every day that we have been spending together, I have been falling more in love with you because of how much I have grown to care about you. I don't care if you don't feel the same way. I just care if you'll be okay. I am so sorry for lying to you."

I stand up and tell him, "I am okay knowing that, but what I want to know is do you promise not to lie to me again?"

Greg looks at me with an expression of complete sincerity on his face. "I promise I will not lie to you again. I don't want to hurt you again. I just want to be by your side to make sure you will be okay no matter what happens."

****

A few hours later

The jury is finally back from trying to decide a verdict. They file back into the courtroom and take their seats in the jury box.

After they have given Judge Connors the verdict, he stands up and quiets the courtroom.

"The jury has come up with a verdict and they have determined that Michael Smith and Bruce Daniels are guilty of negligent driving and attempted voluntary manslaughter. They are being charged with ten years prison time without the possibility of parole. Bailiff, take them away for booking."

Once the judge announces the verdict, everyone in the courtroom claps their hands, including me.

Chapter Sixteen

Jade's POV: As soon as the judge announces the jury's verdict, I grab Derek in my arms and hug him tight. *I can't believe this! They are actually getting locked up for what they did to Destiny!*

"Thank you so much, Derek, for your help in this trial. I can't believe how easy it turned out to be. That those douche bags are actually getting locked up for what they did. Especially considering what Bruce wanted to do. That was fucked up, but I'm so glad that they are both getting their karma."

Derek gives me a smile. "I am, too."

After he says that, I notice his eyes looking over my shoulder and turn around to see what he's looking at: Greg. As soon as I see him, I can feel the mixed emotions coming up from everything he told me during recess. Derek walks away as Greg comes over.

He walks over with an apologetic look on his face. "Jade… I am so sorry for not telling you the full truth about what I saw when I got to Destiny. I should have told you as soon as I told you I was the officer who went to her accident on the highway. I'm sorry. Is there any way that you can forgive me?"

I let out a deep sigh. "I don't know. Can you promise me that you won't lie to me again? About anything."

"Yes. I promise. And if I do, you can punch me. I don't want to lose you as a friend because you are the best friend

I have ever had... the closest friend I have ever had. I don't want to lose that."

"And what about your feelings? I don't feel the same way towards you. Are you sure you're okay with that?"

I see a small hint of pain cross over his eyes before it goes away. "Yes. I'm sure. I'll be okay. I promise. Do you want to go see Destiny now that the trial is over?"

I nod my head as I take my phone out of my pocket to check it. As soon as I turn the screen on, there are at least a dozen missed calls from the hospital and from Dr. Drew. My eyes go wide as I feel myself starting to panic.

My breath starts to speed up and hyperventilate as my brain goes into complete panic. I can feel my heart starting to race as I collapse to my knees. My phone drops to the floor in front of me as Gregory races to grab ahold of me.

All I can think of is that the worst has happened. My vision is blurry and I can't hear anything. I can barely see Greg's lips moving as he tries to ask me what's wrong, tries to get my attention. But all I can hear is my heart and my breath echoing in my ears. All I can see in front of me is fuzzy shapes and colors.

Before I know it, everything in front of me goes black.

Greg's POV: "Are you okay, Jade? What happened?"

She just checked her phone while we were talking and then started freaking out and panicking like she did at the hospital.

I reach out and grab her as soon as I see her collapsing to the floor. I keep trying to talk to her, get her to tell me what's wrong, but she faints in my arms.

I yell, "Somebody call 911! Please! She's having a panic attack and fainted."

As soon as I yell for help, her lawyer Derek runs back over along with a dozen other people.

He pulls out his phone and dials the number, putting it on speaker while asking, "What happened? What did you say?"

The operator answers a few seconds later. "911. What is your emergency?"

Derek tells the man, "I have a friend here suffering from a severe panic attack. Her name is Jade Shay and we're at the city courthouse. Can you please send an ambulance?"

"Yes, sir. They are on the way. Would you like to stay on the line?"

"Yes, sir. Can you give me advice on what to do until the ambulance gets here? I've got a friend holding her right now. Is there anything we need to do until they get here?"

"Is she warm and is she still breathing?"

Derek turns to me and asks if I can check. I lean my head down near her mouth to see if I can hear her breathing. I place my hand on her face after I check for breathing. Once I finish checking if she is still breathing and see if she's warm, I nod my head to tell him that she's breathing still and that her face is warm.

Derek tells the operator, "She is still breathing, and feels a little warm. What should we do until they get here?"

"Just make sure that she continues to breath. When they get there, a cold rag will be placed on her forehead to try and cool her down. They should be there any minute."

As soon as he says that, paramedics rush through the doors. "Move! Move!"

They hurry over to where we are and start checking Jade's blood pressure as they put her onto a gurney.

"Is she going to be okay?" I try not to panic myself as I ask the paramedics this.

One of them looks at me and says, "She should be, but we won't know until she gets to the hospital, and we can get her on a nicotinamide adenine dinucleotide or NAD drip. This should help calm and control her symptoms of anxiety."

They get Jade's blood pressure and get her outside and into the ambulance after a few seconds. They get her hooked up to a temporary IV and a heart monitor, then start getting ready to take her to the hospital.

As soon as they start getting ready to shut the doors and take off, I stop one of them and ask, "Can I please ride with her to the hospital? I'm her friend and want to make sure that she's okay. That nothing happens to her."

"You can. You'll have to sit in the front though so that we can be able to take care of her until we get to the hospital."

"That's fine. I just want to make sure that she'll be okay and be near her the entire time so that I know nothing bad has happened."

I follow the paramedic to the front as she gets in the driver's seat. I get in the passenger seat and buckle up before she starts to drive.

As soon as we're hauling ass down the road, all I can think about is that look of panic that was on Jade's face right before she passed out. How she looked like something horrible had happened. I didn't see what was on her phone before she started to have the panic attack, but whatever it was, it couldn't have been good.

A few minutes go by before we reach the hospital and the paramedics rush Jade inside. The woman who drove tells me that I'll have to go inside to the waiting room until they can get Jade set up in a hospital room with a doctor.

I go inside to the waiting room and sit down, watching the news that's on the TV monitor.

I try to get my mind to stop worrying while I wait for someone to come out and tell me what's going on with Jade. But all I can think about is what could have been on her phone when she checked it.

After a while, my eyes start to fall closed. I eventually fall asleep in the chair I'm sitting in.

****

I wake up to someone nudging me on my shoulder.

"Hello? Are you awake?"

My eyes open after I blink a few times. I sit up and look in front of me to see a doctor standing there.

"What's going on? Is Jade okay? Is she in a room now?"

"I'm Dr. Sharp. She is in a room now. She's still unconscious, though. Would you like to come see her?"

I stand up and follow her to Jade's room. It only takes a few minutes to get to her room, and as soon as I'm inside, I rush over and start to check on her.

Dr. Sharp comes inside and tells me, "It seems like she had a sudden aneurism burst through her brain right before she fainted. Her fainting helped her to not have a more severe reaction to the aneurism. She's stable now and is set up with an NAD drip and saline drip. She should wake up soon."

"Okay. Is it all right if I stay with her for a little while?"

"Of course. I'm going to be back in a bit to see if she has woken up."

The doctor leaves me by myself with Jade in the room, and I sit down in a chair next to her bed. As I look at her, I can't help but think that this happened because of me. That she had the panic attack because of me.

I sit thinking about what she could have seen on her phone that made her panic so badly, and the only thing that I can think of is it was something with Destiny. And as soon as that thought hits my brain, I jump up.

I look over at Jade before I leave the room and tell her, "I'll be right back. I'm going to go check on Destiny and see how she's doing. I'll be back as soon as I can."

I hurry out of the room and go over to the elevator, hitting the button for the second floor.

The elevator arrives after a few seconds. I get on and as soon as the doors are closed, my foot starts tapping impatiently on the floor.

After what feels like hours, the elevator finally stops and lets me out.

I make my way to Destiny's room as fast as I can. As soon as I get there, I push the door open and walk inside. And what I see when I am inside the room shakes me to my core.

Destiny is sitting up and awake.

My mouth drops as I try to say something. "W-w-what? You're awake!"

Destiny looks at me and says, "I am. Who are you, and where is Jade? What's going on?"

"I'm Greg. I'm a new friend of Jade's. Jade, she's in a room here. What all do you remember from the last time you were awake? Do you remember anything?"

"All that I can remember is that one minute I was driving home from work, and the next minute I'm here talking to you. What happened?"

I take a deep breath before I start to explain everything to Destiny. "Well you got here about a month ago after getting into a car accident. You've been in a coma since then. Jade has been visiting you every day to make sure you were okay. I met her the first day she was here with you and have been helping her be able to not worry too much that something was going to happen to you. She's been staying in my apartment with me because staying at your apartment had been making her depressed, worrying about you.

"Her and I just finished a trial against the men who hit you when you were driving, and when she'd checked her phone afterwards, she had a severe panic attack that sent her here. Did you call her?"

Destiny looks at me as she says, "I tried calling her a dozen times. I didn't know what was going on. After I woke up, my doctor was in here to make sure that everything was okay, but he didn't tell me where Jade was, so I was panicked and worried that something had happened to her. Is she going to be okay?"

"She should be, especially once she sees you. Right now she's still unconscious after fainting. But once she wakes up and she sees that you're awake, I know she'll be okay. Do you want to call your doctor back in here so that you can ask if you can go see Jade?"

Destiny picks up the control next to her bed and hits the call button repeatedly until somebody comes into the room.

A nurse comes in and asks her, "Is everything okay? Do you need anything?"

"I need to go check on a friend who's here. Can I please go see her?"

"Let me go get Dr. Drew and he can determine if you are okay to go see her. I will be right back with him."

The nurse leaves the room to go get Dr. Drew. A few minutes go by before she comes back into the room with him.

As soon as he's in the room, he asks Destiny, "So what's going on? You told Jackie that you want to go see Jade? As far as I can tell, you seem okay enough to leave the room and go see her. But you'll need to use a wheelchair to maneuver to her room because I don't want you hurting yourself trying to walk."

"Okay. That's fine. I just need to go see her as soon as I can."

Dr. Drew leaves the room for a few seconds to go grab a wheelchair for Destiny to use. After he gets back, he unhooks her IV and I help her get off the bed and into the chair.

I help get her settled in the chair and stand behind it so that I can start pushing her. I take Destiny to the elevator and take her up to the sixth floor so she can see Jade.

We go to room 638 and I push her inside through the door. When we get in, Jade is still laying unconscious on the bed, her breathing steady in her chest. I push Destiny's wheelchair to sit right beside Jade's bed.

Destiny looks at Jade laying in the bed and reaches forward, placing her hand on Jade's.

"Jade, it's me, Destiny. I'm awake, really awake. I love you so much. I don't know what all you went through while I was in that coma over these last few weeks, but I want you to know... need you to know... that I am okay. That I am not going to fall back into a coma."

As Destiny is talking to Jade, she's rubbing her hand up and down Jade's arm. Destiny does this for a few moments longer after she finishes speaking.

I stand to the side, observing. While Destiny is moving her hand along Jade's arm, goosebumps start to appear on her skin, making the hairs on her arm stand up.

I decide to leave the room so that Destiny can be by herself with Jade.

Destiny's POV: I sit in the wheelchair just looking at Jade lying in the hospital bed. *I can't freaking believe that Jade stuck by my side through all of this. That she didn't want to leave me alone or abandon me at all.*

"Jade, I love you so goddamn much. You are my best friend, and now my girlfriend. I remember me asking you if you would be my girlfriend when I was awake for a little bit a couple of weeks ago. I just want you to know that I am okay. That I should be able to go home soon. Please try and wake back up soon. I want to see your beautiful eyes and your smile that I know will show up as soon as you see that I'm awake."

I lean down and give Jade a small kiss on her lips. After I kiss her, I grab her hand to hold in mine, holding it close to me.

I sit with her like that for an hour, just watching to see if there's any movement coming from Jade.

After a while of sitting with her, Jade's doctor comes in the room. "Hi. I'm Dr. Sharp. I'm Jade's doctor. Are you her friend?"

"Yes. I'm her best friend. Do you know when she's going to wake up?"

"She may wake up within the next hour or two. When she arrived here, I had to inject her with NAD+ to help calm down the symptoms that were causing her to have a panic attack and faint. Her heartrate and breathing has calmed down too, so she should wake back up soon."

I tell her okay before she leaves the room.

After she's closed the door behind her, I sit and just watch my baby laying peacefully in front of me. Her chest is moving up and down evenly as she breathes. Each time she breathes in and out, her mouth opens slightly with each exhale.

Her eyes are moving rapidly behind her eyelids, letting me know that she's dreaming right now. I roll my chair as close to the bed as I can and place my hand on her chest so that I can feel her heartbeat.

Jade just looks so peaceful laying like she is despite the cause that put her here. I just hope that she wakes back up soon and is happy to see me.

****

Jade's POV: My mind feels fuzzy as I try to open my eyes. I have to squint them after I get them open because the light in the room is bright, white, and blinding.

I manage to get my eyes open, and when I do, I think I see Destiny sitting in front of me. *I must be seeing things, because she's still in a coma.*

"Destiny? Is that you?"

She reaches towards me, placing her hand on my cheek. "Yes, baby. It's me. I woke up this morning around eleven. That's why you had so many calls from me when you got done with the trial. And I'm okay, baby. I feel a lot better now that I'm awake. How do you feel?"

I jump into a sitting position and wrap my arms tight around Destiny's neck, hugging her as tight as I can.

"Holy crap! It's really you, babe! You're really awake! I'm so fucking glad that you're awake. I was so miserable with worry that you weren't ever going to wake back up. How do you feel, baby?"

Destiny lets out a laugh as she says, "I'm feeling good, baby. I'm so glad that you stayed by my side this entire time. Oh and do you want to tell me more about your friend Greg? Because I have a feeling that there's a little something more to him than either of you have told me so far."

"Well the first day after I came to see you, I was sitting outside the hospital, crying in the rain when he found me. He took me to his apartment to warm up and sleep for the night. After that, he started helping be my shoulder to cry on while you were in the coma. Well, I didn't know this until he told me this morning, but he said that he's starting to get feelings for me. I don't have any feelings for him except as a friend, and I let him know that."

My baby looks at me and a big smile crosses her face as she says, "I kind of thought that he had some sort of feelings for you when he came to my room and told me who he was. I vaguely remember meeting him for a day when I had woken up for a little bit. He's a really sweet guy and it makes me happy that he was with you this entire time so you weren't alone."

"I'm so freaking glad that you're okay now. Hopefully within the next day or two we'll both be able to go home finally and work on getting you officially moved into our apartment."

Destiny leans forward and gives me a kiss on my lips. As she kisses me, it feels like we have been doing this every day since the day we met, and it's amazing. Her lips are so warm and soft against mine.

We kiss for what must have been five minutes before we both pull away.

Destiny smiles warmly at me and says, "That kiss felt just like the ones in my dreams: amazing. Like the best kiss I could have ever had. From the only person I could ever want to kiss and be with. I love you so fucking much."

I hug her close, squeezing her in my arms before I let go. As I sit back up in the bed, the door opens and my doctor walks into the room.

"Well hello, Jade. I'm your doctor, Dr. Sharp. How are you feeling?"

I turn to him and say, "I feel absolutely amazing now since this woman is here. She is my girlfriend who has been in a coma for the last month. That's what caused me to have the panic attacks that had me in here the last couple of days, my worry for her."

Dr. Sharp walks over and tells me, "That is fantastic. Can I check your vital signs right quick? If they are good, you should be able to go home shortly."

I nod my head and he gets the blood pressure cuff to place on my arm. Once it's velcroed onto my arm, he turns the machine on and it starts to tighten. About twenty seconds go by before it loosens back up.

After the cuff has loosened, Dr. Sharp looks at the monitor and tells me, "Your blood pressure is 114 over 72. That's really good. I'm going to check your heartrate and breathing now, and if they are good, I can put in your discharge papers and let you go home."

She puts the stethoscope on and holds it against my chest to listen to my heartbeat.

After a few seconds of listening, she tells me, "Take a deep breath."

I open my mouth and breathe in deeply a few times before she removes the stethoscope ear pieces from her ears.

"Well Miss Shay, your heart and lungs sound really good. If you're ready, I will go put in your discharge and bring them back so you can sign them to go home."

After Dr. Sharp leaves, I ask Destiny, "Have you found out from Dr. Drew when you'll be able to come home?"

"He told me that so long as I stay good and am feeling good before tomorrow morning, I should be able to come home. Then I can come home to our apartment so that we can start officially getting me moved in."

"Awesome, baby. I can't wait for us both to be home so that everything can go back to normal again. Do you think that you'll want to go back to work after you get home? Or do you want to wait a few weeks to go back?"

Destiny pauses for a few seconds before answering me. She has an expression on her face that slightly reminds me of how I felt when I first came to see her at the hospital.

After a few seconds, Destiny opens her mouth and says, "I don't know if I want to go back to work for them because the day that I was in the accident, I had a shitty day at work because I had a panic attack and got yelled at by Jeff. I don't know that I ever want to go back there or see his face ever again. Honestly, I think that I want to find a job in an office where I won't have to deal with shitty assholes like him ever again."

"Okay, baby. Well, after you've been home for a week or two, I can start helping you look for an office job."

Once I finish talking, the door opens and Dr. Sharp comes back inside with my discharge papers.

"Here you go, Miss Shay. If you could just sign these, you will be good to go home."

I take the papers and pen from her and sign where I need to before handing them back to her. "Here you are, Dr. Sharp. Thank you for taking care of me after I had that panic attack. Hopefully I won't be back with another one."

She laughs as she says, "Let's hope so."

She leaves the room after I hand her the papers. Once she's gone, I get up from the bed and grab my clothes that are folded on the chair.

I untie the robe and let it fall off my body before putting my underwear back on. As I'm doing so, I catch Destiny looking at me.

"What, baby? Why are you watching me?"

Her cheeks turn red as soon as I call her out. "Well... when I was in the coma and dreaming, there were a few times during the dream that you and I... were intimate with each other. Like, really intimate. And seeing your body right now is turning me on a little bit."

I laugh lightly when Destiny says this. "Well, I don't know if Dr. Drew would want you doing any strenuous activity. At least not until you are okay to go home. Do you think that you can wait until then, baby?"

Destiny continues watching me as she says, "Maybe. Just so long as you finish getting dressed nice and slow."

I smile while I put my bra on, sliding it over my breasts as slow as I can. Then I grab my t-shirt and pull it over my head. Lastly I finish by grabbing my pants from the chair, bending over as I do so, putting my ass up in the air towards Destiny.

As I do this I can hear her let out a gasp of breath. I start pulling my jeans on one leg at a time, my ass in the air the entire time. Each time I move, I can feel it slightly jiggling behind me.

I finish getting them on, then get my sneakers and slide them onto my feet, bending over to tie them.

I finish getting dressed then stand up and look at Destiny. "Are you ready to go back to your room, baby?"

She bites her lip as she nods her head yes. "Oh, yes. I wish so bad that we could have some fun right now, because god was that sexy as fuck. *You* are sexy as fuck. I love you so fucking much, babygirl. You're amazing, you know that?"

"I know. Now let's get you back to your room."

We get to Destiny's room after a few minutes and find Greg in there with Dr. Drew.

I push her wheelchair up next to the bed and Greg comes over to help me get Destiny back onto it. We get her onto the mattress and help her get centered. I grab the blanket and slide it over her to make sure that she doesn't get cold.

After we get Destiny comfortable and situated on the bed, Dr. Drew asks her, "How are you feeling, Destiny? Are you feeling okay so far after just waking up a few hours ago?"

"I am. I'm feeling really great after getting to see Jade again. When do you think that I'll be able to go home with her?"

"Well, if you are still feeling really great in the morning after breakfast, you can go home then. How does that sound?"

Destiny smiles big, her face lit up with pure happiness. "That sounds great, doctor."

"I'm glad. I'm going to go for now because the nurse will be in soon with your dinner for the night. I hope you have a good night's rest, and I'll be back in here around eight to see how you are feeling after the night."

"Okay. Thank you, Dr. Drew for taking such good care of me this last month."

After he leaves the room, Greg asks us, "Do you guys want me to stay with you for the night? If not, I can go home and come back in the morning to pick both of you up and take you home."

I look to Destiny and let her answer him.

"You can stay. That way you don't have to drive back again in the morning. But I'm just warning you, you may or may not end up seeing things happening that you don't want to see. So if you're okay with that, you are more than welcome to stay the night up here."

I can see his face turning as red as a ripe tomato and laugh when I tell him, "Nothing's going to happen here. I don't want Destiny getting hurt or over-exerting herself. Besides, she's got a broken leg and I don't want it to get hurt again. So we'll be good tonight. Don't worry."

He lets out a sigh of relief after I say that. "Okay. Well I am probably going to go back to your apartment and grab you some clothes to change into in the morning. That way you won't have to wait then or leave in the hospital gown."

"Thanks, Greg. I appreciate it. And if you want, you can just grab me a shirt and sweatpants. That way you don't get creeped out by my panties."

He visibly shivers when Destiny says the word panties and we both start laughing at him.

Once we stop laughing at him, he looks down and starts pouting. "You guys are mean. I never knew that being friends with two girls would get me bullied so much."

I walk over and give him a hug. "We're sorry, Greg. We'll stop being so mean. I promise."

He stops pouting after a few minutes and sits down in one of the chairs next to the door. I sit down in the chair next to Destiny's bed and get comfy.

Once we're all sat down, a knock comes at the door. A nurse walks in a few seconds later carrying a tray with food.

"Are you ready for dinner, sweetie? I've brought a few pieces of fried chicken, some corn, and some French fries, along with a sweet tea to drink."

She sets the food down on the table tray and pulls it across Destiny's bed.

Once she gets Destiny's food set in front of her, she asks Greg and I, "Would either of you like any food? I can go down to the cafeteria and grab you something to eat. That way you aren't starving while watching her eat."

I smile as I tell the nurse, "Could you grab us each a bag of potato chips and a sandwich?"

"Of course. I'll go right down and grab them. I should be back within a few minutes."

After she leaves, Destiny reaches out her arms, moving her fingers for a hug. I laugh and stand up, walking over to her. I wrap my arms around her and hug her tight to me, squeezing her in my arms.

"I love you, baby. I'm so happy that you're awake now and okay. I can't wait for you to be able to come home in the morning."

A few minutes later, the nurse comes back with mine and Greg's sandwiches and chips.

She hands them both to us. "Here you go. Enjoy your food, guys."

I unwrap my sandwich and start eating.

Greg stands up with his chips and sandwich in his hand. "I'm going go ahead and go to your apartment so that I can grab Destiny some clothes. I'll eat my food on the road and be back in about thirty minutes or so. If you guys need anything, call me."

****

When Greg gets back thirty minutes later, Destiny and I have finished our food and are on the verge of falling asleep in the bed and recliner.

My eyes open slightly as I say, "Hi. We're both about ready to go to sleep for the night, so if you want, you can put something on the TV to watch."

Chapter Seventeen

Destiny's POV: The next morning, I wake up around six to the nurse bringing in breakfast. I sit up and stretch for a few seconds while she's setting the food onto the tray and sliding it in front of me.

"Good morning. Here's your breakfast, hun. Did you sleep well?"

I answer her, saying, "I did. Thank you."

I look over at Jade and Greg in the chairs and see that they're both still asleep. I let out a small chuckle as I tell the nurse, "They did, too. Theirs just isn't over yet."

She smiles at me as she says, "That's all right. I brought them a little bit of food on the tray, also: a couple of biscuits with a piece of sausage and cheese on them along with a carton of milk for each of them. Your doctor should be in to see you in less than thirty minutes to see how you're doing."

"Okay. I'll wake them up in a minute so they can eat their food before he gets here."

After she leaves and closes the door behind her, I turn the TV on and put it on to a channel that's playing *Act of Valor*. As soon as it comes on, gunfire starts blasting from the TV and both Jade and Greg jump up from their chairs like they heard an explosion.

I look over at them and smile as I turn the volume back down some. "Well good morning, sleepy heads. The nurse just brought in food and said that Dr. Drew would be in here to see how I'm doing in about thirty minutes or so. I just wanted to make sure you were awake before he gets here."

Greg turns to me with furrowed eyebrows. "You're mean. I was dreaming about riding a nice boat in the deep sea."

Jade laughs as she gets up and comes to give me a hug. "Good morning, baby. How was your night?"

I start eating my eggs as I tell her that my night was good. Her and Greg each grab their biscuits and start eating, too. Before either of them have finished their biscuit, I finish my eggs and start eating my sausage.

As soon as I bite into it, the grease runs from the patty into my mouth. "Mmm... this sausage is really freakin' good." I finish it after a few bites.

After I'm done with my sausage, I chow down on the biscuit and chug my milk that the nurse gave me.

When I finish everything, Jade looks at me with a bewildered look on her face. "You were hungry. Jeez. I've never seen you eat so fast in my life."

"I just ate so fast because the sooner I finish eating, the sooner we can leave after Dr. Drew comes in."

They both laugh at me as they finish their food. Once they're done eating, we sit and relax for a few minutes while we try to wake up. Greg stands up and yawns, stretching his arms out in front of him, and Jade sits up in the chair, stretching her whole body out before she stands up to stretch her legs some more.

Five minutes later, Dr. Drew comes in. "Good morning, everyone. How are you all feeling? Specifically, how are you feeling, Destiny?"

I tell him, "We're all doing great. We just finished our breakfast. I'm feeling fantastic this morning. Like I'm just seeing sunshine for the first time."

"That's great, Destiny. I want to check your vital signs so that I can make sure that everything is still going good and you can go home. Is that okay?"

He hooks me up to the blood pressure machine, placing the cuff on my right arm. After he presses a couple of buttons, it starts tightening on my arm. It takes about twenty seconds before it loosens back up and puts me blood pressure on the screen.

Dr. Drew looks at if for a second and tells me, "Well your blood pressure is a little bit high at 174 over118. But that's not bad considering you were recently diagnosed with high blood pressure. Now I'll check your heartrate and your breathing before I decide if you're ready to go home."

He uses the stethoscope for a few minutes as he checks me heart and breathing. After he's finished, he puts the stethoscope back around his neck and tells me, "Your heart sounds really good, and your breathing does, also. If you feel like you are ready, I can go down to the nurse's station and print out your discharge papers so that you can go home finally. Otherwise, you are more than welcome to stay and visit for a while longer."

I let out a laugh as I tell Dr. Drew, "No, thanks. I think that I have stayed more than long enough. Now it's time for me to go home with Jade and unpack my things finally and finish getting moved into our apartment."

He smiles as he tells me, "I will go get your discharge papers and be back in a few minutes if you want to go ahead and get changed out of the gown and get your things ready to go home."

After Dr. Drew leaves the room, I ask Greg, "Can you leave the room for a minute so I can get dressed? I'll be quick so you don't have to stand out there for too long."

"That's fine. Just holler my name when I can come back in." He walks out, closing the door behind him.

Jade comes over to the bed after Greg is out of the room and helps me stand up. She grabs my hand as I put my feet down and slowly get to a halfway standing position, my left leg propped on the bed in the cast.. As soon as I'm up on my right foot I can feel myself starting to wobble, but Jade grabs me before I can fall back onto the bed.

She holds me hand as she helps untie the hospital gown and pulls it off of me. Once the gown is off, she picks up my shirt and helps slide it over my head. I get the collar on and put my arms through the sleeves with somewhat ease. I get the shirt pulled down over my stomach as Jade picks up the sweatpants and carefully helps me get each leg into them. She pulls them up over my thighs and my butt and makes sure that they're all the way up to my waist.

After I've got my clothes all the way on, Jade smacks my butt lightly.

"There ya go, babe. You're all dressed and sexy. Are you ready for me to call Greg back in here?"

"Yeah. I can call him." I pause before calling him and give Jade a kiss. As soon as I pull away, I call out, "Hey Greg, you can come back in here!"

He comes back in a few seconds later. "How are you feeling? Still feeling okay, Destiny?"

"I am. I'm just ready to go home so that I can help Jade with unpacking some of my boxes and get moved in finally since I was supposed to do that a month ago. That way me and Jade can start our lives together and work our way to starting our future together."

A few minutes later, Dr. Drew comes back into the room with my discharge papers and a set of crutches.

"Here, Destiny. As soon as you sign these papers, you'll be free to go home."

I take the papers and place them onto the tray table and start signing them. As soon as I'm finished, I hand them back to Dr. Drew.

"Thank you so much for taking care of me this whole time. I hope that I won't have to come back again anytime soon. At least not for anything serious." I stand up and put my shoes on while Jade helps me keep my balance.

Once my shoes are on, Jade, Greg, and I go down to his car so he can take us home. The entire way to the car, both Jade and Greg hold onto me to make sure that I don't lose my balance.

As soon as we get to the car, Greg opens the door for the back seat and Jade helps me get in.

After they both get into the car, Greg starts driving down the road. Once we're on the road, Jade reaches over and turns the radio on. She turns it up and *Drops of Jupiter* by Train starts playing.

Jade and I start singing along to the radio as loud as we can. We sing to every song that plays on it until we get to the apartment building.

When we get there, Jade and Greg help me get out of the car and hand me the crutches that the hospital gave me. They help me stand up on the crutches and go upstairs to our apartment. When we get to mine and Jade's apartment unit, she unlocks the door and opens it.

I make my way into the apartment and go to the couch to sit down.

"Is it okay if I sit and rest for a few minutes before I come help with unpacking my stuff? My leg is killing me."

Jade looks at me and says, "Of course you can, baby." She turns to Greg and asks him, "Do you think that you could help me with starting to unpack Destiny's boxes? I would really appreciate it."

"I can, Jade. I'm your friend. I can help unpack everything. That way Destiny can just rest until she can get the cast off and be able to fully walk again. And that way you're not doing this by yourself."

"Thank you, Greg."

Before he and Jade go to my room and start unpacking, she comes over and places a pillow under my leg on the couch. "That way your leg is propped up at ease."

Jade's POV: After I get Destiny settled on the couch, Greg and I go into her bedroom to start unpacking her stuff.

"Let's unpack her clothes first to get them out of the way. If you want, you can do the shirts and I can do her pants and undergarments."

"I can put her shirts up. Do they all go in the closet? Or do some of them go in her dresser?"

I think for a second then tell him, "Everything except her tank tops and crop tops go in the closet. Here's a package of hangers for you to use."

I toss him the hangers and open the box that has Destiny's shirts in it before sliding it across the floor to Greg. He starts taking out shirts and putting them on hangers while I open the box that has her jeans and other pants.

After I get the box open, I start taking pairs out and start to organize them.

I put her jeans in one stack, then her shorts in another. Her leggings in the next stack with sweatpants and yoga pants beside them. The last stack I make, I put Destiny's pajama pants in.

Once I have them all organized, I put each stack of pants into their individual drawers. It takes me about twenty minutes total to get them all organized, folded, and put up.

When I go to open the next box, the one with Destiny's panties and bras, Greg comes over and asks me, "What drawer do you want me to put the rest of Destiny's shirts in?"

I point at the top middle drawer of the dresser. "That one. That's the only one that will be able to fit them in there.

"Got it. After I finish getting the shirts put up, what do you want me to do next?"

I look around the room for a few seconds before deciding what he can help with next.

"Hmm... You can help with unpacking her books and pictures. While you're doing that, I'm going to start unpacking her knickknacks and random things after getting her underwear into her nightstand. Do you think that you could also help hang the pictures up once you get them unpacked?"

As Greg starts bringing over Destiny's tank tops and crop tops, he tells me that he can. "Of course I can hang them up after I get them unpacked. Is there any particular way she would want them hung up? Any particular order? Or can I decide how they go on the walls?"

I laugh before saying, "I'll show you once you're ready to start hanging them. Because if they're put up wrong, she'll blame me."

After I tell Greg what to do after her shirts, I finish putting away Destiny's bras and underwear into their drawers, then grab a box that's full of various knickknacks, figurines, trinkets, etc.

I tear open the box and start organizing everything before I start placing them on her shelves and tables. I go through each thing and put them where Destiny would put them. By the time I finish setting them all up, it's taken me almost an hour.

When I'm setting the last figurine where it goes, I look up and catch Greg staring at me.

"What? Why are you staring at me?"

He smiles at me as he says, "I finished getting the books and pictures unpacked thirty minutes ago. I figured it'd be interesting to watch what you were doing until you were done, and it was. You being so meticulous with where each little thing goes. It was cute."

I give him a fake mean look when he calls me cute. "I am not cute. Besides, if I was, it's only for Destiny. Now first let's get the books alphabetized by title, but series together on their own shelves."

I spend the next hour and a half working with Greg to get all the books in alphabetical order on the shelves.

Once we're done with the books, I help him with the pictures and posters.

"Pictures of family and friends go on this wall next to the bed. The ones of her mom and dad go at the top, pictures of her grandparents and extended family go next, then pictures of family pets. On the other side of the wall is where the pictures of her friends go. Those can be in an assorted order on the wall."

Greg hangs up each picture where I tell him to and finishes this wall within twenty minutes.

We move to the next wall where I tell him, "This wall gets the framed paintings that she has. Portraits up top, images and landscapes in the middle, and abstracts at the bottom."

He hangs each one up as I tell him to until all the paintings are on the wall.

Then last, I show him where to hang up Destiny's celebrity posters that have pictures of hot actors and actresses and pictures of singers that she likes.

"These ones go by category: actors and actresses together by genre, and singers together by genre in their own section."

Once Greg finishes getting the pictures hung up, I help him unpack the couple of boxes that have her stuffed animals in them, placing them on her bed and on the backsides of the tables and dresser, in between the knickknacks.

"There. I think we've got everything. I'm going to let her worry about where she wants her makeup."

After Greg and I finally finish putting all of Destiny's things where they should go, we go back into the living room. As soon as we get in there, I see Destiny asleep on the couch, snoring quietly.

I look at Greg and put a finger to my lips, telling him to stay quiet. I grab a blanket off the ottoman and drape it over Destiny's sleeping body.

I whisper to Greg, "You can go home and get some sleep. I think I'm going to lay down on the other couch in here for the night. Thank you so much for helping me get her boxes unpacked. I really appreciate it, and I know she'll appreciate it when she sees her room in the morning."

"It's not a problem. You don't have to thank me. Text me or call me in the morning if you guys need anything. I mean it. Or even if you just want me here to pick on while you drink your coffee together. I'll be here."

He gives me a quick hug before walking out the door to go back to his apartment.

As soon as the door is shut, I go to my bedroom and grab a pillow and blanket before making my way over to the loveseat. I set the pillow down at the end before laying down for the night.

****

Destiny's POV: I wake up the next morning, opening my eyes to see that I'm in the living room at our apartment. I pull the blanket off myself as I look around the room.

When I look around, I see Jade laying on the other couch sleeping.

I grab the crutches and use them to help me stand up so I can walk over to Jade. When I get to her, I use one of them for support and bend over to give her a kiss on the lips. As my lips touch hers, her eyes flutter open.

I smile as I tell her, "Good morning, baby. How did you sleep?"

She sits up and says, "I slept amazing, babe. Now that your home, I'll be able to sleep great every night. I am so happy that you're here and okay."

"I am, too. You have no idea how glad I am to be awake, actually awake, and home with you finally."

Jade stands up as she says, "Do you want to come see your bedroom? Last night, Greg and I managed to get all of your boxes unpacked and everything put up. I tried to get everything put up how I know you would do it."

I put my crutches back under my arms and follow Jade over to my room. She turns the light on when she opens the door and as soon as I walk through the doorway, my mouth drops.

"Holy crap, babe. This looks great. You guys even put my stuffed animals up right. Thank you so much for doing this. You know you didn't have to. I could have worked on this today after I woke up. It would have gotten done a lot slower, but I could have gotten it done."

"I didn't want you to worry about it after everything you've been through. I want you to be able to relax and let your leg heal as long as it needs to until you can be able to fully get around without my help. And that way you can try to start working on your writing, start working on getting your career up and going."

I walk into the room and look around at everything. "Thank you, baby. I see you already set up my laptop and notebooks on the desk. In order of which ones are the most important, too."

Jade walks with me to the desk and says, "Of course. I know how you like your things to be organized. We lived together in college. You have a specific way that you like everything, and I wanted to make sure that I organized your room the way that you would."

After I finish looking around my newly unpacked room, I follow Jade to the kitchen.

I sit down at the table while she starts making some coffee. "So baby, what do you want to do today after we drink coffee and eat breakfast?"

"We can go out to Shelby to visit the girls. We haven't seen them in a few months and they'd probably be happy to hang out. How does that sound, baby?"

I smile at Jade. "That sounds great, baby. Chloe, Deanna, and Terri will be happy to see us."

Jade starts making some scrambled egg, bacon, and toast for breakfast. She cracks the eggs into the skillet first and starts cooking them. As they cook, she opens the package of bacon and puts a few pieces into the other pan then turns on the burner.

After a few minutes, Jade finishes cooking the eggs and bacon, then puts the bread in the toaster to cook. When the toast is done, she grabs a knife and butters each piece.

I smile as Jade sets up our plates and gets our cups of coffee. She sets my plate down in front of me first, then sits down next to me with her plate.

I pick up my fork and start digging into the eggs. As soon as I put the first bite into my mouth, it starts watering from how fluffy and tasty they are. Each bite that I take makes my stomach feel happy.

"These eggs are so good, Jade. Thank you for making breakfast this morning." I pause to take a sip of my coffee. "And this coffee is amazing. What creamer did you use?"

Jade looks over at me as she swallows a bite of toast. "Thank you, baby. I used the Irish crème with some of the French vanilla creamer. I figured that we could have a simple breakfast, so I'm glad it tastes good."

"It's so good being able to eat food at home with you now, baby. I mean, I ate with you in the dreams I had while I was in the coma, but that wasn't real food. This is a thousand times better than any five-star food I could ever wish to have. Thank you so much. For everything you've done so far and everything you're going to do."

"I love you, Destiny. I have loved you since the day we met, even if I didn't realize how much I loved you back then. I would do anything for you. I will do anything for you. I just want you to be happy, baby."

I reach my hand over and place it on Jade's as I say, "I love you, Jade. I want to be able to make both of our dreams in life come true."

I finish eating my food after ten minutes, and grab my crutches to stand up, but as soon as I do, Jade stops me.

She points at the chair I was sitting in and tells me to sit. "I can throw your plate away and wash your fork and coffee cup. You just sit and look pretty. Is that okay, baby?"

"Fiiine. I'll sit on my ass and let you wash everything. But after your done washing the dishes, can I go to my room and get dressed by myself? I should be okay doing some things by myself, including walking."

Jade laughs. "You can. As soon as I finish washing the dishes and getting them put away."

After she says that, she grabs my plate and throws it away. She takes our forks and coffee cups over to the sink, then grabs the pans and spatulas she used to cook with and puts them in the sink.

I watch as she turns on the water and puts some soap on the sponges, scrubbing the grease off of each dish. Once she's gotten them all scrubbed with soap, she runs them under the water to rinse, then places them into the draining rack.

Jade walks back over to me once she's done with the dishes and gives me a kiss. "There, baby. Now you can go get dressed. I'll go to my room and do the same, and if you need any help with getting anything on, just call me."

I get my crutches and hop to my bedroom. When I get into my room, I hop over to the closet and start looking through my shirts.

I look through each shirt before deciding on a dark blue t-shirt that has a picture of a penguin sitting on an iceberg printed on it.

After I get the shirt out of my closet, I make my way to my bed. I sit down so that I can get the shirt that I'm wearing off and put on the penguin shirt.

Once I get the shirt pulled down, I hobble over to my dresser and get out a pair of underwear and a pair of yoga pants. I get out a pair of pink cotton underwear and a pair of black yoga pants.

I go back over to the bed and lean against it so that I can pull off the pants I'm wearing.

I grab ahold of the right pant leg and pull it off, then move my left leg as close to my body as I can so that I can pull it off.

Now comes the hard part: getting the other pants on.

I get my underwear and bend down as much as I can so that I can slide them over my feet and pull them up over my legs. Once I get them up to my thighs, I lay back on the bed and carefully put my legs up in the air so that I can pull them all the way up.

I finish getting my underwear on then slide my pants over my feet and carefully pull them up over my ass. I get a pair of shoes from next to my bed, then grab my crutches and hobble back to the living room.

When I get in the living room, Jade's sitting on the couch waiting for me.

I make my way over to her and ask, "Can you help me get my shoes on, baby? Then I'll be ready to head out to see our friends."

"Yes, baby. Sit down right there, and I'll help get your shoes on."

I do as she tells me to and sit down, leaning the crutches against the side of the couch. Jade grabs my shoes and puts them onto both my feet, then ties them for me.

"There you go, baby. Are you sure you're ready to go?"

I look at her with one eyebrow up as I say, "Yeees. I'm sure I'm ready to go. I want to go see everybody so that we can tell them what's been happening since we last saw them. I want to tell them about what all happened with me this past month."

"Okay, baby." Jade walks over to the counter and grabs her keys and wallet as well as my wallet.

I get up from the couch and go out the door with Jade behind me as she locks it.

When we get to the stairs to go down, Jade stops for a second and asks me, "Are you sure that you can make it down the stairs? I don't want you missing one with one of the crutches and falling down them."

"You can walk in front of me to make sure that nothing happens. I'll be slow and careful, though."

She lets out a sigh as she goes down the stairs in front of me. We spend the next thirty minutes going down the stairs as careful as we can. Once we get down the stairs, I follow Jade out to the parking lot and climb in the car with her help.

As Jade starts driving, I ask her, "Have you called or texted one of them to let them know that we're coming to visit? Or are you planning on surprising everyone?"

"You can call Chloe to let her know we're on the way. Just put it on speaker phone so we can both talk."

I pick up my phone and dial Chloe's number.

After a couple of rings, she picks up. "Hey! It's about damn time you called me. Where the hell have you been?"

"There's been a lot going on over these last couple of months. Me and Jade are coming to see you, Deanna, and

Terri for a little while. We can explain everything once we get there in about thirty minutes."

"Okay. I'll call them over to my apartment so that we can all hang out for the day. It better be a good reason that you guys haven't called or came to see us."

"Oh it is, don't worry. We'll see you guys soon."

I hang up the phone and set it down after Chloe and I finish talking.

I turn the radio up as I set my phone onto the seat next to me. The rest of the ride, Jade and I jam along to early 2000s rap music until we get to Chloe's apartment.

When we get there, Jade parks the car in front of the building and helps me get out of the car. I get my crutches situated under my arms and start walking with Jade inside. I follow her over to the elevator and we ride it up to the fourth floor.

Jade and I get up to Chloe's apartment, and she knocks on the door. Barely five seconds after Jade knocks on the door, Chloe opens it and lets us inside.

As we're walking through the door, she looks at me and asks, "What the hell happened to you, Destiny? Are you okay?"

I let out a laugh before saying, "It's a slightly long story. I'll explain to everyone once we get inside and say hi."

Chloe moves to the side and lets Jade and I in. "Okay. Well, Deanna and Terri are in the kitchen. You can sit down on the couch so that you can put your leg up, and we'll all come sit in there so you guys can tell us what happened."

Chapter Eighteen

I use my crutches to hop over to the couch and sit down as everyone comes to the living room. Jade sits next to me, and Chloe, Deanna, and Terri sit down on the other couch.

After everybody is in the living room, Chloe asks, "So what happened to you?"

I take a deep breath before answering her. "About a month ago, I got into a car accident with a semi-truck. I was having a really shitty day and got sent home from work for having a panic attack. I ended up in a coma and with a broken leg. I spent the last month in the hospital until I finally woke up from the coma yesterday morning. I'm okay now, though. I've just got to wait for my leg to heal all the way so that I can be able to walk again."

Deanna, Terri, and Chloe all look at me with worry on their faces.

Terri asks me, "Are you sure you're okay? Do you feel okay?"

"Yes. I feel okay. Jade and I also have some other news. Her and I are dating now."

"Holy crap! Are you serious!? When did that happen? I thought you guys were just moving in together?" Chloe asks me, her eyes widened.

Jade looks at me for a second before answering her. "This happened after Destiny had woken up briefly from the coma. She woke up and told me how she had dreamt that we were together and wanted it to be real, so she asked me to be her girlfriend and I said yes."

All three of our friends look at us for a second before they jump up squealing in excitement. They come over to the couch that Jade and I are sitting on and give us both hugs."

Deanna tells us, "I'm so happy for you guys. What are you going to do now? Are you guys going to move into the same bedroom at your apartment?"

Jade answers her with, "For now until Destiny's leg is healed and out of the cast, she's going to stay in her bedroom and I'll stay in mine. Afterwards, we'll probably alternate bedrooms. Sleep in my room one week, then stay in her room the next week."

Chloe turns to Jade and I and asks, "Do you guys want to do something to celebrate your new relationship? I can go open a bottle of wine and we can have a game night together. Board games, card games, the Wii..."

"That sounds like a lot of fun."

Chloe gets up and goes to the kitchen to grab the wine while Deanna goes over to the stereo and turns on some music. After Chloe gets the wine, she grabs five glasses and opens the bottle so she can pour some for everybody. Then she goes to the closet and pulls out the board games and card games.

"What do you want to play first? I have Monopoly, Sorry, Clue, Life, or Candy Land in the board games. I have Uno, Phase Ten, Cards Against Humanity, and a deck of playing cards in the card games. And for the Wii, I have Mario Kart, Wii Sports, Rock Band, and a few other Mario games. Choose your poison."

I look at Jade and she nods her head to tell me it's my choice. So I sit and think for a second before deciding on Uno.

"Let's play Uno first. That way I can kick all your asses."

Chloe gets the box of Uno cards and takes them out to start shuffling. She gets them shuffled a few times, then deals five cards out to each of us.

I pick up my cards to look at them after she's done and see that I have a red five, a yellow nine, a green two, a skip card, and a wild card.

Chloe tells me that I can go first since I just got out of the hospital and moved in with Jade. I look at my cards for a few seconds before deciding to play my yellow nine.

Next, Jade plays a yellow five, then Chloe plays a blue five. Deanna plays a blue six, then Terri plays a draw four on me.

"Ugh really, Terri? What the hell?"

She laughs as I draw my four cards begrudgingly.

We play for almost an hour before somebody wins. Jade ends up losing first, then Terri loses. Then it's just me, Deanna, and Chloe.

Chloe loses next, leaving just me and Deanna.

We go back and forth, playing card after card. Colors, wild cards, draw fours, until I end up having three cards left, and Deanna one.

The last card that she played was a red eight. I have a green ten, a green six, and a blue eight. I put down my eight and watch as her mouth drops.

"You son of a bitch!" Deanna throws down a blue three.

I start cheering in victory. "Boo yeah! Boo yeah! Boo yeah! I won! You lost!"

Jade grabs me and hugs me close. "Hell yeah, babe! *You are the champion, and she is the loser!*" She sings a line from Queen's *We Are the Champions* mockingly at Deanna while she pouts.

We all spend the next few hours playing games and drinking wine until we start getting tired. By then, it's already past midnight, and none of us are in any kind of state to be driving home. We probably drank four bottles total while playing games.

Once we're finally done playing games for the night, Chloe tells Jade and I that we can sleep in the spare bedroom, and Terri and Deanna can sleep in here on the couches.

Jade helps me wobble my way to the bedroom, trying not to fall over her own feet and puts me under the covers before she lays down next to me. As soon as she gets in the bed, I wrap my arms around her, pulling her close.

****

Destiny's POV: The next morning, I wake up to see Jade still lying next to me in the bed. I smile as I lean towards her and plant a sweet kiss on her lips. As soon as I do, her eyes open slowly.

"Good morning, baby. How did you sleep?"

She turns and looks at me with her beautiful eyes as she says, "I slept wonderfully, baby. I loved having you next to me all night in my arms. Were you able to sleep well?"

I wrap my arms around Jade, hugging her close to my body. "I slept great, baby. Having you by my side all night was amazing. It felt just like it did in my dreams. Like I was sleeping next to the love of my life for the first time."

Jade stands up from the bed to stretch before helping me up and handing me my crutches. Once I'm up and stable, we both go out to the living room to see if everybody else is awake yet.

When we walk out to the living room, Terri is the only one already up and awake.

"Good morning, guys. How are you both feeling? Did you get plenty of sleep and rest?"

I make my way over to the couch that Terri slept on and sit down before answering her questions. "We slept really well, and we're feeling great. I'm feeling great. My leg is a little sore, but I'll be okay."

Terri stands up and goes to the kitchen as she says, "That's really good. Do either of you want some fresh coffee to help you wake up? Or do you just want some water or tea?"

Jade goes to the kitchen with her and helps get down a couple of coffee mugs. "We'll do some coffee, babe. I can help you pour them and get them mixed if you want. That way you can sit back down with your coffee."

Terri nods her head and hands Jade the coffee pot before coming back to the living room to sit with me on the couch. When she sits down, Terri looks at me with a slight worried look on her face.

"Are you sure you're okay?"

I turn my torso slightly so that I can look at her. "I'm sure I am okay. It honestly just feels like I was asleep for a while and woke up with a broken leg and slightly bruised ribs. But seriously, I'm okay. I am going to have to go back to see the doctor in a couple of weeks to check on my broken leg and change out the cast, though. But so long as I don't suffer any more head trauma, I should be okay."

Jade comes into the living room with our coffees and hands me mine before she sits down next to me and Terri.

After she sits down, Terri asks us, "Are you guys excited to be in a relationship and not just friends anymore?"

Jade and I both smile brightly at her as I tell her, "We really are. When I first asked her to be my girlfriend and she said yes, I knew that this was going to be the best thing that I ever did. In fact, when I asked her, she said yes almost immediately. It was the most wonderful feeling in the world."

"I'm so happy for you guys. You both look so cute and so happy together."

Jade blushes, her cheeks turning a warm shade of pink. "Thanks, Terri. We are so happy, and so excited to be starting our lives together as more than just friends."

As Terri, Jade, and I continue to talk about us being girlfriends now, Chloe comes out of her bedroom.

She walks into the living room where we're all sitting. "Good morning, everyone. Well, almost everyone." Her eyes dart over to where Deanna is still laying on the other couch passed out.

She makes her way closer to the couch and leans down next to Deanna's head before opening her mouth, yelling, "Ollie Ollie oxen free! Wake up!"

Deanna darts up quick as a bullet and smacks her head on Chloe's forehead. Chloe jumps back, grabbing her head with her hand.

"Ow! You hit my forehead!"

"I wouldn't have hit your fucking forehead if you wouldn't have yelled in my ear. What the hell was that for anyway? I was still sleeping."

"Exactly. Everybody else is awake, therefore you have to get your lazy ass up." Chloe pushes Deanna's legs off the couch and sits down next to her.

After Chloe sits down, Deanna sits up and rubs her head. "Is there any coffee? I am going to need some to try and help this headache go away. Do you need any, Chloe?"

Terri points to the kitchen. "In there. Her coffee cups are in the cabinet in the corner."

Deanna leaves to the kitchen and gets her and Chloe each a cup of coffee to drink and comes back a few minutes later.

She hands Chloe her coffee and sits down before asking all of us, "So what are we going to do today? I've got to go to work at one, so I'll have to leave around twelve. That way I can have time to go home and get ready."

Terri answers her first with, "I'm probably going to go home around twelve too so that I can work on some laundry and run some errands that I have to do." She turns to Jade and I and asks, "What about you two? What are you guys going to do for the day?"

I look at Jade before answering her question. "We're probably going to go home for a little while, then call a new friend that Jade met when I was in the hospital and ask him to come hang out for a bit."

Deanna is the first person to look at us and ask, "Who is this friend and how did you meet him?"

Jade tells her, "I met him the first night that Destiny was in the hospital when I was leaving to go home. I was a mess of emotions and he saw me sitting outside crying and stopped to ask me what was wrong. I told him about what happened to Destiny, and he offered to take me to his apartment so that I wouldn't be by myself.

Me and him became close friends and he spent every day with me while I was visiting Destiny and waiting for her to wake up. I found out shortly after I met him that he was actually one of the cops who showed up at the accident."

When Jade finishes talking, Deanna tells her, "That's pretty cool. But what I want to know is why the hell didn't you call any of us after Destiny was in the accident and in the hospital, heh? We would have been there for you."

"I know, I know. But I didn't want to bother you guys since we hadn't called any of you to talk or hang out in a few months."

Deanna looks at her and says, "Listen girl, I love you. Both of you. All three of us love you guys. Don't ever think that because you hadn't called or we hadn't called that you don't have us as a support system. Because if anything ever happens, big or small, we will be there. Just like I know you will be there for us."

Jade and I smile at all of them. "Thank you, guys. We promise to never do this again. In fact, if you guys want, when we all have free time, we can introduce you to our new friend, Greg."

Chloe takes a sip of her coffee. "That sounds great, babe. We would love to meet this mystery support man. Hopefully we'll like him as much you both do."

I laugh as I tell her, "You should like him. He's a pretty cool guy. And it's fun to pick on him and give him shit. It's kind of like having a brother."

As soon as I say this, Chloe, Terri, and Deanna all look at me before they all say, "Call him now."

Jade looks at each of them to see if they are being serious before she gets out her phone and starts dialing Greg's number, putting it on speaker phone.

After two and a half rings, he answers the phone with a groggy, "Hello?"

We all get close to the phone as we say together, "Hi, Greg!"

"Whoa! Who all is this? Is that you Jade?"

"It's me, Destiny, and our friends that we want you to meet. This is Chloe."

Chloe grabs the phone. "Hi, Greg. I'm Chloe. Here's Terri."

"Hi, Greg. Terri here. Now for Deanna." She hands the phone to Deanna last.

"Hi, Greg. I am Deanna. Were you good to Jade while you were with her visiting Destiny in the hospital?"

He chuckles quietly. "I was. I made sure that she was okay every day. I was there any time she needed me. And after Destiny woke up, I was with both of them, and they were both mean to me."

Jade laughs as she tells them, "Destiny was mean to him first, threatening that we were going to do things during the night that he might not want to see."

Chloe speaks next, saying, "Well that just shows that she accepted you as one of us. Being mean is a part of being friends with them as well as the rest of us. In fact, this morning I woke up Deanna by yelling in her ear."

"Yeah, and my head's still ringing, thank you very much." Deanna sticks out her tongue at Chloe.

Greg laughs at all of us as he says, "Well, I can't wait to meet all of you in person. You seem like really fun girls."

Terri, Deanna, and Chloe all chime in with, "Thank you!"

Terri tells him, "Maybe this weekend, we can all go out for drinks together. Have a getting to know each other get together at the bar."

"Maybe. I should be free this weekend."

Jade and I both say, "That sounds good, Greg."

I tell him, "We'll let you go for now so that you can get back to sleeping or get started on your day with whatever you need to do today."

"Okay. Well, it was really nice meeting all of your friends, and I can't wait to meet them in person this weekend."

We all tell him bye before Jade hangs up the phone. "Did you all like Greg from what you heard of him through the phone call?"

Deanna says, "I did. He seems like a really nice guy."

Terri pipes up with, "He seems like he's a really good friend to you guys. I'm glad that you met him and he was able to be there for both of you while Destiny was in the hospital."

Chloe tells us, "Yeah, he seems like he'll be a great friend to all of us. And he definitely sounds like he'll be a lot of fun to pick on and make fun of."

I laugh after she says that. "Oh yeah. Hell, after I had teased him about Jade and I possibly doing things during the night, he turned dark red and got all quiet."

We all continue talking about Greg and how we plan on picking on him once we hang out this weekend and all start hanging out together. We talk and drink coffee for a few hours before Deanna and Terri have to leave so that they can get ready for work.

After they leave, Jade helps Chloe put up the pillows and blankets that Terri and Deanna slept on the couches with. Then she goes to the room we slept in and makes the bed while Chloe washes up the coffee cups that everyone used.

I sit on the couch with my leg propped up while they are both cleaning everything.

They both finish with everything at around twelve thirty. When Jade gets done, she comes over to me and gives me a kiss.

"Are you about ready to go home, babe? That way we can get ready to go see Greg for a little while before I have to go talk to my manager about coming back to work?"

I sit up on the couch, putting my feet on the ground and tell her, "I am, baby. Besides, I need to get a shower before we go see him. Because I feel gross."

Jade helps me stand up and get my crutches, and Chloe comes over to give us hugs before we leave.

"Bye, guys. I hope you have a good day. Call me later when you get a chance to. That way we can decide what time we're all going to meet up at the bar with Greg on Saturday."

Chapter Nineteen

Jade and I leave Chloe's apartment and we ride for about twenty minutes until she asks me, "Do you want to go get something to eat for lunch, baby? Because I'm getting a little bit hungry."

I turn in my seat to look at her and say, "We can, baby. What are you feeling up to eating?"

"We can stop at Valerie's Diner and eat some sandwiches and fries. Possibly get a couple of milkshakes to eat. How does that sound, baby?"

"Let's go. Valerie's has great food, and fantastic milkshakes. Especially since she puts extra chocolate syrup in them."

Jade drives for a few more minutes before she pulls into the parking lot in front of Valerie's diner. As she gets the car pulled into a parking spot, she puts it into park and turns it off.

After she gets unbuckled and gets out, she comes over to my side and opens my door to help me climb out and get standing with my crutches. We walk slowly to the front of the diner and Jade grabs the door, letting me walk in first.

We go in and are greeted by Sally, one of the waitresses.

"Good afternoon, gals. Y'all can take a seat anywhere and I'll be right over to take your drink orders."

Jade and I go over to a booth next to the front windows where she helps me get seated. I pick up the menu in front of me and look at the lunch menu for a minute, scanning over each item.

After looking at it for a few minutes, I decide on getting a Pepsi to drink with a toasted ham and cheese sandwich and an order of fries with ranch dressing on the side. I set my menu down after deciding what I want, and sit while I wait for Jade to figure out what she wants.

Sally comes back after a few minutes with a notepad and asks us what we want to drink.

"I want a Pepsi, please. What do you want, baby?"

Jade sets her menu down and tells Sally, "I'll take a diet Dr. Pepper."

"Okay, sweeties. Are y'all ready to order your food yet, or do you need a few more minutes to decide?"

Jade turns to me and says, "I know what I want, baby. Have you decided what you want to order yet?"

I smile at my baby before looking over to Sally to tell her, "I'll have a toasted ham and cheese sandwich and fries with a side of ranch dressing. What do you want, baby?"

"I'll take a grilled chicken quesadilla with a side of tater tots."

Sally writes down both of our orders. "I'll be right back with your drinks and your food, ladies. If you need anything else before I come back, you can come to the counter and let Jeff know."

After Sally leaves with our orders, I reach across the table and grab Jade's hand. "I love you so much, babygirl. I still can't fucking believe that we are together and are going to start our lives together."

"As soon as we get home, I am going to treat you like the queen you are. I'll pamper you, help you shower, and do whatever you want to make you feel good, baby. I just want to make sure that you are happy and okay. I love you so much, baby."

I pull her hand across the table and kiss it softly. "You are amazing. You have been making me so happy every day. Especially since I was dreaming about us every day while I was in the coma. It was amazing getting to spend every day with you in my subconscious, and it felt so real. And now it is real. It's absolutely amazing."

Jade gives me a big smile as she says, "I want to do everything I can to make your dreams become reality. How does that sound, baby?"

"It sounds amazing, babe. I love you so much."

As Jade and I continue talking, Sally comes back to the table with our food.

"Here you go. Your toasted ham and cheese with fries, and your grilled chicken quesadilla and tater tots. Enjoy your food. If you need anything, just find me at the counter and ask."

I grab my sandwich and bite into it, the warm cheese melting in my mouth as I eat it. While I eat the sandwich, I look towards Jade and see her eyes closed in satisfaction as she's eating her quesadilla.

She looks so cute, enjoying her food. I can't believe how cute she is.

"What? Why are you staring at me like that?"

My face grows warm as I beam at her. "You are just so darn cute, baby. I just love looking at your beautiful face, especially when you're eating."

She grins at me, looking as happy as she can be. "I love you so much, sweetie. You are the best girlfriend I could ever have. You are absolutely amazing."

As we both finish our plates of food, Sally comes back over to take our plates and asks, "Do either of you want something for dessert? We have cakes, sundaes, milkshakes, and brownies. A variety to choose from."

"We'll both have a chocolate milkshake with chocolate crème."

Sally smiles at me as she tells us she'll be right back with our milkshakes.

Jade and I both spend the next few minutes staring into each other's eyes while we wait for Sally to come back with our milkshakes.

As soon as she's back with them, we start drinking our milkshakes through the straws. While we are both drinking our milkshakes, we sit and continue staring into each other's eyes.

I finish mine within fifteen minutes while staring seductively into Jade's eyes.

She finishes hers shortly after I do, and asks me, "After we pay for our food, do you want to go home and get that shower? Then have a little careful fun in the bedroom?"

I bite my lip slightly before telling Jade, "Oh yes, baby. I would love that a lot."

Jade gets up after I say that and takes her debit card to the counter to pay for our food and dessert. When she gets back, she grabs my hand and helps me get my crutches to walk out to the car.

As soon as Jade gets me in the car and gets behind the wheel, she hauls ass down the highway to go back to our apartment.

We make it back in less than ten minutes. She helps me out of the car and back up the stairs to our apartment.

When we get inside, I go to the bathroom so that Jade can get the shower started. I sit on the toilet lid while she turns on the water and waits for it to get warm.

After a few seconds, Jade pulls my shirt up over my head and pulls it off. She undoes my bra, then moves down to my pants and underwear. I lift my butt up so that she can get them off me, then watch as she slides them carefully off of my legs. Then she grabs a plastic wrap that the hospital gave us for my cast and wraps the plastic around my leg.

She finishes with me before taking off her clothes. She pulls her shirt off over her head, slow and sensual. Then she takes her bra off and slides her leggings and panties off of her butt, letting them fall to her ankles before she takes them all the way off.

As soon as we are both completely undressed, Jade helps me climb into the shower.

"Do you want to wash my hair, baby, and I wash yours? Or do you want us to each wash our own hair?"

Jade looks at me with a sexy darkness in her eyes. "We can wash each other's hair. I'll wash yours first, then you can wash mine. After the shampoo is gone, we can wash each other's bodies together. Does that sound good, babe?"

"Oh, yes."

I lean against the wall while Jade gets the shampoo bottle, squeezing some out into her hand. She rubs her hands together to lather it up before starting to rub it into my hair.

She runs her fingers through my it, massaging my scalp to make sure that it goes all the way through every strand. Once she gets the shampoo massaged all throughout my hair, she grabs the sprayer and slowly rinses the shampoo out until it's completely gone.

Then she does the same with the conditioner until my hair is completely clean. By the time she has finished washing out my hair, my brain and my mind feel completely relaxed.

As soon as she's done, I wash Jade's hair, massaging the shampoo and conditioner through her hair and against her scalp. I lather the shampoo deeply into her hair before using the sprayer to rinse it out. I run my fingers through her hair until there are no bubbles left in it.

Once I am done, Jade looks at me and asks, "Are you ready for me to wash your body off? Or do you want to wash me off first?"

"You can wash me off first, then I'll do you, baby."

As I say this, Jade picks up the bottle of body wash and squeezes some out into her hands. She then proceeds to rub her hands across my entire body, soaping it up. She squeezes my breasts with her hands as she puts soap on them, rubbing my nipples slightly, before she runs her hands along the entire length of my body.

Once she finishes washing my body, she puts her hand between my legs and starts massaging my pussy with her fingers. Her fingers move in and out of me slowly as she washes me. They feel so amazing inside me as she moves them in and out.

Jade keeps doing this for a few more minutes before she grabs the sprayer and rinses the soap out of me.

"How did that feel, baby? Did it feel good?"

"Oh yes, babe. It felt so fucking good." I take a deep breath through my mouth before asking her, "Are you ready for me to wash off your body?"

She smiles at me, nodding her head as I grab the body wash and start to wash off her body.

I soap up her entire body, rubbing my hands across every inch of her skin. I massage the soap onto her breasts and torso before starting to rinse it off of her. Then I use my fingers and slide them between her legs and slowly push them inside her pussy, moving my fingers back and forth slowly until I have tickled her g-spot.

When I'm done, I rinse the soap off of her entire body and use the water to rinse out inside her.

Jade turns the water off after I'm done and helps me climb out of the shower. She grabs the towel off of the hook and dries my body off before drying herself off. We both get dried of, then Jade helps me make my way to my bedroom and helps me onto the bed.

As soon as we're both on the bed, Jade starts to kiss me. Her lips so warm and soft against mine. She moves her body carefully with mine as our bodies start to grind against each other. Her legs spread open, letting me rub my pussy against hers as our bodies move with each other.

I kiss her neck, my lips moving up and down every inch as her head tilts back in ecstasy. Her fingers move down and slide inside me as she starts to finger my insides.

After what feels like hours, we both orgasm from each other's touch and lay next to each other on my bed, breathing heavily.

I turn towards Jade and tell her, "I love you so fucking much, babygirl. That felt so amazing."

"I love you too, baby. How do you feel?"

A smile covers my face. "I feel fantastic, baby. Your touch felt wonderful on my skin. It was just how I imagined it in my dreams."

We lay with each other on the bed for a few more minutes before Jade gets up and gets us both some clothes. She helps me get dressed first, then gets her clothes on.

As she finishes pulling her pants up over her cute butt, she asks me, "Do you want to go sit in the living room and watch a movie, snuggling under a blanket?"

I sit up and grab my crutches. "Yes, baby. What do you want to watch?"

"Can we watch Beauty and the Beast? It's my favorite and we haven't watched it in a while."

"Of course. I can go in there and turn it on while you make some popcorn and a fresh pot of coffee. That way we'll have tasty movie snacks and something to keep our insides warm."

Jade helps me make my way over to the couch and hands me a blanket and the remote so that I can find the movie and turn it on. Once I'm comfortable under the blanket, she goes to the kitchen and gets the popcorn in the microwave before starting pot of coffee.

After she finishes getting the popcorn and coffee ready, Jade comes and sits next to me with a bowl of popcorn and two mugs of sweet coffee. She sets the coffee cups down on the table in front of the couch and places the bowl of popcorn in between us as the movie begins.

We lay together, spending the next few hours watching the movie together until it's over.

As soon as it's over she turns on Toy Story, and we end up having a Toy Story movie marathon, watching all four of them for the rest of the night.

****

When Jade and I finish watching the movies, I let out a yawn and tell her, "I'm ready for bed. Are you, baby?"

"Okay, babe. Your room or my room?"

I think for a second before telling her, "Let's sleep in your room tonight. Tomorrow we can sleep in my room. Just so long as we're next to each other, I'll be happy."

Chapter Twenty

Jade's POV: I wake up the next morning and turn onto my side to see my baby laying next to me, and I smile as soon as I see her beautiful face. I continue to lay on the bed gazing at Destiny's sleeping figure for another twenty minutes before I decide to get up and go make some coffee along with cinnamon rolls and bacon for breakfast.

I move the covers off of myself slowly so as not to wake her up. I put on my fuzzy slippers once I am standing and quietly pad out of the bedroom, closing the door behind me. Once the door is all the way closed, I make my way into the kitchen and go over to the counter.

When I get into the kitchen, I grab the coffee pot and fill it up with water, then fill the filter in the machine with coffee grounds. After I get the machine started, I open the fridge and take out a roll of cinnamon buns and a new pack of bacon.

I grab the cast iron skillet and turn on the front burner to get it warmed up while I get the bacon open. I plop a few strips into the pan, then turn the oven on and get a baking sheet out of the cabinet.

While the bacon is cooking, I pull the tab on the package of cinnamon rolls and open them as quiet as I can, trying not to let the package pop too loudly. Once I get them open, I pull them apart and place them in rows on the baking sheet and put it in the oven.

After getting the cinnamon rolls in the oven, I get a paper plate and use a spatula to get the bacon out of the pan and place them onto the plate. I put a few more pieces of bacon into the pan and let them cook for a few minutes until they are nice and crispy like the others, then put them on the plate.

While the cinnamon rolls finish baking in the oven for the next ten minutes, I sit down at the kitchen table and put on some music from YouTube on my phone. I search up the song *With Arms Wide Open* by Creed and hook it up to my Bluetooth speaker. As soon as the song starts playing, I begin singing along with it, singing as loud as I can.

Not even halfway through the song, I hear Destiny coming out of the bedroom on her crutches. When I look up at her as she enters the room, I see a big ol' grin on her gorgeous face.

"Were you trying to serenade me awake, babe? Because it worked. What are you in here doing?"

I stand up from the table and walk over to my baby, my arms wide open as I say, "I'm just cooking us some breakfast. Cinnamon rolls and bacon. And coffee. Would you like me to make you a cup?"

Destiny nods her head as she sits down in one of the chairs, leaning her crutches against the table.

I grab her favorite coffee cup, the one that's shaped like the face of a sloth, and pour some coffee into it. I get the French creamer out of the fridge and pour some into the cup until the coffee is a light brown color. I add a few spoonfuls of sugar to it, then mix it with the teaspoon and take it over to Destiny.

After I give her her coffee, I grab a couple of pot warmers from the drawer next to the oven and get the pan of cinnamon rolls out. I set them on the stovetop and grab the package of icing to squeeze onto each of them.

I finish icing the cinnamon rolls and grab a couple of them to put onto a plate for Destiny. I put a few slices of bacon for her, then get a fork and bring the plate to her.

"There's your breakfast, baby. I'm going to get mine, then I'll be right over to sit and eat with you."

"Okay, baby. No hurry." She takes a bite as I go to make my plate. "This is great, babygirl. You know how much I love cinnamon rolls."

I finish making my plate, then sit down next to Destiny. "Thank you, baby. I figured that you would like having this for breakfast instead of just eggs and bacon or sausage. I just want to make sure that you are happy."

I grab my fork and start eating my food with Destiny while music continues to play from my phone.

We listen to Linkin Park, Journey, Queen, Black Sabbath, and others the entire time we eat, singing together between bites of food. As I'm eating the last bite of food from my plate, *Faithfully* by Journey starts to play.

With each lyric, we both look into each other's eyes deeply.

This song makes me feel so happy now that I am with my baby. It shows everything that I feel for her with each and every word, and it makes my heart feel so warm and happy.

After a few minutes when the song ends, I reach across the table and grab Destiny's hand in mine. "You make me so happy. Right now I feel so much in love, I can't freaking believe it. Being with you these last few days has made me feel so much closer to you than I have ever felt with anyone else in my entire life.

"I cannot picture my life ever not being with you because you are the one person for me. The one woman for me. I just want to spend the rest of my life with you until the day we die in each other's arms."

As I continue to hold Destiny's hand in mine, I lean down and kiss the back of her palm.

"Destiny baby, I know that you have only been awake for two days from the coma, but I want to ask you something? I want to ask you if you will be mine forever. My woman. My queen. My forever. I want to ask you for your hand in marriage."

Her eyes look at me, getting wider with each word that comes out of my mouth. Her mouth slowly drops open, an expression of shock and pure happiness covering her entire face.

A few minutes after I finish speaking, she grins the biggest smile that I have ever seen on her face.

"Yes, baby! Yes! I will absolutely give you my hand in marriage. I don't care that you didn't give me a ring, or if you ever do. You make me so fucking happy. This is so much better and more intimate of a proposal than I ever could have imagined. I love you so goddamn much! You are so fucking amazing, and the best woman I could have ever wished to be with. I would love to spend all of forever with you."

I smile the biggest smile as soon as Destiny finishes speaking. "You are so fucking amazing. I can't believe everything that has happened. I can't fucking believe that you said yes!"

My eyes fill with tears as I jump up and wrap my arms around my babygirl. I nestle my head in her shoulder and start to sob tears of joy. I hug Destiny as tight as I can before letting go a few minutes later.

"You have been the best thing to ever happen to me. I love you so, so much, baby, and I cannot wait to spend the rest of my life with you by my side."

After we stop hugging each other, I grab a couple of napkins from the table for Destiny and I to use as tissues. I hand her one as I use mine to blow my nose, snorting like an elephant as I do.

She lets out a laugh at my snort, and I laugh with her until I can't breathe.

When we're both finally able to catch our breath a few minutes later, I look at Destiny with the biggest smile on my face. I can feel my cheeks turning a rosy shade of pink as I look into my baby's face.

"I love you so fucking much, baby and can't wait to celebrate our future together with you. To be able to work towards having the perfect life with you."

She smiles back at me, her face the most gorgeous shade of pink in the kitchen light. "I love you with all my freaking heart. We should call the girls and Greg to tell them that we have something to celebrate."

I nod my head in agreement as I pull out my phone to start calling everyone.

I dial Deanna's number first and put it on speaker while I wait a few rings before she answers.

When she picks up her phone, she answers by saying, "What's going on, girlfriend?"

Destiny and I both smile big as we squeal into the phone, "We have some exciting news that we need to tell everyone, but we all need to get together so we can tell you guys."

"Okay. I can come hang out after if get off at five. Does that work for you guys?"

Destiny tells her she can meet us at Francisco's Italian Grill at six before I hang up the phone call and get ready to call Terri. As the phone is ringing, I can see the happiness radiating off of Destiny's face.

Terri answers her phone on the second ring with a, "Hello. What's going on, babes?"

"Hi, hun. Destiny and I were wondering if you could come out with us and everyone else tonight. We have some really fucking good news that we need to share with all of you. We already called Deanna, and she said she can go out after she gets off."

"Of course I can. Do you want to meet at Durk's Bar? Or where are you wanting to meet up?"

Destiny answers her, saying, "We're actually thinking of somewhere nicer, like Francisco's. Because tonight is going to be a celebration."

"Oh. Okay. Well I can definitely be there. What time are we all going?"

"Six o'clock."

Terri tells us that she will be there at six, then we get off the phone.

As soon as I hang it up, Destiny smiles at me and says, "Just two more people to call. Then we're going to have to go out for the day to celebrate by ourselves before we go out tonight. How does that sound, baby?"

I look at my baby and tell her, "That sounds great. What do you want to do to celebrate?"

She turns her eyes up in thought for a few seconds before she says, "Let's go downtown and see if there's anything fun to do over there for the afternoon. Possibly find something to buy each other as a symbol of our engagement, too."

"Okay, baby. Let's finish calling Chloe and Greg, then we can go get dressed and head downtown."

Destiny nods her head as I put Chloe's number in and wait a few seconds before she answers it.

"Hi, hun. What's up?"

I smile at Destiny as I say, "Destiny and I were wondering if you could meet all of us at Francisco's at six because we have something exciting we want to share with all of you. And it's not news that can be shared over the phone."

"I can. Is everything okay?"

"It is very okay. We'll tell all of you when we get to dinner and have glasses of wine."

"Okay. I can't wait to hear what your exciting news is."

Destiny gives me a big hug as we get off the phone with Chloe. Now it's time to call Gregory and ask him if he's okay with coming out and meeting everyone a night early. Because he's honestly part of the reason that Destiny and I got together, even if she was the one to ask me.

He's a big part of mine and Destiny's relationship coming to fruition, so he should be a part of our exciting news. Even if it might make him sad considering what he told me at the trial.

"Hey babe? Are you okay?"

My thoughts are broken by Destiny's sweet voice.

I look towards her as I say, "I'm okay. Let's call Greg."

I pull his number up on my phone and hit the start call button. I sit staring into Destiny's beautiful eyes until he picks up his phone."

"Hi, Jade. How are you doing this morning?"

"Hi, Greg. Destiny and I were wondering if you could come out to dinner at Fransisco's with us and the girls tonight? Because we have something we need to share with all of you, and it can't be over the phone."

"Uh, sure. I should be able to come to dinner."

"Okay. Well, we will see you tonight at the restaurant."

As soon as I hit the button to end the call, Destiny reaches over and wraps her arms around me in a hug.

I hug her back tight and give her a kiss on the cheek. "I am so fucking happy right now. I can't fucking believe that we are engaged to each other now."

Destiny lets out a laugh. "Well, you better fucking believe it, missy. Because it's true. We are engaged and we are going to be together forever, baby."

I lean my head back and give her a kiss on the lips. As Destiny kisses me back, I can feel myself melting into her lips.

My lips move with hers as we kiss each other with sweet, slow passion. The kiss moves into more than just a kiss, becoming a slow make-out session as we grope each other's bodies. I move my hands up and down her torso as we kiss, and her hands grab my hair as her fingers become tangled in it.

Our lips move together as we kiss each other, our hands moving all along both of our bodies until we are finally able to pull out of the kiss a few minutes later.

Destiny bites her lip as she smiles at me. "Let's go get dressed so we can go downtown and m celebrate before tonight's dinner."

I nod my head at her as I stand up and help her get the crutches so that she can stand up.

Once Destiny is on her feet, I follow behind her to her bedroom so that I can help her get dressed. When we get in there, she sits her cute butt down on her bed while I go to her closet to pick out a cute shirt for her to wear.

I look through her closet for a few seconds before deciding on a cute lacy purple top. Once I get it out of the closet, I set it on the bed next to Destiny and go to her dresser. I open a drawer and get out a pair of black leggings. Then I grab out a pair of hot pink satin underwear and a lacy black bra.

I bring the leggings, bra, and underwear over to Destiny and help her get out of her pajama t-shirt. As soon as it's off, I caress her breasts for a few moments with my hands before helping her get the bra and top on.

I pull the top down over her head, letting it slide down her body before I start to help her with getting the new pair of underwear and leggings on.

Destiny lays back on the bed, carefully lifting her butt up so that I can pull the underwear and pajama shorts she is wearing off of her. I grab the waistband and pull them off of her nice and slow, sliding them carefully off her legs over the cast on her left leg.

Once the shorts and underwear are off and on the floor, I grab the new pair of underwear and slide them over her feet and up over her butt. I then get the pair of black leggings and slide them over her feet and pull them up over her legs and her cute buttocks, squeezing it as I do.

After I finish helping Destiny get dressed, I help her go out to the living room while I get dressed.

I grab a blue t-shirt and tie dye leggings and change into them quickly before going to the living room with Destiny. I gather my keys and purse, then she and I head out the door.

We both make our way down the stairs slowly and get down to the lobby in ten minutes time.

When we get to the car and get in, I put the key in and start the ignition, the radio cranking up loud. Elton John's *Crocodile Rock* plays and we both start singing along with it.

We ride for about twenty minutes, singing as loud as we can along with the radio until we get there.

I drive over to The Cantina and park us close to the door. As soon as I get out, I go over and help Destiny get out of the car. We walk up to the door together and go inside where we're greeted by Frankie, the owner.

"Hello, ladies. I haven't seen you two around here in a while." He stops when he notices Destiny on the crutches. "What happened to you? Are you okay? Did she beat you up?"

Destiny smiles at him. "She didn't beat me up. Don't worry. I was in a bit of a car accident. That's why we haven't been coming around this last month. But I'm okay now."

"Okay. Well let me get you guys to a table so you can sit down and order your drinks."

Destiny and I follow Frankie over to a table near the bar and sit down.

He hands us each a menu before asking, "Do you know what you want to drink?"

I think for a second, then tell him, "I think I'll take a pink lemonade with a little extra sugar."

Destiny smiles at him as she says, "I just want a sweet tea with honey in it."

Frankie writes down our drinks as he says, "I will be right back with your pink lemonade and your sweet tea with honey."

Once he walks away, Destiny and I start looking over the menu.

"What do you think you're going to get, baby?" I ask Destiny.

"I'm looking at the burgers and the ranch burger with a side of curly fries is sounding pretty good right now. What about you, babe?"

"I'm thinking just the regular cheeseburger with lettuce, onions, and Swiss and cheddar cheese with a side of tater tots. That sounds pretty freaking good."

I set my menu down before asking Destiny, "Are you really excited that we're engaged, baby? Because I cannot wait for the day we get to say our vows and get married to one another."

Destiny looks up at me, her eyes shimmering in the light as she tells me, "I am beyond excited, babygirl. It will be the best day of my life. Right next to the day we first met in high school. Because I can still picture that day like it was yesterday."

I smile as I say, "Oh yeah. I was a mess that day. I remember that I dropped my books because I didn't have a backpack, and you offered to help carry them for me. Then after the day was over, you bought me a backpack from the dollar store down the road. I think I still have it, actually. It's buried in the back of my closet with everything from my last year in high school still in it."

"Damn. I thought that you would have thrown that old thing away after all these years."

"Of course not. It was the first thing that you ever gave me as a friend. I'm not letting it go. It will be buried with me when I die."

As we sit at the table talking about memories from being in high school together, Frankie walks over with our drinks in his hands.

"Here you guys go. Pink lemonade with extra sugar for you, Jade, and a sweet tea with honey for you, Destiny. Have you figured out what you want to eat yet? Or do you need more time?"

I turn to him and say, "I think we're both ready to order. I'll have the cheeseburger with lettuce and onions on it, Swiss and cheddar as the cheese, and a side of tater tots."

"I'll have the ranch burger with a side of curly fries, please."

After he writes our orders down, we both hand him the menus.

"Okay, ladies. I will get those out in a jiff."

After Frankie walks away, I tell Destiny, "I have kept every little thing that you ever given me since the day we met. None of it is ever getting thrown away. Especially now."

I laugh before I continue. "We'll have to get a bigger apartment so we can have a spare room for everything we give each other."

She laughs. "Oh, probably. But we can manage. For now it'll just have to look like an apartment that houses a couple of hoarders."

I smile at her when she says this. "You are absolutely amazing, baby. We will have the best life together, and I can't wait for the day that we get married in front of all our friends and family."

Destiny squeezes my hand in hers as she says, "It will be the best day ever. Nothing will be able to top it. And afterwards, we'll go on the best honeymoon. To Norway where we can see the snow and the northern lights shimmering in the night sky. We will be in a wooden cabin up in the mountains together where we can snuggle under a blanket in front of the fireplace together."

My cheeks turn a dark shade of pink as she describes our honeymoon. "That sounds wonderful, Destiny. How long have you been thinking about that for our honeymoon?"

"Since the moment you proposed to me. I think that I dreamed about wanting that for our honeymoon when I was in the coma, also. I just want it all to be perfect."

I stand up from my chair and go over to Destiny, giving her a kiss. Our lips press against each other's, moving together, as we kiss passionately for a few moments. My hands reach up and grab the sides of her head until we both pull away.

I sit back down in my chair as Frankie comes back over with our plates.

He sets each of them down in front of us. "Here you go, ladies. Enjoy the piece de resistance. If you need anything else, just holler my name."

Destiny and I start eating our food, savoring each and every bite of our burgers for the next twenty minutes. We eat each and every bite off our plates until they are empty.

As soon as we both finish our food, I go over to the bar and pay Frankie for the check, thanking him for the delicious food.

When I get back to the table, I help Destiny stand up, and we go out to the car.

"Where do you want to go now, darling? Anywhere special? Or do you want me to decide?"

She gives me a cute little grin as she says, "Let's go to the craft store. I want us to each pick out a cute, artsy ring for each other."

I grin back at her, the dimple in my right cheek showing. "Okay, baby. Let's take the car so you don't have to walk for very long."

We go out and get into the car, driving for a few minutes down the road until we reach the craft store.

As soon as we get there, we both get out of the car and go inside. Destiny starts walking towards the back where the craft jewelry section is. I follow behind her until she stops in front of a shelf filled with rings, bracelets, and necklaces.

I start looking through them with her, looking at all of the beautiful jewelry to choose from. I look at the rings, trying to find one that pops out and catches my attention.

They have gemstone rings, rings with animals on them, colorful rings made with lots of different colors on the band.

All of them are so beautiful, but none of them are really catching my eyes. At least not until I see one in particular.

A ring that has a violet gemstone on it with a green and blue band. It looks gorgeous. I pick it up from the shelf so that I can look at it more closely. The light inside the store bounces off of the stone as I hold it up, making it sparkle and shimmer brightly.

I smile as I ask Destiny, "What do you think of this ring, baby?"

She comes over to me and looks at it in my hands. "It looks beautiful, Jade. Is that the one you're getting for me?"

"It is. Have you found one for me yet, baby?"

Destiny reaches onto the shelf and picks up a ring. "This one. The fiery orange gemstone is what caught my eye because it matches your fiery spirit. Do you like it, baby?"

My face lights up. "I love it, baby. Do you like the one that I picked out?"

"I do. It's perfect and unique just like I am. It matches me just right. Do you want to go pay for them? Or do you want to keep looking at things?"

"We can go ahead and pay. That way we can go home and relax before we have to get ready for dinner out with everybody."

Destiny and I make our way over to the registers at the front and pay for our rings.

Once we finish paying for them and go out to the parking lot, Destiny stops me on the sidewalk with the ring in her hand.

She grabs my left hand in hers as she says, "Jade, I cannot wait for the day that we can stand in front of our friends and everyone when we get married. And I want you to wear this ring to show that we have made that promise to each other. Until I can put the wedding band on your finger."

I smile as she slides the ring onto my ring finger. "I love you so fucking much." I grab her hand as I tell her, "This ring represents my love for you and the promise that you have my love for all eternity. And then when we get married, I'll add your wedding band next to it."

Destiny smiles the biggest smile. She holds her crutches under her arms as she leans in and gives me a sweet kiss. "You are the love of my life, baby. I love you so goddamn much. Now let's go home so we can relax and get ready to go out and tell everyone about our engagement."

****

Destiny's POV: As Jade and I finish getting ready for dinner, I look over at her and smile. She's wearing a beautiful sapphire colored dress with her hair pulled up into a wavy bun on the back of her head. She has her black leather purse hanging over her arm as she walks over to me.

"You look gorgeous, baby. That little black dress is my favorite. And your hair looks amazing with it curled like that over your shoulders."

Jade grabs my purse from the counter and hands it to me. "Are you ready to leave, baby?"

"I am. We can go ahead and leave to meet everybody at Fransisco's."

Chapter Twenty-one

Jade and I get to Francisco's at around ten till six. We go inside to the host's stand and wait for a few moments before the host walks up to greet us.

"Hello. Would you like a table for two?"

I tell her, "We have four more coming soon, so we're a party of six."

"Okay." She grabs six menus and takes us to a table near the left side of the restaurant.

Jade and I sit down next to each other on the side facing the wall before she sets down the menus in front of each chair.

"What would you ladies like to drink?"

"Can I get a Dr. Pepper to drink?"

"Yes, ma'am. And you, ma'am? What would you like to drink?"

Jade tells her, "I'll take a Dr. Pepper as well. Also, can we get a bottle of strawberry wine for the table with six glasses?"

She smiles at us as she says, "Okay. I will be right over with both of your Dr. Peppers and the glasses and wine."

Jade and I sit together, listening to the soft music playing from the speakers until our friends get to the restaurant a few minutes later.

Chloe sits down next to Jade on the left side of the table. Greg sits on the right side across from me, and Deanna and Terri sit next to him.

Terri is the first to speak after everyone sits down. "Hi, guys. Do we get to find out what you invited us all out for? Or do we have to wait?"

The waitress comes over with mine and Jade's drinks along with the wine and glasses as soon as Terri says that. She sets the wine glasses in front of each of us before asking everyone else what they want to drink.

Terri eyes the bottle for a second before telling her, "I'll have a diet coke."

Deanna tells her that she wants a Pepsi. Greg asks for a coke, and Chloe asks for a Pepsi, also.

She writes their drinks down before she opens the bottle of wine and pours it into the glasses in front of each of us.

After she walks away, Jade and I pick up our glasses.

I smile before I tell everyone, "The news we have to tell you guys... This morning after breakfast, Jade asked me to marry her. This is a celebration dinner celebrating our engagement."

As soon as my mouth is closed, everybody's eyes widen.

Deanna opens her mouth wide before she says, "Oh my god! Holy crap! Are you serious?!"

Jade and I smile, our teeth showing as she says, "Oh, yes. She's serious. This afternoon we went downtown and bought rings from the craft store to be engagement rings."

Greg smiles at Jade and I. "Damn! I'm happy for you guys."

Chloe tells us, "Congratulations, you two. I never could have imagined before that you guys would end up together and engaged, and not just best friends. I can't believe this."

Terri grins as she says, "I can't believe that you guys are going to get married. Just the other day, we didn't even know that you two were dating, and now you're engaged. I'm so freaking happy for both of you."

Jade smiles at all of our friends. "Thank you, guys. We are beyond happy that we're engaged. And we bought the strawberry wine to toast with."

She lifts up her glass, and we all clink our glasses together as we toast.

All of our friends cheer, "To Destiny and Jade's engagement!"

Each of us take a sip before setting the glasses down.

Terri asks Jade and I, "When are you guys going to start planning?"

I look at Jade before I answer. "We'll probably start planning soon. We were thinking of having a Halloween themed wedding in October. We haven't really talked about any details yet except for what we plan to do for the honeymoon."

Chloe smiles and asks, "What do you guys want to do for a honeymoon?"

Jade tells her, "We were thinking about trying to go to Norway for a few weeks so that we can spend time skiing and see the Northern lights. We want to rent a wood cabin so that we can spend time in the evenings inside in front of a fireplace, staying nice and cozy."

Deanna's face lights up. "That sounds wonderful, babes. I'm sure you guys will be able to get there for your honeymoon."

A few minutes later, the waitress comes back with everybody else's drinks.

She sets them down, then asks, "Have you all had a chance to look at the menu yet? Or do you need a few more minutes?"

I tell her, "We still need a few minutes."

She nods her head, then walks away. I pick up my menu a second later and start to browse the options on the dinner menu.

There's steaks, chicken, pork. I look at the steaks, and they have filets, Porterhouse, New York strips, and a few other options. They all sound so good. After a few seconds of looking at the menu, I decide to get a 5-ounce filet with a baked potato and a Caesar salad.

Once I finish looking at the menu, I set it down in front of me and turn to look at Jade.

"Have you figured out what you want, baby?"

She sets her menu down and closes it. "I think so. I'll probably get the grilled chicken, green beans, and potatoes. What are you getting?"

"I'm going to get the 5-ounce filet, baked potato, and Caesar salad."

Jade squeezes my hand as everyone else sets their menus down. While we wait for the waitress to come back and take our orders, we all start talking about what we're going to do for wedding plans. What we want to do for the wedding.

Jade tells everybody, "I just want the wedding to be perfect. We'll probably have the ceremony in the evening time, close to dusk."

I nod my head. "It's going to be an outdoor wedding, probably somewhere surrounded by trees that we can hang lights in. Bat garland in the branches, a purple aisle runner with black lace on it."

Deanna smiles at both of us. "That sounds really nice. We'll all do everything we can to help get everything ready for your wedding."

After Deanna finishes talking, the waitress comes over with our food on a cart. She sets each of our plates down in front of us, giving Jade and I our food first. Then Terri, Deanna, Greg, and Chloe.

I start eating with everybody after we all thank her for bringing our food.

I cut my filet into bites before starting on my salad. I dig into the salad, the lettuce crunching as I chew each bite. The Caesar dressing coats each bite I take until I'm finished with the salad.

Once I finish the it, I move the plate to the side and start eating the cut up pieces of steak. It's nice, tender, and juicy. Cooked medium rare so that it's still a little pink in the center. Each bite is so soft and easy to chew.

I savor each bite of my juicy steak until it's gone.

I look in Jade's direction as I swallow the last bite of steak. "How's your chicken taste, baby?"

"My chicken was delicious. It was really juicy and tender. How was your steak and salad?*

I scoop up a bite of potato as I answer. "They were really good. My steak was medium rare, how I like it. It was juicy and tender, too. And the salad was really good."

Jade and I continue eating our food with everyone until we're all finished.

After everyone finishes their plates of food along with the drinks, the waitress comes over and asks if we want any dessert.

I ask her, "Can I get a slice of chocolate cake in a to-go box?"

"Yes, ma'am. Would you all like me to go ahead and bring the check over?"

"Yes, please. Can we split it into five checks?" I point at Jade before telling her, "One for both of our meals and one for everyone else's. And she'll pay for the strawberry wine."

She smiles at me as she says, "I can do that. I'll be right back with the cake and your checks."

Jade and I sit with everyone talking for a few minutes until the waitress comes back over with the checks and the to-go box with the cake.

As she hands the checks to each of us, we hand her our debit cards to pay for our meals.

A few minutes go by before she brings our cards back with our receipts. "There you go. Have a great evening."

"Thank you so much for the great service." I thank her as we all stand up to leave.

Jade helps me pull my chair out and stand up as she places my crutches under my arms. I turn to her with a warm smile on my face.

I love her so freaking much. I still cannot believe that Jade and I are really engaged to get married.

As I walk with everyone out to the parking lot, I stop for a moment before we split off to our own cars and say, "This was a really great night. A really great day. I'm so glad that you all are happy for us."

Chloe smiles as she tells me, "Of course we are. You guys are our best friends. I am incredibly happy for you two, and can't wait to see you get married to each other. I can only imagine what your future together is going to look like."

Jade wraps her arm around me and pulls me close. "I cannot picture a life without Destiny in it. Especially not a life without us being together. It's going to be amazing. "

"Yes, baby. We're going to have the best life together."

Chloe comes and gives us both a hug. "I am so happy for you guys."

Terri and Deanna walk over to Jade and I and wrap their arms around us in a big group hug.

Terri smiles brightly as she tells us, "You guys are perfect together. You were made for each other, babes."

"Yeah. You two are the only people that I could ever picture staying together forever."

Jade laughs happily as she says, "Thank you, guys. You're the best."

Greg walks over to Jade and I and tells us, "I can't ever picture you guys not making it together. Not after everything that you have already been put through. You're both strong and I know that neither of you will let anything get in your way."

"Thank you, Greg. You're a really great friend."

Jade and I give him a hug before we all say our goodbyes, then we all go to our cars to go home.

****

After we get home, my baby and I go to her bedroom for the night. I sit down on her bed while she goes to get me some pajamas from my room.

She comes back with a black t-shirt and a pair of red flannel pajama pants.

"Will this work, baby?"

I smile at her. "Of course, babe."

She comes over to where I'm sitting and hands me the t-shirt so that I can change into it.

I pull off the shirt I'm wearing and set it on the foot of the bed before putting on the t-shirt. Then Jade helps me stand up so that she can help me change my pants before she changes her clothes.

Once we're both changed a few minutes later, she helps me climb into the bed and under the covers.

She slides close to me and holds me in her arms as we both drift off to sleep.

"Goodnight, my sweet baby. I love you so freaking much."

I lean my head forward and give Jade a small kiss on the lips. "Goodnight, my love. I love you with all my heart."

I fall asleep a few minutes later, laying in my baby's arms.

****

The next morning, I wake up to Jade still laying in the bed asleep next to me.

I think to myself, *She looks so cute and peaceful like this.*

I get up from the bed as quietly and carefully as I can so as not to wake her. I grab my crutches once I'm up and go to the kitchen so that I can start a pot of coffee.

Once I'm in the kitchen, I go over to where the coffee pot is and start filling it with water. I fill it up to the twelve marker, then pour the water into the machine. Then I grab a coffee filter and place it in the basket and fill it with the coffee grounds.

After I hit the button to turn the machine on, I make my way to the living room and sit down, turning on *Friends*.

I lay back on the couch, propping my leg up with a throw pillow as I start watching the show.

I lay there watching the TV until I hear the coffee go off, letting me know that it's done brewing. When I hear it, I get up from the couch, grunting as I push myself into a sitting position. I grab my crutches once I'm sitting on the edge of the couch and use them to stand up.

When I get back into the kitchen, I grab down a couple of coffee mugs. I fill them both with coffee, then grab the creamer from the fridge. Once I finish putting creamer into both cups, I grab a spoon and scoop a few spoonfuls of sugar into each of them.

I grab my cup first and carry it carefully to the living room while I walk in there using my crutches. I set it down on the coffee table, then go back to the kitchen and grab Jade's cup to bring into the living room. I set it down next to mine and lay back on the couch again while I wait for Jade to wake up.

By the time she gets up and comes into the living room, I have finished almost the entirety of my first cup of coffee and watched almost three episodes on the TV. She comes over to where I am on the couch and bends over to give me a kiss.

"Good morning, babygirl. How was your night?"

I smile as I kiss her back. "My night was fantastic, getting to sleep next to you all night. I made you a cup of coffee, but it might need to be heated back up."

She picks up her cup of coffee and takes a sip. "Thank you, baby. It tastes really good, but I will go heat it back up. Do you want some more coffee?"

I hand her my cup. "Yes, please. Thank you, babe."

She goes to the kitchen to heat hers up and comes back a few minutes later with both cups in her hands.

"Here you go, sweetie." She hands me back my cup and I take a sip.

"Mmm, thank you, baby. This is good."

Jade sits down next to me on the couch and gets comfy. "You're welcome, baby. You just want to have a relaxing day before everyone comes over to hang out tonight?"

I wrap my left arm around her shoulder, squeezing her close. "Yeah. Just have a relaxing day watching *Friends* with my baby by my side."

She smiles as she says, "That sounds great."

I spend the rest of the morning and afternoon watching *Friends* on the couch with Jade, drinking coffee with her.

By the time 4:00 hits, Jade and I get up so that we can go to our bedrooms and get dressed and ready for everybody to come over around five.

I go to my closet and look through my shirts until I find my maroon colored Metallica t-shirt. I pull it off the hanger then sit down on my bed and change into it. Then I grab the crutches and make my way to my dresser.

I open the drawer that has my leggings in it and pull out a pair of dark violet ones.

After I pull out the leggings, I make my way over to my bed and sit down so that I can change my pants.

I grab the waistband of my pajama pants and pull them down off my butt, then pull the legs down and slide them off onto the floor. Once my pajama pants are off, I grab the leggings and slide them carefully over my legs and up over my butt.

I stand up once I finish pulling my leggings on and make my way back into the living room where Jade is sitting.

As soon as I enter the living room, I see Jade sitting on the couch, now wearing a royal blue shirt and black jeans.

I make my way over to her and sit down on the couch. "You look really great, baby."

She smiles at me as she says, "Thank you, sweetie. You look really great, too."

A few minutes later, a knock comes at the door. Jade stands up and goes over to it so that she can answer it. She opens the door and Deanna and Greg are the first ones to come inside.

"Hi, guys."

They both come inside and sit down on the other couch.

Greg speaks first after he sits down. "How are you guys doing today? Did you do anything fun? Or just hang out here?"

I tell him, "We just relaxed here all day watching TV and drinking coffee."

He nods his head in approval as another knock comes at the door.

Jade answers it and lets Chloe and Terri inside. After they're through the door, everyone sits down on the couches and chairs.

When everybody gets settled, Greg opens his mouth and asks the girls, "So what do you all want to know about me. I am an open book."

Terri asks him, "I was wondering, the night that you met Jade, you really just wanted to help her out and make sure that she was okay? Because most guys would have seen her and tried to take advantage of her."

He looks at Terri with an expression of honesty on his face. "I saw a woman who was obviously hurting and looked like she had no one to go to for support. I honest to god just wanted to make sure that she was okay and nothing would happen to her. Because I could see that she wasn't in a good enough mental state where she should drive herself home."

Terri nods her head at him. "Okay. That's really good that you did that for her even though you were complete strangers to each other."

Deanna pops in and asks, "Were you really one of the officers that went to the scene of Destiny's car accident after it happened?"

"I was. I was the first one there, actually. And the reason why I didn't tell her right away that I was one of the officers on the scene was because I didn't realize it until a few days after Jade and I met."

We all spend the rest of the night hanging out together and talking while the girls continue to ask questions to get to know Greg.

By the time it's 9:00, the conversation starts to taper off until everybody is ready to leave and go back home.

Jade and I tell each of our friends goodbye as they leave. After everybody is gone, we make our way to my bedroom and lay down for the night.

Neither of us worry about changing our clothes, and just climb into the bed and under the covers. Once we're both comfortable, Jade and I turn towards each other. We kiss goodnight, then close our eyes and fall asleep.

Chapter Twenty-two

Monday morning, I am woken up to the smell of a fresh cup of coffee. I open my eyes and see Jade sitting next to me on the bed with two cups of coffee in her hands.

"Good morning, babygirl. I made us both some coffee this morning. That way we both have energy fuel before we have to leave for your appointment at ten to see if your leg is finally healed enough to take off the cast."

I grab my coffee from her, cupping it in my hands. "Thank you, baby." I take a sip of it, letting the warm coffee run down my throat.

Jade and I sit on the bed together, drinking our coffee until we have to get ready to leave for my appointment.

After we both finish our cups of coffee, Jade gets up from the bed and grabs me a t-shirt and sweatpants out of my closet and dresser. She helps me get dressed, then helps me walk to the living room so I can wait for her to get dressed.

I sit on the couch, looking at Facebook on my phone until she comes out with the keys and our purses in her hand.

"Are you ready to go, babygirl?"

I grab my crutches and stand up as I tell Jade, "I'm as ready as I can be. I definitely hope that they can take this stupid cast off. Because I want to be able to start walking again soon."

She nods her head in agreement as she helps me out the door so we can go down the stairs to the car.

It takes fifteen minutes after we leave to get to the hospital for my appointment. Jade gets the car parked close to the door, then gets out so she can help me out of the car. She grabs my crutches from the backseat and helps me stand up with them.

We both make our way inside and I sit down in one of the chairs in the waiting area while she signs me in. When she finishes getting me signed in for my appointment, Jade comes and sits next to me.

I turn and look at her once she's sitting and ask, "Do you think that they'll be able to take this cast and bandages off today? Because I want to be able to finish healing from the stupid accident and put it behind us. Be able to start moving forward instead of worrying about if I'm okay all the time."

Jade gives me a serious look as she tells me, "I don't know if they are going to take it off today or not, but either way, we will start moving our lives forward. And maybe in a few months, we can try to take a trip and visit our parents in Scotland. See how retirement has been treating them."

I smile at her, thinking about how much I miss my mom and dad. "That sounds wonderful, baby. I would love that. In fact, after we get home from the appointment, we should both call our parents since it's been at least four months after the last time we called them."

Jade wraps her arms around me in a hug. "I love you so much, babygirl."

We sit with each other, leaning against one anther until a nurse comes out to call me back.

"Destiny Morgan? Are you ready?"

As my name is called, Jade helps me get standing with the crutches as we walk over together and follow the nurse through the doors.

She stops me in the hallway and tells me, "Please step onto the scale so that we can get your weight and your height. Then I will have you sit right here next to the scale and check your blood pressure."

I do my best to stand on the scale, using the crutches to prevent me from falling. She measures my weight and height the best that she can with me not being able to stand up straight. Then I go over to the chair and sit down so that she can get my blood pressure checked.

After a few seconds, she tells me, "It looks like your blood pressure is doing really well. Now I'll get you into a room, and the doctor will be in shortly after."

Jade and I follow the nurse down the hall and go into Exam Room 4 so we can wait for the doctor to come see me.

I climb up carefully onto the exam bed and slide back as much as I can without hurting my leg, and Jade sits down in the chair against the wall. While we wait, I sit there looking at all of the posters and pictures on the walls. There's a few posters with pain scales on them and pictures of flowers. Also a few posters with diagrams showing the anatomy of an adult sized heart, and one showing the anatomy of the entire torso.

As I am staring at the posters, my thoughts get broken by the door being opened. I look over and see Dr. Drew walk inside.

"Hello, Destiny. Hello Jade. How is the patient feeling since getting out of the hospital last week?"

I give him a half smile as I say, "I'm feeling alright. I am just ready to have my leg back again so that I can finally start to walk again."

He comes over and carefully grabs my leg. "I am going to check it for a minute and see if your leg is healed enough to be able to remove the bandages and cast. I'll have to do a quick x-ray to check the bone. But if it's healed completely, I will grab the scissors and cut your leg free."

Dr. Drew and Jade help me stand up and lead me to the x-ray room down the hall. Once we get there, he has me sit down in the chair as he gets the machine ready to scan my leg.

He finishes the scan after a few minutes, looking at my leg carefully before telling me, "Well Destiny, I think that it's safe to say I can remove the cast and bandages from your leg. It looks like the bones have completely healed from the accident. I am going to go get the scissors and cut them off with as much care as I can, then unwrap the bandages."

He goes over to the counter and grabs the scissors out of the drawer then comes back over. He sits down after pulling his chair in front of me. He picks my leg up carefully then starts to cut the cast free. It takes him about thirty seconds of cutting before it tears free from my leg. Then he grabs ahold of the end of the bandages and unwraps them from around my thigh.

Once the bandages are completely removed, he tosses them into the waste bin. I look down at my leg, and it's a little purple from bruising.

Dr. Drew sees the look on my face and reassures me by saying, "Don't worry. The bruising should be gone within a week or so. Your leg is only bruised because of having it wrapped up for a month to mend the broken bone that you had. But I can prescribe you some pain cream to rub on it every morning and night to try and ease the pain. And you will have to go to physical therapy once a week for the next month to make it easier starting to walk again."

"Okay, Dr. Drew. Thank you. Do we need to go to the front to get my first appointment scheduled?"

He stands up, picking up some paperwork off of the counter. "Yes. Just go to the front reception window and Fran will get your next appointment set up for you."

I nod my head at him as Jade helps me stand up with the crutches so that I can walk to the front.

Once I am steady on them, Jade and I make our way back through the halls to the lobby. We walk over to the reception window after getting to the front and are greeted by Fran.

"Hello. So he wants you to come back next week so you can start physical therapy on your leg. What day would work best for you?"

I think for a second, then tell her, "Wednesday around midday can work."

She taps on the computer for a second before she says, "Okay. There is an 11:00 on Wednesday, August 9th if that works for you."

"Yes, ma'am. That will work. Thank you."

After she puts the appointment in, she hands me an appointment card, and Jade and I go out to the parking lot so we can go back home.

Jade helps me climb into my side before getting in on the driver's side. Once I'm settled in my seat, I buckle my seatbelt.

When Jade gets in and gets buckled, I ask her, "Are you ready to call our parents yet? Or do you want to wait until we get back to the apartment?"

"We can call them after we get home in a few minutes. That way we're not on the road."

"Okay, babygirl."

As we're riding through town, Jade asks me, "Do you think that you'll be okay doing the physical therapy appointments? I've never done any type of physical therapy, but from what I know, it can be pretty intense and pretty painful."

"I know that it'll hurt, but I should be okay. If not, you'll just have to push my limits outside of the appointments so that I can be able to handle them."

Jade lets out a cute laugh when I say that. "Oh, really? How do you want me to push you, babe?"

"I'm not sure yet, but it has something to do with being in the bedroom."

As we pull into the parking lot, Jade turns to me and says, "I'm sure that I can do that, babe. I'll do everything I can to help with at home physical therapy."

We both get out of the car and walk upstairs together. Once we get to the apartment and go inside a few minutes later, I sit down on the couch and pull my phone out of my purse.

I look towards my baby and tell her, "I'm going to go ahead and call my parents if you want to call yours, baby."

As I start dialing my mom's phone number, Jade pulls out her phone and starts calling her parents. I wait a few rings before she picks up and answers her phone.

"Hello, baby. How have you been doing?"

I smile when I hear my mom's voice. "Hi, mom. I'm doing good. I'm sorry I haven't called in a few months. There's been a lot going on. How have you and dad been doing? Is he home?"

"I'm doing great since you called. Your dad is right here. Do you want me to put the call on speakerphone so that we can all talk?"

"Yes, mom. If you don't mind. Because I need to talk to both of you about what's been going on since the last time we talked to each other."

After a few seconds, I hear my dad's voice. "Hi, sweetie. What's going on? Are you doing okay?"

"I am, dad. I wanted to talk to both of you because there has been a lot going on over these last few months since the last time I called you guys."

My mom asks me, "What all has been going on? Is everything okay?"

"Yes, mom. Everything's okay. But a couple of months ago when I was supposed to be moving in with my best friend Jade, I ended up getting into a car accident after having a shitty day at work."

I hear both of them gasp before they ask me, "Are you okay, baby? Are you in the hospital? How badly were you hurt?"

"I'm okay now, but for almost a month and a half, I was in the hospital in a coma. And I had a broken leg and bruised ribs from the impact. I just got the cast and bandages off my leg today. But I promise I'm okay. Jade was by my side the entire time. And she's the next thing that I want to talk to you about."

My dad asks, "What? What about Jade?"

"Well, at one point shortly after I had gotten put in the hospital, I had woken up. And because of the dreams and thoughts that I had been having while in the coma, I ended up asking Jade to be my girlfriend."

My mom squeals in delight. "Oh my god! I'm so happy for you two!"

My dad tells me, "Congratulations, honey!"

"Thank you. Actually, I have a little more news on that front... The other morning, she actually asked me to marry her and I said yes. So now we are engaged."

My dad whoops out in enthusiasm after I tell them that Jade and I are engaged. I can hear my mom squealing even louder after I tell them the news.

"We are both so happy for you girls."

"Thank you, mom. And we were thinking about trying to fly out and come see you guys and her parents in a few months once I'm finished with physical therapy and am back on my feet long enough to be able to fly without any worry."

My dad tells me, "That sounds great. If you would like, we could help with the tickets to get you both out here to Scotland. That way you don't have to save up for a long time."

I smile as I tell him, "Thank you, dad. I really appreciate it, but you don't have to."

"I insist. How much would both of your tickets cost?"

I let out a sigh. "Fine. I know you're not going to give in, dad. The cost for both of us is $1,308 to fly to Edinburgh. It's about the same amount to fly back."

I hear my dad talking to my mom for a few seconds before he tells me, "Your mom and I can help with the cost to get here if her parents can help with the cost to fly you both back home after the visit."

"Okay, dad. Thank you. I'll talk to Jade in a minute after I get off and see what her parents told her."

Both my parents tell me okay and say goodbye before hanging up the phone. After I get off the phone, I stand up with my crutches and go to the kitchen to see if Jade is still on the phone with her parents.

When I get in there, Jade sets her phone down on the counter and walks over to me with a smile on her face.

"So my parents are thrilled that we want to come see them. What did your parents say about us coming to visit?"

"Mine said that they are really happy that we want to visit all of them. But they said that they want to help pay for our tickets there. And they wanted to know if your parents would be able to help with the money to get us back home."

Jade smiles at me. "They said they would help get us there or back if we need them to. They just want to be able to see us because it's been so long."

I wrap my arms around her in a big hug. "I am so freaking happy, baby. I can't believe any of this is real. Everything that has happened since getting home from the hospital has been so amazing, and it's all because of you, babe. I love you so fucking much."

Jade gives me a kiss on the side of my head. "I love you so freaking much, babygirl. We will do everything we ever dreamed of together and more. You are my one and only."

After she tells me that, I feel my face stretching into a huge grin. "Baby, I want to get married to you as soon as possible so that we can be able to start our life together, really start our life together."

She sits me down on one of the chairs next to the kitchen counter and places her hands on my shoulders. She looks me in the eyes as she tells me, "We will get married before the year is over, baby. I promise. That just means that we'll have to fly out to see our parents soon and try to save up as much as we can so that we can still go to Norway for our honeymoon. Otherwise, we'll have to do something else here in the states and save up to go to Norway another time."

After Jade finishes speaking, I smile at her and say, "Babe, I just want to be with you. We can do what we need to in order to have our dreams. Even if we have to have a small wedding with our four best friends and our parents. We'll just have to fly them here to come to the wedding."

She leans forward and gives me a deep, passionate kiss on my lips, my eyes closing as soon as I sink into it. I kiss her with every ounce of love and affection that I have for her before we both pull away.

I look at her as I say, "Let's call our parents back and see if there's any way that we could possibly have the wedding in Scotland when we're there visiting them, and ask our friends if they would want to fly out there with us and be our wedding parties."

"That sounds wonderful, baby. I love that idea. We can call our parents back right now, then call the girls and Greg to find out if this is an idea that could work for them."

Chapter Twenty Three

As Jade and I finish speaking to our parents about possibly getting married in Scotland when we come to visit, she sits down next to me at the kitchen table with the biggest blushing smile on her face.

"My parents said that they would love if we got married in Scotland. What did your parents say to you, baby?"

I grin as I tell her, "Mine said the same thing. I am so fucking excited. They said that they could even try to get The Royal Botanical Gardens reserved as a wedding location for the ceremony and the reception." I squeal out as I finish talking.

Jade wraps her arms around me in the biggest hug. "Oh my freaking god. We are really going to do this. I can't fucking believe it."

Tears fill my eyes as I start to cry from happiness. My body starts to shake in Jade's arms as I hear her starting to cry, also. *We are really going to get fucking married.* In *Scotland, of all places.*

I cry tears of joy with my face buried in Jade's shoulder until I am able to catch my breath.

When I sit up from her shoulder, Jade hands me a few napkins from the table to use as tissues to wipe my face. I clean the snot from my nose and around my mouth, then grab another napkin to dry my eyes.

After we both finish wiping off our faces, I look up at Jade and ask her, "Do you want to call our friends in a few minutes? Tell them about what's going on."

"Yes, baby. In fact, we can try to group call them. Tell them all at once."

Jade picks up her phone and dials Deanna's number.

After a few seconds, she picks up. "Hi, Jade. What's going on?"

Jade puts it on speaker phone as she says, "Destiny and I have something we want to ask you and everyone else, but we're going to create a group call so we can tell you all at once."

"Okay. If you want, I can add Terri to the call, and you can add Chloe and Greg on here."

Jade pulls up Chloe's number after Deanna finishes talking and dials it up.

Chloe answers after the first ring, saying, "Hi, hun. How are you doing?"

"I'm doing really good, babe. We've got Deanna on here, and Terri, and we're going to add Greg to the call. Because we've got some fucking fantastic news that we want to ask your opinions on."

When Jade finishes speaking, she starts adding Greg to the call and waits for him to answer.

He answers almost immediately. "Hi, Jade. Is everything okay?"

"Oh, yes. Destiny and I were just calling because we wanted you to be in the group call when we tell everyone the great news that we have. We called our parents earlier because we're planning to visit them in a couple of months. And we had suggested to them that we might want to get married there, in Scotland. And we were wondering if all of you guys would want to fly out there with us when we go, because we want all of you to be in our wedding parties. Have you all as our bridesmaids, and groomsman."

As soon as Jade is done explaining everything to everyone, a cacophony of screams and whoops sound off through the phone. Deanna, Chloe, Terri, and Greg all cheer for almost a minute straight before any of them actually says anything.

Terri is the first to speak up after the hollering calms down. "I for one, would absolutely love to be part of your wedding party. What about you guys?"

Chloe tells us, "Hell, yeah. I am not going to miss you two getting married just because it's going to be in Scotland."

Deanna says, "I'm with them. I am going. And so are you, Greg. You are part of the reason they are together, because you were there when it happened."

"Oh, yeah. I'm going. I may be a new friend, but I am an official friend. I will be there, Destiny and Jade."

Jade and I continue talking to everyone for another fifteen minutes, talking about what all we need to get done in order to get the wedding set up. We talk about catering, what type of food that we want to be served for everyone to eat. We talk about what music that Jade and I want the DJ to play for the reception, for Jade and I to dance to for our first dance, and what music we want when we go down the aisle and leave the reception.

Then we talk about what we plan to wear and how we want to decorate the trees around the botanical gardens, as well as what we plan to do for the cake. By the time we all finish talking, Jade and I almost have a complete plan on what we are going to do for everything.

Once we get off the phone, Jade and I start talking about what we need to do first: dresses.

I ask her, "Do you know what kind of dress you want to wear for the wedding, baby?"

"I think that I want to wear a sleek, black dress that has layers of purple in the skirt. One that has sheer, satin sleeves. I wan to wear a dress that's cut down the right side from the knee all the way to the ankle."

As I picture it in my head, I tell her, "That sounds amazing, baby. I was thinking maybe a dark purple gown. One with layers in the skirt, and a black leather jacket over the shoulders because the gown should be strapless."

Jade smiles at me. "That sounds beautiful, baby. I'm glad that we're not doing the traditional white dresses. Because that is over-rated and definitely not us. We are unique, and our wedding should show that."

"Do you want to go online so that we can start trying to find our dresses? See if we can find any that suit what we want."

I nod my head as I get onto my phone and start to look for my dress. As soon as I pick up my phone, I go to google and search up royal purple wedding gowns and wait to see what pops up.

I go to the shopping category and see dress after dress. There's poofy violet gowns with short skirts. Poofy ballgowns. Purple nightgowns. And there's straight purple dresses. I scroll for almost twenty minutes before I finally find one that I think would be perfect.

I find a deep violet colored gown that has different shades of violet and blue in the skirt. Layers of lacy satin fabric. And the body looks like it's smooth satin with no straps. It looks perfect. And what's great is that I don't have to order the jacket for my shoulders because I already have one in my closet.

As soon as I find the dress, I call Jade's name so that I can show it to her.

She looks up from her phone to look at mine and gasps when I show her the dress. "Holy crap, baby! That dress looks amazing. It will look stunning on you. Do you want to see the dress that I have found for myself?"

"Of course. Let me see." She hands me her phone so that I can see the dress she's decided on.

I look at her screen and see a gorgeous black dress. It looks like it will fit to her body, and conform with her shape. It has translucent black sleeves that go down the arms, and the entire dress goes all the way down to the mid-calves. It also has lacy violet layers in the skirt.

I smile at Jade after I finish looking at the dress. "That dress looks amazing. You will look drop-dead gorgeous walking down the aisle in this dress. When do you want us to order these?"

"We can order them Friday after I get paid. I want us to be able to get everything we need for the wedding as soon as we can."

After we finish looking at each other's dress choices, Jade stands up and asks me, "Do you want me to make some dinner for us to eat? Or do you just want to make grilled cheeses and snack for the night?"

"Let's just snack and relax on the couch, watching TV together."

"Okay, baby. I can go ahead and get the sandwiches made right quick if you want to go to the living room and find something to watch. You can grab a blanket and get comfy for when I bring the sandwiches and snacks."

I nod my head at her as I stand up using the crutches and make my way to the living room. When I get in there, I grab a thick blanket from the ottoman and grab the remote from the coffee table. I plop my butt onto the large couch, letting the blanket cover me before I turn the TV on.

I start scrolling through channels until I find something good. I put the TV on to HBO because they are about to play Sweeney, which is one of mine and Jade's favorite movies to watch.

I lay on the couch watching commercials until Jade comes into the living room with food, right before the movie is about to start. She hands me a plate with a couple of sandwiches, chips, and some snack cakes on it, then sits down next to me with her food.

We spend the next couple of hours watching people being bloody murdered by Sir Sweeney, a vengeful sailor. Watching people get drowned and slaughtered by him.

Before I know it, I can feel my eyes starting to fall closed with my head laying against Jade's shoulder. I turn my head slightly to see if Jade is still awake.

Her eyes are closed completely and her mouth is slightly open as she snores quietly in her sleep. I lay my head into her shoulder and close my eyes, letting myself drift into slumber with my baby next to me.

****

I wake up the next morning to the smell of coffee brewing in the kitchen.

I sit up from the couch and holler towards the kitchen, "Did you make coffee, baby? And if it's finished brewing, can you bring me a cup?"

A laugh sounds from the kitchen as Jade hollers back, "Yes, baby. I made coffee. I'll bring you some in a second. Then I'll be in there with you so we can watch some TV together until I have to get ready to leave and go to work at the office for a few hours."

"Okay, baby. I just want to be able to spend as much time with you as I can every day until I am able to start working again, and get started on my writing career."

Jade comes into the living room a few seconds later, holding two cups of fresh, hot coffee. She walks over to where I am and hands me my coffee before she sits down next to me with her cup.

We spend the next couple of hours relaxing together until she has to get up and get ready to leave for work.

When she stands up, she tells me, "I love you so fucking much, baby. I am going to try and get through this day at work as quickly as I can so that I can get back here to be with you. Will you be okay spending the day here by yourself?"

"Of course, baby. I'll probably spend it listening to music, watching shows and movies, and trying to practice walking some. See if I can. But I'll only try to walk near the counters and the walls so that I have something to fall against."

Jade gives me a look that could kill after I say the last sentence. "Be. Careful. Don't try too hard. And do not try to hurt yourself. Because I don't want to get a call telling me that you had to go back to the hospital after hurting yourself."

I half-smile as I say, "I'll be careful, baby. Don't worry. Now go get ready for work. I'll be okay. I promise you, baby. I don't want to end up going back to the hospital either."

Jade leaves the room for a few minutes to go get dressed for work, and while she's out of the room I start to try standing against the kitchen counter.

I get up using the crutches and make my way over to the counter. Once I am next to it, I set the crutches down next to me and grab onto the countertop while I slowly let my left leg move down to rest on the floor. I lean against the counter as my weight begins to rest on both of my legs and feet.

As soon as my weight starts to settle, I can feel my left leg wanting to give out underneath me. I hold onto the counter tight as I try to fight to keep standing for a few more seconds. But my leg can't take it anymore and decides to collapse underneath me, making me fall to the floor.

"Gah! Dammit!" I smack the floor right as Jade runs back into the kitchen.

She rushes over and grabs my arms to help me stand back up and places the crutches back under my arms. "What the hell happened? How did you fall?"

I look at her with a frustrated expression on my face. "I was trying to stand while using the countertop for support, but my leg gave out. It decided that I did not want to try standing. I just want to be able to stand and walk already."

As Jade helps me walk back into the living room, she tells me, "I know that you do, but you have to give it time.

And the physical therapy treatments will help a lot. Just be patient, baby. Please. I don't want you hurting yourself because you're so stubborn."

"I know. I'll be careful. I'll only try standing for the day while you're at work. But I'll only try a few times. And I'll make sure that I have a chair or cushion like the couch to land on if I fall, with the crutches being in reach."

After I get seated back on the couch, Jade leans down and gives me a quick kiss. "I love you. Please don't push yourself harder than your leg can take. And if you need anything while I am away at work, please call me. I will be back here faster than you can say *I love you, baby.* I don't want to come home and find you lying on the floor because you fell and couldn't get back up."

I give her a hug as I say, "I promise I won't hurt myself. I love you. So much, babygirl."

Jade gives me a kiss and a tight hug before she grabs her purse and keys. "I love you so much, babygirl. I will be back in eight hours. Maybe less if I can sweet talk Daniel into letting me come home early. And again, if you need anything, call me."

"Okay, baby. I should be okay."

She walks out the door, blowing me a kiss as she closes it behind her. As soon as the door is closed, I grab the TV remote and turn it on so that I can watch something all day while I am here by myself.

Jade's POV: As soon as I am out the door, I can't help but feel a sense of worry about Destiny being stuck at the house by herself all day. Because I know that she is going to try standing again, and probably end up getting hurt. But I know that she just wants all of this to be over, and the sooner she can walk right and have muscle strength in her leg again, the sooner that will come.

I make my way down the stairs and walk out to the car in the parking lot. As soon as I get to it, I grab my keys off of my purse and unlock the car.

Once I am in the car and start driving, I spend the next fifteen minutes until I get to the office thinking about all the different ways that Destiny could hurt herself while I am gone. I just don't want her to try too hard to stand or walk and end up snapping her leg again from her weight putting pressure on it. Because that will take her back a step in being able to finish healing.

When I get to the office, I go inside and go to my office where there is a manuscript sitting on my desk.

I pick it up and look at the title. *Killing My Mind.*

I start reading it, and it's about a woman named Marie who is dealing with mental illness in the form of demons taking over her thoughts and mind. As I am reading the first chapter, I can't help but think about how Destiny must be feeling.

She has to be feeling similar to Marie to an extent because her mind is stubborn and powerful. And when she wants to do something like walk, she will do whatever she needs to in order to get what she wants. Even if that means hurting herself in the process.

I continue reading the manuscript, taking notes as I do, until I have made it almost halfway through the pages. I finish the eighth chapter and note down that Marie is trying to come to terms with the fact that the demons in her head are only in her imagination. I write down how the author describes Marie's mental battle with herself while trying to cope with everything that is happening in her life.

After I finish writing my notes, I pick up my things and go over to Dan's office. I knock on the door before he tells me I can come inside.

When I walk through the door with the manuscript in my hand. "Hi, Dan. This manuscript is really good. But I find it a little funny that you gave me this one today."

He looks up from his computer with a curious look on his face. "Why is that, Jade?"

"Well, it just touches a little close to home. There has been a lot going on lately. And it just feels a little similar to how the main character of this manuscript is feeling. It is really good. I just can't believe how much it touches on how I have been feeling with everything going on in my personal life."

Dan nods his head. "Ah, okay. Are you going to be able to finish this manuscript and it not bother you too much? Because if it does, I can give it to somebody else to finish."

"I'll be okay. I should be able to finish it. I'm almost halfway through with it."

"Okay. And if you need somebody to talk to about what's going on at home, you can come find me in my office and talk to me about it."

I give Dan a small smile as I thank him. "Thank you, Dan. I really appreciate it. I'll be okay."

I talk to Dan for a few more minutes before I leave to go home. Before I go, I tell him bye and that I will be back first thing tomorrow morning.

After I leave work, I drive the fifteen minutes back home to the apartment. I have to deal with some traffic and slow drivers on the road, but I make it home within less than twenty minutes.

As soon as I pull into a parking spot, I put the car in park and get out. I go inside and climb the stairs up to mine and Destiny's apartment.

I go inside once I reach it, and see Destiny laying on the couch asleep. I smile at the sight of her laying there, and walk over to her. I grab a blanket from the ottoman and place it over her body, giving her a kiss on the side of her head after I tuck the blanket around her body.

"I love you so much, baby," I whisper to her before I stand up.

Chapter Twenty-four

Destiny's POV: It has been just over a week since I got the cast removed from my leg, and I still can't really balance my weight without trying to fall over. All week, I have been trying to stand without the crutches, but every time I end up losing my balance and collapsing onto whatever chair or cushion I have near me. But today is my first physical therapy appointment.

I make my way from the bedroom to the living room, using the crutches to help me walk. When I get to the living room, Jade is sitting in there with two cups of coffee in front of her on the table. As soon as she sees me, she stands up and walks over to me with a smile on her face.

"Good morning, beautiful. How was your night?"

"My night was great, baby. I slept like a rock. And thank you for making me a cup of coffee this morning."

Jade grabs my hand and helps me maneuver carefully over to the couch. "You're welcome, sweetie. I wanted to make sure that you could have a cup of your wake-up juice before we have to leave for your physical therapy appointment."

As I sit down next to her, I tell Jade, "I hope that this appointment isn't too difficult. But I hope that it helps me gain progress towards being able to walk. Because I want to be able to walk before we fly to Scotland to see our parents and get married in a couple of months."

"Don't worry, baby. I'm sure you'll be able to walk by then. You'll be running and jumping off of walls before we fly out. I can just see it."

I sit back on the couch and hug Jade. "Thank you so much for being my support, baby. You're amazing."

She gives me a cute smile as she says, "I would do anything to make sure you're okay, baby. And I'm sure that you will do great at this first appointment when we go to it. Because you are so fucking strong. So much stronger than you tell yourself."

When Jade says that, I feel my cheeks start to blush. "I am trying to be strong, but every time that I can't stay standing up or try to walk I feel like I'm never going to be able to fully walk again."

I take a few sips of my coffee as Jade looks at me and says, "You can do this. You will do this. You will be able to walk again, baby. I know it."

We spend the next twenty minutes drinking our coffee and talking until we have to get dressed and ready to leave for my appointment.

I go to my bedroom after I finish drinking my coffee and make my way over to my closet so that I can find a shirt. I look through it for a few minutes before I decide on wearing a white t-shirt that has a picture of a cute pug on top of a blue circle.

I go over to my bed and sit down while I take off my shirt from last night and pull on my shirt from the closet. I slide it onto my arms then pull it down over my head.

Once I have my shirt changed, I get back up with the crutches and go over to the dresser. I grab a pair of panties out of my underwear drawer, then open the drawer with my yoga pants in it. I dig through it for a few seconds before I find my navy-blue yoga pants.

I make my way back over to the bed and sit down as I take off my pants and underwear that I had on last night. I slide them down off of my butt and pull them down my legs. I let them fall onto the floor once they reach my ankles. Then I grab my clean underwear and pants to pull them on.

I pull the underwear over both of my feet and pull them up my legs. I lay back and lift my butt up so that I can pull them the rest of the way up. Once I get my underwear on, I pull my yoga pants over my legs, and slide them up over my butt after I use the crutches to stand back up.

When I finish getting dressed, I slide on a pair of sneakers that don't have shoelaces and go back into the living room.

Jade is in there when I walk out of the hallway, and she smiles as soon as I am in the living room.

"Hi, babygirl. You look cute."

I go over to the couch as I say, "Thank you, baby. Are you ready for us to leave for my appointment?"

She stands up and walks over to me with her keys and both mine and her purse in her hands. "Yes, baby. Are you ready to leave for it?"

I nod my head as I follow her out the door.

****

When we get to my doctor's appointment, Jade signs me in while I sit in a chair in the waiting room. After she finishes getting me signed in, she comes and sits down next to me on the couch. We sit together until one of the nurses calls my name to come back.

Jade helps me stand up and helps me walk back to the exam room.

We follow the nurse down the hall and into the second room on the right. She gets my weight and my blood pressure, then tells us that the doctor will be in in a few minutes to take me to start trying to do the physical therapy.

Jade and I only have to wait for a couple of minutes before the doctor comes into the room.

She walks inside and greets us, saying, "Hello. I am Dr. Shekner. I will be helping you with your physical therapy treatments over the next month. Can you try to stand up and show me how much balance and movement you have?"

I nod my head as I stand up with the crutches. "Is it okay if I use these to get next to the wall or the counter?"

"Of course. I just need to see what you *can* do so that I know what all we need to work on."

I grab the crutches and make my way over to the counter and slowly place my left leg down onto the floor. Once I get my foot flat on the floor, I lean the crutches against the counter then grab onto it so I can try to stand.

I can feel the pressure starting to grow in my calf as I stand with my weight on it, and end up having to grab the crutches before I fall over. I use them to walk back over to the chair and sit back down.

Dr. Shekner watches me the entire time until I am sitting back down in the chair. Once I am sitting, she tells me, "It looks like you have no muscle strength in your leg whatsoever. So we are going to have to work on helping you regain strength by doing simple exercises with your leg. And once it begins to get a little bit stronger, we can slowly start working on walking until you don't need support anymore.

"First, let me see you try to lift up your leg and move your ankle in small little circles. Just try to do it as easily as you can. Don't try to hurry yourself."

I use my hands to lift my leg up into the air and start trying to turn my ankle in circles. But after I do it for almost fifteen seconds, I can feel my leg starting to burn from working the muscles. As soon as I start to feel pain, I let my leg slowly go back down to the floor.

After I finish trying to move my leg, Dr. Shekner asks me, "How much pain did you feel while trying to do that? Because if it was a lot, we are going to have to get you a compression boot to try to ease the pain and help you start getting to where you can walk."

"Pardon my language, but after the first few seconds my entire calf was starting to fucking kill me from pain shooting through it and my ankle."

"Okay. Well, I can order you a compression boot for your ankle and foot as well as a brace to wrap around your leg from the knee down to help ease the pressure as you slowly start trying to walk again."

Jade and I nod our heads at her after she finishes speaking.

I tell the doctor, "I just want to do anything I can to be able to walk again soon. Because this fucking sucks. And I want to be able to walk before her and I get married in a couple of months. Because I want to be able to walk down the aisle."

"I will make sure that you can. How about this? I believe that there might be a boot and brace in the supply closet down the hall near my office. I can grab them for you and lend them to you until you have your wedding. Then you can bring them back and it will be as if they were never missing."

I smile at her. "Thank you so much, Dr. Shekner. I really appreciate this so much."

She stands up from her chair and tells me, "I will go grab them right quick for you, and then you can go get your next appointment set up for next week. That way I can see if your range of movement has improved any after a week. For now, I hope that you have a great week until you come back to see me."

After Dr. Shekner leaves the room, Jade turns towards me. "Baby, I know that you will be able to walk without any support by the time that we have to leave for the wedding."

"Oh, I know. I just have to work at it until I can without feeling any pain or limping at all. But I'll do it."

As we are sitting and talking about the work I am going to put in to start walking again, Dr. Shekner comes back into the room. And she has the compression boot and leg brace in her hands.

"Here you are, my dear. Would you like some help with getting them on before you go?"

"If you don't mind. I really appreciate it."

She comes next to me and wraps the brace around my leg, pulling it tight against my leg before fastening it. Then she has me take my shoe off before sliding the boot onto my foot. Once it's pulled all the way up, she fastens the Velcro and secures it on my foot.

"There you go, hun. Now you're free to go."

Jade and I both thank her as we go to the front to get my next appointment scheduled. When we get up there, the woman behind the window tells us that Dr. Shekner said that she wants me back in a week. She asks us if Wednesday at ten works for the next appointment.

I tell her it does, so she schedules it in the computer and gives me an appointment card before Jade and I go to leave.

As soon as we get out to the car, I pull out my phone and tell Jade that I am going to text everyone and tell them how the appointment went.

I pull up each of our friends numbers and start to type into a group text, *Hi, guys. I just got out of my first physical therapy appointment. The doctor had me try to move my leg and show her what my range of motion is. And it fucking hurt after a few seconds. A lot. She gave me a compression boot and a leg brace to help with the pain and pressure as I start trying to walk. She said that so long as I ease myself into it and work at it, I should be walking again before we fly out to Scotland for the wedding in a couple of months.*

A few seconds after I send out the text to everybody, my phone pings with texts back from everyone. Texts saying, *Awesome!* and *You got this, babe!* and *We know you can do it.*

I smile as each one comes in because that just motivates me even more to work as much as I can to get walking.

When Jade and I get back home to the apartment, she helps ease me out of the car and onto my feet. She hands me the crutches to help me walk upstairs to the apartment. As

I work on walking some between using the crutches to help, we slowly make our way up the stairs and into the apartment.

She opens the door to the apartment, unlocking it to let me inside. As I walk into the apartment with the crutches, I go into the kitchen and sit down at the table. Jade follows me into the kitchen and sits down next to me.

As she sits down in her chair, she asks me, "Do you want me to make us anything to eat for lunch? Or do you want me to call in something for us to have delivered or go pick up?"

I think for a second before I tell her, "We should go pick something up. What do you think about picking up burgers and milkshakes from Sherry's Homestyle Diner? Because my stomach has been craving that a lot."

Jade smiles at me as she says, "That sounds delicious, baby. They have some good ass burgers and milkshakes. We can leave to go over there as soon as you are ready."

As soon as she says that, I stand back up and tell her, "Let's go, babe. We can go get burgers and milkshakes, then come back home to eat and relax for the day."

We leave and head out to go to Sherry's and pick up food. It's only a few minutes down the road from the apartment, so it doesn't take us long to get there.

After Jade parks the car, we both get out and go inside to order our food to take home. As soon as we walk through the door, we are greeted by Claire, one of the servers. She's standing behind the service counter where she's finishing up someone else's order.

"Hi, guys. How are you two doing? I haven't seen you two here in a hot minute. Do you know what you want to order?"

I look at the menu behind the counter before deciding what I want.

I tell Claire after a few seconds, "I think that I am going to order just a cheeseburger and onion rings. And can I get a chocolate shake with extra chocolate syrup?"

She writes down my order then turns to Jade and asks her, "And you, hun? What would you like to eat?"

Jade smiles as she tells Claire, "I want the same thing. I'm going simple today."

"Okay. Well, I will have both of your orders out to you shortly. Do you want to eat here, or are you going to take your food to-go?"

I answer her saying, "We're going to take it home today, I think. I have to rest my leg because I recently had a cast removed from it."

Claire peeks over the counter to see my leg with the brace and the boot on it. "Oh shit! Are you okay?"

"Yeah. I am now. I had gotten into a car accident that put me in the hospital for about a month. But I'm okay now. I've just got to work on getting back to being able to walk again in a couple of months, because I want to be able to walk again soon."

After I tell Claire a little bit about what all has been going on, I go over to a table near the window and sit down to rest my leg. Jade sits down with me while Claire has the cook get our orders made so we can go home.

We sit for about ten minutes listening to the music playing from the diner until Claire calls us over to grab our orders.

Jade gets up from the table and grabs them. Before we leave to go home, we both thank Claire and tell her we'll see her later.

By the time we get home a few minutes later, I have already started digging into my milkshake. I tell Jade that it's really freaking good and really rich. That it is the best milkshake I have had in a long time, considering.

When we get home and go into the apartment, I sit down on the couch with my milkshake and my food. Jade comes and sits next to me, turning on the TV before she starts eating her food.

She puts on a horror movie before we both sit back and relax while we eat our burgers and onion rings.

I lay back next to my baby and finish off my food within twenty minutes of the movie. As soon as I am finished eating all my food and drinking my milkshake, I grab a blanket and lay back next to Jade.

She wraps her arm around my shoulder as she lays back into the couch, finishing off her food and milkshake.

We spend the rest of the afternoon and evening until it starts to get dark outside.

Once dusk starts to fall, Jade and I go into her bedroom and change into some comfortable pajama clothes. She helps me with getting my pants changed before she finishes changing her clothes. As she does, her hand slides across my thigh moving up my skin towards my pantyline. My cheeks turn dark as she does this.

"Oh, baby," I moan out. "I love you so freaking much."

After she finishes helping me get my clothes on, I sit down on the bed, pulling her down with me in a kiss. Her face falls into mine as we kiss each other gently. I reach my hands up into her hair, gripping it as I pull her closer.

We both fall back into the pillows, our hands moving up and down across each other's bodies. We continue kissing each other for a few more minutes before we climb all the way onto the bed.

I slide towards the pillows and pull the blankets over me as Jade climbs all the way onto the bed. She climbs underneath the covers next to me as we both lay down. We both get comfortable, laying against each other as we fall asleep together. I wrap my arms around Jade's body before I fall asleep, and she wraps hers around mine.

Chapter Twenty-five

Destiny's POV: I wake up the next morning and get my boot and knee brace on before grabbing my crutches to go into the living room. I try to walk some with my left foot, carefully placing it on the floor as I walk down the hallway.

When I get to the living room, Jade is coming from the kitchen with two coffee cups in her hand. She looks up and sees me when I get to the living room. She sets them down on the coffee table, then walks over to where I am and gives me a kiss, wrapping her arms around my waist.

"Good morning, baby. I see that you're already trying to walk. How's your leg feeling today?"

I smile at Jade as I wrap my arms around her waist. "It's feeling a little better this morning. After wearing the boot and the brace all yesterday afternoon, the pain has gone down some. There's still a little bit of soreness, but it's definitely better than yesterday."

Jade helps me get to the couch so that I can sit down with her and we can drink coffee together before she has to leave for work in a couple of hours.

Once we are both sitting on the couch, my mind wanders to everything we need to do in order to be ready for our wedding. The first thing that pops in my head is our dresses. We need to order them so that we can make sure that they fit us just right.

As my brain is thinking about the dresses, I ask her, "Baby, while you're at work do you think that I can get online and order our dresses so that we have them for the wedding? That way we can be able to try them on and get them tailored if necessary before we fly out to Scotland."

"Of course, baby. I'll send you the link for mine and leave my debit card home with you."

Jade pulls out her phone and gets the link to send to me. "There you, baby. You should get it in your texts in a second."

I pick up my phone and check it when the text makes it ping. I pull up the link and open it, making sure that it came through. Once I get it open and loaded, the image of her dress pulls up along with the purchase options.

I turn my phone off after I finish looking at her dress. "Thank you, baby. This way the sooner we have our dresses, the sooner we can figure out everything else that we need to get done to prepare for our wedding."

Jade takes a few sips of her coffee before telling me, "Definitely, baby. If you want, while I'm at work I can do research to try to find a baker and a caterer to do the cake and bring the food to the wedding reception."

"Okay, baby. I'll even do some research to try and find a DJ that could play the music for the ceremony and reception."

As I start drinking some of my coffee, Jade says, "That sounds great, baby. We each do two things so that we can try to get everything figured out. Hopefully it won't be too much of a pain in the ass for either of us. That way the only thing we have to worry about is you working on walking, then having to get our bags packed when we're ready to fly across the ocean."

I sit with Jade as she finishes drinking her coffee. When she gets up to get dressed for work, I follow her to the bedroom so that I can sit on the bed and watch.

When we get to the bedroom, I sit down and set the crutches next to me on the bed. Jade goes over to her closet and goes through her shirts for a few seconds, pulling some out. She sets them next to me once she's pulled them out of the closet. Then she goes over to her dresser to pick out some pants or leggings.

She sets a few pairs next to the shirts and asks me, "What do you think I should wear? I've got this black patterned long sleeve shirt, this blue shirt with flowers near the bottom, and this plain hot pink shirt. Then I've got black leggings, dark denim jeans, and white jeans."

I look at everything for a few seconds before I tell her, "I think that you should wear the pink shirt with the blue jeans. That would look really nice on you, baby."

"Okay. I'll do that."

Jade pulls off her black t-shirt that she wore to bed and grabs the pink t-shirt. She slowly pulls it on over her head, letting the fabric fall down across her body. Then she slides her pajama pants off her butt, letting them fall to the floor. She picks up the blue jeans and slides them over her legs and up over her thighs until they reach her butt. She has to bounce a couple of times as she finishes pulling them up, then she zips them and buttons them.

As soon as she's finished getting dressed, Jade looks over at me with a smile on her face. "Did you enjoy that little show, baby?"

I grab my crutches and stand up, making my way over to her. I wrap my arms around her neck and pull her in for a kiss. Jade places her hands around my waist as she leans in close to me. We kiss each other for what feels like forever before we stop.

After we both pull out of the embrace, Jade and I go back to the living room so that she can finish getting ready for work. I plop myself back down on the couch while she grabs her keys, purse, and water. I grab my tablet from the table and open up my writing app to start working on a new story idea when Jade walks over.

She gets my attention by placing her hand on my head. "I've got to go for the day, baby. Will you be okay until I get back home?"

"Yes, baby. I will. Oh, and can I get your debit card so I can order our dresses while you're at work?"

Jade grabs her wallet out of her purse and pulls her debit card out of it. "Here you go, baby. And I'll do research on caterers and bakers in Edinburgh that could be able to help do the food for the reception and the cake. I'll try to find the highest rated ones, that way it can be perfect."

"I love you so much, babygirl. We will have the most perfect wedding."

Before she goes to leave for work, she gives me a quick kiss. "I love you with all my heart, babygirl. I'll see you as soon as I get off. Let me know after you order the dresses when they should be able to get here."

As she heads to the door, I tell her, "I love you so much, baby. I will. See you this afternoon. I hope that your day goes well."

She smiles at me as she shuts the door behind her. Once it's closed, I open the link for my dress from my phone so that I can get it ordered.

I choose size medium and click on the option for the cheapest shipping, which will get here in about two weeks. Before I click to put in the payment information, I double check the price. It'll cost $129.89 after the cost of shipping.

I click the button to purchase and put in Jade's card information. After I finish and confirm the purchase, I text Jade to let her know that I just ordered my dress for $130, and am about to go to order hers.

I pull up the website with her dress and choose her size before clicking to put in the card information. It only takes me a few seconds to enter everything, then I choose the cheapest shipping option, which is also about two weeks, and confirm it. Hers costs about $115.99, so it's almost fifteen dollars less than mine.

After I text her about her dress order, I go to Google on my phone and start trying to look up DJs that work in or around Edinburgh, Scotland. I go through website after website for at least thirty minutes before I find a few that could maybe work.

There's one guy named Jeffrey Sanders who is highly recommended online. He works in Edinburgh and the surrounding areas. He's able to play a wide variety of music, from rock to pop music to alternative to slow music.

I put his name in the back of my head as I continue looking for a few more minutes. I find a few others who have high ratings and write their names down, too. After I get at least five names, I get off of Google and turn on the radio so that I can listen to music for a little while and try to relax my muscles.

Jade's POV: After I get to work, I get to my office and find *Killing My Mind* sitting on my desk. I sit down and open it to where I left off yesterday and continue reading it and taking notes.

I spend the first half of being at work finishing up the notes. As soon as I finish it, I write down in a large note on the title page that says, *Highly insightful into the human mind. Recommend for publication using my suggested notes.*

As soon as I close the manuscript and set it to the side, I grab out my phone so that I can try to find a caterer and someone to make our wedding cake. I go into Google and look up five-star catering in the Edinburgh area. I look at caterers who can do steaks, chicken, and a variety of other things. There are so many to choose from who are highly recommended by everyone online. But one that catches my eye is a restaurant in Cramond hat can cater a wide variety of food options to anywhere from Vermont to Connecticut or even New York.

They have amazing, mouth watering steaks and grilled chicken, as well as a large variety of sides such as baked potatoes, macaroni and cheese made with cheddar jack and Muenster cheese. Steamed vegetables and salads. Steak fries and fried potatoes. It all sounds so delicious that it's making my mouth water.

I pull up their phone number after deciding that they seem like the best option out there and give them a call.

After two rings, a man answers the phone. "Hello. This is Charles from Dapper Steakhouse. How can I help you?"

"Hi. I was wondering about your catering. Is there any way that you could cater a wedding for fifty?"

"Yes, ma'am. We could do that. When will the wedding be and where is the location going to be?"

"It will be on October 23 in the Royal Botanical Gardens near Edinburgh, Scotland. Is that enough time for your restaurant to be able to prepare the food?"

There are a few moments of silence before Charles answers me. "That should be plenty of time for us. Would you like us to cater a little bit of everything for your reception? Or do you have a specific menu in mind?"

"I was thinking a bit of everything, but set up buffet style if that's possible. That way our guests could choose what's on their plates. Does that sound like something you could do?"

"We can do that. We will just need tables for everything."

As Charles and I finish discussing the catering, I let him know that we will be able to provide tables and an area for the food to be set up.

After I get off the phone, I go online to see if I can find anywhere that rents out tables and chairs for events. I end up finding Event City and they have all kinds of tables and chairs. From regular plastic ones to fancy wooden tables and chairs with designs on them.

I decide on the regular plastic tables and chairs with black and purple table cloths. I put in that our wedding will need thirty tables in total, plus sixty five chairs, and order them.

For the rest of the afternoon before I can go home, I spend it looking at websites for bakeries in the Edinburgh area that could make us the perfect wedding cake. I call probably twenty places before coming across one that can bake what we want: a three-tiered chocolate cake with purple and black icing, little cobwebs and bats in black on it, and a black wedding cake topper that is shaped like two skeletons.

Once the bakery and I finish going over what all Destiny and I want, I hang up the phone. I gather all of my things before going to Michael's office to let him know that I'm headed home for the day.

****

Two months later

Destiny's POV: As soon as I wake up, I jump out of bed in excitement. *Today's the day that Jade and I are finally flying to Scotland to see our parents and have our wedding with all of our friends and close family.*

I run to the bathroom where Jade is and give her a big hug. "Good morning, baby. Are you ready to go to the airport soon?"

I hear a smile in her voice as she tells me, "I am beyond ready and really fucking excited. We're going to see our parents and get married in front of everyone we know and love. I just need to get dressed and get my coffee to take with us."

"Okay, baby. I'll go ahead and get our bags into the car before I get dressed."

Jade turns around to look at me as she gives me a quick kiss on the lips.

I leave the bathroom while Jade finishes washing her face and go to our bedroom, which used to be just her bedroom, and start gathering our suitcases and carry-on bags. I grab her suitcase that's turquoise with pink frogs on it along with her black carry-on bag in my right arm, then grab my purple suitcase and my carry-on bag in my left arm.

Once I have all of our bags, I take them and set them next to the front door so that I can get my shoes on. I grab my black converse sneakers and sit down on the couch so that I can pull them on my feet. I get them on and tied in just a few seconds, then open the door so that I can get out with the bags easily.

I get down the stairs and to the car, then put the suitcases into the trunk. I put the carry-ons in the backseat and go back upstairs afterwards so that I can get dressed.

After I get inside, I go to the bedroom and start rummaging through the closet and dresser. I find a dark blue t-shirt and a pair of black sweatpants to wear so that I can be comfortable on the flight.

I pull off my pajamas and put on the t-shirt and sweatpants quickly. Once I'm finished getting dressed, I go out to the kitchen and help Jade with getting our coffee to take on the road.

"Hi, baby. I got the bags down in the car."

Jade finishes stirring her coffee and hands me the pot. "Awesome. We can leave to the airport as soon as you're ready to go. That way we'll get there early enough before our flight."

I place my hand on hers, sliding it across the top of it. I pour my coffee into a red metal tumbler and pour some creamer and sugar into it before mixing it together.

Once I put the lid onto my cup, I tell Jade that I'm ready to hit the road.

****

We reach the airport in less than twenty minutes with two hours left before our flight is supposed to board. When we get there we go inside and get our bags checked before we start making our way through the security lines.

As I walk with Jade through the airport, I can feel the excitement teeming through my body. I haven't been in an airport since I was in high school. It feels almost surreal that this is really happening. There are so many other people around us, bustling through the security lines, baggage claim, and going to the gates.

The line in front of us slowly moves forward as people get their carry-on bags checked and go through the metal detector. It takes us probably about forty minutes before we reach the front of the line where we have to put our things into the bucket to be scanned on the conveyor belt.

The TSA agent who's directing the security checkpoint comes over once we get to the front of the line and tells us, "Take your shoes, cellphones, jewelry, and anything else metal that you have on, along with your purses and place them into this bucket on the belt. Once you've set everything in there, I will have you both walk through the metal detector to make sure that you don't have any weapons on you."

I take my shoes off and place them into the bucket before taking off my ring and necklace that Jade gave me. I place them in the bucket along with my cellphone, purse, and keys. Jade does the same, then we both follow the agent and walk through the metal detector.

As soon as we're through, we step to the side and get our shoes back on and gather all of our things before heading over to where Gate 22B is. Jade and I set our things down next to a couple of seats before we sit down in the boarding area.

After I get seated next to Jade, I turn towards her and ask, "Are you ready for this?"

Jade turns to me with a huge grin on her face as she says, "I am beyond ready. I can't wait to get there and see our parents. And I really can't wait for tomorrow afternoon when we're going to get married to one another. It will be amazing."

I smile back at her and lean in to give her a big hug.

We talk for the next hour about everything that's going to happen over the next few days, talking about what we'll do with our parents, the wedding, spending time with our friends and family. And we talk about the honeymoon that we'll be going on after the visit is over.

By the time our flight is called to board, we have talked about almost everything that we expect to happen throughout this trip and how amazing it will all be.

As we finish talking about everything, we hear, "Boarding call for flight 361 to Edinburgh," sound off from the overhead intercom. Jade and I both gather our purses and carry-on bags then make our way to the gate.

"Hi. May I see your boarding passes and your passports, please?"

We both show them to her before she lets us pass onto the jet way to get on the plane. Once she lets us go by, Jade and I make our way through the doors and onto the plane.

We go down the aisle until we reach row 14 where our seats are. I help Jade place our carry-on bags into the overhead compartment before we both sit down in our seats.

I ask Jade after we put our bags up, "Do you want the window seat, babe? Or the aisle?"

"I'll take the window seat because I know that it will probably freak you out sitting where you can see the sky outside."

I laugh as she sits down next to the window then sit next to her in the aisle seat.

We wait for another twenty minutes as everyone finishes boarding the plane. Once everybody's on and seated, a flight attendant goes over the safety protocols for during the flight. She tells us what to do in case of loss of cabin pressure, what to do in case of a crash or a water landing. By the time she's finished with the safety speech, the seatbelt light turns on and the plane begins taking off into the sky.

As we start going up into the air, I can feel my lungs starting to breathe a little heavier because of my anxiety. I feel Jade's hand on my arm as she tries to help me calm down while the plane rises into the air.

"It's okay, baby. I'm here. Don't worry."

I swallow a large gulp as the plane hits some turbulence. "I know we'll be okay. I just can't help it. I really don't like flying and being up off the ground in the sky."

Jade and I spend the next seven hours on the flight watching movies and napping until we get to Scotland. When we get there, it's already six in the evening with the change in time zones.

Once the plane lands and we are able to get off through the gate, Jade and I are both met with our parents in the airport. They all come over to Jade and I and wrap us both in hugs.

When they finally let us both go after a few minutes, my mom is the first person to speak.

"Hi, baby. How was your flight getting here?"

I smile at her as I say, "The flight was great. There wasn't too much turbulence, but it still freaked me out some. I ended up sleeping for most of it, though."

Jade speaks up and tells my parents, "I made sure that she was safe, too."

Her dad smiles at her. "You were always extra protective of her back in high school. I'm glad to see that you're still protecting her. How are you feeling, babygirl?"

"I'm feeling really good, dad. Glad that we're finally here. And really excited for tomorrow."

Her mom pipes in, saying, "We are, too. None of us can believe that you two are going to get married tomorrow afternoon. It's wonderful."

As we all continue talking, we make our way to baggage claim and grab our suitcases so that we can go with our parents to their houses. My dad grabs my bags from me and Jade's dad grabs her bags from her.

Once we have all of our things, we follow our parents out to their cars. We walk outside with everybody, making our way across the rainy parking lot.

When we get to the both cars, my dad asks Jade and I, "Do you girls want to go get some dinner before we take you home to rest for the night? We can go to a diner that's just down the road from our houses."

As I'm climbing into the backseat of my parents' car, I tell him, "Of course, dad. We'd love to go out to eat with you guys. Besides, we haven't eaten anything except peanuts and crackers for the last seven hours."

"Well then, we're taking you to get some food. That way you'll have plenty of energy for tomorrow."

After we all get into the two cars, we ride through town for about twenty minutes until we reach the diner, Amos's Home Diner.

When my dad pulls into the parking lot, he turns around and tells me, "This place has the best chili cheeseburgers and fries you'll ever have. As well as the best chocolate lava brownies, which I'm going to order for you two as a night before the wedding celebration."

I laugh at my dad as I climb out of the car. Jade and her parents walk over a few seconds later, and we all make our way into the diner. We're greeted by the hostess when we walk inside and she takes us over to a table near a window. She hands us each a menu before asking us what we would like to drink.

We each give her our drink orders once we have all decided what we want. Once she finishes writing them down on her little notepad, I start looking over the menu.

There are so many sandwich options and burgers, as well as chicken and meal plates. They all look and sound so good, I don't know what to choose.

As I'm looking at the menu, I turn to Jade and ask her, "What are you thinking of getting, baby? I'm not sure what I want because it all looks so freaking good."

"I'm thinking about that fried chicken and gravy sandwich with some chili cheese fries."

I hear her dad let out a chuckle. "You take after your dad, don't you? That's what I always get from here."

I laugh a little before I say, "You know what, I think I'll get the chili cheeseburger and fries that you suggested, dad. Because those sound fucking good."

It takes a few more minutes for our parents to fully decide what they want before the waitress comes back over with our drinks.

As she sets them down in front of us, she asks, "Are you all ready to order your food? Or do you need another few minutes?"

Jade's dad tells her that we're ready to order. He lets me and Jade order first. Then her mom orders the turkey club sandwich with a side of tater tots. My mom orders the regular cheeseburger with lettuce and tomato, and our dads order the same as Jade and I.

While we all sit and wait for our food to be ready, we talk about everything that's going to happen for the wedding tomorrow. From getting ready to the ceremony to the reception and flying off for the honeymoon to Norway after we finish visiting with our parents in two weeks.

By the time the waitress comes back with all of our food, we have already talked about everything that's going to happen over the next two weeks. Once she leaves after giving us all our plates, we start digging in to our food.

My chili cheeseburger is drippy and greasy as shit, so I have to use a fork and knife just to keep from making a mess everywhere while I eat. As soon as I take the first bite, I can feel the chili and cheese oozing in my mouth.

After I take a few bites, I tell my dad, "Thanks for suggesting this, dad. It's freaking good."

"You're welcome, honey. I figured I'd suggest something delicious because I know how you like greasy food."

We all continue eating our food in almost complete silence until our plates are clean. By the time I'm finished with my burger and fries, my stomach is full and feels like it wants to pop from this fattening meal. I didn't realize how hungry I was until I started eating and couldn't stop.

When we're all done with our food, our dads split the bill and pay for everything before we make our way back out to the cars and head to our parents houses for the night.

Once I get to my parents' house with them, I send out a group text to the girls and Gregory to find out if they made it okay and if they're in their hotel. A few seconds after I send the text, my phone pings with responses from everyone, letting me know that they have made it safe and sound.

I finish reading the texts then get up from the living room where I'm sitting with my mom and dad. I tell them that I'm going to go lay down for the night so that I'm nice and rested for tomorrow.

I go to my bedroom after giving both of them a hug and kiss goodnight. I shut the door behind me and climb into bed after turning off the light.

Before I doze off, I think to myself, *I can't freaking believe that Jade and I are really going to get married tomorrow.*

Chapter Twenty-six

The next morning when I wake up, I go downstairs to the living room and find my parents sitting in there watching the news and drinking their coffee. As soon as I walk into the room, they both look over and greet me.

My mom smiles at me as she says, "Good morning, sweetie. There's coffee and tea in the kitchen if you would like any."

"Thank you, mom. I definitely need some to give me energy for the day before I have to start getting ready in a couple of hours."

I go into the kitchen and grab a cup from the counter, pouring some coffee into it. I open the fridge and get the bottle of creamer and pour some into my coffee until it's a nice tan color. I put a few scoops of sugar in, then stir it together with the spoon on the counter.

Once I finish making my cup of coffee, I go back into the living room and sit down on the other couch with my mom and dad.

"How did you guys sleep last night?"

My dad answers me, saying, "We slept great, sweetie. Especially since you're here. Before we fell asleep, we kept talking about how much we love that you and Jade are getting married. You two were made for each other."

I smile as I tell him, "Thank you, daddy. I cannot wait to be married to her and starting our lives together."

As I drink my coffee, I ask my mom, "Do you think that after I finish my coffee in a little while that you could help me do my hair and makeup for the wedding?"

"Of course, honey. I would love to help you with your hair and makeup. How are you wanting it done?"

"I was thinking that I could have my hair done in ringlets at the bottom that fall around my face. And my makeup with subtle blush and dark shadowy eyes with some violet on the lids, and dark lipstick for my lips. Could you do that, mom?"

She smiles at me as she tells me, "I can definitely do that. I will make your hair and makeup look amazing, sweetie."

I spend the next few hours hanging out with my mom and dad before I actually have to start getting ready. Once it's almost 11:00 in the morning I go to my room and grab my makeup and hair things so that my mom can help me get started with getting ready. I bring everything to the living room where my mom is and sit across from her on the couch.

I set everything down as I tell her, "This is the makeup and hair stuff that I brought with me. Do what you think will look the best with my dress. You can look through it for a minute while I go grab the dress from the closet. I'll be right back, mom."

After I set down all my makeup and hair supplies for my mom, I go back to my room and get my black and purple dress out of the closet.

I take the dress downstairs and carry it over to my mom. "This is the dress, mom. Both of our dresses are black with purple for our Halloween themed wedding colors."

As I sit down in front of her on the couch, she tells me, "I will do my best, baby. I will turn you into a beautiful dark princess. But either way you'll still look gorgeous, because you are always gorgeous."

My mom starts digging through my makeup supplies and pulls out some eye shadows, my mascara, black eye liner, foundation, lip liner, and lipstick. Before she starts to put any makeup on my face she grabs a few face wipes and wipes my face off to try and get all of the oils from the night off of my face.

Once she finishes cleaning my face, she starts putting foundation and concealer on it. She rubs it in after covering all of the important spots. When she's finished putting foundation and concealer on my face, my mom grabs the dark grey eye shadow and tells me to close my eyes. She uses one of my makeup brushes and puts the eye shadow on the bottom of my eyelids.

Next she gets some dark purple eye shadow and brushes it along the middle of my eyelid, filling some light purple eye shadow on the top of my eyelids. After she finishes putting on my eye shadow, my mom gets the eye liner pencil and draws on a dark line along the edges of my eyelids. Lastly my mom puts the mascara on my eyelashes.

When she finishes doing my eye makeup, she puts a bit of blush on my cheeks, then does my lipstick and lip liner. She puts a full layer across my lips before handing me a napkin to blot my lips on.

I place it between then and hold them together for a few seconds to get off the excess makeup before setting the napkin down and grabbing the mirror to look at my face.

I hold it up at different angles as I look at myself, opening and closing my mouth in different expressions.

After a few seconds of examining myself I give my mom a big smile.

"This looks great, mom. This is probably the best I've ever looked with makeup on ever. Thank you so much."

My mom smiles back at me as she says, "You don't need to thank me, sweetie. I would do anything for you. Are you ready to do your hair in a second? Because we'll have to do that in the bedroom so that I can use the curling iron and the mousse." She glances at my dad on the other couch before continuing. "And that way we won't disturb your dad anymore with the girly stuff."

I laugh at her as I stand up and follow her upstairs to the bedroom. When we get there, my mom goes into the bathroom and grabs the spray bottle, hair dryer, curling iron, and mousse, along with a couple of brushes and hair barrettes.

My mom runs a brush through my hair and sprays it quickly with the spray bottle before plugging in the hair dryer. She dries my hair after she finishes brushing through all the tangles. As she's doing my hair I can feel my brain relaxing.

Once she finishes getting my hair dried, she plugs in the curling iron and begins curling the bottom length of my hair. She goes over each piece a few times before she's done. Then she turns the curling iron off and grabs the mousse, spraying some into her hands before running them through all of my hair to make sure that my curls hold.

After she's finished, she puts a couple of barrettes into my hair. "There. I'm done, baby. Go look in the bathroom mirror to see what you think."

I stand up and make my way into the bathroom, turning the light on before I look at myself in the mirror.

As soon as I look in the mirror, my mouth drops in awe. *Holy crap. I look amazing.* I look at myself for a few seconds more before going back into the bedroom.

"Thank you so much, mom. This is amazing. I never thought that I could ever look like this."

My mom stands up and walks over to me. "Babygirl, you look amazing without all of this. This just adds to your beauty. Now it's time to get you into your dress and everything else so that we can get down to the park and finish getting you ready. Your dad and I, along with Jade's parents will help make sure that everything is set up and ready for the ceremony and reception."

I smile at my mom as I stand up and start getting out of my pajamas while my mom takes the dress off of the hanger and fluffs it up a few more times.

Once I've got my pajamas off and set on the bed she helps me get the dress on, being extra careful around my hair and makeup. She helps slide the skirt over my head and slowly pulls the top down over me before I slide my arms through the top of the dress. After I finish getting the dress on all the way, I go over to my suitcase and get out my black leather jacket to put on over my arms.

I finish getting my jacket on before I grab out my knee-high leather boots. I sit down on the bed and pull up my skirt so that my mom can help me with getting them on over my feet.

She pulls them up over my feet and helps me stand up and closes the door so that I can look at myself in the mirror.

"What do you think, sweetie? Is this good enough for your wedding?"

My face starts beaming as I look up and down at myself. "It definitely is. Thank you so much, mom. I never could have done this by myself."

After I finish looking in the mirror, I follow my mom downstairs to where my dad is so we can tell him that we're ready to go to the park. As soon as we enter the room, he stands up and comes over to me with a huge smile on his face.

"You look amazing, darling. You're mother did an amazing job. Are you almost ready to leave for the park soon?"

I grin as I give him a big hug. "I'm ready, daddy. Let's go so I can get married and you can give me away to my wife."

****

After we get to the park, I meet up with Deanna and Chloe so that I can help them get lined up for the procession. Terri and Greg come over and join them, Terri standing next to Deanna and Greg standing next to Chloe.

Once they're set up how they're supposed to go down the aisle, I go back around the back of the aisle runner and meet my mom and dad on the left side of the trees behind the area.

We wait for a few seconds with their arms wrapped around mine. I have my bouquet in my hands, holding the flowers in front of me before the processional music starts. As it starts playing, I watch Terri and Deanna walk down the aisle, going to each side when they reach the front. Then Greg and Chloe make their way down the aisle.

The music continues playing as my parents start walking me down the aisle. Every eye turns to watch as I make my way towards the front, the biggest smile on my face by the time I go over to stand next to Deanna and Chloe.

Once I'm up there under the arch, I look down the aisle and wait for Jade to come down with her parents. When I see her starting towards the aisle, I can feel the brightest smile covering my face from cheek to cheek. She looks so gorgeous in her dress, almost radiant as the sunlight hits her face.

When she reaches the arch and her parents give her a kiss, she has the most radiant smile on her face, her cheeks blushing even more pink through the blush.

As the processional music winds down, the minister begins the ceremony.

"We gather here today to join Destiny Morgan and Jade Shay in marriage. These two women have the most wonderful bond with each other. They have been with each other through everything over the years. Now I would like to ask Jade if she would like to say her vows."

Jade looks over at me with a huge smile on her face as she says, "Destiny, I love you so much. We have known each other since the first day of school and have been best friends ever since that day. You have shown me so many things and taught me so many things ever since we met that have helped me grow closer to you each and every day. You are my life, my everything."

As she finishes speaking, I can feel tears welling up in my eyes as they roll down my cheeks.

The minister turns to me and asks if I am ready to say my vows. I tell him that I am as I take a deep shaky breath.

"Jade, even though I didn't know it at the time, you have been the love of my life since the first day we met. You have been my best friend by my side every day. You helped me through every struggle since the day we met, and that helped my love for you grow more and more each and every day. You are amazing. You are the only person I could ever see myself spending the rest of forever with. I love you so much I can't even describe it. You are my one and only."

When I finish saying my vows, the minister gets the rings from Greg.

He asks Jade, "Do you, Jade Shay, take Destiny's hand in marriage? As your wife for better for or for worse until death parts you?"

She smiles as she takes my ring and says, "I do." She places the ring on my finger alongside my other ring.

"And do you, Destiny Morgan, take Jade's hand in marriage, allowing her to be your wife for better or for worse, until death parts you?"

I feel my voice break a little as I tell him I do. I place Jade's ring onto her finger with her other ring.

Once I finish sliding the ring onto her finger, he tells us, "By the powers vested in me by God and the town of Edinburgh, I now pronounce you wife and wife. You both may kiss the bride."

I drop my bouquet on the ground as I pull Jade forward, kissing her deeply. Her lips meet mine as her eyes fall closed. Our mouths move together for what feels like forever as we hold each other in embrace.

After we finish kissing, we make our way down the aisle, everyone cheering.

We make our way over to the reception area with everyone and go to the center of the dance area so that we can have our first dance together. As the music starts to play, we start to sway together in front of everyone.

As we dance, all I can see is Jade swaying in front of me. All I can hear is the music. All I can feel is my love for my wife. Even though it's chilly outside, being fall in Scotland, my heart is making me feel so warm that I can't even tell that it's cold.

We dance for what feels like an eternity before the song ends. I wrap my arms around her and give her another sweet kiss before we make our way over to the tables to cut the cake and get some food.

Jade and I pick up the knife together and cut through the cake. As soon as the knife reaches the bottom of the tier, I scoop my hand in and throw some into her face. When I do that, she laughs and does the same.

We spend the rest of the reception eating, dancing, and talking with everyone, having the time of our lives.

****

Jade and I spend the next two weeks with our parents visiting and doing things around town. We spend every day together, having fun with everyone, laughing and seeing sights and checking out everything around Edinburgh.

By the time the two weeks are over, Jade and I are beyond happy. But we're also ready to be able to go to Norway for our honeymoon.

On the last day, we gather our bags and everything that we got during the trip and go with our parents to the airport so that we can fly off for our honeymoon. Our parents help us pack up our bags into the cars and drive us to the airport.

When we get there, it only takes an hour for us to get through security and get ready to board at the gate. We say our goodbyes to our parents when our flight is called for boarding, then get on the plane together. We spend the next few hours flying to Norway.

When the plane finally touches down to land, it's almost 7:00 in the evening. We get off and make our way through the airport, going to baggage claim to get our luggage. Once we have our luggage, we go outside together to get on a shuttle to our hotel.

We reach the hotel after about twenty minutes, and get our bags set up in the hotel room. We hail a cab and take it to the nearest empty park so that we can watch the Northern lights going across the night sky.

We lay together in the grass, holding each other as we stare up at the sky. We lay like that for twenty minutes before the sky starts to light up in purples and greens and yellows.

As the lights start flashing across the sky, I can feel the most incredible feeling spreading through my heart as I hold Jade in my arms. This is the best night of my life, being with my wife under the Northern Lights. I can't freaking believe that this is real. That Jade and I are actually married and here watching these lights in the sky.

As Jade and I are lying together watching the lights, all I can think to myself is, *I can't believe this all happened because of my car accident and coma. If that wouldn't have happened, all of this wouldn't have happened. And I'm so glad about everything that has come from that accident*

About the Author

I am an up-and-coming new author. I was born in Carlsbad, New Mexico, but grew up in Savannah, Georgia because my dad moved us there through the military. I have always loved reading and writing since I was a child. I just want to share my stories and characters with the world.